HULA

BOOKS BY ARMINE VON TEMPSKI

HULA · DUST · FIRE · LAVA

HAWAIIAN HARVEST

RIPE BREADFRUIT

BORN IN PARADISE

THUNDER IN HEAVEN

ALOHA

Juveniles

PAM'S PARADISE RANCH

JUDY OF THE ISLANDS

BRIGHT SPURS

HULA

A ROMANCE OF HAWAII

BY
ARMINE VON TEMPSKI

OX BOW PRESS
WOODBRIDGE, CONNECTICUT

1988 reprint by:

OX BOW PRESS
P.O. Box 4045
Woodbridge, CT 06525

Library of Congress Cataloging-in-Publication Data

Von Tempski, Armine, 1892–1943.
Hula : a romance of Hawaii / by Armine von Tempski.
p. cm.
I. Title.
PS3543.O647H8 1988
813'.52—dc19 87–36899
CIP

ISBN 0–918024–64–1
0–918024–60–9 (pbk.)

Printed in the United States of America

I DEDICATE THIS BOOK

TO

MY DAD AND UNCLE EDWIN

AND TO ALL THE GREAT LOVERS OF THE WORLD

CONTENTS

PART I

PART II

PART III

HULA

There are localities in Hawaii beautiful as Eden—isolated from the bulk of the island by lava outpourings and mighty ravines—that constitute little worlds to themselves. In them people live as they please, victims of their exotic environment and the subconscious realization that they are beyond the censorship of onlookers.

Hana, on the island of Maui, is such a place.

Great headlands face the unbroken sweep of the Pacific. The thousand greens of the Hawaiian forests go back into the blue mass of Haleakala. Mountain streams fall thunderously through the amber and jade of forest sunlight and shadow. Bronze of banana and crimson of young *lehua* mingle together. Rain showers move like ghosts across the sea. *Halas* cling with octopus-like roots to the windswept brows of the bluffs. Cane fields flutter beneath a guava-scented, brine-impregnated breeze. The immense blue swells of the Pacific smash at the base of thousand-foot cliffs and from every fold of the boldly outlined landscape a heady sort of freedom seems to assail one.

Until recently the entire district was owned by one Island family, the Calhouns. Sugar planters, ranch owners, lovers of blue-blooded horses. . . . Royal livers; prodigal; open-handed. . . .

And this is the story of Uncle Edwin and Hula; the tale of an old half-Hawaiian cowboy's devotion that set itself in opposition to mighty forces—blood, environment and inheritance—that the soul of the girl-child he loved might be saved from destruction.

PART I

THE ALTAR OF INNOCENCE

HULA

CHAPTER I

"I'm going to consult with that fellow Haldane we met the other day at the Club. He's a first-class engineer and the sort of man that I want."

There was a silence. The words seemed to hang in the air like a puff of smoke discharged from a gun. The speaker, a long-limbed, gray-skinned man, stretched back in his chair to observe their effect upon his companion.

"That's not a bad thought," conceded Mitchell, mopping his florid face, "but isn't the idea a bit presumptuous? Haldane seems a tremendous sort of man in his quiet way. Still," he heaved his thick body into a more erect position, "that's the kind of fellow we need. He'll have no sentiment about Hana or the Calhouns. It'll just be a business proposition to any one who doesn't know the place or the people. Old Bill's doomed to go under. It's on the books. If we don't get hold of his land some one else is bound to."

The gray man sat up.

"No one else is going to. After the trip I made last week through the 'Ditch' Country I'm more convinced than ever that it can be done. It will mean millions if that water can be taken around to irrigate the plains of East Maui. But until this fellow came there hasn't been any one in the Islands whose decision I'd attach any weight to. This man knows his business. I want him."

Mitchell looked at the expressionless gray face opposite

him. God, what a fellow Howard Hamilton was! From nothing he had risen to be the first man of the Islands, though there were others whose fortunes entitled them to places of greater prominence.

"Well, let's call Haldane up. He might be interested to look into the proposition for us even if he doesn't actually want to undertake it."

Mitchell's red face got redder with suppressed excitement.

"Wonder what he's here for? He doesn't appear to be doing anything."

"I don't imagine he has to," Howard said, "but if I'm any judge of a man he isn't the kind who will be satisfied to loaf very long. I'm going to give him a ring."

With the deliberation of movement characteristic of tall men Hamilton rose and picking up the receiver he directed the operator to call the Moana Hotel.

"Since meeting Haldane I've made some inquiries about him. He's done some pretty big things for British companies in Africa. Got knighted or something for his services in a government deal—" He broke off to talk and when the conversation ended set down the telephone with quiet triumph.

"He's doing nothing this afternoon and will be glad to see us now. Let's go."

Talking, they descended the stairs, entered the waiting automobile and drove away through the flowered streets of Honolulu. It was May and every shrub and tree was ablaze with color, but the two men were oblivious of their surroundings. Carefully they went over the ground they were intent upon breaking, blind utterly to the lavish beauty about them. The car turned into the white pillared entrance of the Moana and halted. At the office the clerk informed them that Mr. Haldane had directed that they be taken to his rooms.

The door opened to the discreet knock of the Oriental who had conducted them to it and a tall man, with thoughtful brown eyes and a generous mouth, met them. He wondered a little what was afoot for he had been in Hawaii long enough to know that both these men loomed large in Island affairs.

Greetings over, he asked them to be seated and ordered drinks. While he busied himself with the preliminary rites of hospitality he took the opportunity to study his guests. Mitchell, he classified and dismissed with a glance: a typical promoter, shrewd, probably inclined to be somewhat of a gambler, in all likelihood born lucky in matters of business and chance. Howard Hamilton was more of an enigma.

Fully six feet four, angular, quietly but faultlessly dressed in shades of gray, he sat back in his chair as far as possible, as though to get perspective of his fellow beings. Gray-haired, gray-eyed, gray-skinned, he appeared passionless; but Haldane suspected him of deep passions. There was a terrific repression about him. Every ounce of superfluous flesh and feeling had been burned away in a grim concentration upon some definite end. Haldane knew he was rated as the first business man in Hawaii.

"Well," he said, smiling a little as he seated himself at length with a drink, "to what in particular may I attribute the honor of this visit?"

He addressed both men but his eyes were fixed upon Hamilton.

"We have come to consult with you, Mr. Haldane," commenced the gray man, "about a pet project of ours that deals with the lands of East Maui—"

"About which I have not the foggiest knowledge," smiled the Englishman, "but about which I shall be most interested to hear."

"For years," Howard commenced, and the pupils of his eyes contracted almost to the point of invisibility, "I have had a scheme to get control of the watershed of East Maui, with a view to collecting all the streams of that region—and it abounds in them—in a main ditch to irrigate the cane-growing lands of West Maui.

"Every island of this group, Mr. Haldane, has more or less two distinct types of climate and topography, the combination of which gives every island a similar agricultural problem to cope with. The windward coasts, where the moisture laden trade-wind clouds first strike the high mountain masses which compose the bulk of the islands, possess a tremendous rainfall, but are cut into ravines so deep and sheer that cultivation of any sort, except in limited and isolated areas, is impossible. The leeward sides, protected from erosion, have ample space for cane and pineapple growing but do not possess sufficient water for proper development. On Maui, the island on which I live, this feature is unusually developed. I have thought upon this matter for years and am convinced, that, with an able engineer, it will be possible to tunnel, ditch, siphon and flume the water of East Maui to the plantations that are now operating in limited areas on the western portions of the island. With an adequate supply of water their expansion will be enormous, and the more land that is put under cultivation the more water will be needed." He paused and waited attentively.

"Why hasn't this been attempted?" inquired Haldane.

Hamilton smiled. "If you knew the type of country I propose to bring that water around you would understand.

"The greater part of the lands of East Maui is owned by a family called the Calhouns. They have been residents of Hana for nearly three generations. Old Bill has mortgaged his plantation and all pertaining to it, several times over, to a fellow called Dehan, a half white who lives on an adjoining estate in Kipahulu. He can never square his debts to him. Dehan is nobody's fool; perhaps he has some such scheme as we have, under his hat, but I fancy that his real motive is to get Dick Calhoun, Bill's son, sufficiently into his debt for a more personal reason."

"Yes?" prompted Haldane as the man came to a stop.

"For reasons of friendship and sentiment, neither Mitchell nor I want to go over personally to offer to buy the plantation or the water rights of the place if they won't sell outright. The money will be welcome enough but the plantation will, for all practical purposes, cease to operate if the water is taken away. Both Mitchell and I are prepared to pay a fair price. We should prefer to purchase the land outright but will agree to other terms if we must. The Calhouns come from great stock but they are run down. Worn out. They will have to go, for they will not keep pace with the development of Hawaii. Hana is absolutely cut off from the rest of the island of Maui. Life in the district is much as it was fifty years ago, idyllic but not in step with the times. We've all been royally entertained by old Bill and it makes it extremely difficult for either of us to make a move to possess ourselves of his land. You, as an outsider, with no previous friendship or association with these people can act without bringing sentiment or friendship too strongly into the deal. The Calhouns are delightful, one cannot help liking them, but they are all wasters. I don't think Bill has been really sober for years. If I were absolutely satisfied that the water could be taken to West Maui I'd go up now, in spite of everything, and offer to buy, immediately; but I must have expert advice before I undertake to put this thing through.

"May I give you more details?"

"I'm waiting for them."

"Providing that you decide to look into this for us, I suggest that you go to Hana as soon as it is convenient. I'll get a good topographical map of the country for you. Let Dick know what you've come for, intimate that you are prepared to make a six-figure offer. It'll set him thinking. They are up to their ears and about to go under. He knows it as well as his father. Later, if you are assured that the water can be got around we can come to definite terms. It will be the biggest engineering project ever staged in these Islands. You'll appreciate the magnitude of it when you see the country—and it will be worth millions and millions if it can be done."

Haldane watched a long wave break across the bar. The smoke of its crest trailed backward and was dissipated in the gold of the waning afternoon. He caught the ring of passion through the iron sound of Hamilton's voice, and again he was subtly aware that this man had fought for all that he possessed. Poverty, obscurity, had hampered him, but his determination had overcome all obstacles.

"And why can not the Calhouns share in some of the profits of this undertaking if, after all, they pioneered the land and have possession of it?"

The question dropped like a stone into a pool of deep water. The rings of its disturbance spread far before Hamilton answered.

"Because," and his cold voice came slowly but with weight, "because, no matter what one might attempt to do for them they would undo themselves and, with themselves, us."

"Are they really such profligates?"

"Yes. I dislike to say it for I've known Bill Calhoun all my life. He is a man much older than I am, a royal liver. Generous. Hospitable. But life, for them, consists of four things—"

"And they are?"

"First, last, and always, race-horses. In spirit the Calhouns are fourlegged. Then cards, wine and women. It's a pretty layout. You'll have an experience when you meet them. . . . Going to Hana will be worth the trip if nothing else."

Perhaps some vibration of Howard's brain-pictures reached Haldane. He looked up slowly. Eyes met eyes.

"I'll go," he announced, thrusting his hands deeply and determinedly into his pockets. "When does the next boat sail?"

"Two go next week. Are you in earnest?"

"Absolutely."

"Then we can discuss . . . terms . . . to-morrow."

Mitchell sat up. "I'm sure, Mr. Haldane," he said, "that a time will come when we shall all look back upon this afternoon as a momentous one in our lives."

He spoke with a fat man's pompousness, nodding a little.

"I have a feeling, even now," said Haldane, "that it is." His eyes were serious though his lips smiled. "Sometimes," he went on, "I am pleasantly or unpleasantly aware of destiny's finger in the little pies of our lives."

Both men looked at him curiously. There was solemnity mingled with whimsicality in Haldane's brown eyes, and Howard wondered, for the first time, what turned-down pages this man's life held. No one would ever get a look at them. Men such as Haldane had no confidants and craved no confessionals even in the most difficult passages of their lives, and because Howard, too, had played a lone hand he liked him.

Outside the afternoon had waned to a daffodil evening. Lilac shadows lay on the sea. Far horizons burned. Hamilton waited for Haldane to speak but he sat silently contemplating the square of beauty that the opened window imprisoned. Beauty of sky and sea such as only islands know. Clear-washed, coolly yellow, the sky showed above the crawling gray sea. An almost audible harmony seemed to rise from smoking reefs and cloud-shadowed islands.

"Tell me a bit more about Hana," said Haldane at length; "what little you've detailed has interested me tremendously."

"The Calhouns are typical of one faction that used to inhabit the Islands. I belonged to the other, the missionary element."

That explained it, the repression, the austerity, the quiet force of the man.

"Between the two yawned a great gulf." Howard spoke without interest or emotion. "Do not expect to be able to talk any business with Dick or old Bill inside of a week. In a way this is a bad time to go. The Kamehameha Day races come off shortly and they won't be able to think of anything else until the meet is over. On the other hand it's a good time for you to go, as it will give you an excellent opportunity to size up the whole situation and you'll realize the impossibility of including the Calhouns in matters that entail responsibility."

"By Jove," broke in Mitchell, "madly as they love horse racing, when the day of the race comes they usually get drunk and leave everything to Edwin."

"In any other hands Hana plantation would be a paying concern," continued Howard, "but they've got the ungrown crops of the next five years borrowed on as well as a huge standing debt. The place isn't worth a fourth of what Dehan's lent them on it. He's Dick's closest friend; they've grown up on adjoining plantations. I suspect that for all Dehan's seeming generosity he has an ulterior motive. He's clever, and he's got a clever partner in Kipahulu with him—von Erdmann, a German. Dehan's likable, an indecently handsome beggar, too, but I stand by my first guess, Mitchell, don't you? It's Hula."

"Without a doubt."

"Hula?" questioned Haldane.

"Yes, Hula Calhoun."

"Not knowing the young woman in question, for I presume it's a woman, the statement conveys little to me."

"Nor will it—until you've seen her"—Hamilton's voice was as even as the flow of cold water— "only she isn't, as yet, a woman. She's only a child, but beautiful—"

"Nothing like her on two legs has ever been made," said Mitchell, and after uttering the statement he leaned back with a peculiar expression upon his red face. Compassion was largely mixed in it, compassion that sat oddly upon the coarseness of his features. "Poor kid," he added like an afterthought, "she's never had the ghost of a chance."

"Hula?" inquired Haldane as if he knew her.

"Yes: too much beauty, too much inheritance, too deadly an environment. She'll go straight to Hell as soon as she's old enough. As yet she's unspoilt, thanks to old Edwin, just a baby and rather a marvelous one at that; but he can safeguard her only so far. After that—the deluge. He knows it, too, poor old devil. It's—damnable." Mitchell rose from his seat and walked to the window, his face betraying a capacity for emotion characteristic of stout men. "I'm rather an ass about her," he finished, "I've kids of my own."

Haldane nodded comprehendingly.

"Hula is rather an odd name for a girl, isn't it? I thought it was some kind of dance."

"It is. It's not her real name. The cowboys gave it to her because of her dancing steps as a baby. Every one's used it to the exclusion of her given one. Come to think of it I don't know what her real name is. Don't think any one else does, and that's a fact."

Mitchell made the statement with an expression of surprise in his voice.

"Funny, but positively I can't think of it. Hula suits her somehow. The cowboys—"

"Cowboys?" interrupted Haldane. "I thought you said that it was a sugar plantation."

"It is, but every plantation of any size in these Islands

has some kind of ranch attached to it to raise meat for the laborers. Calhoun has about fifteen hundred head of stock, most of them running at large on the bluffs and in the forest. Lots of them have gone wild. Ruinous business that, letting them into the forests. It'll spoil that end of the moutain for a watershed, if it isn't stopped. But he doesn't or won't see it and Edwin—"

"Who is Edwin?" asked Haldane, finding himself growing more and more interested.

"Edwin's the foreman, a part Hawaiian. Magnificent old fellow. He's brought Hula up. Her mother died when she was born. Best thing that could have happened under the circumstances too. If it hadn't been for Edwin, God knows what would have happened to her by now. It's an extraordinary situation."

"I'm inclined to believe so from what you've outlined. Why doesn't her father or brother—"

"Hell, they pay more attention and devote more care to the poorest thoroughbred colt they raise than to that kid. By Jove, I believe I envy you, Haldane, going over to Hana for the first time." Mitchell regarded him thoughtfully, interestedly, then added half-jokingly, "Take care you don't go under. It's a dangerous place for any one to be in too long. I've wasted considerable portions of my life there. In fact most Islanders have—except Howard here. He had too much sense."

Haldane realized that this gray descendant of missionaries in all likelihood had had little occasion to be invited there or inclination to go if he had been. And yet sometimes these cold men. . . .

"Hana and the Calhouns," Mitchell went on, "are indirectly responsible for the wreck of more than one young fellow's life."

"So you propose sending me there, or do you think my age safeguards me?"

"You'll go through unscathed," said Hamilton.

"I wonder?" Mitchell said it speculatively. He looked at his partner, then at the Englishman, "I wonder if any one can go there and not be influenced somewhat by it?"

"What's so deadly, Mr. Mitchell? The people, the place or the mode of existence?"

Amusement glinted in Haldane's brown eyes.

Mitchell divined his thought. "You smile; you doubt. Well and good. Let me tell you that there is something in the very land over there that goes to one's head. It's subtle but deadly. Even a fat and unimaginative man like myself is conscious of it. One has the feeling that anything, absolutely anything, can happen to one in a place like Hana. And it's not the only one of its sort in the islands—there are others . . . Ulupalakua . . . Waimea . . . places that are invested with the same peculiar atmosphere. I cannot attempt to describe or explain it but it's there. How about it, Howard? It's true, isn't it?"

Hamilton nodded.

"Well," said Haldane straightening up, "I'm keen to go. I want to look into this ditch proposition; it's a job after my own heart. If this thing is feasible I'm your man, Mr. Hamilton. I've been run down, tired; I've been traveling to find rest and distraction; but, after all, isn't work the best cure for all ills?"

He got to his feet to light his pipe. Lanky, unmistakably well bred, he stood over his guests looking at them with direct eyes, brown as earth. Hamilton experienced a moment of deep satisfaction. This man was a fighter. He would do. This afternoon had exceeded his highest hopes.

"Mr. Haldane," he said rising, "when may I expect to see you at my office?"

"To-morrow. I'd like to see a good topographical map of the country."

"I'll have everything you need. Figures, estimates. If you decide, after looking at the country, that the Ditch can be built, Mitchell and I can guarantee unlimited financial backing for it. Every one will want to be in on it and we'll be in on the ground floor!"

A quick exultation flamed through Hamilton's voice; then it subsided, leaving him as cold and gray as before, but Haldane realized that this man's whited exterior was a covering for a deep and passionate nature. His passion was work. This Ditch was in all likelihood the great dream of his life. That he shrank a little from the absolute despoiling of the Calhouns made Haldane like him better. He was big, forceful, compelling. He would be a man worth working with and for. Haldane had no sentiment in regard to Hana or the Calhouns though he had become interested in them. He was sorry for them in an abstract way because his own life had not been happy. They were without doubt weaklings, and it is written in the pages of progress that all such must go. Perhaps it would be possible to devise some scheme whereby they might reap some of the profits without endangering other people's interests. Time enough for that later. After all they or their immediate forbears had pioneered the land. It would only be just to give them something from it. Elation pricked through his veins. Life once more seemed to pick up and move on.

"Well, I have a dinner engagement to keep, unfortunately, or I would ask you both to dine with me. I'll have to be dressing. I shall be down at your office to-morrow at ten."

"I shall be waiting for you."

"We can line things up a bit," broke in Mitchell, "and next week you can go over, that is, unless you have plans to prevent."

"I have none."

"Good. You see it's imperative that we waste no time. Every one knows Bill's standing. Some one might slip in ahead of us with a proposition like this. I don't doubt that Dehan will advance cash as long as he has it to spare. But I'm a bit afraid of von Erdmann. He may try to check things, and Dick—or the old man—might be only too glad to jump at any offer that would make them feel they could repay Dehan a little of what he's lent them. I can't afford to let some one slip in ahead."

"I understand. Then the sooner I get off the better?"

"Yes," assented Hamilton.

"Curious to see Hula?" asked Mitchell facetiously.

"I'm woman proof," answered Haldane a trifle contemptuously, "besides you said she is only a child and I'm—"

A peculiar expression crossed his browned features and his face seemed to close up.

"My error," conceded Mitchell laughing, "but no talisman, however powerful, makes a man safe against Hula. She will take possession of your soul. Remember this when you meet her, when you get to know her. She is the spirit incarnate of Hana. Deadly. Destructive. There's no withstanding her. It's been the same always, even when she was a baby. She's a boy and a girl in one. A woman and a baby."

"I shall be interested to make the acquaintance of so remarkable a child," said Haldane quietly. "Good evening. I shall see you both to-morrow at ten."

CHAPTER II

Steaming along the coast of East Maui, Haldane's eyes went constantly to the mass of Haleakala that bulked high above the polished sea. He knew it was rated to be the largest extinct volcano in the world and that its dome composed two-thirds of the island. The rays of the noonday sun fell revealingly on its weathered and titanic slopes. Jungled ravines cleft back and were lost in lavender distances; gorges yawned their jaws on the sea; streaks of white high under the cloud-line suggested cataracts, and Haldane appreciated the volume of water the country must hoard. Howard had not misestimated the wealth that might be derived from it, and Mitchell made no mistake in deciding to back up the undertaking.

Haldane stretched in his chair and watched the shore as it slipped past the ship's rail. The boat was due to arrive in Hana at three, and it was only a little past noon. The route lay close to the land, and he was able to see the country in detail. It was a coast of a thousand greens, of a thousand streams; some dropping like transparent veils from cliff to cliff; others rolling down thunderous sheets of yellow foam; others wrestling fiercely with ragged volcanic rocks; still others winding placid, *hau*-shaded, through peaceful valleys, beached with white sand and met by a fiercely-blue and satiny sea.

A coast of dreams . . . unreal . . . stupendous.

A woman, walking by, gave him a passing look of interest. He was moderately broad of shoulder, slim-hipped, and had about him an air of aloneness which is characteristic of a certain out-door type of man. His eyes were serious and smile-wrinkles made their outer corners delightful. He had a careless and casual air but, passing a second time, the woman knew him to be determined and suspected that he had had a difficult life.

Haldane's eyes appreciated the grace of her figure. She walked flowingly. There was ease and softness about her and, though he had been in the Islands only three months, he knew that Hawaiian blood ran in her veins although her skin was gardenia-white. Her eyes, dark-lashed, had in them the expression of one who has loved too long and too well. In all likelihood this girl was not, according to the world's rating good yet, without knowing her, Haldane felt liking and compassion for her. He wondered who she was, where she was going, what her life had been.

At lunch the steward seated them at the same table. They smiled as friends smile who have known each other a long time, understandingly.

"We seem to be the only passengers," observed Haldane. "Where are you going? To Hana?"

"Yes. You are too?"

The man smiled, "Yes."

"To visit the Calhouns?"

Haldane nodded.

"Where have you known Dick? I am sure you are a *malahini* (a newcomer) and I suspect you are British. Are you?"

"I am British; to be more exact, I am English. My name is Haldane. I have not, as yet, met Richard Calhoun, Miss—" he stopped.

"Miss McKaine. Helen McKaine. I have known the Calhouns always," said the girl looking at him; "they are the dearest friends I have. I'm going to stay with them over the races."

"I am going on business."

"Well, you'll not be able to do any until after the 11th of June," observed the woman; "but you'll have an excellent opportunity to size things up a bit."

"That's what I want to do," said Haldane as they rose from the table. "Are you going on deck?"

The girl nodded.

"May I walk with you?"

"I'd like you to. You've been in the Islands how long?"

"Nearly three months."

"I wonder if you can imagine, in the slightest degree, what's ahead of you? I suppose you've come to see Dicky about his land." She paused and looked at him, then added like an afterthought, "Poor Dick."

"Is he so—unfortunate?" asked Haldane as they walked the slowly lifting deck.

"He has been cursed from birth with a terrific inheritance and a treacherous environment."

"Which, to your thinking, is the more deadly?" asked Haldane.

"In Dick's case, environment, though he has a surplus of the other too. Look at it," she gestured toward the Island, "look at those teeming forests, at those headlands, at those smashing seas. Don't you feel the untrammeled spirit of the place? Wait until you get ashore! Purple roads with yellow plumaria flowers starring them; green fields of cane—"

"Careful," warned the man smilingly, "don't lay it on too thickly."

The woman smiled. "Let me finish! Race-horses, music, leisure, leis. . . ."

The girl sighed with the gusty sweetness of a tropic breeze then lifted her eyes to the man's. "They couldn't survive it, any of them—any one for that matter—if they stay long."

In her eyes Haldane could see memory pictures moving.

"They've had too much beauty, too much joy, been too cut off from everything. I've lived a life somewhat similar to theirs. I know."

There was, for a moment, an aching beauty to her face; then her spirit seemed to shrug its shoulders dismissingly. "You'll like them, Mr. Haldane. They are fine people. They've loved their life. It's been gorgeous. But it's ruined them. Dick may have a come-back in him. I doubt it. He's a darling; but," she gestured expressively with her hands—lovely hands with rosy palms and slim, pointed fingers— "but I know Uncle Bill hasn't, nor Hula—"

"I've heard of her," interrupted Haldane.

"Have you?" asked the woman quickly. "How?"

"Mr. Mitchell, of Honolulu, happened to remark that she was the loveliest child that he'd ever seen."

"She's utterly beautiful, unique, and as yet unspoiled; but she'll go the way of Dick and Uncle Bill unless some man marries her and takes her away within the next two years."

"How old is she?"

"Nearly fifteen," replied the woman. "It'll break old Edwin's heart if she reverts to type. He's loved her so, guarded her so jealously. She owes him—everything."

"You've made me curious to know these people and experience the life they lead," said Haldane.

"You'll experience sufficient of it in these next two weeks," observed Helen; "it'll be something you'll never forget." She smiled amusedly. "I shall enjoy watching your reaction to it."

"There'll be little, if any," said the man. "I don't boast that I'm bullet proof; I've lived too long to make such a rash statement, but what feeling there is in me has been—felt."

There was a note of finality in his voice and a sort of fierce desolation flashed into his face, then subsided. Helen darted a quick comprehensive glance at him.

"Burnt out," was her thought, "like me, but differently. He's loved some one terribly and has been short rationed. Whoever she is or was, she's a fool." She studied him for a moment: "I wonder how long he's been like this. It'll make a difference."

"At any rate, Mr. Haldane," she said aloud, "it will be an interesting experience; this phase of life in Hawaii is passing away. A few years more will see the end of it, and if you know yourself to be safe from it—"

"Are you—mocking me? I did not mean to boast, as I explained, when I spoke as I did. I am interested by many things but not affected by them."

"Hana will affect you," said the woman, "perhaps not vitally, but you'll be influenced a little by it."

"I shall be interested to see, Miss McKaine."

"Call me Helen, first names are an institution in Hawaii."

"I should like to. Thanks. Mine is Anthony."

At three the steamer dropped anchor. A canoe came out before the whale boat to take passengers ashore had been lowered. A brown-bodied Hawaiian brought a note up the ship's side and handed it to Helen.

"Dick's gone to Kipahulu. He'll be back about sundown, with a mob," she informed Haldane when she finished reading. "He says his father is not well. Poor Uncle Bill; he has them periodically. And Hula's with Edwin in Kaupo getting steers. That leaves Diana to greet us." The girl grimaced prettily and continued in explanation, "Dick's married recently a trained nurse who came to take care of his father. I believe she's fascinating, but I fancy she's difficult. Men like Dick possess a positive genius for marrying women who cannot understand them and who are not suited to them."

"Well, we'll have one another until Dick comes," said Haldane.

He wondered why Dick had not married this girl. She could have been fittingly part of the highly-colored life of Hana as it had been portrayed to him. Perhaps they had known each other too well and too long.

On the wharf a second Hawaiian, old, with a flower-decked hat and a wrinkled face, greeted Helen and led them to a carriage.

"Beauties, aren't they?" asked the girl getting in, and she gestured toward the horses.

"By Jove, yes!" agreed Haldane, then added, "So Hana has not, as yet, been invaded by automobiles?"

"Not yet. There are not more than a hundred cars on the whole island of Maui."

They drove through the town at a smart trot under spreading *kamani* trees; past shrubbery-smothered cottages. Rustling rivulets, fragrant with four-o'-clocks, flashed on the sides of the streets; a sugar mill filled the air with vast vibrations; and the deadly sweet odor of molasses drifted to their nostrils. In the yards about the mill straining teams of mules and blue-coated Japanese laborers swarmed about loaded cars of cane. Cries, the mighty rumbling of machinery reached their ears . . . faintly . . . persistently. . . .

They turned into a short tree-shaded avenue and came to the Calhouns' gardens. Spacious. Spreading.

Helen looked affectionately and with recognition at them; at Norfolk Island pines of mechanical precision, at purple mango trees, at the intense blue of the sea where it showed between the dark fingers of cypresses.

Haldane looked about with the intense interest with which one first regards a place much talked about. Truly if this generation of Calhouns were wasters the previous ones had been noble builders.

The carriage halted before the steps of a white house of many spreading wings. Baskets of fern hung between the pillars of the verandas; ginger and Chinese violets exhaled a damp and heady fragrance from below the railings.

A step sounded and a woman came out. Haldane knew she must be Dick Calhoun's wife, a woman with odd, secretive eyes and an unhappy face. Her features were interesting but irregular. Wine-red sprays of color showed below her high cheek bones. Haldane felt that she held the whole world in distrust.

He mounted the steps, hat in hand.

"Mrs. Calhoun?"

"Yes."

"My name is Haldane. I wrote to your husband by the last mail that I would be coming to see him, on business, by this steamer, and he directed that I should come here."

"He is expecting you. Will you come in?"

"Thanks. May I present Miss McKaine; she was a fellow passenger on the *Klaukina* and is, I believe, one of Mr. Calhoun's guests—"

"How do you do? Father mentioned you would be coming."

Diana Calhoun spoke politely but her eyes were distrustful.

"This boy will take you to your rooms."

She spoke to a white-coated Japanese who took up the suitcases.

"Dick will be in about six. We dine at eight."

"Who's there?" a thick voice called boomingly from upstairs. "Here, Di, bring 'em up I say!"

The woman's form grew rigid.

"Just a minute—father." She brought out the word reluctantly.

"Is that Mr. Calhoun?" asked Helen.

"Yes."

"May I go up?"

"He—isn't—well."

"I know." Helen's face was compassionate. "I've known him all my life. He was my father's best friend."

"That you, Helen?" called the great voice.

"Yes."

"Come up. Hell! but it's great to hear you again!"

"I'd better go. Poor old man." Helen looked at her hostess, then without waiting for permission ran up the stairs.

Haldane waited. Diana Calhoun did not move. The spots of color in her cheeks flickered and her eyes grew as watching as a cat's.

"Shall I go with this boy?" Haldane asked, for the Japanese waited expectantly with a bag in each hand.

"Yes"—the woman recollected herself with an effort.

Helen appeared at the stair-head.

"Uncle Bill insists on seeing you for a moment, Anthony," she laughed; then in a lower tone, "Please come up."

"Pardon me, Mrs. Calhoun," said the man. The woman did not answer. She inclined her head in acquiescence but her lips tightened.

Haldane mounted the stairs and Helen's hand fell lightly upon his arm.

"You are a dear. Poor Uncle Bill." Her eyes were wet and she wiped them resentfully. "I ought not to mind seeing him like this. He's had what he wanted from life."

They entered a spacious room. A jowled, blue-faced man lay in a four-poster bed propped up by a quantity of pillows. His face and surroundings reflected the life he had led. Silver racing cups, photos of men and women and horses adorned the room. Beside his bed was a small table covered with medicine bottles. A nurse in a white uniform stood looking out of the window.

"Hello, glad to see you—Haldane. That's the name isn't it, Helen?"

"Yes."

Haldane took the outstretched hand and shook it.

"Sorry I couldn't be down. Damn sorry. Don't like to be inhospitable. But you understand. Sit down. I'll be right as a bank in a couple more days. This," he gestured toward the table, "is all bosh. What I need now is a drink. Hair of the dog that bit you—"

He chuckled, then glancing at Helen tipped his head toward the white figure at the window. "Send her out," he signaled.

Helen went to her. She possessed the gift of being charming; even her dismissal of the woman was graciously done.

"Thank you awfully;" her hand fell lightly upon the nurse's for a moment. Her words, her acts, seemed to forge a bond of understanding between them.

Old Calhoun heaved a windy sigh of relief when she disappeared.

"Damn fine woman, Helen, but depressing. Like Di. Makes you feel like a corpse." He turned to Haldane. "Did you meet Diana?"

"Yes."

"She's a fine girl but no wife for a man like Dick. Doesn't belong in our stable. It's tough for her. Been brought up pretty strictly I imagine. Can't stomach our life and won't adjust herself. Looks like a caged animal sometimes, poor girl. Is afraid that Dick's going to be a replica of his drunken old Dad. Helen!"

He reached out and drew the girl down to his bedside. She laced her fingers compassionately through the old man's. He had been a hard-liver, a spendthrift, a gambler, a drunkard; but he was a great figure in his own way. He had lived life joyously; generously. She had known him always. "Old Man Calhoun." It had been a name to conjure up pictures with when she was a child; pictures of race-horses and *leis* (wreaths) and *luaus* (feasts). He had always been in the forefront of everything, with a wreath around his hat and another about his shoulder. Walrus-mustached, merry; pinching little girls' cheeks; putting his arm about women; running purplish hands over horses to ascertain their condition. . . . With a "Hey, damn you, but it's great to see you again. Come on in and we'll have a drink! *Aloha ka ko!* (Love to all)." And he had loved them all; horses and men and women. Open armed, open hearted he had embraced life as it came to him. Race-horses' hoofs had beaten their tattoo upon his heart; the perfume of women and flowers filled his nostrils; the great headlands of Hana gladdened his eyes; the sonorous music of the Islands rung in his ears.

Now, he lay, lavender, worn, like a tired old hound that, hearing a younger generation going out, rouses itself for a last run.

"Now you're here, Helen, I begin to realize that the races are near. Have you ever missed coming to us for them?"

"Never, Uncle Bill."

"I'll stake my life on it. Fond of horses, Haldane?"

"What Englishman isn't, Mr. Calhoun?"

"Right! Damnation, what would we do without horses. Bless their hides. Long from home? Helen, how's to rustling some drinks?"

The girl looked dubious.

"It won't set you back?"

"Hell, no! A little good whisky never hurt any man. All that keeps an old fellow young. Ring for Fugi, and—don't tell her," he rolled his eyes toward the door, "or Di."

The Japanese appeared.

"Three glasses, Fugi. Whisky—and soda."

"I'll take mine straight," said Helen when it was being poured.

Calhoun slapped his thigh.

"True to form! Here's to you, Helen, and to you, Haldane. Aloha ka ko!"

"And to Silver Wings," said the woman, lifting her glass

toward the picture of a great-thighed gray horse. "May he never lose a race."

"We are racing him for the last time on the eleventh. Tom's imported a new horse from California, 'Hurricane.' Thinks he'll beat our nag. Can't be done. Silver Wings is a descendant of Isonomy and his dam's pedigree traces right back without a break to the Godolphin Arab. Don't breed 'em any bluer. Wait until you see him, Haldane. Dick or Hula will take you through the stables to-morrow. Wish I could but I'll be down in a day or so now. Well, Aloha!" he lifted and drained his glass.

"Now, Helen, my pipe. I'm beginning to feel like myself again."

The girl attended to the old man's wants, then seated herself in a chair by his bed and held his hand. Haldane watched her. So they sat, sipping their drinks while the old man grew increasingly garrulous. He talked of race-horses and racing, of records made on every track in the world. His eyes burned like live coals; blood suffused his hanging jowls.

"You've come on business, Haldane," he said turning to his guest, "well, forget it until the races are over. Live. Enjoy yourself. A man only lives once. Take everything. I have. I've paid for it but it's been worth the price. I have no kicks to register. I wouldn't have missed or changed a moment of my life. I have no regrets save that it's so nearly done. But some sparks of me will live on to enjoy when I have gone. Wish I could guarantee those two kids of mine the time I've had. . . ."

The light died for a moment behind his eyes and his spirit seemed to look regretfully back at the path it had trod, lingering briefly among the trophies of the valiant past that filled the room: racing cups, sets of "plates" taken from hoofs that would ring no more upon any track . . . goblets, photographs, whips and caps. Then it seemed to come back.

The sound of steps arrested the old man's flow of thought.

"Di," he said; "she's a good girl. Damn good. But she can't understand. It's too bad. Sets too much store by appearances. Don't have to bother with them in a place like this. Ditch the glasses, Helen," he winked like a huge boy. "Well, Di, come to rescue your guests? It's about time they were toddling off to clean up. Dick ought to be along presently."

Dressing in his low ceilinged spacious room Anthony's mind went back to the old man upstairs. He thought of his ringing words, "I wouldn't have missed a minute of my life. I've loved all of it. I've no regrets, save that it's so nearly done."

What a triumph for any one to be able to feel that he had had the uttermost—according to his own way of thinking—from life.

Haldane scraped savagely at his jaw with the razor and wondered what benefits he had ever reaped by essaying to live his life according to accepted standards of what was wrong and right. He had tried to play the game, to carry on, to use the phraseology of his school days, in a marriage that had been the supreme blunder of his life, that had warped and weakened him and discolored his outlook. . . . Just out of college with no experience to guide him he had met a girl whose beauty dazzled and dizzied him. He succeeded in attaching himself to her only to find out that she had neither sympathy nor understanding for his work or for himself. Besottedly as he had loved her at first it did not take him long to discover her true character. She was selfish, shallow and disloyal. She had forced him to give up his chosen career to follow stocks in order that she might pursue the social life of London that was her ambition. Haldane had possessed limited means of his own and had hoped to increase them. . . . City life had been insupportable, but he had loved her and was ready to make any sacrifice to have her love him in return. He learned with time she had no real love for any one but herself. When he failed to achieve the success she had expected of him she had not scrupled to show her contempt. Bewildered, disgusted, hopeless of ever being able to please her he decided to take up the profession for which he had fitted himself, engineering. It was his passion; for her he had relinquished it, wasted valuable years, but he knew that he must return to it if he were ever to make a mark for himself. He informed his wife of his decision and she told him should he really elect to go into the field he could go alone. She would remain in London with her mother. Reluctant to leave her, although they seemed to call out everything that was worst in each other by living together, he had yielded a second time, and driven by the ferocity of his feelings he accomplished some moderate successes. But Margaret Haldane brushed them aside. What were paltry thousands when Haldane's younger brother George had made millions in the stock market?

Haldane had known his wife's fierce contempt because of his inability to achieve wealth on an equal scale. Heart-sick, disgusted, he had finally written to an engineering company in East Africa asking for employment. The man at the head of it had been a college chum. To his astonishment he was informed after some months' delay that they had no place for him. Years afterwards he had met his friend and learned that Margaret also had written. . . . Then he left her.

With time success had come. He sent her a generous allowance, sometimes smiling ruefully, thinking of her dissatisfaction with the amount, ample though it would seem to most women. Occasionally she wrote to him, usually to ask for more money, and once, after he had accomplished his most notable undertaking, to inquire when he would be coming back to England. He answered that he did not know, but he determined he would never see her again. Margaret would not be averse to playing the rôle of a great man's wife; she could do it rather well, but he did not intend to come under her influence again. She destroyed his faith in himself, lessened his morale, made it impossible for him to accomplish anything. Affectionate, craving love and understanding he had writhed under her cruel and consistent punishment in those early years and now he did not want her approbation. He had schooled himself to aloneness, devoted himself to his work. He knew better than to risk being with her. She would destroy him once again. . . .

He stood for a moment, razor in hand, thinking. Work. It had been the saving grace of his life, yet overwork, combined with a rotten climate, had temporarily disabled him and filled him with a great distaste for living. The combination of mental and physical condition had produced in him a peculiar state that made everything seem unprofitable. A great bitter hatred for life swept through him. He had tried to play fair and had been cheated. He knew it. He had given full measure to Margaret and had got nothing in return. She once had utterly possessed him and still did in an intangible way. He knew her caliber, despised it and yet could not shake himself mentally free of her. She still held him, somehow. When things happened his mind involuntarily leaped back, thinking . . . wondering . . . how it would affect her. He did not, could not love her. Love, if one might call the feeling he had had for her love, had been killed; she had hurt his mind, and the scar of her destroying influence remained.

He threw up his chin and proceeded shaving. He was an ass to be unable to shake himself free of her. He had been loyal and disloyalty had been meted to him. He had mistaken outward beauty for the inner sort. He owed her nothing . . . yet fragments of his father's teaching lingered to hamper him. . . . "Play a losing game as you'd play a winning one. . . ." Margaret was his wife; he had no one to thank for his marriage but himself. He must go through with it, face it as he would have faced any other difficulty. . . . Decency demanded it of him, yet what had he got in return for his effort to do the right thing? Nothing! How old Calhoun's heartily expressed sentiments knocked on the head all the generally accepted tenets of living. He had undoubtedly broken every commandment; had lived madly, badly and gladly. He had had to pay the price of his gladness; but at least he had had it, and he declared that the price justified what had gone before. No one, decent, could ask for any more.

He checked the dangerous trend of his thought, peered into the glass and finished shaving.

People were beginning to arrive. He heard voices, greetings, the quick steps of Orientals. Laughter. Dick and his guests, back from Kipahulu. He wondered what manner of man his host's son could be.

Somewhere outside a dog was barking, persistently, defiantly as if it both challenged and denied the spell of its surroundings. Haldane had always been conscious of a peculiar charm about the Islands. They possessed a beauty compounded of opposing elements. Combined with the lavish abundance of the tropics was a vigor characteristeric of colder lands and an impression of space such as one is confronted with in deserts. It is a space resulting from the great altitudes of the volcanically formed islands . . . a space that dizzies and intoxicates with its suggestion of unrestricted freedom. Blue seas, blue distances, lofty blue mountain tops that arouse in one longings for things constructive and destructive, and in this locality the spell was more potent than in Honolulu.

Of a sudden the man distrusted his surroundings; they worked in a subtle but deadly manner, hand in hand with the frustrated fulness of his life.

He strode to the door hastily.

Opening it he stepped into the hall. Some one collided with him, and so violent was the impact of the small body that he was compelled to embrace it to avoid being knocked down. He looked and knew at once it was Hula that he held. The face upturned to his was heart shaped, the mouth a crimson rose, the eyes luminous, silken lashed.

He had never seen anything that even remotely approached the rare quality of this long-legged child in her breeches and boots. She was like a hibiscus flower, flaming, tropical, and like a valiant unawakened boy. He knew her life thus far must have been wholesome and vigorous. Her face was vivid, browned, with candid eyes and beseeching brows that tilted above the bridge of a delicate little nose as tantalizing as the red lips beneath it.

A moment they stared at each other then fell apart laughing good-humoredly.

"Hurt your nose on my sternum?" asked Anthony as the child rubbed it ruefully.

"Yes; who are you?"

"Anthony—" he began.

"Oh, I know about him," Hula interrupted; "that was one of the books Uncle Edwin got for me to read. He found it on a table inside. We had trouble learning from it. The words were hard and I used to cry because I wanted to ride and not read. But when we got to know it the words were beautiful. The lady was Cleopatra."

"Wonderful primer for a child like you," observed the man laughing, tremendously intrigued.

"But you aren't that Anthony, of course," the girl said,

then studied him intently, "but I've a feeling that you sort of look like him."

Haldane bowed playfully. "And you, I'll venture, will be a second Cleopatra."

"What's your other name, Mr. Anthony?"

"Haldane. And yours?"

"Hula."

"They couldn't have named you better. Where were you off to in such a hurry?"

The girl's hand flew to her mouth.

"My dog! I was chasing a puppy I took from a man in Kipahulu yesterday. He was a damn Portuguese and he was beating it. Nishi, the second houseboy, let it out of my room when he brought milk up to it. I was trying to catch it when I bumped into you."

"May I help you to look for it, Hula?"

The child's eyes opened wide.

"Oh, will you, Mr. Anthony?" she cried in a throaty and thrilling voice.

Later, when the guests began to assemble in the *lanai* (a sort of glorified veranda) Haldane came out of the garden.

"What have you been doing?" asked Helen. "Looking at the garden?"

"I've been helping Hula to find a dog."

Helen and the other guests chimed their mirth.

"Trust Hula to rope in the first comer! Dick, this is Mr. Haldane."

Helen beckoned imperiously with her head and a man detached himself from the group about the table and came forward.

"Sorry I wasn't down to meet you," he said thrusting out his hand, "but I'm glad you're with us."

Haldane looked into a clean-cut face with dark-lashed blue eyes. Dick's legs were straight, his shoulders erect, his chin square. He was forceful, vigorous. . . . Haldane was quite taken aback.

"You've met my wife? Then let me present my other guests. Dr. Fitzmaurice, the Island veterinarian, and Mr. von Erdmann."

Haldane's eyes passed from the Irishman's long, aristocratic face to that of the German. Tall, blue eyed, with something unpleasantly suggestive of a shark's belly in the quality and pallor of his skin, he acknowledged the introduction and Haldane knew why Howard Hamilton and his partner distrusted this man. Were he to get the slightest wind of their scheme. . . .

"Deanie!" Dick called to a voluptuous looking woman, "your attention for a moment. I want to introduce you."

The woman looked over her shoulder archly.

"Seeing it's to a man, I'll come."

She moved toward them. Small, dimpled with a smile and with eyes that were covert invitations she looked up at Haldane. He had encountered her type before and despised it.

"And this is Jack, Mrs. Lightfoot's husband." Dick made the statement roguishly as a boy.

Deanie laughed and her husband, a big red man with a head as tawny as a lion's but less noble, lounged forward. Haldane rather pitied him. He knew his lot was not enviable.

A Japanese waiter arrived with cocktails, and a maid followed with caviar on a silver tray.

The guests grew congenial. A second and third round of drinks was served.

"Where's Harry?" asked Dick looking around.

"Upstairs with Uncle Bill, I think," Helen said.

"Hey! Dehan! You're losing out!" shouted Lightfoot in an effort to be convivial.

"I'm not either. The old man's decided he's coming down," a voice shouted in answer; "we're getting up steam."

"Shall I go up and try to stop him?" asked Diana hastily.

"As you like, my dear." Dick shrugged his shoulders for he knew the futility of such an attempt. When his wife had gone he moved toward Helen.

"Where's Mrs. Bane gone to? I'd forgotten about her. Fine neighbor you are! Thought I'd invited you to help Kay to entertain this gang. Why don't you look out for my guests, Deanie?"

"Mrs. Bane's still dressing, I suppose," Deanie giggled; "she'd be flattered to know you'd forgotten about her being here. She thinks she's a knockout where men are concerned. Wait till you meet her, Mr. Haldane: the Golden Widow, the Sunbeam Lady. She plays the rôles to perfection. Take care. Here she comes. A late but effective entrance."

Haldane could not suppress an instant of mirth at Deanie's good-humored maliciousness. There was some likable quality in her after all.

A golden-haired woman, clad in a dull gold gown, came slowly across the *lanai*. Nameless sorrow, an appeal for protection and understanding, seemed to emanate from her.

"Oh, I'm sorry I'm late. Forgive me."

"There's nothing to forgive, Beautiful Lady." Fitzmaurice hastened forward. "I saved a cocktail for you. Here it is."

"How good of you. I," she laughed deliciously, "really need a keeper. Isn't that what the guardians of the feeble-minded are called?"

"I should think another sort of a keeper would be more in order—how about a husband?"

"Don't." The woman's eyelids quivered downward, registering tragedy. "I don't want to, ever, entrust my happiness to other hands than my own. It's too risky."

"Some man's been a brute to her."

So flashed the thought into the Irishman's expressive face and Haldane did not doubt that the aristocratic and easy-going fellow felt murder in his heart, as Mrs. Bane roused his chivalrous nature to her defense.

"I hear Dad. Excuse me, I must give the old boy a hand."

Breaking away from his guests, Dick mounted the stairs and reappeared after a few minutes with a man Haldane guessed to be the half-white, Dehan. Between them old Calhoun walked. At his appearance a hubbub broke out.

"Bring on the fatted calf!" cried the old man; "the prodigal's returned. Thanks, boys; capital! Now, girls, come and kiss me. Lovely, Deanie. Capital, Helen. I feel better every minute. Who's the vision?" He waved toward Mrs. Bane. "Come nearer. I want to see if you are real. By Jove, you are. Introduce me, Dick. Can't keep her all to yourselves. Must let an old fellow have his inning too."

Mrs. Bane expanded. She felt that, thanks to this old man, she was going to be a success, that her visit to Hana might result in something worth while. She applied herself to him.

"Drinks, Dicky, drinks!" ordered Calhoun; "must celebrate such an occasion."

He pressed the white fingers of the widow's hand which he had detained in his possession and Haldane saw Diana's involuntary recoil. He did not doubt that, to her, her father-in-law's behavior appeared amorous, but he knew it was compounded of many subtler essences. This old man loved women as he loved horses and good times. They were all part of the fabric of a highly-colored life that was fast slipping from him. There was a pathetic quality in old Calhoun's open-armed liking of his fellow creatures. His geniality, his hospitality were kinglike. From the moment of his entrance a different atmosphere had taken possession of the assemblage.

"Hey there, *Pelikani* (Britisher)," he waved his arm at Haldane, "have you met every one? No, you can't have met Harry for he's been upstairs with me. Here, you son-of-a-sea-cook, come over and be introduced. Haldane, this is Harry Dehan. Prince of a fellow. Don't make 'em any finer. Grown up with Dick; just like my own son."

The two clasped hands.

Dehan had a gallant bearing and an insolent grace. In his long black eyes volcanic fires burned. His voice was resonant, gold-lined; his hair glossily black. He was brown skinned and possessed a leisurely manner of speaking but had a violent mouth.

Haldane was both attracted and repelled.

"Well, boys and girls, here's luck!" Calhoun lifted his glass. His eyes swept the room. "Where's Diana, Dick? Find her. We can't drink without your wife."

Dick departed and returned in a few moments, alone.

"Di's busy, Dad, with the cook, and asks to be excused. She's detained by some matter."

His faced was flushed, his eyes angry.

"Very well," cried Calhoun, knowing well enough that the Chinaman who had cooked for him all his life was quite capable of proving equal to any emergency that might arise. "Too bad, it's hell to be a hostess. Well, good people, here's *aloha ka ko!*"

"Aloha!" responded his guests.

To Haldane, drinking his third cocktail, the ringing toast seemed symbolic of Calhoun's whole life. How he brought it out! Like a great battle cry— "Love to every one! Love to all!"

"Dinner serving."

The deferential voice of Nishi, the second boy, penetrated through the babel in the *lanai*.

"I'm hungry, by Jove, and didn't know it. Bed kills a

man. Here, Harry, here, Dick, let's be moving. That's it. Thanks. There's life in the old dog yet."

Supported between the two of them he preceded the company to the dining-room and took his place at the head of the table. Chairs were drawn back. Guests seated themselves. Laughter, conversation broke out. Calhoun's spirit dominated the gathering as he roused his guests to the same pinnacle of enjoyment as his own.

Diana came in and took a late seat, apologizing for being detained. Her eyes glittered and the sprays of color seemed to throb in her cheeks. Her manner was tense from inner pressure, though she strove to hide it by assuming the rôle of gracious hostess.

Mrs. Bane, although she was busy creating an impression, was conscious of an empty chair beside Dehan and she wondered for whom it had been placed.

"Deanie, it was just wonderful of you to write and invite me to this beautiful place," she cried cooingly.

"I always try to stand in well with my men friends," laughed the little woman, "so occasionally I give them a treat by importing some new material to Hana for them to whet their hearts upon."

"Well, you got the real stuff this time!" cried Calhoun looking admiringly at the blond woman by his side.

Mrs. Bane was stifled with excitement. Truly fate had flung her into the right environment. In this place anything might happen. Already she was invading half-a-dozen new fields. Fitzmaurice hung on her words. Calhoun seemed to turn a tide of admiration and attention toward her. Dick smiled at her. Haldane, seated beside her, was delightfully attentive.

She held the center of the stage.

She grew wittier, more fascinating with the stimulus of success. Deanie looked on amusedly. The widow dismissed her hostess with a thought. Jealous! She looked at Dehan. He of them all was the only one who did not seem intent upon her. Then she looked at Haldane. She must make inquiries concerning him. Of them all he seemed the most worth her time. The intangible aura that surrounds men who have accomplished something worth while hung about him. A second husband, carefully chosen, was the objective of her life.

She turned the battery of her brown eyes and golden hair upon him for a moment, then took them away. She was too wise to specialize early in the game, but she wished him to know that she was aware of him.

Deanie, watching, squealed with glee and her hand fell upon Helen's.

"Oh Boy, there's going to be fun. The Sunbeam Lady thinks she's going to bring down that big man. Delish! Nothing gives me such joy as to see another woman fail."

Helen smiled, "But she may not fail." Then her eyes went worriedly to Dick. A line showed by his mouth. Diana looked remote. They had been quarreling and instinct told her that it was partly about Dick's father but also about herself. She wanted to say something, to make the situation less tense—that she had known the Calhouns all her life, that their liking for her had in no wise lessened because of the way she lived, that she was a welcomed, a loved guest in their house, that no one had Dick's welfare so at heart as she had. . . .

She clenched her hands beneath the table. Instinct warned her that things were about to go wrong.

Mrs. Bane glanced at the tense face of the beautiful half-white. Helen was a silent destroyer but not to be genuinely feared because of the life she had led. Virtue, so-called, had its compensations. It carried weight with men like Haldane. Mrs. Bane had been wisely careful in her widowhood, careful that the world should know her for a good woman, one who bore her troubles bravely and who, subjected to temptation because of her beauty, was too innately fastidious to be attracted by it. A man such as she intended to get would feel no call for anything that was not above reproach. For instance, this Haldane. English, with rigid principles regarding his own mode of life and a woman's. She studied him guardedly, then became aware that his attention was focused upon the doorway and not upon herself.

A slim girl, who was still lingeringly a child stood in it, clad in riding breeches and with a dog clutched in the crook of her arm.

"Hello, Toppie," cried Fitzmaurice rising. Haldane half rose also and the girl advanced. Dehan pulled out the chair beside him and the child sat down, deliberately. Her eyes wandered over the guests, then fixed themselves upon Mrs. Bane.

"Hula," called Dick, "this is Mrs. Bane, Deanie's guest."

The child acknowledged the introduction, but the woman knew instantly that Hula disliked her.

"And this is Mr. Haldane."

"We've met."

"Already?" laughed her brother. "Hula, you're coming on. Look out, girls, when she leaves the wire."

There was a careless brotherly pride in his voice.

"We'll be numbered with the 'also-rans'," shrieked Deanie; "any one as destructively lovely as you, Hula, should be compelled to go veiled."

Hula looked at Deanie with a sort of polite disdain, then her eyes went to Haldane. She smiled at him and the man received the impression that she came toward him with outheld arms. Dehan looked at her, then lowered his lashes to veil the flash of his eyes, and Haldane realized that Hamilton had not been wrong in his surmise.

Hula!

Dinner progressed, but the attention of every one was no longer centered upon Mrs. Bane but upon Hula. Between violent tussles with her half-grown dog she essayed to eat. Without effort she commanded attention, evoked interest and provoked laughter. No wonder people predicted disaster for her. She had too much appeal. She was at once intensely friendly and aloof, as only a child can be. Haldane longed to see the man who was responsible for her being as she was. Uncle Edwin . . . a name to conjure with.

Calhoun called jovially to her and she answered him in a like vein but Haldane perceived that there was a fine distaste in her feeling for her father's state.

Had any one asked Hula whom she loved best and admired most she might have, out of deference to her father, hesitated in replying; but her heart would have answered unswervingly for the old cowboy. He had taught her to ride and rope, to be cool in tight places. His code had been a hard one, but she knew it to be a good one. More than once it had reduced her to stormy tears—tears she had wept out on his breast. She had been chided and schooled and comforted there, but she loved her goodly life with the hard-riding, neck-risking *paniolas* (cowboys) of the Islands. In a child's dim way she appreciated Edwin's effort to safeguard her from the easy manner of living that existed in her father's house.

After repeated efforts to accomplish a meal and retain hold of her dog Hula thrust it into Dehan's lap.

"Hold it," she commanded.

His sullenness vanished at her notice of him. The meal progressed toward its end. Fresh courses were served. New wines poured.

Mrs. Bane knew her hold upon the evening had ended; without trying Hula had taken it from her. Her hands clenched. Eclipsed by a child! She looked at her fixedly, at the dark, wide-open eyes, at the crimson lips. She was beautiful and possessed a quality of appeal that was destructive.

Suddenly, the puppy, which Dehan had been carelessly holding, escaped.

Hula dived under the table to catch it. With shouts various guests pursued it. White-coated Japanese with inscrutable faces darted upon it unsuccessfully. Old Calhoun wiped tears from his flat, purple cheeks, Deanie clapped her hands and screamed shrilly. Helen leaned back and smiled. Only Diana and Mrs. Bane sat aloof from the uproar.

The dog dashed through a partly open door, and Fugi grabbed it by its hind legs. He returned it to Hula, and the laughing, breathless guests resumed their places.

"Take it away and lock it up in my room," commanded the child, handing it back to the Japanese. "It makes me mad always trying to get away when I only want to love it."

"In all likelihood, dear child," laughed Haldane, "it doesn't know what affection is. Give it time and it'll learn."

The girl regarded the man thoughtfully. He wasn't like the others. He was Uncle Edwin's kind. He enjoyed fun, but he had sense. She felt a sort of possession of him waking in her. She had intended to go back to the stable when dinner was over, but she lingered with the rest when they adjourned to the *lanai*.

"What's biting Dick?" she asked, sharply observing her brother.

"I don't know, Hula," answered Haldane.

"It's Di," flashed the child; "she thinks we are a bad lot because we race horses and Dad and Dick play cards and drink. But it's all right so long as you don't cheat. I love it, Mr. Anthony"—her eyes lighted—"it's such fun. Are you going to be here for the races?"

"Yes, Hula."

"Oh, good. I love it all so. The pretty ladies from Honolulu, the horses, and the fun. I love the ride over to

Waikapu through the Ditch Country with the cowboys and pack horses and thoroughbreds with their grooms coming behind."

How the beautiful eyes shone and the little face glowed.

Dick, restless and unhappy, conscious that his wife was, in spirit, holding him off with the rest of his guests, picked up a guitar and commenced singing and playing a hula. Deanie was immediately on the floor, tantalizing some one into dancing with her. Fitzmaurice was easily caught. The other guests stood in groups talking. Conversation turned to the races. Hula was all attention and interest. Jumping from the floor near her father's chair where she had been seated, she disappeared, returning almost immediately with a silver-framed photograph of a gray horse. About its neck was a *lei*, upon its back the damp mark of a saddle just removed.

"Silver Wings," she announced to Haldane, "and," she lifted a gold cup in her left hand, "this is what he won for us and this and this and this." She indicated graceful vases and cups placed about the *lanai*. "He's wonderful, Mr. Anthony. He's never been beaten. I adore him."

The man smiled.

"And when am I to see him?"

"To-morrow. We can't go to-night. You see we start over in a few days, and he has to have his rest. He's got a long journey before him."

"Where are the races held?"

"At Kahului; on the other side of the island. Wait. I'll get you a map."

Like a firefly she was gone. Returning she spread it upon the table, and with a slim finger she traced the route overland. The first fifty miles of it lay through the heart of the Ditch Country. Haldane bent over it interestedly. He knew every gulch of it from study of his own map.

The child watched his face.

"What are you thinking of, Mr. Anthony?"

"Many things, Hula. I'll tell you about them some day when the races are done."

She nodded and stood looking thoughtfully at him.

"Come inside and I'll show you the race-horses' pictures."

Haldane followed her into a room that opened onto the *lanai*. Hula stared back at Mrs. Bane, and the woman felt singularly like a child caught stealing jam. Hula had not missed her following look.

Busy indoors with albums and cups, Haldane was still conscious of the scene being enacted outside. Dick and Helen were sitting together playing their guitars, devils of laughter in their eyes and at the corners of their mouths for the words of the song they were singing. Deanie, not so many years from the mainland, was executing a hula that would have evoked much mirth from a Hawaiian. Angered by his wife's attitude of withdrawal, Dick incited his guests to greater efforts, and old Calhoun watched delightedly. This was the sort of evening he loved.

"Whoop it up, Dick!" he cried, re-living in his son the days of his own alcohol-drowned youth.

Hula looked out of the doorway at the posturing figures. Fitzmaurice danced well; slim, graceful, his feet moved easily through the weaving hula steps, and his hands were eloquent.

"Can you do it?" asked Haldane.

"Yes, but Uncle Edwin won't let me."

"Who is Uncle Edwin, Hula?" asked the man, to see what it would bring from her.

The child's face grew radiant.

"He's Daddy's head *paniola*. The best one in Hawaii."

Her little brown hands, lasso-hardened, rested for a moment upon the photographs. "He teaches me to ride and rope. He taught me to read—" For a minute she looked at the lighted *lanai;* at Deanie kicking off her shoes and picking up her skirt that she might move with greater abandon; at her lion-headed husband watching resentfully; at Helen, exquisite above her guitar; at old Calhoun, the gayest, greatest spirit of them all, and she sighed gustily.

"I love it, Anthony," she said regretfully, "but Uncle Edwin says I can't do both; that if I want to be a first class *paniola* I musn't sit up late or drink. It spoils your eye and judgment—"

"You bet it does, kiddie," agreed Haldane; "he's quite right."

Haldane appreciated the old man's ruse to wean her away from the things of her heredity.

"Do you like it, Anthony?"

"What?"

She tilted her head toward the *lanai.*

"I like outdoor things better, Hula. They last."

The little girl slid her hand into his and laced her fingers through it, giving it a firm, comradely pressure that expressed, more than the most eloquent words, her liking for him.

The impulsive little act, the touch of the small, warm palm, for a moment upset Haldane. It was so intimate, so affectionate, so trusting in its innocent frankness and faith. Almost he might have had a daughter Hula's age.

A step roused them. Dehan stood in the doorway.

"Edwin wants you."

He spoke shortly.

"All right," said the girl, then, noting the sullen expression of his face, she observed him more closely.

"Did you go and tell him to get me? There's dew on your shoes."

Dehan paused to light a cigarette before replying, but the flame had not burnt half the match before a curt voice called from outside.

"Hula!"

"All right, Uncle Edwin."

The girl released Haldane's fingers and replaced the racing-cups on the table.

Haldane looked out. A fierce old man with burning eyes stood at the bottom of the veranda stairs. His snow-white hair was in direct contrast to the undimmed youth of his sturdy figure. Fifty years in the saddle had not lessened the accuracy of his arm and eye. Before Hula had been born his life had been anything but circumspect. Traces of those early years lingered about his eyes. Now he was as hard a taskmaster for himself as he was for Hula. In soiled dungarees with the cowboy knife of the Islands in his legging, he waited.

"*Wikiwiki!*" (Quickly.)

His face was a trifle stern. He looked appraisingly at Haldane, then transferred his attention to Hula. Nodding good-by, the child crossed to him. Fiercely, contemptuously, Edwin's eyes swept the merry-makers; then he took a jealous and affectionate hold of the little girl's arm, as if he feared she would be lured away from him. His whole being was set in opposition to the life that he feared and knew would some day claim her.

Haldane watched with a great compassion.

He appreciated the caliber of the old *paniola's* love. It would have to be taken into account and reckoned with when the final show-down came, for there were no lengths to which it would not go. The old fellow knew the child's nature. It was beautiful, perilous, profligate, ready to squander the wealth of its loveliness in the space of a day. She should not go the way of her father and brother. . . .

If he could not somehow achieve rescue for her, he would sooner see her dead.

So Haldane read the thought in Edwin's face and was conscious of the tragedy attendant on all the world's great loves.

CHAPTER III

Anthony waked to the great clean morning of the windward coasts of Hawaii. He saw the blue sparkle of the sea through the tree tops, caught the fragrances of the garden as it waked to the sun. The rumblings of the sugar-mill produced a pleasant, slightly exciting vibration in the atmosphere that somehow fittingly merged into the possibilities of the day.

Anything could happen in a place like this.

He dressed hastily. Going down, he wandered about the garden for a while. The great breath of the sea came invigoratingly to his nostrils. Palely blue, polished, it showed between the tree trunks, and above their sun-gilded tops the hills of the Ditch Country rose one behind the other until they vanished into the mass of Haleakala. A very sponge of moisture, the forest showed wetly green, impenetrable. He stood looking at them. As chance would have it, he was to ride through the very sections of the Island that he most desired to see. The delay caused by the races was not, after all, without compensation. And he was sportsman enough to feel keenly interested in the fortunes of the animals that the Calhouns set such store by and which had ruined them.

He moved off, and instinct directed his footsteps toward the stable.

Turning into a great quadrangle formed by loose-boxes and saddle rooms, he came upon Dick, Fitzmaurice and Dehan. Beyond them, with swinging legs, Hula sat on a hitching rail, strumming on a ukulele. Cowboys lounged about her. Horses with twice-tied heads were being groomed in their stalls.

Sighting Haldane, Dick called out good morning, and Hula slipped off the rail.

"Dicky, tell them to bring out Silver Wings."

"Right, sweetheart. Well, Haldane, you are like a pointer; your nose guides you faithfully to where the birds flock. Want to see Hula's horse?"

The girl looked at her brother quickly.

"If only he were!"

"He's the property of the estate, Hula," laughed her brother; "we all have a leg on him. He's the only asset we have. Mahiai, bring him out."

The boy addressed, an exceptionally dark Hawaiian, thick set, with a smile that would have influenced Peter to unbar the gates of Heaven to him against his better judgment, departed. The great stallion was his special care, and he would have laid his body down for the horse or Hula to walk over.

"Whom were you serenading at this early hour?" asked Haldane looking at Hula.

"That's her morning song of thankfulness," Dick broke in; "she's like the larks you hear up above us, so damn happy she must tell the world about it or burst."

"It's a great way to be, Hula," said the Englishman with a vague moment of envy and loneliness. "It's going to be hard for you to grow up. Skirts won't compensate for all this," and he tilted his head toward the stable.

"No," said the child, "not if one loves riding and shooting and roping as we do."

"Do 'we' do all these things?" teased Haldane.

"Not the ladies—"

"But you, Hula?"

"Of course, and I don't want to grow up, Anthony, because of the horses and Uncle Edwin. I would rather stay his little girl."

There was a beat of hoofs on the wooden flooring; then

like the blinding flash of a striking wave Silver Wings leaped out of his stall. Hula danced about the high-spirited animal, and Haldane marveled at her beauty and enthusiasm.

Like a joyous god exulting in his strength, Silver Wings circled about on the tips of his hoofs, whinnying and shaking out his mane. His tail shimmered; a ribbon of light ran like quicksilver from withers to ears. He rocked and danced; blew out his rosy nostrils. Prominent eyes shone; ears pricked back and forth. Mahiai jerked upon the leading rope soothingly. Hula went and embraced the horse's head with such vehemence that it drew away startled. A quick hurt showed in Hula's face; then it vanished as the horse reached toward her again.

She pressed her face against his nose, inhaling the fragrant body odor of his well-kept skin.

"Look out," warned Dick, "he might step on you, sweetheart."

The child laughed derisively.

"Lead him about a bit, Mahiai."

"By Jove, he looks fit," commented Fitzmaurice, looking at him critically.

Dehan studied him through half-closed eyes.

"Umph," he observed, "even if old Collins has got an imported horse, my money goes up on Silver Wings."

Hula darted to his side, and her small hands clasped his arm.

"You are a darling, Harry!" she cried; then she turned back to the horse, oblivious of the expression that leaped into the half-white's face.

Dehan drew a deep breath and turning aside lighted a cigarette.

"Fitzie," cried the little girl turning to the veterinarian, "if Silver Wings gets beaten in his last race, I'll die."

"I believe you."

"He's so beautiful, so proud. When he comes out of the stable like that it makes tears come." Laughing, she shook them out of her eyes.

Haldane's face grew tender. So much of happiness for a heart like that—so much of sorrow, too, perhaps.

A cowboy cantered past, driving a mob of work horses before him. The stallion whinnied imperiously, and the band wheeled and halted; but with a clap of his spurs and a flourish of his lasso the man drove them on. Silver Wings called again, mightily, thrillingly, until even the mount the Hawaiian was riding hesitated, but the man was inexorable.

Hula danced about, as excited as the thoroughbred.

"Isn't he a king! He knows they all belong to him!" she cried, her cheeks crimson at the spectacle he afforded.

"Look out, Hula," warned Haldane, putting out a long arm and drawing her aside, "he might knock you down without meaning to.

Hula looked up, laughed, and clung to his arm.

"All right, Mahiai," said Dick, "take him in. Like to look at some of the youngsters, Haldane?"

"Yes, indeed."

For a while they inspected the young animals: slim-legged, big-eyed babies with fluffy foretops lifting in the breeze and coral pink nostrils that flared in alarm at any untoward sight or sound. Dick's face bore the intense expression typical of a passionate lover of horses. He inspected each animal point by point—though he had seen them a thousand times—and Haldane appreciated how these thoroughbreds and all that went with them had been responsible for the downfall of these people. The stables were palatial; thousands upon thousands of dollars were represented in the buildings and in the beautiful but unprofitable horseflesh they housed. The feed bill for hay and oats, imported three thousand miles, alone must total five figures at a year's end.

"Is there any market for this type of stock in the Islands?" he asked.

Dick laughed. "Absolutely none. They don't breed 'em any bluer than we do in Hawaii; but only a few fools like ourselves and Tom Collins in Waikapu, John Garrison in Makawao, English chap—introduced polo and racing to the Islands—the Parkers on Hawaii and a few others keep thoroughbreds. They ruin us, but life isn't life without them."

Haldane studied the man as he stood in his smartly cut breeches and boots. About the crown of the felt hat he wore was a wreath of crimson roses, feathered with maidenhair, sparkling with dew. But his flower-crowned headgear did not detract from the quality of his manhood; rather did it emphasize it. He could not believe that there was no come-back in Dick, although his face was beginning to reflect the mode of his life. Haldane guessed him to be not over thirty-two.

He looked down at the girl who still clung possessively to his arm while she eagerly and accurately called his or Dehan's attention to this or that—flexible long pasterns and short cannons of some colt that denote speed in a thoroughbred, or a too steeply sloped rump that indicates a sprinter and not a stayer. Then he looked at the country above them, a country that had a fortune in it if only these people could rouse themselves from their absorption in horses to the fact. No wonder Hamilton was loath, even with his great desire to possess this land, to bring an end to the Calhoun régime. It had something magnificent to it . . . something monarchical.

"What are you looking so serious about, Haldane?" asked Dick laughing good-humoredly. "Computing the cost of maintaining this establishment?"

"Not exactly, but I was thinking about your life."

Dick laughed again. "I know it gets you nowhere, but it's the way I've always lived. I like it."

"Who wouldn't," said the Englishman.

"Glad you are human enough to appreciate the fact. A lot of Island people look on us as a set of rotters, but they've missed a lot of real living, let me tell you. Have you ever had your own horse, one you've bred and watched grow up, come in first under the wire? No. It's something you can't beat. Puts other thrills into the shade. . . . Well, it must be about breakfast time—"

"Wait," cried Hula, "let's have out the dogs."

"More animals," laughed Dick turning to Haldane. "All right, sweetheart. Turn them loose."

The girl darted eagerly toward a detached wing of the stables. At the sound of her steps a delirious chorus of dog-voices broke out. She threw the door open, and a pack of fox terriers swarmed about her legs. She succumbed instantly to their importunings. Dropping upon one knee in their midst, she embraced them in turn while they whined their pain and delight at the pressure of her arms.

Haldane watched, his brown eyes full of compassion. What a nature, what a nature, the child had! Abundant, showering its wealth of affection upon everything, saving nothing. The girl felt the friendliness of his spirit for her, and, rising from the clamoring dogs, she went to him with the mongrel puppy in her arms.

"It likes to stay with me a bit to-day," she said. "I love its long sad yellow face. You're a mess, Topsy, but I love you! Don't you, Anthony? She's one of *my* things—"

Dick laughed. "You may not understand it, Haldane, but when Hula commences to get fond of anything she thinks she owns it, body and soul, and nothing can convince her to the contrary. When you, for instance, pass a certain point in her affection you will become 'My Anthony.' From that hour she will possess you utterly, as Uncle Edwin and many others have found out to their cost. She takes a persistent and pestiferous interest in the people and animals to which she becomes attached, whether or not they like it. So be warned!"

Hula's face was a comical mixture of expressions. Her enchanting eyebrows seemed higher above her eyes than ever.

"Oh, Dicky," she cried protestingly.

"Never mind, kiddie," laughed Haldane, "the honor of being 'your' Anthony—and I hope I shall be in time—will amply compensate for any restrictions the distinction may entail."

He looked at the flushed little face framed in its raven curls.

"Oh, Anthony," she said adoringly and her voice grew throaty and rich. The husky vibrations sent an odd tremor through the man. Exquisite, glowing little being. How she could shake a man with sudden and disconcerting gifts of herself!

Dehan's face grew pallid and his eyes glittered. Haldane felt uncomfortable and angry. Surely Dehan could not regard him as a rival. Enough years gapped between him and Hula to make the thought ridiculous. To him she was only a child: unique, adorable.

An impulse to laugh replaced his annoyance, then his face grew thoughtful. This man had a nature as headlong and reckless as the blue water that assaulted the coast. Passionately, selfishly, destroyingly, he would love, and if he married Hula she would go headlong the way of her fathers.

As he stood thinking, while those about him inspected the dogs, he became conscious that he was under an intense scrutiny of some sort. Turning, he saw old Edwin, one thumb hooked in his belt, his hat cocked over his eyes, watching him.

Haldane returned the look with interest. Doubtless this

old Hawaiian had a great eye for a bull or a horse, but he knew he had a greater eye and a greater heart for the fine things of life. His face was lean, with savage eyes, his body whalebone and steel from a lifetime of riding, but beneath the faded blue of his *palaka* (a cross between a coat and a jumper) Haldane knew he had a love for Hula that would put to shame that of most parents for the children of their bodies. There were no lengths to which it would not go. He chanced alienating her affection by the rigor of his rule rather than weakening her nature by indulgence. By his severity, he sought to build in her a strength not hers by inheritance.

Then the foreman's face changed, as if he appreciated, instantly and correctly, the caliber of affection that Haldane had for Hula.

He moved toward them.

"Hula," he said curtly but not angrily.

"Are you ready to go, Uncle Edwin?"

"Ai," he nodded, then added, "but more better you *kaukau* (eat) first."

"All right." She turned to Dick, "I'm going to eat with Uncle Edwin."

"Right, sweetheart."

A look of content grew in Edwin's eyes. He could never have Hula with him enough. He knew that with him and his *paniolas* she was temporarily safe.

Their lusty life was responsible for Hula's inviolate soul.

The girl bent among her dogs for an instant, then straightened up.

"Dick, will you take Topsy and give her to Nishi? Tell him she mustn't get out."

Her brother took the puppy and lifted his hand to arrest the departure of the foreman.

"Edwin! In four days we start for the other side. Have

the horses shod. We'll need a dozen for the boys and let's see—there'll be Fitz, Tancred, Father, Diana, Helen, this *haole*," he indicated Haldane, "Harry from the house, then a *malahini-wahine* (a woman from away) called Mrs. Bane, Jack, and Deanie. That's about ten not counting myself. I want to look at the saddle horses, myself, to-morrow. Have them brought up."

"Ai."

"What do you think about this Collins horse? Think he'll beat Silver Wings?"

Edwin gave a grunt that was half a laugh and tipped his hat farther down over his eyebrow.

"Huh! old man Tom'll be *poho* (out of luck)."

Dick laughed.

Edwin placed his hand possessively upon Hula's shoulder, and they strolled away, the girl's steps dragging in unconscious imitation of the old cattleman's. Haldane, observing it, could not repress a smile, for he knew in reality they were as light as thistledown. It was evident that this child worshiper sought to model herself upon the lines of the grim-visaged, white-headed man who had brought her up.

Reaching the corner of the quadrangle, Edwin turned and sent a long glance back at Haldane, and the Englishman was aware of his friendliness, a friendliness that the foreman had for no other present. It was as though the cowboy understood how different Haldane's life had been.

He said something to Hula, then they disappeared.

"Well, she's off until sundown or later," laughed Dick. "Let's go in."

Haldane was conscious that the day had somehow lost its luster with the departure of Hula. She seemed the very spirit of the beautiful and violent country to which he had come.

After breakfast Haldane halted Dick and asked him if he might have a few minutes of talk.

The man smiled good-naturedly.

"I'll not promise to talk any business before the races are over," he warned.

"I shall not expect you to," said Haldane, "but I should like to tell you a little more in detail why I've come and what the people I represent propose doing."

"Let's have it."

"I've been sent by Mitchell and Hamilton to offer to buy the water rights of your land, if after I've inspected them they appear to justify the figure they propose to offer. It is somewhere in the neighborhood of three hundred thousand dollars, and if you sell outright they'll make it six."

Dick looked at him.

"They want the whole plantation?"

"If you will part with it."

"Hell! we need the money; we owe Dehan more than I care to think about, but I'll be damned if I could think of parting with this place."

He looked about him.

"They understand that, hence their offer to buy the water rights if you can't think of giving them clear title to the property. That, of course, would be more to their advantage."

"What do they propose to do with the water? All the land that's tillable is under cultivation now, and it doesn't come anywhere near being enough. We've been going behind for years. You see, Haldane, this place is so hilly that, except in a few scattered localities, it's impossible to grow cane."

Haldane looked at Dick. He knew there was no need to intimate to a man like this that what he said was confidential, but he was interested to see its effect upon him. Briefly, comprehensively Haldane detailed the scheme as it had been outlined to him.

"And why didn't the duffers come over to talk to me themselves?" asked Dick, lighting a cigarette.

"For two reasons, Mr. Calhoun—"

"Make it Dick."

"Thanks, I will. First, because I'm the engineer to put it through if it's possible—and I must make the preliminary survey before I can decide—second, I think they realize that you are in a position where you cannot let this opportunity pass."

"They know damn well I can't," laughed the man. "Go on."

"They realize that, once the water is taken, the plantation, to all practical purposes, is done."

"Not a doubt of it. We have to flume all our cane down to the mill with mountain waters. It's impossible to lay tracks in a country of this type except within a short radius of the mill where it's fairly level."

"That is why they instructed me to double the figure for the water rights if you'll let the whole thing go."

"That's a pretty decent offer," said Dick thoughtfully. "Well," he picked up his hat and carefully adjusted a petal of the wreath that lay upon its brim, "I'll think it over. We are pretty hard pushed. I guess Howard knows it. We are looking for an opportunity to make a small clean-up at the races—with Silver Wings. It will relieve the pressure temporarily, but of course it's a mere drop to what we need to get clear. If you'd like to ride up a bit into the hills before we start for the other side, tell one of the cowboys to give you a horse. He can pilot you around."

"Thanks—awfully. I believe I'll take it easy to-day, look around a bit, and write some letters."

"As you like. I'm going to take the bunch over to Kipahulu after lunch. Like to have you come along if you feel like joining us. Please make yourself absolutely at home."

"Thanks, old man, I will."

About one o'clock Dick and his guests departed. When Dehan found that Haldane was not to be of their number, he looked at him suspiciously. He knew Hula had gone off with Edwin and was not expected back until about five. Still, might they not have schemed something? He had never had cause to feel he need worry about Hula. She had never shown more than the most casual interest in any man who had come to Hana, and, for that matter, she had done nothing to justify his unrest in regard to this one. Primitive instinct made him aware that Hula was very much interested in this *haole*, though she herself was not yet conscious of the fact. Somehow he got the vibrations they produced in each other, and jealousy ate him. He had counted Hula as his from a baby. A spicy crimson carnation, she had grown up under his eyes. He knew Edwin would oppose his marrying her, but he counted upon the girl's headlong nature to aid him. When the time was ripe for her to love no power on earth would be able to sway or control her. He would see to it that he should be the first to kiss, to arouse her. . . . He had held back waiting until she was a suitable age. She was almost fifteen, or was she fifteen? The women of his mother's race mated young. Hula was essentially a product of the Islands, even if her body, subjected to constant and rigorous exercise, was as hard and slight as a boy's. But perhaps Edwin and he did not appreciate the fact that her heart was waking. Unknown to the two men who constantly and jealously watched her—one because he loved her, the other because he desired her—it might be that her heart stirred with thoughts and impulses that the child barely understood and yet would be swayed by.

Reluctantly, with a secret determination that he would

return, Dehan rode away with the rest, and Haldane went to his room.

For a while he busied himself with his correspondence, lifting his head occasionally to look out of the window. It framed trees, a vivid field of cane, the sugar-mill and the gaunt headland of Kauiki that seemed to fling itself violently into the sea—cloud-shadowed and flecked with the whitecaps of the Trade.

The over-bright morning had clouded up, and Haldane felt rain in the air. About two he heard spurs and looking out saw Hula dismounting at the gate. He heard her voice rising from regions he suspected to be the kitchen. She was ordering some one about, and occasionally he heard a chuckle and sentences in pidgin English. She was doubtless having a late lunch in the pantry, or more likely in the kitchen itself. Probably regaling the Chinese cook with some adventure of the day's riding and roping.

The overheated stillness of the afternoon grew more intense and culminated suddenly in a torrential downpour. Haldane got up and closed his window just in time to see Dehan gallop to the steps, swing off his horse, and turn it loose. It clattered away stablewards.

He resumed his writing, once in a while lifting his head to watch the sheets of silver water streaming down the panes. The garden was almost obscured by the mist of spray that rose from the beaten ground.

Presently he heard an uproar in the house: doors opening and shutting; hurrying steps; voices. He smiled. Topsy . . . escaped again. He laughed silently. What a child Hula was! How lovable, how upsetting.

Then he heard her voice, raised in angry altercation.

"But Topsy's gone, Di! She'll go back to Manuel, and he'll kill her!"

"But it's outrageous of you to expect Nishi and Fugi to

go out in such a downpour. They've more important work to do than to chase a worthless puppy. With such a houseful of guests—"

Diana's voice sounded overwrought.

"We got on all right before, no matter how many people stayed," Hula cried. "Nobody ever fussed. Nishi!"

"Hula, I must forbid you to send them out again. They're dripping."

"Oh, hell!" the child's voice, sharp with exasperation, sounded above the rain. "You are a regular missionary, Di. Why can't you ever be glad about anything?"

"I'm—"

"Don't look stepped-upon," cried Hula contemptuously. "I know you are Dick's wife and mistress of this house. Put your boys to bed. I'll get Harry to hunt with me," and furious steps stamped away.

In a few minutes an even more furious pounding sounded upon the door, and Haldane got up.

"Anthony! Anthony!"

"Coming, Hula!"

He threw the door open. Drenched, with her black hair sticking to her cheek like wet silk, the child flung into his room.

"Topsy's gone," she cried excitedly, "and Di won't let me have the boys to hunt for her, and that lazy pig of a Harry won't help. I came home early to get you to go for a ride, but we've got to find my dog!"

Haldane could see tears coursing down her cheeks with the raindrops.

"I'll go for you," he laughed.

Her face grew crimson. "Oh, I love you, Anthony!" she cried, and she clasped his arm and pressed it against her. Then, "Let's go! It's no use taking coats; we'll get drenched anyway."

They went into the downpour.

After a search, they saw the little puppy sitting dejectedly in the shelter of an empty barn some distance along the road. Hula cried out and dived upon it. Instantly it was gone, running down a long muddy lane that led to a gulch.

The child stopped, hurt, unbelieving that anything could so rebuff her. Then she burst into tears.

"Why does it run away from me, Anthony! I'll get it! I will get it!"

Panting, sobbing, she raced down the road, and Haldane followed her.

The lane narrowed into a path that dropped down the gulch. Thoroughly terrified by its pursuers, the dog raced along the brink of the stream that had been swollen to a red torrent by the cloudburst. Turgid, tossing, it foamed seaward.

"Look out, kid!" shouted Haldane warningly; "it's frightfully slippery. You might fall in."

Hula paid no heed, her slim little figure in breeches darting on ahead, here and there, after the puppy. Tawny waves tossed and broke; logs swept by; brush jammed the banks. The roaring of the water filled the echoing walls of the ravine. Little waves crested, flattened out, and were swept downstream. Ripe yellow guavas popped merrily along. And underneath Haldane could hear boulders rolling.

"For God's sake, Hula, let the dog go!" he shouted. Wilfully she ran on, and Haldane, perforce, had to follow. He was blinded at times by the furious onslaughts of showers. Mirth and exasperation filled him.

Then a cry broke from Hula:

"Anthony! Topsy's fallen in. Save her!"

Even as Haldane, unable to resist the appeal in her voice, tore off his coat, he was amused that she gave no thought to the fact that he was imperiling his life to save that of a dog.

He knew, well enough, the danger of that raging stream, swelled within an hour to the proportions of a river.

He ran some fifty feet along the bank and, seeing the dog's head appear for an instant above the water, plunged in. He judged the distance to a nicety and grasped the little creature by the scruff of its neck. Angry waves lashed at his head; yellow foam blinded him. He felt himself seized and swung around by the torrent, then swept downstream.

Hula, helpless with horror, was unable to move for a moment; then she darted forward and ran abreast of him, slipping on rocks, sliding on yellow clay. Fighting to reach the bank, Haldane determinedly retained his hold on the puppy. The sediment from the muddy waters weighted his clothes and choked him. A wave smacked over his head. The sides of the gulch, steep, covered with guava, and broken by black outcroppings of lava rock, swept by him. Hula passed him, on a dead run, regardless of danger from yielding banks or missteps. He realized her objective; a sharp turn ahead where he could see that the middle of the current ran up against a bank, eddied, then shot across to the other side.

Flinging herself down, the girl held out one hand and with the other grasped the yellow root of a guava.

Haldane was afraid of pulling her in but estimated that, even if he did so, they would be sufficiently close to the bank for him to get some sort of hold. He grabbed the small hand stretched out to him. The water swung him about and pulled him toward the opposite bank. He knew the strain on Hula's arm must be terrific, but she did not let go. He endeavored to touch bottom without success. Because of the puppy in his right hand, he could not swim toward her and so lessen the strain.

For a moment the man wondered if it was written that all three were to perish in that swollen stream. Ridiculous. Farcical! He knew he must ease the strain or pull her in.

His feet struck something that gave him an instant's foothold; then it rolled from under him and the water closed over his head. Blinded, weighted with sediment, hampered by the dog, he could not assist her. Just above him, two arms' lengths away, hanging over the tossing water, Hula's exquisite little face hung, every muscle in it tense, crimson waves of color flooding it.

"Take the dog, Hula. I can get out," he shouted.

But she did not let go. She drove her white teeth into her lip and strained backward. A dead branch went by, cutting him in the cheek. He could feel the warm blood upon it. Drawing a deep breath he hurled the dog over and behind her, expecting her to let go and grab it. She gave one backward glance to assure herself it was stunned, then resumed her tugging.

"Let my hand go, Hula!" he cried. "I can swim."

But she clung frenziedly.

Relieved of the dog he struck out with one arm toward the bank, and assisted by the drag on his arm he gained the bank and heaved himself out. With legs still in the water, he sat down and commenced laughing.

"Don't!" cried the girl sharply. "There are falls below here, and if you'd gone over them you'd have been killed. I forgot about them when I told you to go in."

She snatched up the puppy and kissed it; then as passionately flung an arm about Haldane's neck and kissed him.

"You are cut! You are bleeding!" and she pressed her lips to the wound in a desperate attempt to express all she felt.

"Hula!" cried the man, shocked at the sight of his blood on her mouth. Her act revealed, as nothing else could have done, the abandon of her nature. Where might it not lead her!

"But, my Anthony, you might have been killed! If you'd gone over, I'd have gone, too!" she gasped sobbingly.

"Hush, Hula. Here, take my handkerchief; it's sopping, but it will get the blood off your mouth. Look out. Give me the dog."

The girl surrendered it and leaning her forehead against his arm burst into fresh tears.

"Don't cry, sweetheart," begged the man; "it's all *pau* (finished), as you say in these Islands."

She caught her breath.

"Here, Topsy, don't lick her face," laughed the man. "Why, Hula, I do believe the little brute is beginning to appreciate you."

The girl gurgled adoringly and leaned closer. So they sat for a few minutes, in the rain, Hula's little arm circled under Haldane's, pressing about his strong back, lovingly, trustingly.

"Great God, what a dear little heart it is," thought the man as he studied the exhausted small face, rain pelted, pale with emotion.

When they got back to the house, Dehan and Diana and even the house boys had gone.

"Mr. Dick's carriage, he stick over in Kipahulu side. Everybody go to get him out. Only Old Man stop upstairs. Sleeping, I think."

The Chinese cook volunteered the information as they came in.

Hula, standing with the dog clasped under her arm, looked at Haldane.

"Change your things, and we'll have tea by the fire in the big room. Ah Sam, you fix things for us."

"All lightee, Miss Hula."

Arriving downstairs half an hour later, Haldane saw Hula sitting thoughtfully by the fire in a gorgeous kimono. Red, orange, purple, the colors sprawled upon it, inter-shot with vivid bamboo greens, dawn pinks and canary yellow.

"Solomon in all his glory was not arrayed like you, dear kid," observed the man as he sat down. Hula tossed a pillow near his chair and sat upon it.

"You pour, Anthony. I want to hold Topsy. Three sugars in mine."

"I see you try to encourage production," laughed the man. "Cream, Hula?"

"Please. Oh, Topsy!" her laughter pealed out as the little dog drew back, sneezing and wrinkling its nose, after contact with the hot tea.

When tea had been accomplished, they sat in silence staring at the fire.

"Do you make friends as easily with every one as you have with me?" asked Haldane.

"If I like them."

"And like them all the same?"

"All differently, but each one best."

The girl stared up at him.

"That's the stuff, kiddie," he said. "If you can go through life in that spirit, you'll never be unhappy."

The girl studied him.

"Have you ever been, Anthony?"

"Been what, Hula?"

"Unhappy."

The man hesitated, then replied:

"Yes, Hula. It gets you nowhere. Remember, kid, the only gifts that are worth having are those that are given generously. I've learned the uselessness of wanting something that isn't for you. I've been terribly unhappy in my life, but I've learned something from it. I believe, now, that the people we are meant to love or like will have the same feeling for you—the others—"

"Oh," interrupted the girl rapturously and she scrambled

to her knees, "I felt your liking coming toward me, into me, last night—"

"When, Hula?" asked the man, smiling.

"When you bumped me."

"So soon?" asked Haldane, amused, and yet he knew there was truth in what she said.

"Yes."

For a moment neither spoke.

"Anthony."

"Yes, Hula?"

"There is one person I want you please not to like."

"Who is it, Hula?"

"Mrs. Bane. I hate her."

"What an extraordinary girl you are. You don't know her."

"Do you like her?" asked the child quickly, suspiciously, and her voice had a quick note of distress in it as though she expected an answer that would make her wince.

"Not particularly, Hula. She's not my style."

"Am I?"

The girl asked it so innocently, so without coquetry, that it enchanted the man. She put the question to him just as she might have asked whether he preferred beans to potatoes.

"Yes, Hula, you decidedly are."

She drew a deep breath, and her eyes adored him.

"Then please don't like her."

"I won't, but tell me why you dislike her. You just met her last night."

"She wants to marry you, and you are my Anthony. She can't have you."

Haldane shouted his mirth.

"Don't laugh, and please don't like her."

"But she can't marry me, Hula. I'm married already."

"Where is your wife?"

"In England. I haven't seen her for years."

"Doesn't she like you?" asked the girl concernedly.

"Not particularly. We don't hit it off."

"She's an ass," announced the child.

"Margaret thinks I am one," observed the man.

"Why?" demanded Hula indignantly.

"Because I hadn't made all the money that I should have in the first years, and afterward, when I did do better, I suppose because I couldn't get on with her."

There was a sort of savage disgust in the man's voice, but Hula's fine sensibilities got other vibrations.

"Never mind, Anthony. Don't feel lonely; I love you!"

Her arms wound impulsively about his neck.

"Good kid," he said a trifle huskily, putting his arm about her.

At that moment the door opened, and Mrs. Bane followed by Dehan and the others entered the room. The widow regarded the fireside group with amusement.

"Cradle-snatcher," she mocked gently. Then, "But I wonder, Mr. Haldane, if you appreciate how fortunate you are to have so lovely a tropical blossom so utterly at your feet."

Haldane was uncomfortably conscious of his arm about Hula, though he knew its hold to be innocent enough. Hula got to her feet, a frown between her brows.

"Don't be stupid, Mrs. Bane," she said sharply.

"Gently, Hula," warned Haldane.

He was aware that Dehan's face was livid. Something must be done to avert a scene.

"I was telling Hula about my wife, and she was kind enough to be sorry," he said stiffly.

"Is she—dead?" asked Mrs. Bane quickly.

"Yes," replied Haldane, his lips closing against explanations.

Hula glanced at him, appreciated the reason for his answer, and began laughing.

"Oh, Mr. Haldane. I'm so sorry—"

"Please don't let us speak of it. What happened to you all?"

"A washout. We started across a gulch that had been solid enough an hour before but it had been cut out. First the horses got in, then the carriage. It was quite an adventure, I assure you," Mrs. Bane cooed.

"She's glad his wife is dead," thought the child watching her, "because she thinks she can get him. And she can't. What a joke."

"Hello, sweetheart," Dick greeted her, coming in; "why you've been wet, too," as his hand touched her hair.

"Topsy ran away and fell into a river, and Anthony went in after her. He nearly got drowned, but I pulled him out."

Dick laughed. "Where did it happen, Hula?"

Briefly the girl gave an account of the incident.

"Hell, Hula, that was a damn-fool thing to do. It's a miracle Haldane isn't dead. By all that's right, old fellow, your body should be miles out at sea by now. Let's drink to your escape."

"Righto."

"And you saved him from drowning, Hula?" asked Mrs. Bane. "What a plucky little girl you are!" Then she paused, an odd expression upon her face.

"What are you thinking of?" demanded the child suspiciously.

"I, Hula? Why?" asked the widow.

"I see by your face you are thinking about me."

"What a strange child you are. A thought did come to me"—she paused effectively, as though she were reluctant to proceed.

"What was it?" demanded Hula. "I don't want you to think about me."

Her little face was hostile.

"Well," began the woman, "if you will have it. I understood you to say that you saved Mr. Haldane from being drowned, did I not?"

"Yes. What of it?"

"Then you'll live to do him a great wrong. It's one of the oldest superstitions in the world."

Hula's face grew deathly pale, and she turned her eyes toward Haldane.

"How horrible you are, Mrs. Bane," she said, then, catching her breath with a sob, ran from the room.

"What an extraordinary child your sister is, Mr. Calhoun," said Mrs. Bane.

"Hula? Maybe she is," Dick answered absently, then began to look about him in an exasperated fashion. "Where's Di! Gone?"

"Evidently," Mrs. Bane laughed. "And I must retire and get into dry things. I cannot appear so perfectly charming in my disarray as Hula does, Mr. Calhoun."

"Make it Dick. Here, girls, have another drink before you go up. You'll feel all the better and look prettier for it when you come down."

At dinner that night old Calhoun demanded accounts of the day's various adventures.

"Well, dammit, it's great to be young. Wish I could have seen my kid hanging onto you and the dog. Must have been a comical sight." And the old man laughed.

"Where is she, by the way?" he asked, looking around.

"Guess she's having dinner with Edwin," said Dick, who, though he adored his sister, never concerned himself much about her.

Mrs. Bane looked covertly at Haldane, for she suspected why Hula was absent.

After the women had left, the men lingered, drinking, about the table. Hula appeared suddenly and sat down in their midst, without speaking.

"Hello, little gel," said Calhoun; "where have you been? You look pale. Take a sip of Daddy's wine. It'll do you good."

The child put out a hand that shook a little. She placed her lips daintily on the rim of the glass and grimaced after the swallow, but color came into her cheeks.

"It isn't wine," she observed.

"Don't, Dad," Dick protested.

"Hell, Dick, I forgot it was whisky. It's a bit strong for the kid, but she looks tuckered out. Are you turning missionary since you married Di?"

"No," said Dick savagely, "she'd drive a man to the devil instead."

"Been havin' a row? Well, son, we've all had them with our wives when we were young. Take a stiff one and go up and have it out with her. More. It'll give you courage."

Dick poured out a half tumbler and drank it straight. He waited until he felt the shock of the alcohol strike through him, then pushed back his chair. He was loath to go upstairs. He disliked quarreling, and yet he was affronted by his wife's attitude toward his guests. Though outwardly polite, he knew they were all aware that Diana resented their presence in her household, and it was as humiliating to Dick as to his father.

"Damn it!" he thought, "she married me, and she's got to lead my life. She saw what it was when she stayed here. She's got to be hospitable."

He rose and left the room.

Calhoun looked after him.

"Well, boys, take warning. To marry or not to marry! that's the burning question. Poor Dickie's made a mess of it. I'm shorry for him. Di's a good girl. Damn good. Too damn good. She doeshn't understand. Hula won't be like that, will you, Hula?"

"No, Dad."

"Nor Helen either, nor Deanie. Deanie there is what I call a good shport. How about it, Jack. You ought to know?"

He glanced at the big tawny fellow and laughed.

"Too good a shport, fellows, maybe;" he shook with mirth. "Well, let's have another. Here's luck to Dick—he needsh it—and to Di. She needsh it, too."

Haldane looked at the half-intoxicated old man. Gin-drenched, still he was fair enough to credit every one with having a right side.

His daughter-in-law's aloof attitude must undoubtedly be a discordant note in an over-hospitable household, and yet he could feel sympathy and understanding for her.

"Glad I'm not Dickie," he said, "it'll be unpleashant ordeal. Well, boys, to our ladies. They'll be waiting for us in the *lanai*. What more could a man ask for. Big fire, pleashant company, good liquor, lovely women. Lesh move."

Dehan assisted him, and Haldane lingered a moment by Hula.

"Kiddie, don't let what Mrs. Bane said upset you."

"She's a wicked, horrible woman. I'd like to lasso and drag her behind my horse."

"Gently," counseled the man.

"But I would."

Haldane laughed. "But superstitions are rot, Hula."

"They aren't," cried the child; "they come true. Oh, Anthony, I'd die if I did you a great wrong!"

"You couldn't, Hula. How could it be possible?"

"I don't know, but nothing's impossible, Anthony."

"No," said the man, marveling at her unconscious wisdom.

"Then—then I might."

"Forget it, sweetheart. I'm not afraid."

He laughed down at her.

"Oh! I love you, Anthony!" she cried adoringly. "You are an Uncle Edwin sort of man."

"And that's the highest compliment you can pay me, isn't it, kiddie? Coming into the *lanai* with us?"

"No, I'd have to be near her. I'm going to sleep at Uncle Edwin's to-night."

"Do you sleep there?"

"Often. 'Specially when there are parties. You see, he always can go after wild cattle then because Dick and Father are too busy to want him for horses. So he says it's a good chance for us to get in some fun, too. Have you ever chased wild cattle, Anthony?"

"No," said the man, his heart going out to the old cowboy with his ruse to remove Hula from an atmosphere that was a greater danger because she had always been unconsciously part of it.

"It's the most thrilling thing in the world, Anthony. Will you come with us some time?"

"Nothing I'd like better, Hula."

"Can you come to-morrow? We aren't going after real wild ones, just steers, but it's fun."

"Sorry, kiddie, I can't. Not to-morrow. I've work I must do."

"Where?"

"I must ride up into the hills behind here to get a rough general survey of the land."

"Well, maybe we will see you up there."

CHAPTER IV

Dick, after having gone upstairs, was reluctant to enter his wife's room. He detested scenes, and there had been more than one in the short six months of his marriage.

He stood in doubt; then decided that he needed another drink. Accordingly he went down and fortified himself from the sideboard. Lighting a cigarette, he waited a minute, then determinedly mounted the stairs. They must have it out, once and forever. Diana had been reluctant to marry him, and Dick had known it, but, carried away by the intensity of his feeling, he had overridden her. Having accepted him, she must accept his life. He was willing enough to moderate his own behavior—to a certain point—but it was outrageous of her to expect his friends to do so. She wasn't marrying all Hana. . . . So his thoughts went.

He knocked sharply on the door.

"Come in, Di?"

Receiving no answer, he entered. His wife was brushing her hair. It was short and somehow very disturbing. Silken as floss, it lay like a short cape upon her bare shoulders. The woman did not turn, but the mirror reflected her expression. It was sultry, half aroused—one Dick knew and dreaded.

"Why did you come, Dick?"

He took off his coat and threw it on a chair.

"What the devil is wrong with you, Di? You are enough to drive a man crazy."

She made no reply. He looked resentfully at the back turned on him and clenched his fists; then, taking a step forward, he placed his hands upon her shoulders. She shook them off and held her brush with a shaking arm. Her husband's attempt to overcome her with caresses enraged her. She was no weak Calhoun!

"Don't touch me! I detest you."

"Well, you needn't inflict your distemper upon my guests, upon Dad's guests. What do they do, what do I do, for that matter, that so affronts you?"

The woman looked at him with glittering eyes.

"I loathe the atmosphere of this house, of this place. It's—disgusting."

"You knew what it was before you married me," cried Dick angrily. "You nursed Dad for seven weeks! And what is disgusting about it?"

"Everything."

"What, the race-horses, the drinking, the cards, or the playing around?"

"All of it. It isn't—clean!"

The man gripped the back of the chair until his knuckles showed white.

"Yet you consented to become part of it."

"Never in my heart. I thought, I felt that maybe I could wean you from it—"

"What's bred in the bone, Di," said Dick more gently, detecting a little break in her voice. His face relaxed somewhat and he continued: "Don't damn old Dad too much—for us being as we are. He's a real sport. He's drunk his liquor straight but he's run his horses straight, too. No man and no woman, either, has been the poorer because Dad has lived. He's squandered his money right and left until we are in so deep we can never get out again, but he's given away as much as he's spent. . . . He's big, God bless him. He never thought less of any woman because she gave her love to him. He never despised any man because he was down. It's always been, 'Well, Dick, what can we do for her? She was good to me when I was young,' or 'Hell, son, how can we give that chap a hand. He's a decent beggar, just unfortunate.' Damn me if you like, Di, but don't damn Dad. You look at him sometimes in a way that makes me crazy. Are you better than he is when you come right down to it, Di? Because you don't drink whisky and don't race horses and he does? What will it matter in a hundred years what either of you did?"

He took a step forward.

The woman looked at him.

"I was brought up to think that those things were wrong."

"Granted, Di. I understood that when I asked you to marry me. Remember that day when I took you out on the bluffs and asked you to be my wife? I recall every word you said. I told you I would try to moderate my life, because I loved you—"

"But have you!"

"I have. Give me time, Di. You can't teach an old dog new tricks over night. Six months isn't any time at all against thirty-six years."

The woman's strong fingers reached out of the window and crushed a spray of the vine that grew outside it.

She stirred slightly under his compelling glance.

"I hoped Dick—that you'd learn—"

"And I hoped, too, Di, that you'd learn to—love it a bit," he gestured toward the garden and purple night; "that you'd be a little more tolerant—of us—when you came to know us better."

"The more I see of your life, the less I can endure it; the more I know I can never be part of it."

"But you'll have to be if you are my wife. You'll have to make concessions for us. We make them for you."

"For me!"

"Yes, for your inhospitality, for your rudeness to people we have loved and known all our lives. Dad may be drunken, but he never makes people feel uncomfortable. Don't you suppose he knows how you feel toward him, yet he's loyal to you—behind your back as to your face. It's always, 'Di's a damn fine girl, Dick, and don't you forget it. She's been brought up differently, that's all. Be fair. Give her time.' Oh, Di, won't you try to understand a little? Don't condemn what you can't possibly know completely. Be decent to these people who are our guests. Try to like them. Try to be just. Don't sit like a frozen statue of disdain. You have it in you to be anything you choose. You have tremendous possibilities. But you aren't waked up. You've never found yourself."

"And does finding myself mean becoming like all of you?"

Diana asked the question, slowly smiling a secret smile that baffled and enraged her husband.

"At least we don't go about condemning other people because they choose to lead their lives differently than we do. Be generous. Be sporting. Try to meet us halfway. Dad hasn't got much more time. In all likelihood this'll be the last big meet he'll ever see—"

Dick broke off and swore to relieve his feelings, then finished:

"Don't spoil it for him."

The woman darted a quick suspicious glance at him. What was Dick's game? She trusted nobody. She thought of the easy hands of Helen and Deanie on the men's arms, of Hula in the living-room in her kimono, of the drinking, of the intimacy. . . . To such a woman as Di, who liked to keep even her soul private, it was all utterly revolting.

She looked at Dick's eyes, darkly blue, with pupils unnaturally dilated from alcohol. His face was pale and strained. She had never realized until that moment the strength in his mouth and chin. He had the strong figure of the born horseman . . . he was no weakling. She felt the concentration of his whole mind upon her, felt the cry of his being. "Di! Di! Di!" But his white lips did not move.

She knew there were no half measures with him. He was a Calhoun. He loved her—wanted her though he did not understand her, and she knew, reluctantly and in her own way, she was not utterly proof against him. She knew, were she wholly to love a man he would dominate her, and she did not want to be dominated by this one. And yet she had been weak enough, mad enough to marry him. . . .

Flashes came back to her of the afternoon he had asked her to ride with him . . . she had known why. . . . She remembered her cool deliberating upstairs . . . a life of ease against one of hard work. . . . Yet she had hesitated to abandon her career, for she had loved it and knew herself to be fitted for it. She had come to no decision . . . had ridden with him . . . explained her feelings toward the mode of his life . . . had refused it . . . and him . . . then ended by marrying him. Although twenty-nine, Diana had had little actual experience with men although she attracted them, and Dick, who had harvested much knowledge of mankind and womankind in his thirty-six years, had known it. No woman had ever appealed to the man in him as had this one, though he had known lovelier ones. She exasperated and enraged him. She was his wife, but he knew her to be aloof from him always. . . . He wanted her. He would force her somehow to accept him and his life, for deep in his heart he knew he would never abandon it. He did not think of to-morrow—to-day was enough. He wanted to be happy. It was insupportable to have discord in his house such as had been so apparent these last two days. When his father was present and his wife away it was like old days, but let Di come. . . .

"Well?" he asked; then, eager to get it ended, temporarily at least, he took her into his arms and kissed her.

She wrenched herself free, the smell of alcohol on his breath arousing her afresh.

"Oh, why did I ever marry you!"

There was a ring of genuine despair in her voice.

Dick looked at her. She was different from any woman he had ever known. He did not know how to break down her defenses. Even Hula, if one quarreled with her, one could win back with a kiss.

"Because I made you!" he said. "Come, Di, kiss me and forget it. You'll get broken into our pace by and by."

"I won't!"

She was like a cornered tigress. Her strange, secretive eyes were bare slits, her face ash white. All her life she had made it a point not to feel things intensely. She had been afraid of life, aloof from it until she married Dick and now she was fearfully embroiled in it. She'd show this man she had as strong a will as he. Her anger rose hysterically and she cried:

"I hate your life!"

Had Dick appreciated the excess of feeling stifled in her at the moment he would not have answered as he did, but, exhausted and overwrought himself, he gave no thought to the words he uttered.

"Well, there are others who don't find it so distasteful. I'll go back to them," and, slamming the door, he went out.

Diana closed her eyes and shuddered. The volcano of fury within changed to ice.

Her eyes dulled. Dick would go back—to Helen or others like her, and if he did so, she would be partially responsible!

"You know he loves you or he would not have married you," a little voice taunted.

"Do I love him enough to justify the battle I must fight to make him what I want him to be? Will he be worth the effort?"

So her thoughts went.

For a long time she sat thinking, then got up. She would go down and try to play the game. She must not let these people be better sports, as they phrased it, than she was. Dick loved her. She must fight for him, show herself to be the woman she had always cherished as an ideal. Big; understanding; with hands to lift others up. She would show Dick she could be big—as his father. Then she checked herself with a shock. Was the atmosphere of this place so deadly that in six months it had made her, Diana Parker, compare herself to a sodden old man whose face had at first revolted her, then commanded her compassion?

She hesitated, aghast.

Then she went down stairs slowly and crossed to the *lanai*. At the farther end sat old Calhoun, spread back in his chair. On the arm of it Deanie perched coyly, holding the old man's arm about her soft waist, while with the other she ruffled his hair.

"Why so glum, Dicky?" she called out, imps dancing in her eyes. "In bad odor at court?"

"Yes," he said violently.

"Poor Dick. It's hell to be married."

"You seem to survive it."

"I don't take it seriously. The trouble with newly married people is they think they are one, when in reality they aren't, any more than before. When you get past that phase things will begin to look up. Eh, Daddy Calhoun?"

"Absholutely, my dear. Wise as you are beautiful."

"I wish Di were more like you, damn it," said the man.

"You should have picked her as you'd pick a race-horse. With an eye to type. She's not sporting, Dicky."

"Here, here!" protested Calhoun, "Di's all right. She's a sport but not sporty. How's that for expressing it? Rather neat, I think. Give her time, she'll learn," and he laughed and blew out his purplish gills. "Shnot fair to judge her. Here, Dick, buck up. Get Helen to sing."

Hearing her name the girl came up out of the dark garden followed by von Erdmann.

"Come, Helen; music."

"What'll it be, Dick?" she turned toward him.

"Anything."

The girl looked at him compassionately.

"Forget it, my dear; it'll all work out," she said softly.

"Drinks, Fitz, damn you. Why aren't you onto your job?" shouted old Calhoun, spreading himself afresh in his chair.

"Sorry, old man. Haldane, give me a hand."

Diana stepped behind the heavy curtains. They passed down the veranda. She could not think. . . .

"Music, Dick!" cried Deanie imperiously, and both guitars rang out as one.

Diana felt the blow of their rhythm upon her heart. How many times had they played together like that.

Turning, she went upstairs.

CHAPTER V

"Let us stop a bit, Kealoha," said Haldane, halting his horse on a convenient ridge, "I want to look around."

The Hawaiian dropped to the rear and, lolling sidewise in his saddle, rolled a cigarette.

Haldane put the reins on his horse's neck and pulled out his pipe.

It had been a great day.

His eyes followed the plunge of the land to the sea. On the right towards Kipahulu, the coast-line was broken into a succession of vivid green bluffs. To the south the island of Hawaii showed, indigo-hued, enveloped in cloud.

Directly below, Kauwiki Point, diminished by distance,

jutted into the flowing Trade Wind sea, and in the curve of white sand to the left Hana lay, peaceful, protected.

Haldane stuffed tobacco into his pipe, his face thoughtful, his brown eyes alight. That day's riding had convinced him that Howard Hamilton's irrigation dream could be realized.

The ground oozed water; ferns and trees dripped it; secret rills gurgled with it; gulches thundered their loads of it to the sea. The whole eastern end of the mountain was a vast sponge. The actual growing of cane could be carried on in Hana well enough without irrigation, but the only means of getting the stalks to the mill—by fluming—would end when Howard Hamilton's Ditch gathered up the flashing streams of East Maui to turn them to the west.

He went over his map carefully again, his eye following the folds of the land.

"By Jove," thought the man, "I'm going to write to Howard and tell him he's got to come up. This thing's getting me. It's magnificent. It'll be a monument to him and to the engineer that puts it through, and I'm going to be the man."

He was conscious of a fresh zest and thrill for life surging through him. It came with the anticipation of the undertaking ahead that awaited his brain, his knowledge, his skill to accomplish it. It came, subtly, in the breath of the clean wind that blew healthily over this jungle country making it a thing of inspiration instead of enervation. It was in the green of the guava-covered bluffs that fronted the sea; in the forested reaches of Haleakala that vanished into the low hanging clouds; in the violent plunge of the whole island from mountain-summit to sea.

Something tremendous seemed to be rushing toward him.

Haldane realized that he desired to live, to feel again. What had he got out of the past ten years? Only a sense of security from being hurt, a security won by dulling his senses to a point where they could no longer feel. Sitting in the saddle facing the inspiration of the blue east, he realized that he had evaded life, this last decade, rather than faced it. He had thought it wisdom but now knew it to be cowardice. He felt that he had outwitted his wife when he mastered indifference, now he knew that he had only succeeded in defrauding himself. . . . Looking at Hana landscape the realization came to him with stunning force. Yet peace and safety had attended his path, but what were peace and safety when measured against what he felt when he looked at this land falling recklessly, spilling itself without care or cost, to the sea?

He picked up his reins and, touching his horse with his heel, started down. The animal chose its way carefully along the narrow path, edged with rank Hilo grass, dotted with the gold of fallen guavas. The cowboy followed behind.

The path wound through clumps of twisted *ohia*, went under shapely masses of mango and breadfruit. It followed swinging ridges; dropped down precipitous gulch sides; crossed mountain streams: olive-green, splintered with sunlight, smelling of moss.

He came out into a small meadow. In the middle of it, deep in the pale Hilo grass, Hula and Edwin sat, their horses grazing behind them, their faces turned to the east.

The wind lifted the hair off Hula's forehead; distant rainshowers moved like ghosts across the sea.

Child and man were talking earnestly, the girl leaning confidently against the old cowboy's lasso-greased knee. Haldane suspected they were deep in some discussion of bull-roping, or riding, or the way of Hula's life. The old man's ragged brows were low over his eyes, his face tender and grim.

Hearing horses, both turned, and Hula waved the hat she held in her hand.

"We thought we'd catch you about here, Anthony," she cried.

The man rode to within a few paces of them.

"What were you two talking so earnestly about?" he asked as he dismounted.

"You."

The reply disconcerted him. Was old Edwin cautioning Hula against him as he cautioned her against all the men who came into her life? He was conscious of no antagonism, for he was sure that the *paniola* liked him.

While he stood talking, Edwin watched him, keenly, appraisingly.

"Sit down, Anthony," ordered the child. "This is my and Uncle Edwin's favorite talking place. We always come here when we have things to discuss. You feel," she gestured toward the falling land and the shifting blue dunes of the sea, "that things are coming toward you. Uncle Edwin"—she placed her hands upon the old fellow's arm—"this is Anthony—Haldane, a *pelikani*."

Edwin acknowledged the introduction with a curt nod of his head, spoke a few words to the cowboy who had accompanied Haldane, then busied himself re-coiling a lasso which he had laid down on the grass beside him during the heat of his talk.

"Well, Anthony, have you had a nice day?" asked Hula. "And what have you found, prowling around in our hills?"

She looked at him, red lips laughing, but Haldane fancied that Edwin was responsible for the latter half of her question. No doubt he dimly felt some change pending, for he must be well aware how matters stood with the Calhouns. He might be an easy-going Hawaiian, but part of him, also, was keen Scot. He might be content to work from day to day, picking up cattle, riding the range, seemingly under the spell of an existence which takes little heed of time; but the wastage which characterized each phase of the Calhoun ménage would never escape him. It was not his place to comment, but that did not prevent him from seeing. Haldane knew that this taciturn shepherd of Hula's soul was always on the alert lest some change of fortune might remove her from his guardianship.

"Well, kiddie," he said, stretching out in the grass at her feet, "I'll tell you what I've been doing, though it's not for the world to know—as yet. I've been looking over the upper benches to see if it's possible to collect all the water here and take it around to West Maui. At present most of it's running into the sea."

Briefly he went into the project, and Hula listened without comment to the end.

"But, Anthony, if they take all our water away—"

"They won't take it; they'll buy it," interrupted the man, "and at a very liberal figure."

Hula looked doubtful, and Edwin, without turning, spoke to her in an undertone in Hawaiian. Evidently his explanation or comment carried more light or weight than Haldane's, for a dawning look grew in her eyes.

"Oh," she observed, "but, Anthony, wouldn't all the digging and tearing spoil it?" She gestured toward the forests, somber now under the vast afternoon cloud of the subtropics.

"To a certain extent, Hula, yes, along the immediate ditch line, but not for long. The cruelest cuts would be covered with green again in a year."

"But down below, where the water won't run any more?" and the man knew she was picturing dying forests below the ditch line, murky pools where once emerald streams had flashed.

"Well, kiddie," the man smiled a little ruefully, "you'll think an engineer is a destroyer instead of a constructor. Of course the gulches will be more or less dry, but I don't think, from what I've learned about the rainfall of this country, that the actual forests will be affected, although the rivers and pools—below—will run only in freshet time."

Hula regarded him thoughtfully.

"I don't think I like the idea, Anthony. I love this place the way it's always been."

"I understand, Hula. Yet if we don't do this, others most assuredly will. Such things are written on the pages of the world's progress."

Again Edwin cut in with a brief comment, and again Hula looked less dubious.

"It will mean millions of dollars, Anthony? Shall we get any of them?"

The man sat up. "If I have any say in the matter, Hula, you most assuredly will."

That brought a quick look from the white-haired foreman. For the first time Haldane got an opportunity to study his face. His features were aquiline and at the same time rugged. The eyes were a living black, deeply set, wide at the nose and narrowing outward, dropping a little at the corner (as do the eyes of every Waimea-born Mackenzie). Edwin was not Maui born. He came from a family that has its seat in Waimea, on Hawaii. It has given four generations of its sons to the great cattle industry of the Islands. Compounded of three distinct strains, the original Hawaiian, crossed with Spanish and later with Scotch, it has bred great men—men who have made landmarks in their chosen calling—and Uncle Edwin was by no means the least of them.

That he had strayed from the fold in Waimea to Maui had its story. As now he was the pattern of propriety, so once had he been the prodigal son . . . but love had worked its great miracle in him, as it has in uncounted others.

In youth he had swaggered; now he carried himself with dignity. A fiery temper and a great love burned in his eyes, and again Haldane realized there were no lengths to which this old man would and might not go for Hula. He had been a drunkard until forty-five, but with the coming of Hula and her subsequent custodianship he had forsworn all forms of alcohol. For her he lived the creed he preached: abstinence, rigor of living, a life out of doors as far removed as possible from the subtle emanations from the Calhouns' big house.

Haldane felt admiration and respect for the eagle-faced, grizzled-headed *paniola.* Without education, almost, he had succeeded in somehow educating Hula. She was no crude young ignoramus, and inward mirth shook the white man as he remembered the primer of her baby days. He could imagine the two of them sitting over it: Hula's stormy tears, Edwin's iron determination that she should learn . . . and afterwards the stately lines falling from the pouting cherry lips—lines that neither teacher nor taugh could fully understand but which both appreciated and responded to in a dim way.

He wondered what other untoward books Hula's young mind had been fed upon. No other could be more incongruous than the first. Was it indicative of what her life was to be? Did the old man realize what he had given to her?

He studied the girl thoughtfully.

"Anthony," her voice roused him.

"Yes, kiddie?"

"When will it begin?"

"Oh, not for ages, sweetheart. Things of that sort take forever to start. It will take a year, possibly two, before we commence the actual work."

"Oh. And will you stay here?"

"If I undertake it, and I have practically decided to do so."

"Then I won't mind much, will you, Uncle Edwin?"

The old cowboy turned and looked at her in a curious way. Haldane felt that the look was reminiscent of something that had already been said between them, concerning him. This old man had been discussing him at length and in detail with Hula—perhaps throughout that day—but he did not in the least suspect in what capacity.

There was a short silence while the horses tore busily at the rank Hilo grass.

Edwin turned to the girl.

"I think more better we go home," he said, and, rising, dusted the grass off his breeches.

As they struck into the avenue-like road that led to Hana from the right, Hula gave a cry.

"Oh, Anthony! they are trying out the horses for the last time before we go over," and, setting spurs to her horse, she galloped toward the green oval of a race-track that lay to the right and behind Kauwiki Point. Edwin cantered after her a trifle more sedately, and Haldane followed him.

Reaching the edge of the meadow, they saw old Calhoun sprawling over the seat of his buggy. Beside him, on horseback, Dick sat, his mind and eyes intent upon the thoroughbreds that were being worked out on the track. Hula had halted her horse beside the white-washed guard rail and was questioning an old Hawaiian who perched like a monkey upon it. Some distance away, Mahiai walked Silver Wings up and down to keep him from getting chilled by the wind. The great animal's ears were pricked to observe the performance of the two-year-olds on the track—his get—but for the most part seemed intent upon the sea that sparkled shoreward or on the white picketed graves that clung to the steep cindery slope of the volcanic headland.

Haldane halted beside Calhoun and his son and they nodded; but the Englishman knew that they were hardly conscious of his presence. Both were intent on a brace of two-year-olds that were being sprinted a half mile. Dick held a stop-watch in his palm, as did his father.

The young horses swung around the turn, raced down the home stretch and finished almost neck and neck under the wire.

"What did you make it?" asked Dick, turning exultantly toward his father.

"Forty-six and an eighth. Check! By Jove, Dick, that's moving! Didn't think that little filly Awapuhi had it in her; but she's got a strain of The Fisherman from her dam. It always comes out! That was a sight for sore eyes, eh, ***Pelikani!***" and Calhoun turned to his guest. His eyes glowed like coals, his vast bulk was animated. "Those youngsters'll give a respectable account of themselves on the eleventh! Damn it, man, I forget I'm old when I see a performance like that!"

"It must be gratifying to see stock you've raised justify your expectations."

"Gratifying! It's glorious—nothing to equal it in the world. Better go over, Dick, and tell those damn boys to blanket them and keep them moving. Never can knock sense into these fellows' heads; good-hearted but regular children."

Dick cantered away to obey his father's instructions, though he knew there was no necessity to do so. But it pleased the old man. . . .

He pulled up beside Hula.

"What did they make it in, Dickie?"

He quoted it.

"I always told you, Dick, that Awapuhi could beat Crusader!" she exclaimed.

"Bah! that was a fluke!" teased her brother; "my colt'd do better than that spindle-shanked, bald-faced weed you're so stuck on."

Hula cut playfully at him with the end of her lasso.

"Sour grapes. I always was better at picking out the good ones than you, Dick. How about it, Opiupiu?" she flashed upon the grizzled jockey. He looked up, and his brow, furrowed as an ape's and bearing the same everlasting query, worked up and down.

"Sure, Hula; you more smart every time. You say Silver Wings going to be winner when he only damn ugly colt."

"Aha, Dickie!" jeered the little girl, "Opiupiu doesn't underestimate my talents. Take your hat off to me."

Dick obeyed. In reality he had a vast respect for Hula's ability to size up a thoroughbred. It was partly woman's instinct but not entirely so. She had watched the Sunday try-outs of colts since she was a baby. She had sat, a fat chunk, on Edwin's hip or on his saddle while he and his father had busied themselves with the training of two-year-olds, forgetful utterly of the little two-legged colt who was growing up with them, without an eighth of the attention and care they bestowed upon the equines of their raising. Hula had absorbed discussion and altercations relating to the different points of a horse; she had listened to the recitals of pedigree that her father and Fitzmaurice had almost chanted, so greatly did they love the noble roll of names that go into the making of English turf history. Isonomy and St. Simon, Flying Fox and Diamond Jubilee, The Fisherman, The Clown, Gallopin and Sceptre and back and back until they came to the great ancestor of all English thoroughbreds, the Godolphin Arab, whose name is inscribed in gold in the heart of every horse-lover. Hula knew the sires and dams of them all, their peculiarities, their outstanding characteristics.

Dick, even while he ordered out the next horses, looked intently at his sister. He realized that she was growing up, that there was a quality to her beauty that pulled at one's heart. Perhaps because he was filled with unrest, jarred out of the easy rut of his life, he gave a little thought to others. He was full of raging anger with his wife, determined to punish her. He felt lonely, sore, like a horse put out to pasture while its more fortunate mates were feasted in the stable.

His life seemed, of a sudden, a mess. Would Hula's be one too?

Motherless from birth, she had been brought up by easy-going Hawaiian nurses. She had wheedled and bullied the *wahines* who had had charge of her. Her life had been without rule. Many a morning when other children would have been in bed she had toddled into the living room to find the men of her household still about the card table, whisky stale in their glasses, matches and cigarette butts on the floor. Without, a pale dawn breaking, within, paler faces about the poker table. She could not have appreciated the contrast of the morning without and within; but had she unconsciously absorbed some of the taint?

He looked back over his life with a furious distaste and yet with a passionate affection. He appreciated the various phases of it, from the idle gaiety and gaming in Hana to the ferocious excitement of their yearly trip to take their race-horses to meet at Kahului. The meet was only one day long, but it entailed a week of celebration before and after. The memory of some of those times reddened Dick's cheeks, though he was not sure he would have forfeited any of them. But he hated to remember Hula had always been there: with the jockeys, about the stables, in and out of the house. Eager, excited, she had danced through those baby years. He and those with him had had little time to waste on her. Save for boisterous greetings and caresses, compliments for her pluck and gaiety, or amusement at the oaths that came sparklingly from her lips to convulse a room with merriment, they had hardly been conscious of her. Then Edwin had taken her for himself.

Dick felt a moment of remorse for the negligence of which he and his father had been guilty. Rather than interrupt the pleasure of their lives, they had shut their eyes and ears and had turned her loose, a motherless colt, to pasture.

He looked at the bewildering loveliness of her little neck and wondered, rather sadly, if some day she would be like the "rest of us." So registered the thought in his mind, and he cursed the wife who had been responsible for putting it there.

"Get Silver Wings out!" he ordered shortly, "and push him for all he is worth, Opiupiu. I want to see what he can do."

Mahiai gave the old man a leg up, and he took the horse out slowly. Gradually he warmed him up while Dick watched and Hula chatted with Edwin.

Dick listened to their conversation.

"Did you make me those whip-crackers, Uncle Edwin, that you said you would, while I was bathing at Aaleli and you were guarding the trail?"

"Ai," replied the foreman, thrusting his hand into his pocket and handing them over.

Dick gave a bark that was a laugh. It had never struck him as incongruous before that his sister should be so utterly in the keeping of this old part-Hawaiian; that he should sit guard while she swam, undoubtedly naked, in some mountain pool. And yet Edwin had been and was the finest influence in Hula's life. From curb to girth, from rope to whip, he insisted that she do everything correctly. That he was equally severe in other matters Dick did not doubt. His code might be a peculiar one, but it was a rigid one, and he trusted to Hula's adoration of him to make enforcement of it and punishment for infringement of it safe. This grim range-rider did not mistake indulgence for love. Battles there had been, many, in those earlier years; but he had known the caliber of the girl he dealt with. She might storm and rage, but she would be ready to forgive and love a moment afterwards.

Dick did not dream of the rigor of Edwin's bringing up, but he might have suspected it if he had ever stopped long enough to appreciate how circumspect Hula's behavior always was in view of the sort of life she had led.

But he had never stopped to think. . . . His hand clenched.

Silver Wings was beginning to stretch out. Dick watched him intently; then his mind went back to the night he had passed. Angry, wakeful, the maggots of alcohol working in his brain, bringing to the surface words and snatches of thought—things his wife had said to him on the many occasions they had had for dispute. Damn Diana . . . damn her anyhow. They had been happy enough before he married her. Life had gone easily.

Opiupiu was getting ready to break. . . .

Dick straightened up in his saddle and leaned forward, tense as a hound. He glanced at the watch in his palm and placed his thumb on the handle, to press down the spring the instant the horse broke from the wire.

"What's it to be, Dick?" cried Hula, reaching over to grasp his arm.

"A mile."

"Fine! Now the old boy will show us what he can do. Oh, I love him!"

Silver Wings propelled himself from under the wire and the stop-watches clicked down on him. With steadying hands and grizzled head buried in seas of mane, the old jockey urged him along the curving ribbon of track. With great limbs hurling the turf contemptuously behind him, the gray stallion went once around. His legs moved with machine-like regularity. Steadily the momentum of his pace increased. He flashed by the half, the three quarter, then hurled down the last stretch for the finishing run.

"Push him, Opiupiu! Push him!" cried Hula, standing in her stirrups while the wind snatched at her hair.

"God! he's going!" cried Dick, glancing from watch to horse. His eyes were keen to note every move, and when jockey and horse flashed under the wire he threw up his hat as exultantly as a boy.

"He did it again, Hula!" he cried. "Look! A mile in 1:43 flat! Bring on your Hurricanes and Cyclones and Tornadoes. Any old wind will do. We can win. Eh, kid, eh! Bet old Dad's turning handsprings!"

He galloped to where old Calhoun watched from his carriage.

"How's that, Dad? Did you get it!"

"Did I! Look!" and he held up the watch, buried in pink palm. "We'll get some big bets against him this time, Dickie boy. Lots of the Honolulu gang will back Collins' horse. Waikapu will rally about Tom's importation. Hey, *Pelikani!*" turning upon Haldane, "what'd you think of our nag?"

"He's all right, by Jove! That was running, Calhoun."

"Don't breed 'em any bluer. Isonomy's his grandsire and on the side of his dam—" and he began to chant what Hula called to herself, "The Song of Pedigree."

Haldane listened comprehendingly, for he had heard the same names fall from his father's lips but not with such ringing gusto.

Triumphantly, lovingly, with all his soul the old man recited the equine genealogy as priests of old recited Biblical ones.

And when it was done he turned to Haldane and his son.

"And now a toast: to Silver Wings and all the great race-horses who have gladdened men's hearts!"

He drew out the flask he always carried and brandished it toward the track and the blanketed thoroughbreds pacing up and down; toward the gaunt headland with the graves at its foot; and toward the flowing blue sea.

"*Aloha ka ko!*" he cried, taking a great swallow, and then he passed it on.

CHAPTER VI

"You'll have to change your tactics, Sunbeam Lady," teased Deanie, clasping her arms behind her head and smiling wickedly; "they don't seem oversuccessful with the big Englishman. He appears to be quite captivated with the youthful Cleopatra of the stables and cattle pens."

Mrs. Bane turned slowly from the window.

"It was a little foolish of me to, well, confide to you that I was—interested. Mr. Haldane is delightful, but I'm not at all sure that I'd want him."

"Sour grapes!" mocked Deanie. "You know you'd give your eye teeth to bag him. And to be beaten by a kid! I'm ashamed of you. Get busy and cut her out. He's an excellent catch. And he's nice. There's something in the wind, and I fancy that he'll be in Hana for some time. I'm a sport. I'll prolong your invitation indefinitely. Don't think we'll fight more than once a year."

Mrs. Bane regarded her companion intently. In negligée, with her hair loose about her shoulders, though it was pinned carefully over a too high forehead, she gave the impression of a charming undress that was, in reality, a studied effect. Mrs. Bane was aware of the fact.

"I like it here," she mused; "the scenery is—exquisite—"

"Never mind the scenery," laughed Deanie; "that doesn't cut much ice with either one of us, though it's pretty enough; but we do have a good time here and there are enough men to make it interesting."

"Yes, but I'm not sure that I'd be content to live here."

Deanie bit her lip and her eyes twinkled behind their silken fringes.

"Oh, wouldn't you!" she thought, then aloud, "Come now, I'll lend a hand. Anthony isn't at all subtle. He's just downright man, and any woman whether she's thirty or thirteen ought to be able to get him if she sets about it right. I'd be shot before I'd let a kid bag the man *I* wanted. She's absolutely monopolized him these last two days. It's outrageous, but I love to see her with him; it enrages Harry so."

She stretched herself, luxurious as a kitten, among her pillows.

"It's nearly tea time. We had better go down. I promised Dick I wouldn't leave him unprotected."

"He and his wife seem pretty seriously at outs, don't they?"

"Yes."

Deane moved to the dressing table. Sitting down she carefully powdered her slender, curved nose, smiling as she did so. "How Diana does love to see us come down like this! Frightful. Immoral! In negligée before men. Wait," she giggled, "wait until she meets 'Dearie' and the Waikapu gang. It will be worth years of my life to see her face when the old girl sails into our midst, terrible with war paint—"

"Who is this 'Dearie' you all joke about?" asked Mrs. Bane, as she interestedly examined the gloss of her finger nails.

"An old inamorata of Daddy Calhoun's. I think the old sport still contributes toward her support—"

Laughing and chatting they moved downstairs.

"Hello, girls," called Calhoun, getting heavily out of his chair. "I was about to dispatch Harry to your rooms on a search party. Been together? Whose reputations have you been ruining? Mine?"

"That was done years ago," said Deanie, perching herself upon the wide arm of his chair. He encircled her waist.

"Not so tight, you old dear, or I'll tell Jack," and she looked across the *lanai* to where her husband sat talking with his hostess. In a dark riding suit, with a severe sailor hat set low upon her forehead, Diana presented a curious contrast to the negligée of the other women. Bright spots of color flamed in her cheeks and her eyes gleamed. She was trying to play the rôle of the gracious hostess, but it was almost beyond her power to do so since her last quarrel with Dick. She felt herself to be among these people on sufferance. She knew, had they had any choice in the matter, that she would have been banished from their midst. She was a damper upon their enjoyment. Setting her teeth, she rallied herself to be witty, gay, delightful, one of them. But her eyes were heavy lidded and her lips straight.

"Beautiful Lady, another cup of tea for our friend of the honey-colored hair."

Fitzmaurice stood over the table with Mrs. Bane's cup. He rather prided himself upon his ability to say things prettily. Mrs. Bane looked across at him, as she slowly turned a large topaz ring about her fourth finger. Her eyes met the Irishman's in gentle appreciation of his gallantry. She always appeared to be in harmony with any man who was nice to her.

A sound of spurs made the woman look away. Hula and Haldane came laughing across the lawn, returning from a day of wild-pig hunting.

"What luck?" asked Calhoun.

"The best. We got a boar and three young sows. Great

sport. How about it, kiddie? Will you back up my account of our killing?"

"You bet I will," said Hula, bending to kiss her father. She looked over at Dick. "Dickie, may we turn them over to the boys who are left behind, to make a *luau?*"

"Anything you say, Hula. Have you people had any lunch?"

"No," said the girl, picking up a plateful of sandwiches and moving to the railing with it. "Here, Anthony," she called, "I'll give you half."

Deanie looked at the widow remindingly, impishly, as Haldane crossed the room.

"Here, Big Man!" she called beckoning imperiously.

He walked over.

"I want to whisper to you."

The man bent his long body, smiling good-naturedly.

"What is it?"

"In that rig, with that big hat on your head you look remarkably Don Juanish—" She said it in a low voice but toned to carry all over the room.

Haldane laughed, straightening up as he did so. "I'm afraid my bark is worse than my bite then, Mrs. Lightfoot."

"I'm not so sure about that," Deanie's dimples deepened; "now go along and devour your sandwiches and desist from cradle-snatching or we'll arrest you."

Haldane chuckled. It had been a glorious day and he felt in harmony with everything, but he wondered a little what Deanie's game was.

Hula held out the plate and he took a handful of the sandwiches.

"Careful, Hula," cautioned Deanie playfully, "he'll be stealing your innocent heart from you. Or is it as innocent as we think it? How about it, Daddy Calhoun? Think your baby is a chip of the old block, or does she take after her mother?"

There was a moment of silence before Calhoun replied, and Deanie, who had only recently married Lightfoot and come to Maui, knew that somehow she had made a mistake. She was not intimately acquainted with the history of the Calhouns, but she determined on the instant she would dig it out.

"Don't know; ask old Edwin," cheerfully came her host's voice.

"Daddy Calhoun?"

"Yes, my dear?"

"There's something I want you to promise me."

"Name it."

"When Hula is eighteen you must put a mask on her, else I'll not have a man left to look at me."

Hula frowned and turned half away as if she were disgusted, but Deanie's speech made the old man observe his daughter more closely than he had ever done.

"I'll always look at you, Deanie," he promised, then added in a surprised tone, "By Jove! the little gel is getting to be quite a knock-out, I do believe."

"Where have your eyes been, Daddy, that you haven't seen it?"

"On you, Deanie, of course."

Helen came slowly into the room, clad in a scarlet and gold kimono, and sat down near Dick's wife.

"Will you pour me a cup of tea, Di?" she asked.

Resentfully Diana obeyed. The common use of her Christian name and its even more intimate diminutive enraged her, coming from the lips of these people who seemed to have taken possession of her house with the ease generated from many other such occasions. She wondered if there was any of life that they kept from one another. . . . She was mad for the overland journey. It would put an end to this unending house-party, and on the road, surely, she and Dick would not be left to the mercy of each other's company. Their life together was an increasing agony. Their time with each other was a succession of battles, none the less violent because they were suppressed, none the less bitter because they frequently ended in his arms, to be resumed when their need of each other diminished.

Helen felt Di's antagonism and smiled inwardly. It was unmerited, for she had just come from a two hours' talk with Dick—in his wife's behalf. As though summoned by her thought of him, the man rose and crossed the room. Across the tea table he faced his wife.

"Have you a cup of tea left for me, Di?" he asked.

"I'll ring for more," replied the woman coldly without looking into the pot. Dick's face flamed like a boy's.

"Don't trouble yourself. I'll take some whisky," and he flung off.

Helen looked at the robin's-egg blue of the late afternoon sea, marveling at the stupidity of which Di was guilty. After an afternoon spent trying to make Dick more understanding, that his wife should bungle the situation as she had! Surely Di knew that her husband never drank tea and only asked for it because she was serving it and somehow it seemed a stepping-stone toward her.

Disgusted, she got up and moved over to Hula.

"Where have you been to-day, baby?" she asked.

"After pigs," replied the child, looking adoringly at the lovely face that bent to kiss hers.

"No, Fitzie, thanks; I'll sit on the rail by the big Kangaroo."

Haldane smiled at Helen's description of himself. It rather suited him. Dick joined them, standing with his back toward his wife who sat, pale with anger at her own clumsiness and resentful of Dick because, indirectly, he was responsble for showing up her lack of finesse to a woman who was an artist where men were concerned.

"Here, Hula," said Dick, taking her hat off, "that *lei* just matches Helen's kimono."

The woman bent her head for the flowers, and Dick stepped back to survey his handiwork.

"It was made for you, Helen," he said; "no woman can wear a wreath as you do."

"Dick," she said looking at him reprovingly.

He stood in front of her, his face pale and strained.

"Well! she hurt me!"

"Infants; both of you."

Haldane glanced at the half-white. Half sitting, half standing, with her scarlet kimono drawn revealingly about her long limbs, she was a picture that must be painful to any watching wife. Yet Haldane suspected that she played fair with her hostess. Strange, beautiful hybrid. Her voice, her every movement, was seductive, unconsciously, fascinatingly sensuous; he knew she was a woman, like her historical namesake, who could take men's hearts at will and break them or make them hers. From across the room, von Erdmann was watching her, his pale blue eyes intent upon the play of her hands. Finished hands with glowing palms and finger tips whose touch was electrical. . . . Made for love and loving. . . . Haldane watched her, too, and knew her heart was full of compassion and understanding for the frustrated woman who brooded above her cups of tea.

And Helen bent her mind upon Diana. Most of her misery was of her own making. She looked intelligent. Was it beyond her to learn? Then she shrugged her shoulders dismissingly.

"Well, are you prepared for the great ride, Anthony?"

"You bet I am. Hula, do I qualify as a *paniola*?"

The child laughed, "Yes, Anthony."

"Does he pass with Uncle Edwin?" asked Dick.

Hula smiled a secret smile. "I think he does."

"You've rather hogged him, Hula, it seems to me," laughed her brother. "Do you remember what I warned you of, Tony—that, if Hula chanced to like you, she'd not give a moment of you to any one?"

"I remember."

"You must let some of us have a chance, too," called Deane. "How about resigning in our favor to-night, Hula?"

"If Anthony wants it."

"The little minx likes him," gloated Deanie to herself. "She's waking up."

"How about it, Anthony?" asked the girl, looking up at him.

"If I'm to be your Anthony, while I'm here, I insist that I have all the privileges that attend being it. Your undivided attention and interest, Hula!"

"You are a darling, Anthony," said the child.

"Quite the nicest man here, next to Dick," said Helen softly, "and I've known him for years."

"We've been sweethearts since Helen was seventeen."

"Don't tell them how long ago that was," laughed the woman, laying her long hand upon his.

"Your beauty is deathless, Helen," said Dick without flattery; "but your secret is safe with me."

Haldane glanced at his hostess. He could not hate Helen, but he could not wholly blame Dick's wife if she hated her. Helen was all Di was not. Subtle, understanding, profound. Had he been in trouble of any sort, he would have gone to her before any other woman there. He realized that Hula adored her—seemed aware of her as she was not of any other person in her father's house. Would she follow in Helen's footsteps? He moved protestingly as he watched the glowing little face. No wonder Edwin kept such jealous watch of her. The life he distrusted had a thousand hands, any one of which might suddenly reach out to take her. He must guard against them all, seen and unseen, and it is not permitted in Hawaii that a cowboy cross the threshold of his master's house unbidden. There were many hours of Hula's life, therefore, that were unguarded. Well, while he remained in Hana he would assist Edwin in his watch. He had entrance to this sphere if Edwin had not.

"Finished, Hula?" he asked, taking the sandwich plate.

"Thanks, Anthony." She gave him one of her quick, caressing looks and slid off the rail. "Well, I guess I'll go and give Uncle Edwin a hand unsaddling."

"Wait," Helen detained her, "will you 'lend' Anthony to me for a little while to-night? I want to talk to him."

"Yes, Helen."

"Thanks, sweetheart." The woman bent and kissed the child.

Haldane looked at Helen when Hula had gone.

"Yes, I want to talk to you—about her."

"I fancied so."

"I do not want her with us, Anthony."

"I'll tell her to console Dehan." The man laughed. He had not been blind to the sullen light that had been growing daily in the half-white's eyes.

"Not Harry," cautioned Helen as she moved away to dress.

Deane did not forget her determination to find out, if possible, why mention of Hula's mother had caused such consternation. The atmosphere of the room had been frigid for a moment. She dressed hastily and dropped in on Mrs. Bane long before the dinner gong was due to sound.

"I'm going sleuthing," she observed; "there's something

shady about your youthful rival's mama, and perhaps if 'Don Juan' hears of it it will lessen his ardor. I'm getting a tremendous kick out of all this. Now be grateful to me."

"It's not so much interest in my affairs as satisfaction of your own curiosity," said Mrs. Bane cooingly. "I shan't make use of any information you may unearth. It wouldn't be sporting."

"Well, you're not so wrong about that," mocked Deane. "I've got to know, and I'll have to tell some one when I do; so it'll probably be you. I know I can find out from Helen. I'm sure she is intimately acquainted with the Calhouns' past. At any rate, Dick's."

She went out laughing.

"Come in," called Helen when she tapped on the door, and Deane noted that she did not ask who it was.

"It's—me," said Deane, moving over to sit on the bed; "can I talk to you for a moment? What are you going to wear? The Nile-green you had on last night? It was wonderful."

"No, black."

"I should imagine you'd look lovely in red."

"That's Hula's color. I never wear it except in negligée."

"I made a fearful contretemps this afternoon," said Deane in an engagingly innocent voice; "I think it was just before you came down. I made some reference to Hula's mother. The effect was electrical. Isn't she talked about? I feel frightful. Tell me about her so I can apologize to Daddy Calhoun if I must."

"Don't you know?"

Deane shook her head.

"Hula's mother was a morphine-fiend."

Deane cried out, "How terrible! Are such things inherited?"

"I don't know. Perhaps the tendency is, but it may never develop unless some fitting opportunity presents itself."

Helen bent to pull on her expensive, long-vamped slippers.

"I should think they would be afraid for her. She'll be a great responsibility in another year or so, with such beauty and such a—possibility. Dick and Daddy may find their hands full."

"They are full now, only they aren't competent to care for her," said Helen, taking up her dress. "I wish her future were in my hands. She's more of a responsibility at this minute than even Edwin realizes."

"Isn't Di competent? She's so good she's uninteresting. Just the sort of woman to bring up a young girl."

"You're wrong there, Deanie."

"How? May I fasten you?"

"Thanks. Di isn't competent to help any one. She has got off, on the wrong foot, to use a racing term. She's out of her stride."

"I guess I had better not even try to apologize—" said Deane, putting her hand through Helen's arm.

"No, Deane, don't."

The little woman's eyes roved about the room as they started out. On the table by the window was a silver match-box. She recognized it as Dick's. Glancing covertly at Helen, she smiled.

Dinner was a noisy meal. Only one day gapped between the night and the morning of departure for the other side. Excitement permeated the atmosphere.

"I got a wire from Hamilton," said Dick, turning to Haldane. "It came just before dinner. He'll be here to-morrow. You must have written to him. Glad the duffer is coming over. The more the merrier, eh, Dad?"

"Absolutely, son."

Hula glanced at her father's suppressed, purple face.

Haldane wondered how his condition affected her. He was more than usually intoxicated. She evinced no concern, it was too usual, but he fancied that he saw a hint of fine distaste in her eyes, mingled with compassion.

When the meal was over, Dick rose, spoke to one of the boys who waited on the table and went to his father.

"Come, Dad, it's time you turned in, old man. Must get a couple of good nights before we start over."

"Rights, sar, Dick, rights, sar!"

As they moved toward the *lanai*, Deane caught Mrs. Bane by the arm.

"I dug out the mystery," she bent and whispered into the woman's ear.

A peculiar expression grew in the widow's eyes.

"Poor child, how terrible."

She looked across to where Hula stood talking to Haldane. Feeling her eyes, the child frowned. The woman crossed the room to her.

"I'm afraid, Hula, that you haven't forgiven me yet for voicing that superstition. It was most unfortunate. I want you to like me, dear."

The girl felt somehow rebuked.

"I told her it was all rot," said Haldane. "Remember, Hula?"

"Yes, Anthony."

"Well, suppose you tell Mrs. Bane you're sorry."

"I will—for you."

"Any reason will suffice, Hula, so long as I am reëstablished in your favor," smiled the woman.

Hula smiled, reluctantly, in return. Had she appreciated the motive that moved Mrs. Bane to make up and the reason for her smile, she would have struck her instead.

Hula departed, almost on the instant.

"Well, Harry," observed Mrs. Bane, "your rival has gone off, for once, with another woman than Hula."

Dehan regarded her with his lazy eyes.

"You notice it, then?" he said as if he were talking to himself.

"Can one help it?"

"I wondered if I imagined that that damned *haole* was stuck on her."

"I'm not so sure about him. I think he looks upon her just as a remarkably lovely child, but Hula is crazy about him."

"You think so?" Dehan turned upon her.

"I'm a woman. I know," said Mrs. Bane, deeply.

The half-white grew rigid.

"What makes you know?"

"When she looks at him there are kisses in her eyes."

Dehan lowered his lashes.

"Where has she gone!"

"Who?"

"Hula!"

"She just went outside."

Dehan breathed with difficulty.

"With him?"

"No, I told you he's out with Helen."

"I remember—I wasn't—thinking. Will you excuse me?" and Dehan got up and lounged off into the dark like a young panther.

Mrs. Bane sat back and listened to the rise and fall of voices outside—Anthony's and Helen's. For a while she talked to Von Erdmann, then, excusing herself, went inside. By a side door she reached another part of the veranda. She must hear what they were saying. Much might hang on it. There was no doubt but that Dehan loved Hula. Jealousy might drive him to talk to Edwin and so make it difficult for

Haldane to be much with the girl. Dehan was volcanic, he would not be likely to let the lava crust under his feet. . . .

From her changed position she could hear better. They were pacing the terrace. She could hear Helen, talking earnestly. Occasionally she was interrupted by Haldane. The sound of their steps on the cement grew louder and fainter as they approached the house and went from it.

After a little Mrs. Bane's ears adjusted themselves to the distance.

"But you do not seem to appreciate, Helen, that Hula is fifteen and I'm nearly thirty-five. Besides—" Haldane's voice got fainter as they moved away.

"But you see," Helen's voice, low, but carrying, came on their return, "if some one doesn't marry her and take her from this environment—"

Voices and footsteps got fainter, then louder again.

"And she's too sweet, too dear. I love her. If I were a man—"

Why did not they cease pacing and stand still!

"But she's only a beautiful child—only a child to me—" insisted Haldane.

"Then what alternative have you to offer?"

"None—as yet."

They paused by the fountain.

"I cannot help but think about her, Helen I cannot understand how she's grown up untouched by all this," and he moved his head toward the house.

"Edwin."

"I know, but his hold on her will be shattered one of these days. What then?"

"Ah, what! That's the question."

"You are clever—think of some remedy."

"There's only one. The one I suggested."

"But it's—unthinkable! It's not possible for a man of my

years to fall in love with a girl of Hula's age, much less to marry her. A bride of fifteen! Great God, Helen, Britishers don't do that sort of thing—"

Laughter that was like a peal of silver bells broke from Helen's lips.

"So," she jeered softly; then more seriously, "If she were older could you fall in love with her?"

"Could any man not do so? But as matters stand such a thing isn't possible."

"Have you ever studied"—Helen halted, then finished as if she were answering her unfinished question to herself—"Why it's the most possible, the most certain thing on earth."

"If I thought that there was the remotest possibility of my being such a fool, I'd leave to-morrow. I'd do anything on earth for Hula—except marry her. Besides you forget—"

"I'm not forgetting anything," interrupted Helen. "If you won't, then you abandon her to Harry, or Von Erdmann, or others like them—"

"I think that, between Edwin and her sweet, wholesome little self, she'll be safe enough until a more logical rescuer comes—"

Helen reached into a plumaria tree for one of the yellow flowers that starred it. With gracefully moving fingers she placed it in her hair.

"Safe only to a certain point, Anthony—until her heart is touched or her passionate nature roused. Supposing she fell in love with you, wanted you?"

"It couldn't be possible."

"It's going to happen, Anthony. The preference she shows for you now is waking love. You may go away, but it won't do any good."

Haldane experienced an unpleasant constriction about his heart. It was not fear but akin to it. Helen's words sounded dismayingly like a prophecy.

"You'll see—" he began.

There was a sound of flying feet across the lawn. Hula came running through the dark. Sighting the two by the fountain, she darted straight as an arrow to Haldane.

"Hold me, Anthony—tight!" she cried.

Her face was damp and pale. Heartbeats shook her.

"What is it! What's upset you, Hula?"

The girl breathed stormily.

"Give me your hankie; no, don't let me go! Get it with one hand. That pig of a Harry kissed me! He wouldn't let me go. How I hate him! I'm going to tell Uncle Edwin. Oh," she shuddered, "I can still taste his horrid lips," and she scrubbed vigorously at her own.

Haldane was conscious of Helen's mocking eyes because he hesitated to do the thing which Hula unconsciously was demanding of him.

"Hula," he said, "would you like me—to take it off for you?"

"Oh, Anthony, yes!"

Haldane bent his head.

"Anthony."

"Yes?"

"Not my cheek—"

Mrs. Bane, watching from the veranda, dug her nails into her palms, and Haldane, even in the midst of his perturbation, had an impulse toward laughter. What an outrageously beautiful creature! What chance had any man against Hula!

CHAPTER VII

Haldane passed a restless night. Helen's prediction troubled him; Hula's act distressed him. It was inconceivable that the child could have misinterpreted his interest for something else. Sufficient years gapped between them, almost, for Hula to be his daughter. The fact must be obvious to her, to every one. He clung to the thought. He wondered if, perhaps, he had showed too much interest in the girl. Her untoward life, her dubious future, compelled one to be concerned about her. Vital, beautiful, abundant, she was a spendthrift, bestowing without thought or stint, the gift of herself upon those whom she loved. Her nature was a reflection of its environment . . . a person was helpless to resist it.

Haldane knew that Helen estimated human nature pretty correctly, but he was prone to think that the mode of her life made her attach too much weight to love in its various guises. She did not misestimate the enslaving charm of Hula's personality: it was potent, undeniable; but he felt that Helen misestimated its effect upon himself.

He did not deny love's ability to surmount almost any obstacle, but the great gap of years was not to be bridged. Concrete, unamenable to any adjustment it yawned between them. He was no hotheaded boy to forget everything because of a girl's beauty. His life held complications enough without his wishing to add anything to them.

He got out of bed and, going to the window, lighted a cigarette. He listened to the wind, to the echo of the sea. The rumbling of the sugar mill came faintly, came loudly, as the wind freshened or fell. At times other sounds surmounted it, a greater wave rushing to the shore, an increased passage of air through the treetops; but Haldane was conscious of the vast vibrations even when he could not actually hear them.

The muffled rings of sound spread, one following on the heels of the other, unendingly. They dominated the night, spreading, enlarging through it, until they broke against the forested hills, mingling with them, becoming part of their mystery.

Haldane smoked his cigarette and lighted a second. He could not even see the lights of the mill, so bowered was the house with trees; but he felt its sound-ripples coming toward him, breaking against him with their muted, continuous jar. They invested the darkness with a quality that was disturbing. . . . The intangible, thousand emanations of the sea and the land about him, the vibrations of the life of Hana, produced some sort of effect, some sort of spell. To choose to deny its existence did not prevent one's reacting to it. It was there; it persisted. It invested the nights with mystery, the days with exhilaration.

He recalled his own sudden response to it the afternoon he had sat on the hill and looked at the leagues of water before him and the stirring country about. Had not even Hula voiced it in a child's fashion when she had said, "Here, things seem coming toward you"? Freedom, such as was suggested by this isolated and magnificent coast, was likely to make one somewhat forget values, so great was its stimulus. Life seemed to rush toward one as the wind and sea rushed to meet the land. Recklessly, magnificently. To refuse to know it seemed to brand one as unfit to experience the glory and fulness of living.

An unexpected turn had brought him to Hana, and he seemed to have become involved vitally in its future and in the future of those who inhabited the district. He thought with relief of Howard's arrival next day. Practical, unimaginative, he would leaven the atmosphere. Haldane longed to commence his tussle with the immense forces of the forest and hills. Work was wholesome; it left no time for anything else.

He listened to a deeper-sounding note in the sea, to the spaced patter of a moment of rain on the cane fields. The shower passed, leaving a damp, gusty fragrance behind it.

His thoughts went back to Hula and the immediate situation

confronting him. He could not believe Helen's prediction to be in any way sound, though Hula's action had been rather distressingly suggestive of it. She didn't love him; it had only been a child's impulse to seek refuge with an understanding person in a moment of pressure.

Haldane was no fanciful woman, he did not for a moment feel that he must leave Hana or abandon the work he contemplated doing—that would be farcical—but to risk Hula's happiness was unthinkable. To bring the tragedy of a love impossible of consummation into her life before she was ready for it was not to be considered. It might drive her to anything. He must safeguard any possibility of such a thing, associate himself with those whose years were more in accord with his own. Without hurting her. Without her being aware of it.

Howard's coming would provide an excellent excuse not to be with her so much. Likely enough, in the excitement attendant upon departure, she would have little time for him. The thought comforted him in the loneliness of the night.

Morning came, bringing a stilled sea and air hardly moving. Before dawn he heard Hula's spurs. They crossed the veranda, descended the steps. There was a crunch of eager hoofs on the gravel driveway, and she had gone to assist Edwin and his cowboys in their work of preparation for the morrow.

"You look a bit fagged," commented Fitzmaurice when Haldane came down. "Have a smoke? I'm off to the stables. Coming my way?"

"Yes, thanks, I'll take one. I didn't sleep well last night."

"I didn't, myself," said the Irishman, as they walked along. "Funny place, this. At times it disturbs one. Can't account for it. After all, it's composed of the same old elements: earth, air and water—but they seem put together differently. Odd, how a place can affect one. What?"

Haldane smiled a trifle grimly. "Yes. Damned odd."

He glanced at the long, well-bred face and figure of the man beside him. What had he had from life? Or was it all still before him? He rather fancied not.

They entered the quadrangle. Dick was standing in the entrance to the saddle room, Edwin and Hula in the flagged yard. About their feet were piles of gear: pack-saddles, saddles for the use of guests, headstalls, tether ropes, blankets. Dick was reading out a list, Hula and Edwin checking it off. The girl's fingers were busy with some intricate knot she was putting into the end of a neck-rope, even while she counted and inspected bridles.

There was not a detail of this sort of work that she was not intimately acquainted with, from turning up the corners of a saddle-blanket to lifting a load from the back or withers of a horse or the fine adjustment of a bit.

Haldane watched her. He felt that he had been correct in his thought that in the next few days of excitement she would give little heed to him. She smiled across at him radiantly but continued with her work. There would be little need to absent himself. He could watch the preparations at intervals of the day and so create the impression of being about her and yet not actually come in contact with her vital personality.

He was conscious of regret that he had determined to be less with her. She embodied the zest of life. Haldane had been born with a universal love of Creation. The world, people, living, had been things of wonder and beauty to him as a boy, as a youth. Life as it had come toward him had had promising eyes. He had embraced it eagerly, confidently, only to find its aspect of fairness a disguise, and Hula, in some profound and inexplicable way, gave back to him some of the vanished feeling of his youth. When he was with her, life seemed joyous, beautiful, exciting . . . as it had seemed to him when he was a boy.

Dick crossed to them to announce that it must be breakfast time, and Hula, dropping her rope, came running like a long-legged boy over the piled ropes and blankets. She caught at Haldane's shoulder with one hand.

"Oh, Anthony," she cried, "you won't mind my not being much with you to-day?"

"Not the least, kiddie; I understand how busy you must be."

"I am, I love it. I love the smell of bridles and saddles. I love all this going away. But I love you, too, and you'll come once in a while to see how we are getting on?"

"You bet I will, Hula."

As he left with Dick and Fitzmaurice he saw Edwin looking at him in a speculative manner. Surely the old man did not cherish any misapprehension in regard to him?

Retracing their steps to the house, they encountered Dehan.

"Had breakfast?" Dick asked.

Dehan made an inaudible reply and passed on.

"What the hell possessed that duffer to try to make love to Hula last night?" Dick said. "She told me. She's only a kid. Harry's a prince of a chap—but he'll have old Edwin on his trail if he isn't careful," and he laughed, as he vanished upstairs to clean up.

"What blind things brothers are," commented Fitzmaurice. "Dehan's been in love with Hula ever since she was a baby. She is only a kid, but a couple of years more will alter that." A thoughtful expression crept into his eyes. "Harry's a decent enough fellow, but I don't like to think of her, somehow, married to him. He's a half-white. Still, the Calhouns, as every one knows, are heavily in his debt. Guess it'll end that way. Can't very well do otherwise. They can never pay him what he's lent them . . . but it's the devil of a shame.

Personally I don't like Dehan. Treacherous cuss, I'll wager, though I've no grounds for feeling that way."

"Some other chap may turn up," suggested Haldane.

"Possibly; but it's not likely. Dehan isn't going to let his opportunity slip. Ah, here Dick comes with the girls."

After breakfast the guests assembled to watch the preparations, which were in full swing. Saddle horses were being tried out, the thoroughbreds groomed. Hula was here, there, everywhere like a scarlet humming bird among birds of soberer plumage. Coiling ropes, letting out headstalls, vaulting onto bareback horses that had to be taken to the smithy to be shod. She had no time or thought save for the work at hand.

Mrs. Bane made the most of her opportunity. She maneuvered adroitly to be with Haldane throughout the forenoon. He would have preferred Helen's company, but she was usually with Dick or Von Erdmann. He wondered a little about the German. He was co-owner with Dehan in the Kipahulu plantation and managed it. A taciturn man, who was given to moments of rapid speech, followed by long silences. He was profound, calculating, perhaps a trifle treacherous.

Old Calhoun came out several times during the morning to see how things progressed. Haldane wondered how he would stand the ride overland. After the first twenty miles he would have to abandon his buggy for a horse. He had refused the suggestion that he take the steamer around to Kahului, which is the chief port of call for West Maui.

"No, Dick," he had said, "I'll ride. I want to cover the old trail, see Kaenae again. Haldane," turning fiercely upon his guest, "I'll show you a sight you'll never forget. Paradise. The Garden of Eden. Oh, the times I've had in that valley as a boy. Why does a man have to grow old? But I've had a good life. A great life. I can't kick, but I hope

I'll die with my boots on, and I'd like to have the sound of horses' hoofs in my ears."

And the ponderous old man had walked away with something suggestive of an over-ridden horse in his wide-straddled gait.

Haldane had looked after him, and Mrs. Bane, noting the thoughtful expression of his face, said softly:

"Isn't it sad?"

"Sad? I don't know. He's had what he wanted from life. One can't very well ask for more."

"Haven't you?"

"Not by a long shot."

"Nor I," said the woman looking away. "I've missed—so much. Why must one?"

"Why must one what, Mrs. Bane?"

"Be given half measures."

"I don't know. Perhaps because we haven't earned a right to more."

"Do you believe that?"

"That we get what we deserve?"

"Yes."

"I suppose I do. I was brought up to think so, but I rather fancy it's all rot."

"I'm inclined to think so, too."

Haldane felt impatient. He had met Mrs. Bane before. Their utterances were echoes of the thoughts and statements of others, which they had heard or read, not mental processes of their own. Politeness compelled him to listen to her, to make the necessary replies, but his mind wandered.

He looked at the scene before him. It was unlike anything he had ever encountered, and he had traveled in many lands. There was a suggestion of an English estate in the stately string of thoroughbreds, but there was an exotic and incongruous mingling of other elements. Pommeled saddles, lassos, men in shirt sleeves working with flowers on their hats, scarlet poinciana trees aflame against the sky, the sound of a ukulele coming from some stall where a groom rested from his labors. Even the garb of the various participants varied in like degree. Dick was in smartly and correctly cut breeches and coat—with roses about his London hat. Dehan was in Hawaiian leggings, tight at the knee and flaring outward, with a gay handkerchief about his throat and a leisurely and insolent walk. It was all a mingling of the tropics and temperate latitudes . . . evidences of lavish expenditure . . . the tragedy of a house built upon sand.

What would come of it all? Would Dick accept Hamilton's offer? If he did so, it would definitely end the Calhoun régime in Hana. Or would he continue in Dehan's debt and let the place gradually wear out? In all likelihood, whichever turn affairs took, Calhoun's death would see an end of this. It was inconceivable that this wasteful but somehow magnificent régime should continue or that it could end. It seemed part of the place, as the forests and headlands were part of the island. He understood why Mitchell and Hamilton had sent him, the outsider, to Hana. His eyes went to the ponderous, purple old man who regarded his race-horses with an almost besotted affection—to his straight-legged, straight-backed son—to Hula—to Dehan. People: their relations to one another, the most absorbing study in the world! Edwin walked into the picture. Squatting on one heel, he examined a saddle. He looked sometimes at Hula, sometimes at Haldane. Dehan, observing him intently, divined what his thoughts were and clenched his hand. There was a curious, intent expression in the old cowboy's eyes. Fierce, speculating they looked from beneath their ragged brows. What was he thinking of? His whole being was concentrated upon something.

Mrs. Bane, feeling the wandering of Haldane's mind,

roused herself to greater efforts. Hula, who had been watching them for sometime, turned and looked at Edwin remindingly. He did not move, and she dropped the rope she held and started to cross the quadrangle toward Haldane and his companion. Halfway to them, she halted, for she saw the amused smile her action brought to Mrs. Bane's lips. She sent a long look of reproach at Anthony, and he was momentarily at a loss to think how he had offended. Then he realized. It was his being with Mrs. Bane.

With storms brewing in her eyes, Hula hastened after Edwin, who had started off toward the corrals. Dehan looked up at her as she passed and grinned. She stared furiously at him. Overtaking the foreman she grabbed his arm.

"*Pehea* (What is it)?" he asked. "Some kind *pilikea* (wrong)?"

The girl shook her head, strode on for a moment, then came toward him again, breathing uneasily.

"Uncle Edwin—last night—he kissed me. I couldn't get away. I hate him! He's laughing because Mrs. Bane's with him! I hate her, and I hate him too!"

"Who? The *haole?*" asked Edwin, with a start of surprise.

"No! Harry!" she cried violently, and she grasped the faded blue *palaka* (blouse-coat) which Edwin always wore and shook it with her small, angry hands. "I wasn't going to tell you—because—I knew you'd get mad—but he laughed at me—he's glad Anthony's been with Mrs. Bane all this morning."

Edwin only heard the first part. An icy blast of anger whitened his face.

"All right, I'll see Harry."

"And, Uncle Edwin—" she broke off, her lips drooping.

"Yes, Hula?"

"No, I won't say it now—"

"All right. When you like, Hula."

For a moment his lasso-hardened hand closed upon her shoulder. He looked at her gallant young body, at her troubled face, and a tender, concerned expression grew in his eyes. He knew the time he had dreaded was upon them. He must be gentle, wise, forbearing, else he would lose hold of her—be unable to help her. His little girl child . . . his little *keiki-wahine* . . . the flower of his heart.

"I think I'm going for a ride."

"Fine, Hula."

"Uncle Edwin."

"Yes?"

"Remember what you said to me on the hill?"

"Ai."

"Well?"

"It shall be so."

The child kissed him with violent gratitude.

He watched her depart, then, with a dangerous face, made his way back to the quadrangle. At the first opportunity he called Dehan aside.

"Well, Edwin?" questioned the young fellow insolently. "What do you want?"

Edwin tipped his hat defiantly over one eye.

"You damn well keep your hands off Hula. She isn't for you!"

Dehan's eyes blazed.

"Hula, when she marries—which won't be for a time—will marry a different kind of a man—and a *haole!*"

He spoke in their common tongue and saw no incongruity that he, who possessed less white blood than Dehan, should speak in such a manner to him.

Dehan's face grew crimson. Edwin waited for him to speak. For a moment he was unable to, then:

"You'll have a lot to say about it when Hula makes up

her mind to love—or marry. 'Uncle' Edwin," he snorted, "will be forgotten like that!" and he snapped his fingers disdainfully.

"I know," replied the old fellow without emotion, but truculent as an old bull, "but she won't pass me up for a bastard like you. Don't try any more of what you tried last night—" Edwin spoke rapidly in Hawaiian, "or I'll rope and drag you till you say *pau!*"

Turning on his heel, he strode off, contemptuously. Dehan looked after him, cursing, for he knew the old *paniola* would be quite capable of carrying out his threat without care or thought of consequences.

CHAPTER VIII

The boat by which Hamilton was expected to arrive docked at three, and Haldane went down to meet it.

"Well, what unexpected developments decided you to come over?"

"After reading your letter, Mitchell and I concluded that we couldn't afford to let sentiment, or anything else, lose us this," and he gestured slightly toward the slope of the mountain. "As soon as the races are over, I'm going after Dick—" He paused as if he were going to ask Haldane a question, then said, "Well, what do you think of Hana? Has it got you? It does most people."

"It has—somewhat."

Hamilton glanced at his companion.

"Think you can survive three or four years of it?"

Hamilton looked at him intently.

"I think I can."

"You'll have a job cut out for you. Even I, when I'm here, become inwardly excited, though no one might suspect it—

of me. My dream of so many years seems already accomplished." He broke off in his abrupt manner, then asked, "Is Helen—Miss McKaine, here?"

"Yes."

Haldane wondered how Hamilton happened to know her.

"She's beautiful," he said in an impassionate manner. "What are we doing this afternoon? Dick's great on entertaining his guests. He's got fine horses and is a wonderful host. He knows how to enjoy life. Ah, here is the house."

"Are you coming with us, Hula?" asked Dick, an hour later, when he was superintending the mounting of his guests.

Hula shook her head.

"Hello there," said Hamilton, crossing to where she sat on her horse; "you're quite a young lady, Hula. It's nearly four years since I last saw you."

"Hello, Howard," said the child, in easy Island fashion; "what did you come up for? The races?"

"Just to see Silver Wings run. You must come over sometime. You could show my boys a thing or two about riding."

Hula looked at him thoughtfully, and the adorable gravity of her face did not relax.

Dick laughed. "I'm afraid Hula would hardly fit into your household, Howard, or, for that matter, any of us."

Haldane looked at him. He had been drinking.

Hamilton smiled a gray smile and caught hold of Hula's horse's mane.

"Well, for all that I'd like to have her come."

"You were here when Silver Wings won his first race," said the child musingly, "and you've come over to see him run for the last time. It's nice of you, Howard." Her eyes wandered over the mounted guests, and, seeing Mrs. Bane's horse drawn up beside Haldane's, her lips grew a little pale. "Yes, I guess I'll come. Don't wait for me, Howard. Go on with the others. I'll get a fresh horse and follow. Which way are you going, Dick?"

"Toward Kipahulu."

"I'll catch you before you hit the first gulch."

She spurred away and the cavalcade moved out after Dick. Haldane smiled at her as she passed, but she disregarded him utterly. The man could not decide if she were really oblivious of his presence or if she wished to give him the impression that she were. If the latter were true, it boded ill. Restive as a horse that apprehends trouble, the man rode, grave-faced, outwardly calm, inwardly perturbed, beside Mrs. Bane. He essayed once or twice to ride up to Hamilton but realized that the gray man intended to retain his place beside Helen. Graceful, with a *lei* of crimson roses about her neck, she rode upon Dick's best horse. . . . What could Howard Hamilton have in common with Helen McKaine? Beautiful, damned. The roads of their lives lay far apart. They could have no meeting. Missionary and . . . but Haldane would not finish the thought. Whatever Helen might be, her heart was pure gold. He knew she had never done a mean or little thing. She gave without care or count of cost because it was her nature. Perhaps it was the very sun of her lavish soul that attracted the chilly man. Having had everything, she had given all; having had nothing, Hamilton had taken all.

It was the attraction that is generated by opposites that drew and held him beside her.

Once Dick glanced back and seeing them together, he smiled. He galloped at the head of the cavalcade with Deanie and Fitzmaurice. Jack Lightfoot rode with Diana. Von Erdmann and Harry lingered somewhat behind, waiting to fall in with Hula when she overtook them. Haldane wished that it had not been his lot to ride with Mrs. Bane. Hula would not like it—might not believe that it was not his doing. But the widow had made it clear from the moment of mounting that she intended to have him for her cavalier. So be it, he thought savagely; the situation, if there were one, was getting beyond him.

Hula overtook them within the half hour. She glanced rather contemptuously at Dehan; then, seeing that Mrs. Bane was riding with Anthony, she began to play up to the half-white in a crude, childish effort to make Haldane jealous.

Her face was suffused with color; storms brewed in her eyes.

Dick led the cavalcade at a hard gallop up and down gulches and finally headed them down a long green ridge that terminated in a bluff fronting the sea. Down the vivid grass the horses ran eagerly into the wind, tossing their heads to get the feel of their riders' hands on the bit.

Of a sudden Hula flashed past, cutting her horse's flanks savagely with her quirt.

"Come on, Dick!" she cried imperiously and headed her horse for the cliffs. Dick drove his spurs home, and his horse leaped free of the encompassing riders. Side by side brother and sister raced. Haldane watched them. Doubtless they knew what they were doing, but, louder than the beat of their horses' hoofs in the long Hilo grass, he heard the hollow thud of a great sea as it burst against the foot of the cliffs. Smoking, it recoiled and assaulted the land again.

Faster, faster, until the wind sung in their ears and tore tears from their eyes, Dick and Hula raced, lashing their horses at each leap, urging, inciting them to greater efforts.

A scream broke from Deane's lips and Mrs. Bane reeled in her saddle. Haldane grabbed at her while he still galloped.

Then simultaneously, on the brink of the bluff, both horses were checked. They propped, poised, reared and wheeled. Hula's eyes were wild and excited. There was a recklessness about her that appalled Haldane. There were no lengths to which the child would not go if she were driven too hard. . . . A deadly coldness swept through him.

Dick faced his guests, laughing. He was quite noticeably intoxicated.

"Well, how's that for an exhibition of well-trained cattle horses? Thought we'd go over, didn't you?"

Deanie laughed nervously, Di was white to the lips, and Haldane saw that even Helen's eyes—the great liquid eyes of her race—were dilated and anxious. She knew Dick pretty well.

Von Erdmann reined in his horse with a jerk.

"Bah! You Calhouns are all crazy," he observed disgustedly—"make us all lose a heartbeat. For what? Supposing something broke? What then! Where would you be?"

"Down there," said Dick, carelessly pointing to where the great seas smoked and smashed. "Let's get off for a while and wind the horses."

He dismounted and lifted Deane off. Haldane assisted Mrs. Bane. Quietly she slipped down and lay limp in his arms. There was a moment's commotion, then she opened her eyes.

"How disgraceful of me—to—faint. But I thought they were both going to be killed. Dick, can you forgive me for being so foolish?"

She asked it with beautiful humility, leaning prettily against Haldane.

"Hell! I'm sorry," said the man, "it's just a little stunt of Hula's and mine, to give our guests a thrill. But you hit a pretty stiff pace to-day, sweetheart," he said, turning to look up at his stormy-eyed little sister.

"By Jove!" he thought; "I wouldn't have cared much if I had gone over, but Hula looks as driven as I feel. What's biting her?"

He looked closely at her; then said aloud casually, "How's to a drink?"

"Put your coat around me, Mr. Haldane, will you? I'm cold," said Mrs. Bane, leaning against him.

"Make it an arm, old man," advised Dick; "don't obey so specifically. Deane and I are quite comfortable. Follow our worthy example."

The little woman giggled and settled back against her host. Haldane felt a moment of intense pity for Diana, then he glanced towards Hula.

Seated between Von Erdmann and Dehan, she was talking to them in a high, excited way. She looked beautiful, but the pupils of her eyes were dilated to twice their natural size. The man felt that her spirit, bewildered as a young animal's at its first beating, was dashing this way and that in a frantic effort to accomplish escape from pain.

An exasperation so intense swept through him that Mrs. Bane—though he neither spoke nor moved—was conscious of it.

What ruse could she devise to change her position without letting Hula realize what drove her to it? Loosing the topaz ring she wore, pushing it down her finger with a hidden thumb, she kneeled up and threw her hand forward.

"Look! there's a whale blowing!" For Deane had informed her that they frequented the windward coasts at some seasons.

Every one followed her pointing arm and she held the graceful posture, then gave a little cry of dismay.

"My ring!"

Haldane saw it flash through the air and scrambled to recover it.

"Oh, dear, my fingers are so slim that it's almost impossible to get a ring sized to fit them. Thank you, Mr. Haldane. Oh, will you take care of it for me until we get home? I'd hate to lose it. Some one I cared for a great deal gave it to me."

"I shall be delighted to, Mrs. Bane," and he slipped it into his waistcoat pocket, without even trying to see if it would go on one of his fingers.

Hula watched, tight-lipped, and the German watched her with an expression of intense interest on his dead-white features.

When a move was made to go home, Hula, disregarding the widow's derisive smile, walked over to Haldane and challenged him to a race. There was a childish hostility in her face, and Anthony stood astounded, appalled at a situation he could no longer be blind to.

"Very well, kid, I'll race you," he said, reining his horse aside.

He had a vague hope that the race might afford an opportunity to talk to her, to attempt to clear matters up a little.

"Wait, let the others get ahead. There's a paddock a little way on where we'll get clear running."

"Righto, sweetheart."

The girl glanced at his mount, satisfied that hers could outstrip it. She watched Dick and his guests depart.

"Now," she commanded, gathering up her bridle.

Haldane felt in his pocket to see if Mrs. Bane's ring were safe and gave an exclamation of annoyance.

"Great God, Hula, I've lost it!"

The girl, who had been more like herself for an instant, became aloof. She dismounted and helped him search for it, kicking at the grass resentfully.

"Look here, Hula," said Haldane grasping her by the shoulders, "what's the matter? Surely you aren't silly enough to be jealous of Mrs. Bane? It's ridiculous."

The child snatched herself free.

"I'll kill her if she doesn't leave you alone. You are my Anthony. Mine!"

"Dear kid," said Haldane soothingly, "of course I am. I wouldn't be any one else's. You adorable, volcanic piece of femininity, what on earth am I to do with you?"

The girl looked at him, a long look that disturbed the man profoundly. He shook her again in a sort of fierce affection mingled with exasperation. She waited for an instant, her eyes upon his face expectantly, then wrenched herself free. She was mounted and off in a second, and Haldane, as fast as he could, followed her.

Satisfied that he was coming, Hula lashed at her horse cruelly. Veering across the slope of green meadow, she deliberately headed for a small, precipitous wash that cut through it. Haldane, following fast on her heels, saw her suddenly vanish. He threw his horse onto its haunches, divining something of what had occurred. It tore up the grass with deep-driven hoofs. Sick, appalled, he dismounted and threw the bridle over its head. Taking a few swift strides forward he came to the brink of the wash. At the bottom of it, jarred out of her saddle, Hula lay limp. A few yards from her, her horse lay—broken backed. Dying shudders passed through it.

Haldane slid down the precipitous side.

"Great God, Hula!" he said chokingly as he fell on his knee beside her.

The girl opened her eyes. "I did it—on purpose—so you'd have to hold me. Don't you love me, Anthony?"

Her face was damp, heated, twisted a little with pain.

He felt her all over in a desperate endeavor to ascertain whether or not anything was broken.

"I'm all right, but I hit a bit hard." Then she clasped him with her strong young arms, straining to him fiercely. "Oh, Anthony, why don't you kiss me, love me? I killed my horse —and still you won't!"

Haldane could hardly believe her statement, yet a glance at the sides of the dead animal verified her statement. Long weals from her quirt stood out on its satiny skin.

"Hula, my dear little girl," he cried his whole being filled with compassion for a nature that endangered her whole life, "don't be utterly crazy. I'm yours, all of me. Set your mind at rest on that score. I'll be your cavalier and no other's, only for God's sake—"

"Promise," she interrupted. "You can't even be polite to her. You can't ride or talk to her, or I'll—"

"Hush, dear," interposed the man hastily. "I'll ride only with you, talk only to you, but for God's sake don't be an ass. I've never in my life known any one like you. I adore you, but I feel like beating you."

The child laughed. "All right, Anthony, but remember"—she looked into his face—"remember!"

"How can I forget!" He spoke hastily, hating to look at the dead horse because of what it stood for, afraid to look at the heated little face lifted toward his own. "You don't understand, you can't appreciate—you're only a baby—"

"I don't care about anything, Anthony, now," she said dreamily, then looking at her horse she pushed him away and went to it. "I had to kill you, Lehua, to make him!" Tears splashed down her cheeks, and she fell upon the animal's dead head, lavishing caresses on it. Then she lifted her face, and seeing the concerned expression of Haldane's face, she laughed.

"Dear kid—that was frightfully cruel," he said, "to it—and to me."

"But I was in agony, I couldn't breathe, I couldn't think, I couldn't bear it. I wanted to be dead."

"I know it, but there's to be no more of this, Hula," he said, making a movement toward her dead horse. "If you don't behave, I'll go away—"

"You sound like Uncle Edwin," gloated the child and looked at him adoringly.

"I'll have to ride home behind you, Anthony," she said when they scrambled up the bank. "I'll send one of the boys for my saddle."

Assured of her possession of Haldane, satisfied that he would keep his promise to her whether or not she was present, Hula slid off the horse with a happy heart when they got home. She sought and found Edwin. He was sitting on the steps of his cottage waiting for her. Cowboys, singing to their guitars and ukuleles, clustered on their verandas or sat on the low stone walls.

"Where you bin, Hula?" asked the man, noting her happy face.

With a sigh of content, the girl seated herself, leaning against his knee. Edwin pulled her silky hair and drew on his pipe.

Briefly, looking up at him the while, Hula detailed the events of the afternoon.

"And he forgot all about her damn ring," she concluded; "he didn't remember even about our not finding it—afterwards."

Edwin nodded.

To his way of thinking, Hula was not too young. It was the way of his people to love early and fiercely. This man was all he desired for her; tender, strong, understanding. Satisfied at the turn affairs seemed to be taking, Edwin listened contentedly to the cowboys' singing, thinking long thoughts as he towsled the head of his child.

"Hula," he said after a long silence, taking his short pipe from his lips, "didn't you tell me, one time, that he had a *wahine*, a wife, in England?"

"Yes."

The foreman did not speak for an instant. Thoughtfully

he looked down at the girl, studying her beauty, appraising its quality.

"It will be all right," he announced aloud, but he was speaking to himself. No man could be proof against Hula . . . none.

"Come, we go see if Silver Wings is all right. Must rest before to-morrow. You, too."

"Oh, let me sit up for a while," pleaded the child, "I'm too happy to go to bed. I want to be with you, Uncle Edwin."

The old fellow grunted.

"All right, kid."

The tour of the stables completed, they returned to the cottage steps and sat down, listening to the *paniolas'* singing in the white night. Silver white as Uncle Edwin's hair shone the sea in the moonlight with shadows upon it. Silver white gleamed the blossoming ginger against the stone walls.

Hula's hand laced and locked the old man's, and she breathed rapturously.

"Oh, Uncle Edwin," she sighed, looking up at him.

"*Maikai,* (good) flower of my heart," he said, drawing upon his pipe until it guttered contentedly.

PART II

WITH THE TIDE

CHAPTER I

Departure took place early. Before the sun had been up two hours, everything was in readiness for the start.

Haldane watched the turmoil of horses in the driveway; cowboys forged ahead dragging reluctant pack-animals after them; watchers called farewell; eager young horses pranced and fidgeted to be off. Edwin sat erect, superintending it all from beneath his tilted hat. Mahiai passed with Silver Wings. The great horse's feet beat an eager tattoo on the hard road, and Huia's heart beat as wild a one in her hard little side. Haldane watched her. Her cheeks were crimson, her eyes shining. With a laugh of carefree happiness, she reined back beside him for a moment.

"Oh, Anthony," she breathed, "isn't he beautiful! Isn't it fun!"

Then she leaped forward to join Edwin who waited determinedly for her. Haldane was nonplussed. She seemed as carefree as a colt, scarcely aware of him, bent only upon horses and the excitement of the journey overland.

Some of the blackness that had filled his heart began to dissipate.

All day they rode through the overheated stillness of the Ditch Country. No invigorating trade-wind struck this section of the island as in Hana; a shoulder of the mountain shut it off. The air was stagnant, heavy, surcharged with moisture and a thousand forest smells. Men rode coatless; horses reeked.

Up and down spray-filled gulches, amber with sunshine, choked with banana and bamboo, tangled with creepers, fringed with fern, the trail wound along. Slippery with mud, crossed with countless streams. Blossoming ginger and begonia flanked every pool; rivers struggled seaward; cocoanuts clustered the coast. Vivid bluffs stood, brightly green, against the fragile, polished blue of the sea.

Horses scrambled and splashed, as they tried to pass one another, only to be rudely checked by the men who rode or led them. Occasionally some cowboy broke into a song, as he rode full-hearted and content, pleasure bound.

Haldane looked ahead, behind, at the line of men and animals; at Dick sitting easily on a nervous bay mare; at old Calhoun, his face blood-suffused, limp upon the back of his gray gelding, Champagne, at Hula, like a scarlet flower; Deanie, dimpled, riding badly, but enjoying it all; at Mrs. Bane, veiled from the sun; at Fitzmaurice easy in his saddle, Helen beside him, with roses about her neck; at Diana, with the suppressed face of one bitterly at odds with life; at Hamilton, gray faced but flaming souled; at Dehan with smoldering eyes; at Edwin, hard-faced, unrelenting.

It was a motley company of human beings riding toward their varied destinies, through a country of green gorges, filled with moonstone lights, bounded above by the somber mountain-mass of Haleakala and below by the blue sea.

"Well, what do you think of it?"

Von Erdmann's voice roused him.

"Great."

"Nothing like it anywhere," observed the German, watching the moving line. Then his eyes moved thoughtfully over the forests. Haldane wondered what was in his mind. Did he, too, cherish dreams? They rode, talking for a while; then Hamilton came up, and Von Erdmann fell back to ride with Helen.

"Is there a doubt but that it can be done?"

Howard's voice, cold, careful but hopeful, fell on the Englishman's ears.

He looked at the ridges, the gorges swathed in green; he visioned their sides, torn, bleeding red clay with men, ant-like, swarming upon them.

"There isn't a doubt," said Haldane.

"It's going to be a big job."

Hamilton spoke tentatively.

"Yes, a big one."

"Dick's pushed. He'll sell. Mitchell and I are prepared to give him a good price, and we've agreed to give you an interest in the ditch that will enable you to live as you please when it's done."

"I appreciate your generosity. I had not expected anything beyond a salary."

"You are to have that as well, while the work of construction is on."

"Your terms are generous."

"We can afford to make them so."

Haldane paused to light a cigarette.

"Is there anything I haven't—"

"No," interrupted Haldane.

"Then you are prepared definitely to affiliate yourself with us?"

Haldane did not reply. He had a straightforward simplicity of soul and a great love for his work, but his whole being was in opposition to the possibilities and the complications that had suggested themselves during the past two days. Better a thousand times to be clear of everything before it was too late. But it was all so preposterous, so impossible. That Hula should be in love with him, or that he could ever fall in love with her. Still he hovered in doubt. The work would take months, years, and it would necessitate his presence throughout the period of construction. Why had Helen ever suggested such a possibility? It had been simple until she had spoken. Had she kept silent, he would have interpreted Hula's act as a passage of unreasoning, childish jealousy. Hamilton was waiting. He must speak. Yet he hesitated, goaded with doubts.

"Oh, Anthony," clear as a bell came Hula's voice, and she cantered up, "we'll be seeing Kaenae in a minute. That's the last turn."

She pointed ahead to a ragged bluff, tree tangled, swathed in vines, that reared against the sky.

"I love it. It's beautiful. I want you to see it with me."

Joyous, unconscious, exulting in the goodly things of her life, she rode beside him. The man had a moment of intense disgust with himself. She was untouched; a thoughtless, headlong child. He all sorts of fool.

He looked at the tumult of horses ahead, checked by a raging little creek. Cowboys dragged at their heads; thoroughbreds reared, pack animals balked. Edwin sat, coolly directing, while hoofs beat the slippery mud and Silver Wings shook his proud head, eager to go on.

"Oh, Anthony! Isn't he beautiful, isn't he a king?"

Again the joyous voice. Horses, horses. Hula was all Calhoun. Her heart would always be with them before any other thing. The unrest that had filled him passed. The day seemed uplifting, as wide as the days before Helen had talked with him on the terrace. It had been a hideous, fantastical aberration. Hula was a baby, he an adult man. Nothing but affection could ever be between them.

He took a free breath. It was as if a sea wind struck him, filling him with its health and purity.

"I'll accept, Hamilton—definitely."

They clasped hands.

"I hope you will never regret your decision. That settled, let us enjoy what's ahead. Like Dick, let us forget that business exists until after the eleventh has been celebrated as His Majesty, King Kalakaua, whose birthday it was, would like it to be celebrated. He was a Merry Monarch and loved a good horse, as these people do."

Hula regarded Hamilton thoughtfully.

"Howard," she observed, "sometimes you are quite nice. What's all this talk? Business?"

The man nodded.

"Well, I'm with the last part of your speech. It's Silver Wings' last race, and we must only think of him and the fun getting there. Now I want Anthony."

"He is yours, young lady."

"Fall back," ordered the child.

Von Erdmann watched from his post by Helen.

"Ah," he said thoughtfully, "Hula likes him. He may find himself in for a lot. April and November. It's amusing, Helen, is it not?"

"I don't see it that way, Tancred."

"But, Helen," Von Erdmann laughed, "the poor man! He surely is as old as I am, and I do not doubt that he is married."

Helen did not confirm or deny the statement. She looked at him.

"I don't believe you would be averse to having her like you, when you come right down to it."

"A man would be a fool who wouldn't like to be Hula's first love. And yet I'm not so sure that I would like to be in his shoes." The German laughed. "He may wish himself well out of it before he is through. These Calhouns! They are extraordinary people. I've watched them for years. Like volcanoes! They disturb. They interest. They destroy. Shall we move on? The horses are across the ford."

Five minutes' more riding brought them to the edge of Kaenae.

Two thousand feet below the valley lay; sheer-sided, tapestried in green. Taro and rice fields, frosted *kukuis*, clumps of mango, groves of cocoanut showed on the wide valley floor. Distant, streaked with water-falls, the *palis* (cliffs) of the farther side stood in a jagged line. Slanting rays of sunlight, pouring through the heavy cloud-masses of the late afternoon, flooded the whole, vast place with opal lights.

Kaenae.

Beautiful, breath-taking, seizing one's heart with violent and possessive hands, its jaws foam-edged, framing a sweep of peacock-blue sea.

Old Calhoun rode up.

An hour's ride brought them to the valley bottom; the trail turned sharply and faced the sea. A breath of wind came freshly from where the surf played outside the bar. The villagers swarmed out to meet them: women in *holokus*, men in dungarees, naked children, shy-eyed girls, bashful boys, mangy dogs.

"*Aloha*, Dick, *aloha*, Hula, *aloha nui*, Old Man!"

They crowded among the horses. Hands stretched up, hands reached down; heads were bent to receive the flower garlands that were raised and placed about the riders' necks.

"Here he comes, Napiha!"

Calhoun cried it in a great voice, "*Aloha, makule* (old man) damn you, but it's great to see you again. And how's Mama?"

First he grasped the vast brown hand of the old Hawaiian, then the wrinkled one of his wife, whose face broke into tears and smiles.

"Ah, *aloha*, Billy," she cried. "Come down. Old bones are tired from a long ride. We got good *kinni* (gin) from that *Pake*, (Chinaman). Ah, Sam, and *okolehao*. First we drink, then we eat; *opihis*, fish, salmon-*lomi*, *poi*. I, too, happy to see you. I, too, happy when you come. Ah, Hula, Edwin, Dick, come down! Come inside!"

The Calhouns and their guests were taken under Napiha's

hospitable roof. His house, rambling, grayed, of weather-beaten boards, reared its two-and-a-half stories high above the grass huts and cottages of the village. Mango trees crowded it; plumaria and oleanders grew against the veranda. A short stretch of natural lawn went down to the lagoon; *halas* sprawled over it, dipping their long sword-like leaves into the water; cocoanuts rustled and whispered; the peace of evening brooded over it.

Strange new food-smells stirred Haldane.

"Great Scott, kiddie," he said, addressing Hula, who sat with swinging legs upon the railing, "I don't want ever to leave. I've dreamed of places like this, as a boy; but I never expected to see one."

The child clasped his arm with both her hands.

"I love you, Anthony. You like everything." Then with a quick change, "You've never eaten Kanaka food, have you?"

"No, Hula."

"It's good. Shall I get you another drink? Gin and cocoanut milk?"

"Thanks, kid; I've had all I want."

Hula looked at him. He was an Uncle Edwin sort of man. It made her sense of possession the stronger. Feeling her eyes, Haldane looked down. Clear, beautiful, candid, they returned his glance. His fingers tightened about her hand where it lay on his arm. She was adorable.

For a moment they stood looking at the lagoon. From somewhere out of sight came the faint cry of bathers. He could hear the uneasy whisper of the sea upon the shingle beach and Calhoun's voice booming from some hidden spot of the garden.

"Let's join them, Hula."

The child jumped down, hugged his arm, and they strolled across the lawn.

"Hey! *Pelikani!* Damn you, come here!"

Calhoun waved at them from the wicker chair in which he sprawled. About him on the grass sat Napiha and other Hawaiians; some drinking, some making *leis*, some preparing dishes of food, some lolling, idle as school boys, in the spreading shade of breadfruit and mango. The fresh water of the lagoon, motionless and gilded by the setting sun, showed in curious contrast to the living sparkle of the sea as it surged blue upon the rocks and fell back broken and white.

"Here, try this tea-root," ordered Calhoun, "made especially for me, by my old *aikane* (friend)," and he looked fondly at Napiha's wrinkled wife who sat with busy fingers sorting and cleaning rubber-like seaweed that smelt as clean as the sea.

Haldane accepted the liquor and looked at it. It was as colorless as water. He lifted the glass to Calhoun.

"Here's to you."

"Drink it down, *Pelikani.* It's the essence of hell—but it's to Silver Wings, and my little gel, and to my *aikanes* (friends) of fifty years. *Aloha ka ko!*" and with a sweep of his arm he seemed to embrace the valley and all that it held.

Haldane drained his glass and gasped. Like the thrust of a white-hot knife, the liquor struck through him.

"Great God!" he gasped.

Mirth swept the group, and Hula danced about like a frisking colt.

"Try another glass," urged Calhoun. "I'll take one with you."

"Thanks, that's all I can manage until I've had food."

Calhoun laughed.

"That was a dirty trick, Daddy," cried Deanie gleefully; "you'll have the good man drunk as a lord if you don't look out."

She watched his departing figure, as he and Hula strolled away in the direction of the beach.

Dehan, lying lazily on his side, sat up.

Helen watched him while she tossed out her hair, damp from swimming.

"Never seen him that way, come to think of it," mused Calhoun, in a meditative manner; "he's a damn fine chap. Good sort and good sport." He stared after him and listened to the sea, then added like an afterthought, "Sort of man I'd like to see Hula—"

Helen's pink palm fell upon his lips. He kissed it, raising his eyebrows inquiringly.

Dehan looked at her as she half knelt and half sat against the old man's knee.

His heavily fringed eyes glittered. After a moment he got up and strolled off in the direction Hula and Haldane had taken.

Calhoun looked inquiringly at Helen.

"Well, my dear? Enlighten me."

Helen glanced behind to determine the pitch of her voice.

"Uncle Billy, weren't you going to say, 'the sort of man I should like to see Hula married to'?"

"I was. What of it, my dear?"

"Well, don't say it in front of Harry. It isn't friendship only that's made Harry so generous to you and Dick—it's Hula."

"But, damn it, she's only a kid."

"She won't be forever. You owe Harry more than you can ever repay."

"I know it."

"He knows it, too. He's generous enough, I'll give him his due, but he's human. Hula will square all you owe. Harry's mad with jealousy now because she likes Anthony."

Calhoun looked harassed and took a drink.

"Harry's a good chap, but I don't like to think of Hula's marrying him, somehow. My little filly's made for a better stable—that big chap's the sort of man I'd like for her. . . . Hell. . . . I want her to have a free choice when her time comes. It's every one's right. Dick's made a mess of his marriage. Well, I'll have to see what can be done. Betting will be high this meet, thanks to Collins' imported horse. Wonder if Silver Wings can bring the bacon home." He paused. "I can make a big clean-up if I've any sort of luck, and I'll pay it all to Harry and borrow enough from some one else to carry me along. Have to talk to Dick. Well, that'll keep till after the races. Pour me a drink, Helen."

She obeyed, for she did not want to say more. Too many were present. She glanced at Deanie, for she suspected that she was straining her pink ears although she was inspecting a bowl of *opihis* (shell fish) with a rosy forefinger and laughing with a doe-eyed Hawaiian girl.

Restlessness filled her, and she got up and wandered away.

Her eyes went to the loneliness of the sea and the headlands. The serried clouds of the trade-wind stood above the horizon, incredibly enormous, polished, white as a tropic-bird's wing.

The evening's peace filled her with misgiving, as if she distrusted its loveliness. Voices came from behind her, faint, unreal. People were gathering for the *luau*. She must go back.

She caught up her rippling hair, tossed it over her shoulder, and retraced her steps to the house. Dick was on the veranda, moody, half drunk. His eyes lighted a little at sight of her.

"Where have you been, Helen? I was looking for you."

"Down on the beach. Where's Di?"

The man's face set.

"I don't know. I suppose she thinks all this," he waved

toward the happy groups collecting for the feast, "is wrong."

"Well?" questioned Helen.

"Oh, I know, some of it's best not spoken about; but after all, it's only human nature—" He broke off for want of words with which to dress his thoughts.

"But you cannot expect a woman like Di to stand for the things we've done. Her life's been too different."

"Hell! I know it," sighed the man in exasperation.

"But you don't take it into account—sufficiently."

"I'm faithful," he said savagely; "she can't expect me to ask all my friends to change from good fellows into a pack of missionaries!"

Helen laughed. "At that, Dicky, I don't believe missionaries are as inhuman as they are made out to be. But remember, what to us is enjoyment, is to her sin. She can't conceive, for instance, how you can kiss me and think nothing of it. Many men kiss me who do not love me, and I kiss men I don't want or love. . . . It's the way we are made, but she is different. You love her or you wouldn't be unhappy; so it's up to you—"

"I'm unhappy enough, God knows. I'm wretched. Can't you talk to her. Knock some sense into her, convince her I love her?"

"I?"

"Yes, you. Ah, Helen, won't you help me?"

She laid her hands upon his shoulders.

"Only you can do that—convince her you love her." Then impulsively, "I'll do what I can, Dick, but it won't be much. But there must be no more of this." She disengaged herself. "She can't understand it. You'll have to cut me out."

"I can't. She must realize that, when I kiss you or put my arm around you it's because you're the best friend I ever had. We've been sweethearts, Helen—though you wouldn't marry me. To her it may seem wrong; but, damn it, I know that a fellow like myself or a girl like Hula could put their last cent on you—"

He broke off.

"But she isn't able to understand, Dick—she hasn't advanced far enough."

"But she'll have to, or we can never be happy. What sort of fellow would I be if I cut out you!"

Helen did not reply. After a minute she said gently:

"It may take years—"

"And I'm to have years of this hell?"

"Possibly."

"Well, I'll be damned if I will. Help me, Helen. I can't get away from it, even when I'm drunk. I haven't been really sober for a week."

"If you love her enough, you'll endure it. Things may some day come right. You'll both have to make adjustments."

Dick stood restive, his handsome face unhappy and dragged.

"Dick."

He looked up.

"I'll try to talk to her—if she'll let me."

"God bless you, Helen."

He threw his arms about her as Hula might have done.

Laughing a little unsteadily, Helen pushed him away.

"Remember, Dicky, no more of this," she reminded him.

He stood, his eyes upon her adoringly.

"You're wonderful—then take this," he tore a ring from his hand and thrust it on her finger. "It's worth a lot, Helen. You need it more than I do."

"Dick, what a hopeless boy you are!"

The woman looked down at her hand. On the fourth finger Dick's ring hung loosely. It was a gold serpent with a great diamond in its head and with eyes of emerald. She recognized it as one his father had won from King Kalakaua in a poker game, years before.

She smiled, and Dick kissed her impulsively.

"I love you, Helen; you are beautiful and good—the best friend I ever had. You should have married me."

"I loved you too much."

"I cannot get your woman's logic, though I have to accept it. Take it, keep it, sell it, do whatever you want with it!"

A sound made them both turn.

Diana stood in the doorway, her face white save for two spots of color that raged like volcanic fires in either cheek. In a clinging gold gown, she looked like an Egyptian queen, but her eyes were those of a woman long dead.

Helen felt Dick stiffen. His nostrils paled and twitched. He sat down upon the railing heavily. When he looked up, his wife had gone.

Helen drew a deep breath.

"I shall have to attempt the impossible. I must—after this. I'll try to talk to her to-night, certainly to-morrow. Take back your ring, dear."

"I will not."

Dick picked up her hand and kissed it.

"Why can't she understand? There are so many kinds of love, Helen. One does not take away from another."

"I know, but few women can understand that fact. Men can—a little. Come, Dick, we'd best go in."

Napiha was assembling his guests about the foot-high, fern-covered table that went the length of the living room.

"Try to sit by her, Dick," advised Helen, and she took Von Erdmann's arm.

Dick looked at his wife's frozen face and in an access of feeling turned to Hula. The child rallied to him, conscious in a dim way of his plight. Inarticulate anger against the woman who set herself so against their life waked in her.

"Well, Dickie," she cried, "here's to Silver Wings." She passed him a glass. "Let's drink. Anthony, sit on my other side. Where are you, Dad? Oh, down there! Tell the boys to sing."

"You tell 'em, Hula!"

"What'll it be, Dad? Your old favorite, Ka Moae?"

"Yesh! Ka Moae, Hula. Well, to hell with trouble. Lesh be gay!"

He raised his glass and drank deeply from it.

CHAPTER II

"Now let's see your horse," cried Calhoun, wiping his mustache; "that drink set me up, Tom."

He turned to his friend, a man singularly like him in appearance, but better preserved.

"All right; come on, folks."

Collins turned to his guests, and they crowded down the steps.

"Well, what do you think of him, Hula?" he asked, turning triumphantly to the little girl, who hesitated on the outside of a circle of cowboys who were inspecting the imported black. The men stepped back to allow her to pass, and she appraised the stallion silently, expertly.

Taller than Silver Wings, heavier, longer of leg, but lacking the symmetry of his rival, Hurricane stood, with half-closed, disdainful eyes. The child drew a deep breath.

It was to be a struggle of giants! She laughed, derisively, as though to give herself courage to face the thought of a very possible defeat.

"He looks like a kangaroo."

"Beauty's only skin deep, Hula," said young Jerry Collins, but his eyes rested on hers with a sort of dazed surprise. Edwin's little humming bird changed almost overnight into a bird of paradise! "Hurricane's got the legs of your gray."

"But not the conformation," defended the girl.

"He'll take one jump to every two of your Silver Wings'! How about it, Dad?" and young Jerry turned to his father.

"Sure as God made little apples," said old Collins exultantly. "Trust your old Dad to pick the real thing! I got him in Kentucky, folks, paid a small fortune for him, brought him to Hawaii just to beat my old pal's favorite—" He laid an affectionate hand upon Calhoun. "We've been in this game all our lives, and Bill's had a bit the best of me. I ain't saying that Silver Wings ain't a good horse. He is. But there's no horse so good that you can't find a better."

"Right you are, Tom," agreed Calhoun heartily; "but I'll beat you just the same. My luck's not all gone, and I'd bet my last cent on an Isonomy."

"Well, you'll have lots of opportunities. My gang from Honolulu," Collins waved toward his guests, "have come all primed to fleece your Hana suckers. *Faites le jeu, Messieurs, faites le jeu!*"

"Well, it looks as though we all ought to have opportunities to make a little money," commented Deanie; "the question is, which horse!"

"Ach, if one could only know!" laughed Von Erdmann.

"Which do you think looks the best bet?"

"Me? Ach, I do not know. It's a toss up. Of course, if anything should happen and Opiupiu did not ride Silver Wings"—the German gestured expressively—"then it would be easy. No man can ride the gray the way he does. They are one. But they lock the old man up in the stall with the horse for a couple of nights before the race so that he will not get drunk. That Edwin! he is hard as iron. Look at his face!"

"He gives me the shivers," Deanie shuddered. "His eyes are like hot coals. How he watches Hula!"

"Goin' to stake me, Billy?" screamed a florid woman, gorgeously arrayed, with blond hair, elaborately and terribly curled, framing a vast expanse of painted face.

"Nothing surer, Dearie!" cried old Calhoun gallantly.

"What! Goin' back on my Hurricane horse!" exclaimed Collins in mock anger; "that's a woman for you. I invite her up here and—"

"Silver Wings has brought me more than one good purse," screamed the woman; "this is his last race. I cannot go back on him. Whew! it's hot. Let's be getting in, or my war paint'll begin to run. Come, Jerry. Here, keep your eyes off Hula, or Edwin will be after you!"

The young man laughed.

"Well, I can look at her can't I, Dearie?" then turning he flung his arm about Dehan. "Come on in, all of you. Dick, you look as glum as the devil. What's wrong? Where's your wife? I missed her in the rush. I hope she won't think me rude. Come, Harry. You look sour as Dick. Thinking of getting married too? Another good man gone wrong!"

They moved toward the house.

"Talking of marriage, Dick, you'd better keep an eye on the kid. She's a knock-out if ever there was one. If she goes on at this rate, I'll fall. Double harness with her on the other side of the pole wouldn't be half bad. Bet Hula'd make a real sort of wife, sporty and game. She'd never hold a fellow to account. But I suppose I'd have you to run against Harry."

He turned his blue eyes on the half-white.

"How about it?" he asked jestingly.

"Ai," said Dehan.

Jerry laughed.

"Hell, Dick, I think the fool is serious. Well, Harry, I'll respect your prior claim. Here's the gang. I'll have to do the introducing, I suppose, as Dad's still looking at the horses. Those old boys are keen as kids. Dick, Hurricane's going to make that old nag of yours look sick."

Dick laughed.

"Prepared to back that statement up in proper style?"

"You bet!"

"Name yours, old man, and I'll double it!"

"Here, wait, you hot young bloods," protested "Dearie," waddling along in their wake. "Wait until after dinner. That's the proper time."

Dick looked around.

"Lost Dad already?"

"Not I, Dicky. I never lost any man, but it's too hot out there for any one as large as I. Who's the big chap with the solemn face? Looks like a stiff. Does he ever smile?"

Dick laughed. "An English chap from Africa. He's a decent sort."

"Sporty?"

"Seems to be."

"Well, the next two days will show whether or not he is. Ah, here come the drinks. After a little 'inspiration' I can dress. It's a long job now!" she sighed gustily, fanning herself with a photograph she had commandeered from a near-by table. "Did you have a good time coming 'round?"

"Yes."

"You're lyin', Dicky," laughed the woman. "What's wrong? Has that horrible German cut you out with Helen —he's been with her all the afternoon—or have you quarreled with your wife?"

Dick laughed, but there was little mirth in the sound.

"Neither! but let's start things going. Get those two old

touts in from the stable! Get out the cards, bring on the drinks."

Dearie looked at him.

"You're nervous, Dicky!"

"Just a bit—" He turned to look at her. "Come on! Let's do something. How's to getting Haldane drunk?"

He turned on the company.

Deanie squealed. "Let's do! I've never seen him anything but cold sober."

"Who's Haldane! The stiff?" Dearie boomed.

"Yes."

"I bet it can't be done," observed Von Erdmann.

Dehan turned on his partner.

"You think so?" His black eyes flashed. "Why?"

"He's got more sense than the whole lot of us."

Dehan's lip curled.

"All right, I'll show you."

He strode out.

Out of doors it had grown dark.

Dehan returned shortly.

"I can't find him, but wait till after dinner."

"Bet he's with Hula," taunted Deane.

The man did not reply for an instant, then suddenly burst out:

"Damn his soul to hell! He shall not have her. I'll kill him first!" and he flung off into the dark.

There was an instant of stunned silence, then "Dearie" observed while she fanned her over-heated face:

"My, my, what a horrible, violent young man Harry's got to be!"

Dick looked aghast, as did the other guests.

"Harry's drunk," he said, after a moment.

"He's as sober as a judge," said Von Erdmann, listening to the raging footsteps on the terraced walk.

"I'd better go after him," said Dick, going out.

His eyes looked concerned. They had the hurt, bewildered expression in them that is in men's eyes when the press of circumstances forces them to mental sobriety while physically they are still drunk.

"Look here, Harry," he protested when he found him, "what on earth made you go off like that? It was rotten taste."

Dehan whirled upon him.

"I'll not stand for that damned *malahini* (outsider) being with Hula all the time. If you don't stop it, I will."

"Cool off, Harry. He's nearly old enough to be her father."

"You think that makes any difference?"

"Of course."

"I know better."

Dehan relapsed into a savage silence.

Dick looked at him. His black eyes were blazing, wide open as they never had been. Realization swept over him of all they owed Dehan.

He laid his hand upon the half-white's shoulder.

"Harry," he began.

"I'll fix him; I'll bust him," raged the man; "then he can't ask her to marry him."

"Harry! You're drunk!"

"The hell I am!"

Contemptuously, shaken with fury, Dehan wheeled upon Dick.

"I apologize, I see that you aren't, but I am, a little, still."

Dick stared at the flagged walk, harried, upset. "If you like, I'll speak to her—"

Dehan laughed shortly.

"Never mind. I'll finish him to-night. No need for you to do anything. Well, I'm going to get dressed."

"Guess I might as well do so too."

Dressing, Dick tried to collect his scattered faculties. He had known Dehan all his life. He had never seen him roused, though he suspected that he possessed the violence that was apparent in his mouth. Sobered, he stood by the window, thinking.

He was unpleasantly conscious of a tension in the air that lingered over from his moments with Dehan. It boded ill for the peace of the Collins household. Dick had all the well-bred man's dislike for anything resembling a scene. That his wife precipitated them in a household that had never known them, upset him for hours afterwards. He always felt thwarted, but he also felt disgraced. Helen's effort to explain had been a failure. Di had become hysterical —and now he felt that he was more than half responsible for Dehan. Why could not people hold in their violence? Dehan was no boor, he was well-bred although his breeding was mixed. In all likelihood he would not lose his head, whatever it was he planned to do. But Dick felt apprehensive, uneasy, distressed. Life of a sudden seemed to have turned its face from him.

The happy, careless years had come to a sudden stop. He must, he must, at the first opportunity talk to his father.

Just before dinner ended, Dehan rose and lifted his glass to the assembled company.

"To Silver Wings!" Then he looked at Hula. "You must drink this too."

The child's eyes grew bright. She was both alarmed and entranced. Uncle Edwin! But surely, once, on such an occasion! She took the glass doubtfully from Dehan and looked about the table questioningly.

"It's a special occasion, Hula," laughed young Jerry watching her admiringly. "Edwin won't mind."

Haldane had an impulse to speak but desisted. He did not

want to make himself ridiculous, and instinct warned him that Dehan had planned things with some definite end in view.

He waited, and Hula gestured toward him.

"Drink it with me, Anthony!" she cried. "It's to Silver Wings."

"Sorry, kiddie."

Her eyes opened in amazement.

"Why not?"

Dehan turned to her. "Guess he's not as much for you and your horse as he pretends to be."

"I'm all for them both," interrupted Haldane, rising from his seat.

The eyes of the entire table were upon the two men.

"Then drink to Silver Wings with Hula!" commanded Dehan rudely.

"Yes, Anthony, yes!" and the child darted to his side and clasped his arm with both hands. He disengaged himself but retained hold of her fingers, as though to guard her from the tentacles of the life that reached for her.

"I will not drink to Silver Wings with you, Hula; but I'll drink to him alone and double any bet that Dehan cares to put on the other horse."

"That's talking!" cried Calhoun excitedly, "take a drink, *Pelikani!* I'll pour it for you."

"Thanks," Haldane accepted the glass without looking at the measure poured. His arm cramped to hit Dehan.

"Come here a minute, Hula," called the half-white.

The child darted to him and he bent and whispered to her.

"Why won't you drink with me, Anthony?"

"Because I'll be damned if I'll have any hand in encouraging you to take your first drink."

"Missionary!" cried Dehan contemptuously, and the guests took up his shout hilariously.

Helen made her way to Haldane.

"I'm with you, Anthony. No drinking, Hula."

With eyes bemused from alcohol and a *lei* of crimson roses slightly awry upon her head Helen was an incongruous figure to voice such a sentiment.

"Here, Helen!" shouted Calhoun, laughing; "you're a fine one to talk!" But his eyes adored her.

In the vibrating atmosphere Haldane was conscious of Howard Hamilton's masked face looking at him speculatively across the table. It was as if Hamilton were taking measure of his man.

"But still Mr. Haldane hasn't drunk to your horse, Hula," mocked Dehan.

"To Silver Wings," said the Englishman, picking up his glass and draining it. Hula, prompted by some imp, snatched it up to drink the drop that remained. Haldane took it from her. The girl looked up at him, then shook her head and laughed.

"I adore you, Anthony! You're like Uncle Edwin. Some day I'm going to marry you."

"Hear, hear!" screamed "Dearie." "Little Red Cherry, this isn't Leap Year."

Hula laughed. "But I'm going to, Dearie."

"Let me be Worst Woman at your wedding, Hula," and Dearie shook with mirth and fanned her vast face furiously with her napkin.

"Well, Dehan, make your bet!" said Haldane, his hand resting on Hula's shoulder.

Mrs. Bane watched the two men tensely.

"I'll take you for—ten thousand," said Dehan deliberately.

Haldane was appalled at the size of the bet. His resources were sufficient but not unlimited. He felt Hula's eyes upon him. He could not go back on her. Double any bet Dehan had cared to make! Those had been his words. He was not by nature reckless, but the alcohol he had taken that afternoon, given impetus by the drink Calhoun had poured, had begun to work in him.

"That makes it twenty for me? Well, I raise you another ten, Dehan."

He looked across the table, and Hula hugged his arm ecstatically.

"I'll take you!" Dehan spoke slowly through clenched teeth. His eyes were narrowed to glittering slits. His estate was enormous; it could stand it. He waited, watching Haldane.

"And I'll raise you another ten!"

"Here, here, that's too high a stake," protested Von Erdmann. "Easy, Harry."

"Take it easy, boys," advised old Collins; "better knock it down a bit."

"Take him, Anthony, take him," urged Hula. "Silver Wings and Opiupiu can beat Hurricane and his California jockey any day!"

"Righto, kiddie. It's my all, but if it goes to please you it's in a sufficiently good cause."

"Bravo. Zhat's the way to talk. Zhe Ladies! God bless zhem!"

Every one took up the cry. The atmosphere relaxed. Liquor circulated. Other bets were made.

Mrs. Bane made her way over to Dehan.

"You've ruined him if Hurricane wins," she said reproachfully.

Dehan shrugged his shoulders.

"What's the odds? He was lost to you the minute Hula came."

"Lost to me? What do you mean?"

"You think I don't know that you liked him?" questioned Dehan; then a thought came to him.

"Mrs. Bane, come outside."

The woman followed him.

"Well, what is it?"

Dehan looked steadily at her.

"I need help. If you can—make Hula doubt him, hate him, I'll whack that bet with you."

"You'll what?"

"I'll whack that bet with you."

"What an extraordinary proposition!"

Dehan snorted.

"You can pull that stuff with the rest, but not with me. Think I don't know what you are?"

"Mr. Dehan, you are curiously rude."

"But you are prepared to talk business?"

The woman stood silent, then said:

"To listen to it."

"That will be a start. You told me in Hana that Hula liked him. I did not believe you, but I know, now, that you were right." His voice vibrated with the intensity of his feelings. "I will give you, as I said, half that bet if you will make Hula hate him, or bust things up between them."

"What an uncouth proposition. How could I do—either?"

"You are a woman; you should know. I cannot think; I hate him so!"

"And if you lose?"

"I will give you five thousand, just the same, if you do your part."

Dehan said it with Hawaiian recklessness.

Mrs. Bane looked at him for a long time.

"I'll see that Opiupiu doesn't ride. We can never dope the horse; Edwin guards him—as he guards Hula!"—the man spoke violently—"and it'll be a job to get the man. I'll do my part; you attend to yours."

He stood furiously in the shadowy, scented garden, then threw up his head and cursed.

"Mr. Dehan, what terrible language!"

"It's not bad enough!"

The woman studied him. He would keep his word. She must devise something. Such an opportunity could not pass. Only a fool, with no sense of the value of money would propose such a bargain. She could not afford . . .

Her hand fell upon his arm.

"Give me—a little time."

Dehan looked down, nodded, and shook her off.

"I won't go back on my word if you do your part."

"I want revenge," said the woman dramatically; "surely we can do this intelligently between us, Harry."

"I attend to Opiupiu; you attend to Haldane."

He looked at her, and his look was an insult; but the woman disregarded it. She had wanted Haldane for a husband, thought Dehan. Now she plotted to ruin him. Undoubtedly she had wanted his money or his ability to provide it more than she had wanted the man. Better so. No sentiment would prevent her from acting, as it might have done had she loved Haldane. And if she succeeded in estranging those two . . . he would not begrudge a cent of the sum. But he despised her utterly.

Hasty steps passed them, going toward the house.

Edwin . . . after Hula.

Dehan laughed.

CHAPTER III

"Dad!" Dick, barefooted and in his pajamas walked over to his father's bed. He looked down at the sleeping man and took hold of him. "Dad, I want to talk to you."

The old man grunted and blew out his cheeks but did not open his eyes.

"Wake up," said Dick.

Calhoun roused himself reluctantly and looked at his son. He seemed very tall and very pale. His eyes were haggard for want of sleep. The line by his mouth was very apparent in the revealing morning light.

"Give me a drink of water, and put a little whisky in it. Not too much."

Dick obeyed and watched the old man drink it.

"Now my pipe. Thanks. Well, what is it?"

Dick sat down on the side of the bed and stared at the tree tops outside the window, gilded by the rising sun.

"I want to talk to you—about Hula," he said, with an effort.

"Hula? Is she sick?"

"No." Dick lighted a cigarette with shaking hands, looked miserable, and then said savagely:

"Damn everything!"

"Not a bad idea," agreed Calhoun, drawing meditatively upon his pipe.

"I don't know how to say it, Dad, but hell!—" Dick broke off again, got up, roved unhappily about the room, looked at himself in the glass and turned away with fierce disgust.

"Well, let's have it, old man."

"Harry—well, we owe him more than we can ever possibly repay."

"What's that got to do with Hula?"

"Everything," said Dick in a sort of futile rage. Then he relapsed into a moody silence, as if he were totally unable to contend with his thoughts.

Calhoun smoked on in the unhurried deliberation of alcohol. The continual saturation of his system endowed him with a sense of remoteness from the troubles of the world and gave him a sense of Godhead. . . . One who looked on magnificently untouched . . . untroubled, secure.

"We can't pay him back, even if any one were idiot enough to want to buy Hana." Dick stopped, and his deadened faculties struggled with the memory of what Haldane had said to him, endeavoring to evolve something concrete relating to their interview.

Calhoun sat up. Helen's words at Kaenae came back to him.

"Hell, Dick!" he said. "Why, damn it all, Hula's only a child."

"I don't know, to be honest, Dad, if she is or not. I don't know anything!" Dick jumped up and ran his fingers through his hair in an exasperated fashion. "What's the matter, Dad? The whole world seems to have gone wrong! Di——"

"I was afraid, Dick, when you married her that it wouldn't pan out."

"Why didn't you say something?"

"Every one has the right to freedom of choice when it comes to marrying, my boy. Who was I to advise you, Dick?"

"Thanks, Dad. Excuse me. I know. I realize. You are the best sport that ever lived. You expect freedom, but you are prepared to accord it to the other fellow too. Most people aren't big enough. That's what makes me so sick about Hula. We've got to do something, Dad, Harry's all worked up. Thinks Haldane is trying to take the girl from him."

"I fancied last night that he was a bit excited when he got to betting so high. Von Erdmann tried to stop him. Had he been drinking?"

"Harry never drinks when he is angry, or if he does it never affects him. What's to be done, Dad? I can't think. It's—it's like selling Hula to pay our debts!" he said violently. "I can't even think of it without wanting to get my hands on some one. Harry's been so decent to us, always coming through, and we"—disgustedly he jerked it out—"so busy having a good time that we have never made any sort of effort to pay him back. I don't blame him for wanting her. Any man who didn't would be an ass. But it's too soon," he raged. "I know so little about her that—"

He broke off.

"That what, Dick?"

"That I don't know if she's a woman or a child!"

He got up and paced the room. All his past life crowded about him, assailing him, bereaving him of thought. He made an impatient movement as though to shake it off.

Calhoun watched his son a trifle anxiously. He had never seen Dick in such a state of nerves. An unpleasant thought came to him.

"Dick," he said, then stopped.

The man looked around with a jerk.

"You've been drinking a bit too heavily these last weeks. You'd best ease up." He broke off, reluctant to voice what he feared.

"Don't worry, Dad."

Calhoun looked dubious. So far his son's magnificent constitution had never succumbed, but his aspect that morning was anything but reassuring.

"Look here, Dick, don't know why—the perversity of human nature I expect—but I couldn't very well stand seeing you with the D. T's. You're on the verge of it, I know, get yourself in hand, old man—can't afford to have you go under with that race and all coming off. We've got to make a big clean-up. Funnily enough Helen spoke to me on this very matter, briefly, at Kaenae."

"What? About Harry and Hula?"

"Yes."

"What have you to suggest, Dad?"

"Let's pile all we can on the old horse and pay it over to Harry. It won't be anything near what we owe him, but it'll show him we mean to pay, and it'll free Hula in a way."

"And if Silver Wings should lose, we'll be deeper in the hole than ever!"

Calhoun looked at his handsome son who sat so dejectedly on his bed. He was conscious of age's compassion for youth. Life in its flood tide was beating against Dick.

"I'll trust the old horse to bring our money home."

"I'll tell Edwin to lock Opiupiu up from now until the race is done. Then he can get drunk for a year if he wants to, or forever. If anything happens to him, we're done for."

He thrust his head out of the door and shouted.

"Fugi!"

The Japanese boy who valeted him appeared.

"Send Edwin to me."

"All right, Mr. Dick."

In a few minutes spurs sounded on the stairs.

"Come in!" shouted Dick in an unnecessarily loud voice.

The foreman entered, his face a mask. What awful blow had life to deal him? His eyes went to his master, disheveled, heavy of eye, bearing upon his person the ravages of the dissolute years. Then he looked at the son. The paleness of Dick's face distracted him, and his fingers grew rigid upon the brim of his sweat-stained hat.

Dick looked at the sturdy figure in its blue dungarees. A

fierce sort of vigor emanated from the old *paniola.* Edwin reminded Dick of a bull, always ready to give fight to whatever crossed his trail. He looked about the room, as if he were debating which corner he would charge first. Dick knew, well enough, that Edwin had little time or patience with either his father or himself. He was all for Hula. He saw contempt for their condition, in the burning eyes, and having some memories of Edwin before Hula was born, he suddenly and, to outward appearances irrelevantly, laughed.

Edwin looked at him, and his lips tightened lest anxiety make him lose hold upon himself sufficiently to voice his anger and disgust. Dick was on the verge. . . .

"Where's Hula?"

The old man felt as though Dick had struck him a terrible, physical blow over his heart. He had not been mistaken then. They wanted his child. But, even as he prepared the necessary outward compliance with a master's will, his whole being bristled and bared its fangs. . . . Never never . . . only over his dead body would he surrender Hula's body and soul to their rotten life.

"She stop—my house." The words came jerkily. "She *moimoi* (sleep) there last night."

He waited for Dick to speak again, but he sat in silence. Dick took out a cigarette, lighted it, deliberately shaking the flame off the end of the match. And anger raged in Edwin for each moment of hell that Dick's waiting brought to him. Was what he had to say so terrible that he hesitated to give it voice? Cowards, blunderers, they had never faced life; now it had cornered them, brought them to bay.

His left thumb clenched his belt; he moved his foot, the spur rang, faintly, sweetly. He examined his hat.

"Where's Opiupiu?" Dick's question made him recoil. From Hula to a jockey!

"He's locked up," Edwin retorted curtly.

What next!

"Well, keep a close watch on him," ordered Dick, "we have an awful lot on the horse. He has to win."

"I know. I look out."

"Are you taking them to the track to-day?"

"No, I think more better stop here. I can take care. To-morrow, early I take them down."

"All right, Edwin, that will do."

The old man turned to the door. He felt suddenly limp, though his erectly carried figure did not reveal it.

"Edwin."

He wheeled back to the pajama-clad figure on the bed.

"Yes?"

"Take care of Hula."

"I take care."

Contemptuously he said it. He was no Calhoun to close his eyes to responsibility. He appreciated well enough how completely these two men, his superiors, depended upon him to keep things running with a semblance of decency during times such as these, when they risked upon the tracks all that they did not possess. He had attended to the details of every important race for years, while Dick and Calhoun magnificently betted, walking around in a lordly way, thinking they were doing it all, their minds hazed, their brains rotted with alcohol.

Why was not Hula his!

He strode down stairs, anger raging in his heart. That two such should have her custody! He spied Haldane pacing a lonely terrace, hands clasped behind him, eyes upon the blue mass of Haleakala just lighting with the sun.

Ass! Fool! what held him back? Didn't he realize that Hula's heart was his! He was her destined savior. He must do his part. Were they all alike, these people of his father's race? Slow to feel, slow to act? Then a closer look at

Haldane's face brought a smile to Edwin's lips. He was fighting, fighting with all his soul, but it had been a lost battle from the start. No man could know Hula's smile, a smile that seemed to light up the remotest corners of one's heart, or look into her promising eyes, and be proof against her. Fight as he might, eventually he would go down. Edwin appreciated, in a small degree, why Haldane resisted, and amusement lighted, for a moment, the grimness of his face.

Then he pursued his way to the stables.

"Well, Dick, that's settled. Edwin can be depended upon. Fine old chap. Hula owes him more than she does us. Lucky he's been about, to care for her. Well, if Silver Wings wins, and he should, though it'll be a hard-fought race, we ought to make something in the neighborhood of fifty thousand dollars."

"About that, Dad, with the purse."

"And we'll turn it all over to Harry."

"Suppose he should press the other alternative?"

"Hell, no man would want a girl against her will. What would he get out of it?"

"Harry's not like you. He's mad to have her, on any terms."

Calhoun considered the statement.

"Perhaps we are jumping our fences before we get to them. Perhaps Hula might not find the thought of marriage with Harry distasteful. She's known him all her life. He's likable and handsome enough to satisfy any woman. But somehow I don't much stomach the thought. Our little filly's for a better stable, as I said to Helen. But it's for Hula to decide. Has Harry said anything to her?"

"He's afraid of Edwin."

"Wonder how Hula feels about it."

"I fancy she's taken with Haldane."

"He's the sort of chap I'd like to see her marry. She'd stand a show of being taken care of—of being happy."

"But he's almost old enough to be her father. There isn't the least likelihood that he'll ever fall in love with her. He's fond of her, interested in her, but it ends there, I'm convinced. He's got a level head."

"Stranger things have happened, Dick, my son. Love knows no laws."

"I know that, Dad," Dick moved restlessly; "that is why I detest the thought that our extravagances, our follies, may rob the kid of her right to choose, when the time comes. It isn't fair that she should have to pay for our fun."

Calhoun lay back heavily upon his pillows.

"If Hula were tied up to Harry she'd head straight for hell. I know that now, Dad. And she's such a ripping kid. Don't know how she's kept that way with our example. Guess she was born straight, but she won't keep that way forever unless she gets out of all this."

"Di been talking to you?"

"No, Helen."

Dick walked over to the window and stood with his back toward his father.

"Dad—do you think you could tear yourself away?"

"From Waikapu?"

"No, from Hana—from the Islands."

"What'd you mean, Dick?"

"I—we've been made an offer for the plantation—I wasn't going to tell you until the races were done—that would enable us to square our debt and go away."

Calhoun looked at his son. His blood-suffused cheeks grew slowly gray.

"It's hard to think of, Dick. I love the place so damnably."

Dick wheeled.

"Then don't consider it, Dad. Damn it, you come first, before Hula or any one. I'll find some other way."

"I can do it, if it's got to be done, Dick."

"No, Dad!" he said emphatically; "don't consider it."

"Stave things off a bit, Dick; don't let them happen too fast. I'm getting old; I don't like to be hurried."

"I'll do my damnedest, Dad," said the man, turning again to the window; but his voice betrayed the quality of his love. His face was bleak, desolate. No one knew how Richard Calhoun worshiped his father. He might be dissolute, a spendthrift, but he was big. They had been comrades since Dick was a little chap, and he loved him with all his soul. The last lap of his race must be untroubled. It couldn't, at the best, be very long.

"Well," he said coming back, "I hear people stirring. Guess it's time I got a bath and shaved." He fingered his chin. "Don't let what I've said bother you. There'll be some way out."

"There always is—out of every mess," agreed Calhoun cheerily.

"Going down to the track to-day?"

"Yes. Bunch of horses arrived from Hilo and Honolulu last night; Tom and I are going to get a line on them. Must see what they've got. This time to-morrow we'll be feeling a bit nippy, eh, Dick?"

"Just a bit. Want your breakfast sent up?"

"Guess I might as well, Dick. And tell Helen to come and jolly me up. Gad! Dick, that's a filly for you. Did you see her last night? Tight as a tick and beautiful enough to make a man drunk just looking at her, standing up there telling the kid not to drink! It tickled me to death. If I'd been in your shoes or twenty years younger, that's the woman I'd have married."

Dick did not reply.

"Don't forget to tell her to come up. Somehow, she seems more my daughter than Hula does."

"I'll tell her, Dad."

About noon Collins gathered his guests and took them to the track at Kahului. The afternoon was spent inspecting horses, examining their condition, speculating upon their individual merits. Hula, with crimson cheeks and dancing eyes, shadowed always by old Edwin, went from stall to stall, talking with the jockeys, teasing them to bring their charges out. Laughingly they obeyed, for they all had known her from babyhood. She was here, there, everywhere, commanding attention without being aware of it, rousing interest and admiration, but so interested in being alive and in all that occurred about her that she was wholly unconscious of herself.

Strangers turned to see her pass; slim, long of leg with a face like a *luau* rose and unawakened eyes. She turned a hundred times to Edwin for confirmation of her statements in regard to horses or for opinions she overheard. Haldane appreciated how the old fellow must worship her.

She was all his life.

The Englishman watched her somewhat sadly. He worshiped her as Edwin did, as unselfishly, as completely. She was not to be found twice in any life. He was aware of vibrations that warned him that the next twenty-four hours would see passages of tremendous living. He had seen enough in the last week to appreciate the deadliness of the intangible menaces that Edwin had fought so long. This was a life with a thousand tentacles that reached for Hula; for every one. He had felt them about himself, in unguarded moments when Calhoun's ringing sentiments had filled him with dissatisfaction for his own strict code. He had felt them in his tingling responses to the lawless landscape, in the thrilling caress of the wind, in the beat of race-horses' hoofs upon the track.

There was a heady intoxication in association with human beings all worked up to a high pitch of excitement. Ruthlessly he and they were swept along by the vibrations generated by the forces at work. The stream of this life swept forward too fast, too far. Events crowded upon one another's heels. Days saw a lifetime's happenings. Would Edwin's love prove sufficient to keep Hula safe?

"Oh, Anthony!" the child's voice penetrated his thoughts, thrilling him with its undiluted rapture. "To-morrow—at this time! I can hardly breathe when I think about it. Wait till you've been through it. And after the races every one goes crazy! I watch . . ." She ended a trifle wistfully, and Haldane hastened to speak.

"I'll watch with you, Hula."

"Will you!" she cried, as if she could not believe that any one could prefer her company to the mad delights of Waikapu.

"Uncle Edwin says"—and the light of excitement in her face dimmed to tenderness— "that such things are nice enough for them, but not for him and me, because we can do more exciting things. But I'd like to try them both; their life and ours. Little prickles go through me sometimes watching all their fun."

"Guess I'm like Edwin, Hula; I prefer the other sort. I once led a life something like theirs, but in less degree—but I couldn't stick it and went to Africa."

"Was that when you had your wife?"

"Yes, kid."

"What are you going to do with her, Anthony?"

"What do you mean, Hula?"

"I'm going to marry you, some day, Anthony," she said smiling up at him.

"I couldn't imagine anything more wonderful than being with you always."

"But you look unhappy when you say it," she teased.

"You'd be a tremendous responsibility, sweetheart."

"Not if I loved you. I'd do anything you wanted, as I do for Uncle Edwin. He asks me to do lots of things I hate, but I do them. Anthony—"

"Yes, kiddie?"

"If Silver Wings loses you'll be bust?"

"Flat as a pancake, Hula."

"And you bet it all—for me?" she said wonderingly.

"Right, sweetheart. I couldn't let you down."

"You are as good a sport as Dad and Dick."

"Thanks, Hula." Or as great a fool, he thought to himself. What would his wife say when, if, she learned that he had staked everything upon a horse-race. The virus of this life had entered his veins indeed.

He stood, holding the girl's hand in both of his, as if to guard her from its spell.

In the very paddock where they stood another phase of it enveloped him. Silk shirts and satiny hides of high-bred horses. Some were being groomed, some exercised, some sprinted out. Others were locked in darkened stalls. Excitement tensed the air. Men stood on guard at the screened doors; others perched, bird-like, on the rails, eyes and minds intent upon all that happened. Men bet heavily, their faces strained; others laughed and slapped each other on the back. Jockeys, small and wasted as undernourished boys, but with wise old faces. Color and movement everywhere. And everywhere men turned to Hula, admiration in their faces, all knowing her, spoiling her.

How had she withstood it?

He thrust his hands into his pockets and turned his eyes toward the keen-ribbed ranges of West Maui, then he looked at the mass of Haleakala in the east; remote, tawny, piled with cloud. At its base fields of green cane, blue cactus land, barren red reaches.

Sight of the uncultivated plains made Haldane remember that he was pledged to stay. He had given Hamilton his word. There could be no backing out. To use a schoolboy phrase, he was "in for it." The thread of his life had been caught up by the fast-spinning loom of the Calhouns' destiny; it was being woven into it for good or ill.

CHAPTER IV

The morning of the eleventh dawned fine. Haldane rose early and was conscious, even while he dressed, of the bustle about the stables. Cowboys from Hana, cowboys from Waikapu were up and about the business of the day; saddling, grooming, seeing that everything was in readiness for the races.

The man had an impulse to see the gray stallion on whose speed, gameness and wind he had risked his all. He wanted, somehow, to establish contact with Silver Wings before he was led away to the track at Kahului.

He finished dressing hastily and went out. Passing down the long corridors, he was conscious of exhausted humanity asleep. Some had not even got so far as their room but were stretched out like hounds upon couches, or collapsed in deep chairs, while the light of day flooded the disarray of the wide *lanais*. He passed a girl, some visitor from Honolulu, small and delicate. She was curled up, asleep, like a kitten, in a deep cushioned chair.

Haldane hurried past—Hula's destiny in all likelihood unless some one took her from here! A queer sharp pang went through him at the thought that she should ever be other than she was. Wholesome, a lover of the out-of-doors, not like that poor drunken little girl.

Again the strange sharp pang went through him. From the moment he had collided with Hula in the hall at Hana the quality of his whole life had changed. He halted in the garden and deliberately went over each incident of the past ten days. Was it only ten days? He could not realize it. It seemed as though all his life previous to this was a dim, unreal dream. His features were oddly grave as he stared at the trees and the garden. First interest had been aroused, then liking, then compassion. Without loving Hula, without having been admitted to the citadel of her rare little heart—as she had never admitted any one save Edwin—he could not have been indifferent to her fate.

If only he might devise some scheme whereby he could give protection and yet leave her free to make a more suitable choice when the proper time came. But she was so shockingly young. Helen's solution of the problem affronted him, filled him with distaste. There must be another way. Even if he were free . . . but he was securely and terribly tied. He wondered if the circumstances of his life had been different if he would have fallen in love with her.

A surge of trampling feet roused him and hastened him stable-wards. The first turn of the driveway gave him a view of the mounted riders assembled in the quadrangle. Dehan, on foot, stood somewhat apart, watching Edwin. With a *lei* of fresh carnations on his hat, he moved uneasily, like a young jaguar; but his insolent youth rose triumphant from the seas of alcohol that had inundated the other members of the Collins household.

Hula was already mounted, also Mahiai. He held the gray stallion by the leading rein while a cowboy gave old Opiupiu a leg up onto a black mare.

Dehan called out jestingly:

"Got a stiff job before you, *makule* (Old One) to beat Hurricane and that California jockey."

"I know. I know. I too *makule* (old), but I try again. That damn Edwin, he no like I get leele drink. *Okolehao* make me like young feller. But he no know. He no ride race-horse."

The cowboys laughed. "Never mind, Opiupiu, after *pau* then we give you *okolehao*. Plenty."

"But I win, sure, if Edwin give me some drinks before I go out to ride."

The old man was plainly a trifle unnerved by the prospect of the race.

"Edwin is a missionary," taunted Dehan, and he glanced at the foreman, but Edwin did not so much as bestow a look at him in return.

Hula called a gay good-by and the cavalcade moved off. Haldane watched the horses go, Silver Wings in the lead, his ears pricked up, his great quarters flashing light as he strode eagerly down the road. He knew what he was heading for, but he could not know how much had been staked upon him that day.

When Haldane got back to the house, he found Helen waiting for him.

"Where have you been? seeing the boys go off?"

"Yes."

"It's going to be a bad day, Anthony," said the girl without preliminary. "Be with Hula as much as possible. Dick's quite out of hand. I can do practically nothing with him. Uncle Bill, so far, is all right, but I never can tell when he'll go under." She paused and her great, dark eyes roved restlessly about. "I have a feeling that something's afoot between Harry and Mrs. Bane. I can't imagine what, but my instinct warns me. Harry would be delighted to ruin you; he has a lot up against Silver Wings, and he hates you." She moved impatiently. "I don't know why I should feel so uneasy. Uncle Edwin has had both horse and man locked up and will be with them until the race comes off."

"If Silver Wings loses, you'll have to stake me home," laughed Haldane.

Helen smiled. "I'd do it."

Then she presesd her lips together thoughtfully, lips a trifle thin but dangerously sweet for kissing.

"The big race comes off at one. Dick will be out then unless he stops drinking. Di's about reached her limit. Her face is terrible—like a dead woman's. Dick'll not stop at anything when he's in this mood, and she couldn't stand a public disgrace. Oh, she is a fool!" the girl burst out in sudden exasperation. "But I'm sorry for her. I feel so worried. Anthony, something is going to happen that will affect us all." Her fingers laced together, then tore themselves apart.

"If I can be of any help, Helen—"

Her hand seized and held his.

"I know I can count on you." She paused and moved her head as though to catch the hinted things that her fine sensibilities warned her were in progress.

"Oh," she cried passionately, "why can't I discover from what direction it's coming!"

"Don't, Helen; you're overwrought. There have been too many nights and days."

"I know. But keep your faculties on the alert. It's only you and me and Edwin against all the rest—against everything."

"You are a marvel to me, Helen," said Haldane; "I can't begin to tell you what I think of you. But you can count on me always as your friend—"

The woman's eyes grew damp.

The man picked up her hand and kissed it in a sort of desperation to express his regard for her.

"Don't feel unhappy, Anthony; I know your affection for me is an honor."

"It is, Helen; you are wonderful."

"Dehan is interpreting this, for he's watching us, quite wrongly," she laughed. "No doubt he'll use it to further his suit, if one can call it such, with Hula. However I can explain it to her. She has absolute faith in me." Then she looked at Haldane. "And what course are you going to take? Are you just going to stand by?"

"What else can I do—I'm married!" Haldane brought it out savagely.

Helen laughed.

"Irreparably so, Anthony?"

"I have always believed so."

"Don't you feel any sense of responsibility toward Hula?"

"Why should I?" cried the man in such a manner that the woman appreciated that he did, although he tried to believe that there was no reason for his doing so.

"Aren't any of us bound to help her, who can? To have Hula's love is to have power to control and guide her. She cannot help herself. Once I was like her, Anthony."

Helen looked at the man in such a way that his heart turned to water. He was conscious of the truth of her words.

"She's so worth somebody's saving! When I look at her, realize her, such feelings crowd into my heart that I feel I could face anything to save her; but only a man can do that—the man she loves."

"But she doesn't love me that way!"

Helen looked at him.

"It's in your hands to make her do so. She's headed that way now. Are you afraid of the responsibility, Anthony? Wouldn't you rush in to save an animal from being hurt or a child from being beaten? Wouldn't you prevent a beautiful statue from being despoiled by vandals?" She paused to give her words weight. "Yet silly fear lest the world misinterpret your motive holds you back! Hula's going to be run over by this life; won't you rescue her?"

"O God, Helen," said the man; "you make me feel a coward."

"Aren't you one? Haven't all the really worth-while people and acts of the world been misunderstood?"

"But—"

"But there are so many obstacles;—let me take your words. There isn't any obstacle so great that love cannot overcome it, if the love be big enough. Time, distance, age, race . . . but there are so few people who are really big. Edwin is"—her voice rang— "the only man I have ever seen who would stop at nothing. He would kill, steal, plunge in magnificently indifferent as to whether or not the world appreciated his motive or his act. Well, the day begins." She turned her head. "I hear steps. People are getting up. I wonder what the end of it will bring."

The Waikapu party arrived early at the track. The first race had not, as yet, been run, but crowds were collecting. Gnome-like Japanese from the Kula corn lands busily unswathed their heads from yards of bandage-like wrappings, intended to keep out dust. Swarms of laborers from adjacent plantations, picturesque companies of cowboys from the cattle ranches of Haleakala, carts and conveyances of every description disgorged their loads. Watermelon vendors, Chinese chop-suey sellers, pedlers, cried their wares. Hawaiian women, like vast calico sofas, grabbed at their broad-brimmed hats; diminutive Japanese mothers hoisted their babies to more comfortable positions upon their backs; Portuguese bragged and showed off.

An occcasional automobile arriving with the lords of the land brought consternation into the surging crowds of animals and pedestrians.

In the paddock and about the grandstand men congregated, in rings betting, or in groups chatting idly. Sleek bodied, iron muscled horses were being "breezed" on the track, attracting momentary interest as they passed, but the day's two chief contestants were locked in darkened stalls.

Excitement tensed the air.

Immediately on arrival Dick made his way to the stables. His gait was a bit unsteady, as was Calhoun's, and Haldane, who accompanied them, wondered if they could survive the day.

Arriving at Silver Wings' stall, they found Edwin on guard in front of it. Calhoun walked up to him. With legs planted well apart, the old man endeavored to focus his eyes on his foreman. The world with all it contained was performing vast, deliberate revolutions. Edwin stood disconcertingly on his head, but Calhoun addressed him, nothing daunted.

"All safe, Edwin?"

"Ai."

"Opiupiu inside?"

"Ai."

"Going to give him a nip before you put him up?"

"One small one."

Now Edwin was standing on his feet, properly; Calhoun was conscious of relief; then slowly he described another circle and appeared to poise on the peak of his stained sombrero. Hula looked at her father and brother anxiously. Her eyes were hurt, bewildered.

On the day of Silver Wings' last race! How could they! So much hung upon it; the horse's untarnished record, Anthony's fortune, their own heavy bets. She wondered with childish exasperation how it would be if she and Edwin cared so little as they did! But they would not fail the grand old horse!

She glanced with quick affection at the foreman. A grim sentinel he stood, his back against the stall. Then her quick eyes flashed to Haldane. She took a step toward him, the sun flashing on her ebony, polished boots.

"Stay with Dick, Anthony, please."

"Don't worry, kiddie; he'll be all right. I'll take care of him."

"But come back before the race."

"I will."

"I'm going to stay with Uncle Edwin." Then quickly, "Where's Harry?"

"He came in with us, a moment ago."

"Guess he's looking at Hurricane. I hate him for betting against our horse."

"He didn't have a choice," said Haldane, who possessed an Englishman's sense of fairness. "I chose Silver Wings."

"That's so—still—"

"Be fair, sweetheart."

"I will, because you always are. Remember, stay with Dick."

Dick overheard her. Her features blurred before his eyes, and he took an unsteady hold of her.

"Fine sort of brother you have, Hula," he said, "a drunken—"

"Don't!" said the girl sharply. "You're all right, but I want you to be on deck when he runs."

"I will be. Come, Tony, this heat's too much. Give me a hand, old man."

Haldane took his arm and piloted him through the surging crowd until they got behind the stand where the wind came refreshingly from the east. Like cool fingers it lifted the hair on his scalp.

"I'm all sorts of a damn fool, Haldane," he said clasping his hat to his chest with both hands, as though he feared he might drop it. "I'm about to go under. If I do, don't let Hula know."

"Look here, isn't there somewhere I could take you for a shower and food? You didn't eat anything at breakfast."

"Drive me back to Kahului; it's that town just outside the track. I know a chap there, a Scotchman. Where's Dad?"

"With Helen."

"God! She's a brick!"

Dick lurched toward the nearest of the Collins' carriages, and with a last, anxious look Haldane scrambled in and drove him away.

When they finally got back, Haldane tied up the horses, and Dick went to the stand. He'd get through the day, but it wasn't likely that he'd have much remembrance of it. His mind was temporarily paralyzed.

Hastening toward the stables and saddling paddock, Haldane encountered old Collins coming from them.

"I've been inspecting Bill's horse. Looks fit. You are in up to the neck, aren't you, old man? Hope your horse wins; we haven't up near what you have. But for all that, Hurricane's got to run his damnedest. Sport, you know."

Haldane nodded, giving a moment of admiration to the old racing man.

"Comin' back when you've had a squint at your nag? We'll be lunching soon. How's Dick? Making the grade? That's good. Too bad you had to go, you missed five good races. Often gets that way, poor boy. Too highly bred. Like some horses. His father goes at it harder but has the constitution for it. Gets him, though, when he hits the pace for too long. But those Calhouns are the real stuff. Can't hide good breeding in a horse or a man. Intangible thing, but you never mistake it. Well, I'll see you in a few minutes. We all need a stiffener and some food before the race comes off. Hell, I feel as limp inside as I did when I was a kid and rode my first race. So long."

They started off in opposite directions; then Haldane turned and hastened back.

"Where's Mr. Calhoun?"

"Helen's riding the old fellow on the curb until after the race. Then she'll let him have his head."

"Tell her I'll be back."

Anthony made his way to the stable.

"How's Dick?" demanded Hula.

"Better."

The man looked at the congregation of cowboys before Silver Wings' stall. Edwin maintained his same position against the door.

A fat man sauntered past and called jestingly:

"Where's Opiupiu? Locked up?"

Edwin nodded.

"Wouldn't that get you?" laughed the man, turning to his companion. "But, that being the case, I'll put some money on the Calhoun horse."

"Who is that, Hula?" asked Haldane.

"Oh, some man from Honolulu; he always jokes us about locking our jockey up, but it has to be done," she ended seriously.

"Have you seen Dehan?" asked Haldane.

"Yes, he's been by several times. There he is now, down by Hurricane's stall."

"Coming to lunch with us, Hula?"

The child shook her head.

"I couldn't eat. When you're *pau* (finished) come back."

"Righto, kid."

"Oh, Anthony"—she darted to him—"tell Helen to keep an eye on Dad and Dick; they must see Silver Wings win."

An ecstasy of love thrilled in her voice, and Haldane's eyes lingered on the disturbing loveliness of her face.

"Kiddie," he said compassionately, "he might—"

"Don't say it. He can't. It would kill me to have him beaten. And don't let Dad or Dicky come here before the race. It makes me nervous when they're like—that. I feel like beating everybody. Tell them that Uncle Edwin and I will attend to everything, but you come back."

"Righto. I'll do my best to see that they stay in the stand; I'll tell them you asked them to—"

"Dick'll understand," said Hula.

"I think he will," agreed Haldane, and a fierce distaste and deep compassion swept him that a girl as young as Hula should face so calmly and so early the unpleasant facts of life. Remembering the jokes, the carousing of the last week, Haldane squared his shoulders as though to brace against a foe. Helen's words of the morning came back to him.

He looked at the eagle-faced man, harsh, condemning, outwardly an uneducated *paniola*, but the bright guardian of Hula's soul. With the flaming and terrible sword of his love he fought for her daily, hourly. That he must know that it was a losing fight made his effort the more magnificent. To the very last he would contest with the enemy for possession of this girl-child.

In the grandstand Helen was waiting for him. The pallor of her face made her eyes appear unusually large.

"How are things at the stable?"

"All right."

She looked around.

"Harry's been up to some devilment. I know by the expression of his face."

She spoke in a lowered voice.

Haldane looked at him; his eyes were narrowed to shining slits; his face looked inscrutable as a lizard's.

"Everything's locked up. Edwin is guarding the stall; I don't believe that he's moved since they arrived."

"Then Harry's meditating mischief when he goes onto the track. I'll try to keep him here with us until the horses are off."

She sighed in a harried way. "Uncle Bill."

"Whash iz it, my dear?" the old man opened his eyes.

"Let's eat; it's getting on toward one."

"Yesh, big race iz comin' on. Let ush fortify ourshelves. Then I mush go to stables and shee Shilver Wings out. Noshin' like sheeing your own horsh out. Boyz might forget someshing."

Haldane caught Helen's eyes.

"If it's possible, Helen, don't let him go—or Dick. Hula asked me to try to keep them away. She's taut as a string, poor kid. I hope to God the horse wins; it'll kill her, in a way, to have him lose."

Helen darted a glance at him. He had apparently forgotten how much he had upon the horse himself. She smiled.

Haldane was conscious that every one's nerves grew tenser as the minutes passed. Sounds seemed unnaturally loud; things startled him that ordinarily he would not even have noticed. A great river seemed to be sweeping him and all that multitude—the very island itself—onward relentlessly. Forward, forward in great leaps and bounds, as torrent-flooded waters toss and foam seaward. He tried to wrench his mind back to the business of eating, of talking. It was ridiculous of him to allow himself to become so wrought up. He glanced at Howard Hamilton's passionless face and felt how far removed he was from the beings about him. He could not feel with them; he could not understand. Race-horses were something aside from his life. They had no part in the meager generations behind him.

Von Erdmann's voice startled him.

"Mr. Haldane, Richard wants to talk with you."

Haldane leaped up.

"Where is he?"

"Down behind the stand. He—"

Haldane cast a wild look back at Helen. She was sitting easily in the Collins box, one hand resting affectionately and detainingly on Calhoun; but her eyes were fixed on Dehan. He lolled back in a seat, one foot on the guard rail, his hands clasped behind his head. Save for the bright, hard glitter of his eyes, one would not have suspected him of anything but the most casual interest in the race.

As Von Erdmann piloted Haldane down to where he had left Dick, he glanced rather interestedly at the Englishman.

"You stand to lose much if Silver Wings is beaten, do you not?"

"Practically everything," replied Haldane mechanically, for his mind was on other matters . . . on Dick . . . on Hula . . . on Dehan.

"You are much of a philosopher, Mr. Haldane. You do not mind?"

"I haven't had time to think about money;" the words came jerkily. "Where's Dick?"

"There, sitting on that box, with his head in his hands."

Haldane took a few great strides and laid his hand on the man's bent back. He looked up, but there was no recognition in his eyes.

"What is it? You wanted me."

"Yes." Dick breathed for several seconds before he could answer. "Will you—see the horse out. I can't."

"Righto. Any instructions for Edwin?"

"Can't—think—"

"Take care of him, Von Erdmann."

The German nodded. These Calhouns! But he felt compassion for Dick nevertheless.

"Come on, old man, pull yourself together," urged Haldane; "the horses will be on the track in a few minutes. There's the gong."

"Hurry."

Haldane did not wait for him to finish but plunged off in the direction of the saddling paddock.

As he approached the stall where Silver Wings was kept, an unpleasant premonition of disaster came to him. He made his way hastily toward it. Blooded horses were being led out of their stalls, jockeys being put up. He shoved through the crowd and saw with relief that the gray horse was out and running in eager circles, Mahiai hanging onto the great ringed snaffle, trying to hold him down. The boy's face was a mixture of emotions, as he essayed to keep his feet, soothe the horse, and somehow participate in what was happening within the stall.

Haldane dived into it. Hula was in the center—her face scarlet, her eyes wet. Edwin was arguing fiercely with her. A dubious looking cowboy stood by with the crimson jacket and cap of the Calhouns in his hand.

"What is it, kid?" asked Haldane anxiously.

At the sound of his voice, Edwin broke into a torrent of broken English and Hawaiian. Haldane got enough. . . Opiupiu . . . drunk . . . Hula say she ride instead of him. No use for a girl to do all same. Better try Mahiai.

Hula stamped and rushed at Haldane. With a furious, shaking hand she pointed at Opiupiu inert in the corner of the deep-bedded stall.

"Harry or Mrs. Bane did it! They want to ruin you. Damn her, damn them all! This is Silver Wings' last race. He shan't lose it. Hold this shirt!"

She snatched it from the hands of the hesitating cowboy and thrust it at Haldane, and while she struggled into it, she talked excitedly.

"It isn't fair! It isn't a test. The odds aren't even. Hurricane is ridden by a jockey he's accustomed to; Silver Wings by me!"

"Hula, Hula," said Edwin trying to calm her. "More better you no try."

"I will; I'm going to ride him. Mahiai is too heavy. Pilipo, shorten my stirrups. I can't, I won't, go back on him. Father's drunk. Dick, too! They should be here. My beautiful horse; he shan't be cheated out of running. My cap." Viciously she pulled it on, tucking vagrant wisps of hair resentfully away. "Kahalewai, my whip! Oh, Uncle Edwin, don't look like that!" She kissed and clung to him. "If he wins you'll forgive me."

The old man held her arm for a moment then made an aside to one of the cowboys.

Hula heard him.

"I'll fix that!" she cried, darting out of the stall. Like a young Greek runner she dodged through the crowd, vaulted onto the back of some cowboy's mount, whipped out a few coils of the lasso that was coiled at the pommel and spurred forward, her intention plain on her face. Grooms rushed valuable charges out of her way; on-lookers ran back. Hurricane's jockey had just been put up on his back. With a single swing Hula roped him; jerked him off; galloped down the paddock some fifty yards, and cast the rope contemptuously away. The man moved feebly. She dismounted, inspected her work hastily, and at sound of the gong straightened up with a jerk.

Odds were even. Both horses would be ridden by jockeys that were strange to them. Running back toward Silver Wings, she collided with Dehan.

"Quick, Hula, you better get up; they're going out."

"You better get up, too!" she cried passionately. "Ride Hurricane! Damn you. You're heavier than I am, but he's the bigger horse."

Dehan was no coward. He was high blooded. The idea appealed to him; he knew young Collins was a sport. He turned and spoke to him.

"By all means. This will be a race that will go down in Island annals. God, what a lark! It'll tickle old Dad to death."

Dehan tore off his coat and leaped like a slim young panther upon the back of the black horse. Edwin, appalled at Hula's headlong behavior, nevertheless gave her a leg into the saddle.

With a spring and a rear, the great horse broke for the track, but Hula grasped the reins in her small hands and curved his neck down. The stallion leaped and reached like a shoreward-striking wave, but she steadied him down. Mahiai ran beside him, reluctant and fearful to have him get out of his sight.

Adoring and disapproving, Edwin stood for a moment watching her go. A running mob of grooms and paddock hangers-on followed in her wake. From mouth to mouth the news flew, reaching the grandstand before the horses were on the track.

Edwin grasped hold of Haldane and strode across the empty stall dragging him with him. He dealt a contemptuous kick at the form of the prostrate Opiupiu and, going to a small window at the back of the stall, lifted the metal screen. It had been cut on three sides.

An icy blast of fury swept Edwin's face.

"Harry!" he said with a fierce snort. "Damned son of a bitch! I fix him some day."

"But Opiupiu couldn't get out of that little window!"

"Hell! no, but Harry give *okolehao* from behind."

Dropping it, Edwin started for the track, followed by Haldane.

The horses were assembling under the wire. A wild confusion of prancing legs, of arching necks, shaking heads and white-glinting eyes. Jockeys in silken shirts pulled their animals around in an effort to get them into place. Excited horses plunged and balked, crashing sidewise into their fellows, or crouched on their haunches like dogs, muscles aquiver, sinews tensed to spring off.

Edwin's face was bleak as he watched Hula struggling to keep the place assigned to her. Eleven horses were lining up. Silver Wings was almost unmanageable. Hurricane, of a different temperament, was cool and wary to get off. The horses broke a dozen times and were called back. Jockeys sparred to wear out their opponents. Hula's face was crimson, strained. She looked as if she would like to cut into the crowding, fighting men with her pliant whip. She had ridden in small races and cowboy races, but this frenzied, unsportsmanlike struggle to cheat for an advantage to win a big purse was to her distasteful, disgusting.

Silver Wings, impatient as his rider, got right away three times and had to be led back. His gray turned to slate blue as he sweated and lathered. Stormy-eyed, Hula sat him, her little face grim as Edwin's, but passionate.

Dehan, although he was riding against her, to beat her, to break the man he suspected of loving her, could scarcely keep his eyes off her. Admiration and passion shone in his face. Alert and eager, he watched his chance to get off; yet his whole mind was concentrated upon her.

"Hell! Hell! Hell!" the word was torn from Edwin's lips with each thump of his heart. "Hell! Hell! Hell!" It was not an exclamation but the echo of each shaking beat.

Then of a sudden the flag dropped.

They were off!

Haldane grasped the guard rails with both hands. Realization swept through him, as the horses leaped away, of all Hula meant to him and to the old man at his side. Another pair of rigid hands gripped the whitewashed railing beside his. If Hula were hurt or killed, life would come to a complete and appalling stop—for him and for the white-haired man at his side.

He rallied himself to watch. . . .

Bunched together, with Hurricane well in the lead, the horses swept around the first corner. Hula's start had been bad, and for a while she felt like a small cork on a choppy sea. Then after a few moments she accustomed herself to the stallion's powerful stride. She rose in her stirrups and pulled on the bit and felt the horse's great soul coming to her through the reins. Reassurance, confidence returned to her, and a passion of love surged through her for the magnificent beast she bestrode. New life swept into tired arms and legs. Eagerly, joyously, the horse propelled himself forward with a stride as rhythmic as the plunging of a machine. Generations of animals bred to this one end went into the making of it.

Once around the half-mile track they swept, the front horses bunched and somewhat in the positions they had had when they started. Hurricane still held the lead and was not, as yet, extending himself.

"Ride him, Hula, ride him!" shouted Mahiai as the horse swept gloriously by. The girl's face was tense, strained, as she flashed past. The pace was terrific. She knew she could not and dared not break through the bunched horses for fear of a foul that might disqualify Silver Wings; so as they rounded the turn she swung wide to take the outside. She was light and could afford to risk it. Dirt pelted her face and eyes; horses struggled forward, dropped back; positions began to alter. Hurricane lengthened his stride as Silver

Wings began to draw up. The last horse fell behind. Hula settled down to fight. She felt a great relief to be free of encompassing bodies. Assuring herself that the two lengths demanded by track laws gaped between her and the bunched contestants behind she swung in recklessly and took the rail. She had it at last, with only Hurricane in front of her.

The track blurred and rushed to meet her like a destroying brown flood. Seas of mane stung her face as she leaned over the horse's great withers. Steadily his stride lengthened. The rush of wind in her face and the roaring of it in her ears intoxicated her. She seemed free of the world . . . flying. . . . At a gathering pace Silver Wings drew up on his rival. Hula was dizzied by the tremendous velocity of his gait. His hoofs seemed to fling the track and all that it held behind him, with magnificent disdain.

"Run, darling, run!" she cried, and the stallion leaped forward faster as if he understood each sobbed and shouted word.

Lower leaned the girl, and faster sped the gray horse.

They were one! they were one! they were one!

So the impact of flashing hoofs rung to her, and the playing muscles sung to her, as they leaned far out for the turn. A strange metallic clash roused the girl from the spell of the song. Side by side, with locked stirrups, Hurricane and Silver Wings raced.

Hula's arms seemed to be tearing out of their sockets; her head reeled; but the iron muscles of her hard little body rallied to the call she put upon them. It had not been in vain that she had lived the life of a boy.

They rounded the corner for the thunderous finish, stirrups ringing, whips flashing. Faster, faster, faster. . . . Hula rode like an Indian upon her horse's neck; Dehan's cheek was by his horse's. Neck and neck, flank to flank, the horses ran, the ringing hoofs and straining lungs of gallant forebears echoing to each stroke and gasp of theirs on the dusty Island track.

A roar struck them like a staggering blow. Spectators in grandstand and bleachers rose as one man to their feet. Hula swayed in her saddle, but drove her teeth into her lip.

"Hula! Hula! Hula! Silver Wings! Silver Wings!"

Each roar struck her like a blow; she felt clubbed, stunned.

Again it came.

"Hula! Silver Wings!"

To the girl it sounded like the concussion of an appalling surf pounding the reefs, jarring the island to its very foundations in the ocean depths. She did not know if she had won or lost but Silver Wings did. His nose had been just a palm's length in front of Hurricane's when they flashed under the wire. He propped and the speed of his deep driven heels jarred Hula as he made his first move to stop. She dropped exhaustedly upon his reeking neck, arms hanging limply; then she straightened up, though mind and vision were for the moment gone. Rough, loving hands pulled her from the saddle; the mists rolled; cleared; and she saw Edwin—heard him crying curtly, tenderly:

"Good kid, good girl, Hula!"

Hurricane blundered and breached back, and young Collins and his men seized him, pulling Dehan off and slapping him enthusiastically on the back.

"Ridden like a professional, by God! Greatest race I ever hope to see!"

Hula clung to Edwin's arm.

"Take off the saddle!" commanded the foreman. "Come, Hula, weigh in. Give me. I carry for you. Look out, you hell-fired fool," he cried, as stragglers began to sweep in to a delayed finish. "Here, kid, this way; get off the track. Go to the scales. Take your saddle. There. *Pau!*" He pulled her aside to make way for Dehan who stepped in to take his place on the scales.

"Weights all correct," announced the Clerk of the Scales in a professional manner; then his duties over he plunged out to participate in the seething excitement.

Dehan dived upon Hula. She was clinging to Edwin's and Anthony's arms, talking eagerly; but, drunk with the excitement of the race, the young half-white saw only her face, like a wet crimson rose. He swung her on to his shoulder and waving his cap shouted:

"Hula! Hula! Hula!"

The crowd took up his shout. Slim, pelted like a leopard with dirt, her face streaked with sweat and tears, she clutched Dehan about the neck with one arm and with the other tore off her confining jockey's cap. The wind lifted her black curls, and she shook her head like an exultant little colt.

Again Dehan shouted her name.

"Oh, Harry, Harry," she cried, forgetful of what he had done. They had been, briefly, one, for together they had experienced a great height of living . . . permitted to only a few. He grasped her slim booted leg with a trembling hand, and she looked down at him and suddenly bent and kissed him.

The crowd went mad. It was a gallant picture, victor and vanquished congratulating and consoling each other. Both were beautiful; both possessed the appeal of youth.

Then Hula slipped down.

"My horse!" she cried, recollecting him.

"Here. . . . I got." Edwin dragged him forward.

Hysterically she laughed and kissed the stallion's blue nose. The horse tore it from the hurt of her embrace; then thrust it remorsefully back again.

"Give her a leg up, Edwin. Mush see my little jock. Zhere's an Isonomy for you," and old Calhoun beat Tom

Collins on the back in a delirium of delight. "Can't beat that blood, I tell you, Tommy." Then he turned to Dick: "Marveloush, marveloush, God damn glorious! Take him away, Edwin—bless his old hide. What was the time?"

The old man was perilously close to tears.

"One-forty-one flat!"

Fifty voices said it at once.

"Hurrash! Did it that day in Hana, didn't he, Dick? Here, kidsh, get off; you mush be done in!"

Dick pulled his sister from the saddle and kissed her.

Excitement and victory had sobered him.

"Dead, Hula?"

She shook her head. Tears choked her.

"Got kish for your old dad?" cried Calhoun.

Hula stepped forward. Mists rolled before her. She looked at the restlessly moving flower-decked horse . . . then the rolling clouds hid him. Mist seemed to rise from the ground. Desperately she fought to rise above it. Recognition came . . . here . . . and there. . .

Seas of faces . . . brown blurring track . . . then:

"Daddy, Uncle Edwin, Dick, Anthony, don't let me fall!"

CHAPTER V

After the race half the Island congregated at Waikapu. Collins greeted them as they came. This was an occasion after his own heart. Hula, determined not to be parted from Silver Wings, even briefly, rode home with Edwin and Mahiai, despite all protests. She was still too excited to realize that she was tired.

When she saw the crowded garden her eyes dilated with excitement.

"Oh, Uncle Edwin, how they love him," and her eyes turned pridefully to the gray horse.

The foreman's heart contracted. How oblivious she was of the gallant part she had played. His unspoiled, adorable *keiki-wahine*. How much longer would she remain so?

"At last, sweetheart!" Dick called from the gate. He pulled her from her saddle to his shoulder, and Dehan looked adoringly at her. His face was flushed, his chin up, his eyes glittering with excitement. Haldane envied him his youth and freedom. He had, to Haldane at least, redeeming qualities; but, looking inadvertently at Edwin he saw the bitter condemnation in the old man's face. To this *paniola* Dehan possessed not one attribute which excused him for living.

"Come, Hula. They are waiting for you," he said.

"For me?"

"Yes, for you," cried Dick; "you're a chip of the old block. First distinct recollection I have of Dad, when I was a kid, was seeing him win a race!"

He carried her triumphantly through the garden and took up a position on the top of the steps.

Bewildered by the ovation given her, Hula sat in a pleased daze clinging to Dick's head, speechless while little waves of excitement pricked through her.

Silver Wings' record was untarnished, his honor safe, Anthony's safe, Dick's bet secured.

The world was beautiful, divine.

"Oh, Dickie," she trilled like a skylark that rises singing delirious with joy into the blue overhead, "I can't breathe; I'm so happy."

"Well, I'll make you happier. Silver Wings is yours. How about it, Dad?"

"Nothing surer. We'll make out the papers to-morrow."

Von Erdmann looked at Haldane, his face expressive of his amused contempt.

"Give away their shirts when the mood is on them, but they'll forget to make the transfer out, I'll wager."

Hula's brain reeled. Haldane, watching her quivering face, felt apprehensive of what all the excitement would do to her. After an instant she opened her eyes and crowed with joy like a baby.

"Oh, oh, oh," she cried, then leaned down to grasp the hands of the cowboys who crowded up to put their *leis* upon her. Adoration mingled with homage shone in their brown faces, and Haldane appreciated the rare quality of affection these Hawaiians had for this little white girl. She was in one their comrade and something to look up to. Edwin had seen to that. For all her hearty participation in their lusty life, the fine invisible line of caste had always been there. Hula was simple, friendly, loving, combining a convincing and unconscious femininity with a wholesome boyishness as no woman of their own kind could have done. She had invaded and triumphed in every field of their calling. What she lacked in brawn she made up for in brain. In the great moments of their life, riding unruly horses or roping wild bulls, she was quicker and surer, for she possessed a keener intelligence and more imagination.

There was no cowboy of Hana that did not feel he possessed distinction because Hula rode with him. She regarded them all as loved comrades; they admitted her into their fellowship because of merited prowess.

And all this was somehow evident as they filed past, joy-filled at her latest achievement. Their Hula, theirs! who had chosen their life in preference to that led by her brother and father.

"Hula, Hula, Hula," they cried as they passed, taking *leis* off their necks and hats to place upon her.

Perilously close to tears, exhausted, elated, she had a word for each of them, and when the last of them departed with sweetly ringing spurs she opened her arms as if to embrace the world and all it held.

"Here, here, Dicky, have mercy on that poor child," protested Dearie; "give her some sherry; take her inside. She must be dead after that horrible and wonderful race."

Like the surge of an inflowing tide, the guests invaded the living-room. Young Jerry Collins seized a glass and, filling it, handed it to Hula. His eyes rested admiringly on her, changed overnight from a child to a girl. She turned involuntarily and looked at Haldane as she would have looked at Edwin had he been there.

"May I, Anthony, just one? I am tired."

Anthony was disturbingly conscious that in some dim way he was, deny it as he would, responsible for the bewildering and beautiful young soul just emerging from its cocoon.

"It's just wine, kiddie; one glass won't hurt you."

The girl sipped it daintily, inhaling its fragrance, appreciating its savor. About her, glasses in hands, the guests gathered, toasting her and Dehan and the two horses. By degrees the wine revived and excited her. Her lips parted and her eyes shone. Haldane watched, worriedly. He was conscious that Edwin, without a word, had handed her into his keeping while she was indoors. A Hawaiian cowboy may not cross his master's threshold save when he is bidden, so, perforce, there were many hours of Hula's life that he could not guard.

Haldane felt restive, apprehensive, responsible. He saw her taking "sips" from Dehan's and Jerry's glasses while they plied her with attentions and flattered her. Perched on the edge of a table, she deliriously re-lived the race with the half-white.

Haldane thought, with a sad, inward smile, that instead of widening the breach between them, the day had bridged it over, had somehow forged between them the bond of a common and great passage of living. Again and again Hula turned in her quick eager way to Dehan for corroboration of her statements, and Dehan gave it, while the light of a great triumph dawned in his eyes and endowed his features with a dazzling beauty that had never been theirs before.

Hula's heart, or at least her reckless nature, was coming toward his. While they had ridden, they had been one. He knew it as one knows intangible things.

Haldane suddenly felt lonely, aside from life, as he had felt before coming to Hana. Youth, imperious and beautiful, was claiming its own. Who was he, with the ashes of the best years of life at his feet, to compete for Hula. How could any one man satisfy the many wants of her joyous, demanding nature? If he might help her a little on her way, know brief moments of her lavish affection, would not that be compensation enough? At least he knew that this would be the only measure accorded him.

Deny it as he might, all life seemed to center about her—his own and that of every one who came in contact with her. He looked penetratingly at her, and then reluctantly made his way to her.

"Kiddie," he warned, "be a bit careful."

"Oh, Anthony, I'm having such fun!"

"I know, Hula; but don't drink any more; you're not accustomed to it. It'll hit you hard."

"Missionary," shouted Dick, clapping him so violently on the back that he reeled; "let the kid have her fun. This is a special occasion. Call off your dogs. It's Hula's night to howl."

"Righshar, Dick," agreed Calhoun heartily, and the guests echoed his shout.

Womanlike, seeing Anthony outnumbered, Hula slid off the table and went to him.

"I love him; he's like Uncle Edwin. Some day I'm going

to marry him." She darted a quick glance to see if Mrs. Bane heard.

Dearie squealed with mirth, and Haldane put his arm about the child, striving to meet the spirit of gaiety about him.

"Rather!" he said, and Dick shouted with laughter.

"Enthusiastic as a corpse, Tony! Laugh, damn you, you solemn Britisher. I'll give my consent when the time is ripe for the fledgling to leave the nest."

"Shay rather for the filly to leave the shtable," advised old Calhoun; "zhat's more 'propriate."

Dehan, watching Haldane, smiled scornfully. Cold fish, to think he dared compete for the fire that was Hula. He looked remindingly at Mrs. Bane, and she slightly inclined her head.

"Shky's the limit!" shouted Calhoun, brandishing his arm.

A sudden thought came to Hula.

"Wait, Dad," she commanded.

In a few minutes there sounded on the steps the trampling of hoofs. Bareback, her slim legs clasping the horse's great ribs, she rode Silver Wings into the living room. The horse reared and quivered at the volume of sound that shook the atmosphere. Hula slid off and spoke soothingly to him.

"Hold him, Dicky; he knows you," she commanded. Then she ran eagerly about the room robbing the willing guests of their *leis*, piling them upon the animal until it was entirely covered with flowers.

"He must have a drink with us," somebody suggested, and Jerry and Dehan darted to the sideboard and filled a chased bowl with punch. The horse bent his flower-decked head and immersed his nose in it. After a taste he desisted and shook his muzzle.

"He's a missionary, like Edwin and Long-Legs," screamed Dearie, helpless with mirth. This was an occasion after her own extravagant old heart. She mopped the perspiration from her streaming face: "Laws, the paint's running this time and no mistake. I'll soon be as ugly as the Lord really made me."

Hula stood breathing uneasily. Suddenly she turned to Dick.

"I'm funny. I feel sick."

"Hula! You're tipsy," cried Dick, frowning. He seized her by the arm and looked at her more closely.

"Like you, Dickie! Like you and Dad."

A spasm crossed the man's face. Involuntarily he looked at his wife. Once, not so long ago, on the cliffs . . . she had predicted.

"Come outside and get some air," he exclaimed in exasperation and alarm.

"No," cried the girl, parrying his hands and shaking her head like a lawless colt. "I'm going to stay. I'm going to do as I want." Then her face grew pale. "No, I guess I'll go out. Anthony! Hold me; take me to Uncle Edwin. Everything is going around."

"For God's sake take her, Tony!" said Dick, pale-faced. "Sober her up. This is ghastly. She hasn't had enough to start a baby—"

Without waiting for the rest, Haldane picked her up and went out. Over his shoulder she waved a small hand.

"I'll come back; I'll come back—when I feel better." Then her arm dropped limply.

"That's the stuff; get some air and come back to us!" shouted the guests.

"You're taking me to Uncle Edwin, aren't you?" asked the girl as they went through the garden.

"Yes, sweetheart."

"Oh, Silver Wings—he's in there."

"Dick'll take care of him."

Hula raised herself with an effort. With a quick gasp, half laugh and half sob, she slid her arms about the man's neck and clung as only such a girl could cling in the innocent fire of her first love. Lifting her vivid face confidently, commandingly, she said:

"Anthony."

"Yes?"

She twined her arms tighter.

"Hold me tight. Kiss me."

Haldane came to a standstill and looked at her.

"I—can't."

"Don't you love me?"

"More than I can tell you."

"Then do it."

"Oh, kiddie, forgive me; you shouldn't have been kissed like that for years!" cried the man when he lifted his head. Hula disregarded his words. With a great sigh of content she relaxed.

"Now take me to Uncle Edwin. Oh, Anthony, I'm so happy."

"What an unbelievable darling you are. Was there ever any one like you!"

Then he stiffened. The garden was silent save for the wind in the treetops. Had he imagined a following footstep?

In the cowboys' quarters, in a house somewhat larger than the rest, set aside for him on such occasions, Edwin waited. Without a word he took Hula into his arms and carried her indoors. He placed her on the hard Hawaiian day-bed and looked at her.

"Are you all right, kiddie?" asked Haldane anxiously.

She opened her eyes and smiled.

"You do love me, don't you?"

"More than I've loved any one in my life, Hula."

"Then you can go. I want to sleep, Uncle Edwin."

"Ai."

"Wake me by and by; I have to go back. Anthony, wait for me in the blue sitting-room about eleven o'clock. I want to see you before we go back to the party."

"I'll be there."

Edwin, with arms locked across his chest, looked at the Englishman, and in his eyes was command; then his grim lips opened:

"You take care of her to-night when she go back."

He knew he could not keep her; they would want her to grace their revels . . . and Hula would want to go. . . . A bitter sea drenched through his heart and subsided, leaving it crystaled with salt.

"I'll do my best, Edwin," said Haldane, his face full of despair.

When Hula woke, Edwin was sitting beside her. She scrambled to her knees and threw her arms about the old man.

"He loves me! He kissed me! He's mine!" and she shut her eyes in bliss.

The foreman put his arm about her.

"Yes, he loves you, Hula, but he thinks he is too old."

The girl laughed. "I love him to be old, millions of years old, it makes him like you, Uncle Edwin."

"Some day he will marry you, take you away—"

"I know, I know. I love him; I've loved him from the minute I saw him. He's my Anthony."

"I, too, marked him as your man from the time he came."

"Yes, I remember that day on the hill while we were sitting in the grass waiting for him to come, you said so. But I'll have to leave you!"

"It is life, Hula, my *pumi-hana*. It is good," said the old foreman, facing without flinching the vision of the emptied years. "He is a good man, the right man for a girl like you. I hoped he would come before it would be too late. Just so far could Uncle Edwin take you; after that the rest has always been in the hands of the man that you love."

"But I'll always love you, too, Uncle Edwin."

"Ah, Hula, I know."

"But you'll ride alone. Oh, Uncle Edwin!"

It was a cry of despair.

"It is life. I am satisfied so long as I know you are in the right hands. I cannot go with you, I belong to Hawaii. But in a measure you will be with me as you have always been." Edwin spoke in Hawaiian as he always did when he and Hula were alone. "You are in every fold of the hills, in the water. You are it and it is you. I shall not be lonely, golden child of my heart."

Hula clung to him, and he placed his lasso-hardened hand on her head.

"Listen. You shall have him. I know it. But it cannot be to-morrow. It will take time. Be with him much, but be as he is. He is not like the other. Follow his example. He is no mad swiller of wine. He can enjoy without casting restraint to the wind. He has led a different life from that of these people you know. I've kept you from it as far as it was possible. You are too fine to become as the rest." He tipped his head expressively toward the big house. "That *haole* loves you with a great love. It will best him in the end, though he thinks now he'll never marry you. Life with him can hold much, Hula, if only you'll tread it the right way."

The little girl embraced him fiercely.

"Darling Uncle Edwin, I'll remember. I'll be good."

She kissed him enthusiastically and hurried away to change her clothes.

Edwin put on his hat and walked slowly into the night. No house could contain his great joy, his satisfaction.

Anthony waited in the blue parlor. It was nearing eleven. Hula must have had a good sleep, and doubtless Edwin had given her a good talking to. He felt restive and had little heart for the celebration in progress. Hula . . . her future . . . filled his thoughts. With shocking aptitude she had leaped into the ring . . . that afternoon had been a revelation . . . ghastly . . . terrible. He could not contemplate it unmoved.

In a measure Helen's prediction had come true.

Hula, somehow, was bound into the very fabric of his existence. He could not abandon her, he could not go although staying meant facing and weaving complications that seemed impossible to untangle. Hula, although a lawless Calhoun, was worth saving, too much worth saving for any man to desert her. She had climbed into his heart before he had realized it—as she climbed into every one's. If she needed him, if his presence was necessary to safeguard her from her own follies, he would stay!

Helen's ringing words of that morning stayed with him with maddening persistency, making him appreciate how pulling were the reasons that made him withhold acknowledgment—even to himself—of his feeling for Hula.

"Have not the great people and fine deeds of this world always been misjudged!"

That had been the gist of them.

He could not forget them. They were truth. Perhaps only one person on earth besides Helen could ever appreciate the quality of his affection for this child. Edwin. *Paniola.* Half-white. Magnificent, fearless, clear-seeing and clean-thinking Edwin. One of the great spirits of the world.

He took a sharp turn about the room, glanced at the clock—ten to eleven—thrust his hands into his pockets and sat down. Ahead were breakers, blackness. He could see no way out, but he must find one.

He had seen sufficient that afternoon to realize how fast Hula would slide the way of her fathers unless some strong influence restrained her.

His thoughts became almost bodily agony as he tried to devise some means by which he could give Hula the protection of his love and yet leave her free. He must talk to her. Soon. But not in this place, Waikapu, nor yet in Hana. The vibrations of all the heights and depths of living that had passed in them disturbed the atmosphere. He felt as harassed as a horse that is cruelly curbed and spur-goaded at the same time. The restraint of his English upbringing held him in check; the unleashed existence about urged him to act.

He must talk to Hula, but he did not know what to say. He was not free to tell her he loved her. Yet life had been flat, stale, unprofitable before he came to Hana.

He burst into a loud laugh. Now—he was wrestling with it as he had never wrestled before. He lighted a cigarette and inhaled the smoke deeply in an effort to dispel the nightmare he walked in. But it would not leave him. Recollection of the kiss he had given Hula brought sweat out all over him. She had commanded; she had overcome his soul. The building of thirty-five years had vanished before her enchanting personality. What had been breathed into the dust of her lovely body. Potent magic . . . beyond the devising of any man.

Had Hula been a boy, the matter would have been simple. He would have plunged in, regardless, to save him or to force him to save himself. But she was a girl, desirable, enchanting, the world would never accredit his motive for what it really was. It would misinterpret it foully.

He knew his feeling for Hula to be the finest thing that had ever come to him. He loved and worshiped her exquisite child's exterior, but more he loved her radiant soul, as Edwin loved it, and differently.

How could he leave it to be spoiled?

He clenched his hands.

Let the world misjudge him if it must. He must keep faith with love.

For a moment he got to his feet, his face intense, his arms rigid; then he sat down limply.

A footfall sounded and he looked up, expecting Hula. Mrs. Bane dropped down silkily into the seat beside him. What damned thing brought her?

He glanced sharply at the clock.

"My debt—of honor," said the woman deliberately, unclasping her purse; "it's the first opportunity I've had."

"Did I make a bet with you on the race? I have no recollection of it!"

"It's gallant of you to try not to remember it, Mr. Haldane; but I cannot allow it. Pay your bets if not your debts, as dear old Daddy Calhoun would say."

"But I haven't the foggiest recollection of having laid a bet with you, Mrs. Bane."

"That's possible; you were, well, a little bit—" she paused delicately and began to take out some bills.

"For Heaven's sake please don't pay me. I was quite a bit drunk." He brought it out brutally as if angered by the life that put some of its meshes upon him. He attempted to rise, but a deftly placed hand detained him.

"But I don't want or need your money, Mrs. Bane. Or Dehan's for that matter. I bet as I did to please Hula and because I was—"

"Don't say it again; I hate to think of it, with you. I shall pay my debt, nevertheless." Slowly she began to count out her bills, playing for time. "Her . . . interest must be . . . rather difficult to deal with. Truly, I feel sorry for you. The situation must be . . . embarrassing. Hula is so evidently a baby. Her methods are pitifully crude."

Haldane's face grew scarlet.

"That's right, isn't it, a hundred dollars?" she went on, gathering the bills into one hand as she glanced at the clock.

"Please!"

"Oh, I must," she said charmingly. She listened intently; then her hand went to her side.

"Oh!"

"What is it?" cried the man in alarm.

She stiffened, arching slightly backward against the seat.

"Oh, the pain; it's dreadful—in my side!"

Haldane glanced up desperately at the clock. He could not do otherwise than support her, and he dared not think of what Hula might be moved to do if she were to come.

Mrs. Bane breathed stormily; then her body contracted forward and her arms clutched Haldane about the neck. Past the brushed, golden head of the widow Haldane saw Hula step into the doorway. A terrible expression grew in her eyes.

"Oh," she cried in the sharp voice of physical agony, and her clenched fist went to her side. "Oh—oh—!"

Her eyelids quivered downward, then flashed up again. With pupils dilated almost to the point of insanity, she watched.

"Hula! for God's sake—"

But at the sound of his voice she was gone.

"Who was that? Whom were you talking to?" asked Mrs. Bane faintly from his breast. "Oh, I'm better now. I can breathe. I'm such a baby; there's nothing really dangerous, just a muscular contraction of the heart; but it's excruciating while it lasts. Could you—but I hate to put you to further trouble."

"What is it?" asked Haldane.

He was stunned, appalled. Apprehension and anxiety raged

in him. Hula would not be likely to believe his explanation.

"Could you get me a glass of sherry?"

"Certainly."

She sipped the wine daintily and deliberately. Haldane sat beside her stonily.

"Now you can go after her and explain, Mr. Haldane."

The man looked around as if he had just recollected her.

"Go after her? Who?" he asked, frowning, in an effort to focus his mind.

"Why—after Hula."

"It would be useless."

"I feel terrible. It was most unfortunate—shall I try to explain what happened to her?"

"Please don't!"

"You are upset, Mr. Haldane."

"Yes, I am—awfully."

"How English that sounds, that 'awfully.' It's so delightfully different. But I am sorry. It was unfortunate that she should come just at the moment she did."

The man looked at her. Of a sudden he wondered . . . but what object would she have in trying to make Hula jealous? He moved, resentful of everything.

"You care—a lot for her," said the woman; "she *is* exquisite. I can understand how a man could lose his head over her. Many will undoubtedly. Oh, I see by your face it's serious. Oh, I'm so unhappy to think that I—"

"It doesn't matter, Mrs. Bane."

"Of course, it doesn't. How silly of me. It couldn't when I come to think about it. Real love couldn't exist between two people so—"

Haldane got up and stood taut. What was Hula doing? Where had she gone to? He was barely aware of Mrs. Bane's voice, it was outside, far away, of no consequence; but it delayed the working of his own mind, with its troubling persistency.

"You look so distressed, Mr. Haldane. I cannot forgive myself for muddling things up between you."

"There isn't anything between us."

"I'm glad to hear you say it. You must realize as well as I do that only misery could result were you to— But you are miserable. I see it by your eyes. I can feel it. I always feel things. After all, my prediction did come true, didn't it? That Hula saved you from drowning to do you a great wrong. An unconscious one, it's true; but it is wrong that you should care so much for her, when there isn't the least likelihood that—"

"Pardon me, Mrs. Bane, if I leave you. I'll have to find Hula."

The woman looked after him as he departed.

"Well, Mr. Harry Dehan," she said, addressing the empty room, "I wish you could have seen that. I rather think I've earned what you promised me," and she moved down the passage like a gilded, resentful snake.

Rejoining the revelers, she saw Haldane among them, his face strained, his eyes as grim as Edwin's. One look at Hula had sufficed to make him realize the impossibility of attempting to talk to her. Dehan had already done that. When she first saw him enter, she had drawn a deep breath, frowned and redoubled her efforts at gaiety.

Young Jerry Collins, Fitzmaurice, Von Erdmann, Dehan, a dozen young men from other islands crowded about her, not understanding her wild mood or its cause, but ready enough to foster it.

Haldane saw the determination in her damp, heated little face. He should suffer as she was suffering! She would go to hell—anywhere to rid herself of the intolerable pain that was life. Pitiful, childish resolve.

Another glass went down.

Her behavior grew hysterical. With a wreath of crimson *luau* roses upon her shapely little head, she looked like a strange young demi-god or a mad Bacchante in from the hills. Pagan. Reckless.

Haldane, with his hands in his pockets, watched from the sidelines. He was afraid to make a move to check her. She incited every one to absurdities. Then Dick made his way to her.

"Well?" she challenged.

"Ease up a bit, Hula; you've had all you can handle."

The girl brandished her glass mockingly at him.

"Sober, Dicky?"

"You aren't!"

"Don't try any missionary stuff with me. Play fair. Give me the leeway you've had. It's my night to howl. You said it, and I'm going to." She looked across at Haldane. "You and Dad have howled all your lives. I have as much right to make a noise as you have."

"That's the stuff, Hula," encouraged Dehan.

Dick looked at him. What did he mean? Was he spurring her on to this mad behavior? His lips whitened with fury and his arms cramped, but he restrained himself. After all they owed Harry . . . everything. Their good times . . . their. . . . All Silver Wings' winnings must be paid to him the next day. He had liked Dehan, but in that moment he hated him. He looked like a black panther, graceful, ready to spring, as he sat, one leg on a table, his eyes fixed on Hula.

A red torrent of distaste and loathing tore through him.

He wanted to be free, to be out of his surroundings, on a high mountain top, with the wind in his face.

"Hula, this damn well has to stop—"

"Look out, Dicky," she warned.

Flamingly her spirit threw his off. The man realized the danger and impossibility of attempting to restrain her.

The night progressed.

Once Helen went to her. She divined that something was amiss. Every atom of the child's body, the very essence of her soul, was quivering.

Searching for Dick, she overheard him talking to his wife. She halted.

Diana's voice, concerned, gentle, subtly changed, came to her.

"Dick, can't you do something to help Hula?"

"Hula! Oh, God, Di. I know in a small way what you've been through. I'm powerless. I could rush in and drag her out, but I'm afraid to."

"Can't you reason with her?"

"Reason with a Calhoun!" Dick exclaimed violently. "What devils and fools we all are. What's she up to? Where is she heading? I'm afraid of and for her. She looks crazy."

Diana looked through the opened door where Hula and Dehan, spurred as if for riding, absurdly bestrode two of the guests, reenacting the race. Foolishly. Grotesquely.

"Do something, Dick."

Dick grasped her hand, but she slowly withdrew it. He looked dashed.

"Wait—there's something I must tell you. I haven't known how. I couldn't till now."

"What is it?" demanded Dick, sick with alarm.

"I'm going away."

"Di! Can't you forgive? Give me one more chance."

"I—can't chance anything." She spoke with difficulty.

"What's that, Di?"

"I cannot run the risk that any child of mine—"

"Oh God, sweetheart!" Dick bowed his black head upon her hands. "Forgive me."

"I do—I will—but I must go. There's no safeguarding any one from this life. Look at Edwin's labor of years—undone in a few hours."

Her restless eyes swam with tears.

Dick clenched his fists, threw up his chin, and said:

"I'm through, Di."

"Through?"

"With drinking, with all this!" he spoke violently.

The woman closed her eyes, shivered and her arms went around him.

Helen, in the shadows, trembled like an overridden horse. Poor Dick. Her great soul leaped to his. What had he taken on! He was sincere enough; brave, foolhardy. He would be tortured, racked. Could he win or would he be beaten?

She commanded herself and went indoors. Almost immediately Dick appeared. A peculiar expression in his eyes made every one turn expectantly.

Hula, glass in hand and riding Dehan pick-a-back, spurred up to him.

"Whoa!" she commanded and looked at Dick with polished eyes.

"Sober, Dicky? Still!"

"Absolutely."

"Drink this—it'll fix you."

"Dry up, Hula; don't be a fool."

"My brother a missionary! There!" she threw her glass of liquor over his head. "Your baptism, Dick."

"You're tight, Hula," said Dick, wiping his face.

"Good way to be, isn't it?"

"Great God—my little sister. . . ." He spoke with a sort of hurt amazement.

"Don't be sorry for me!" She confronted him ripe for violence.

"I'm not, but I can't realize it's you!"

Hula laughed derisively.

Physical nausea threatened Dick, and he made hastily for the garden, colliding violently with Haldane, who was just coming in.

"Sorry, old man. Didn't see you."

"Where're you off to?"

"I'm going in to get Hula."

"Good for you, Tony. I've had my fill, but I daren't touch her. Don't know what she might do."

"I have to chance it."

"Luck to you," and Dick swayed a trifle, his face savage and pale.

Entering the living-room, Haldane crossed to Hula. Her face was passionate, pale. Trembling visibly, on the verge of collapse, she confronted him.

"Don't touch me!" she warned.

A spasm went through Haldane. Memory of her face as he had seen it that afternoon returned to him. Streaked with perspiration and tears but wholesome and sweet. Dusty and radiant.

With a smothered "Damnation!" he picked her up and started out. Dehan plunged after him; but Helen grasped his arm, and her eyes flashed commandingly at young Jerry.

"Don't be a fool, Harry!" he cried pinioning his arm. "Let him take her to Edwin. She's had enough. Only a kid—"

"To Edwin! Like hell!"

He choked with fury, and Von Erdmann took his other arm. He broke into a volley of curses, and Jerry clapped a hand over his mouth.

"Ladies present! Cool off," he warned with simulated good nature.

Dehan struggled, then desisted, and they released him.

Helen slipped out into the scented, sickening dark and sped to Edwin.

Haldane had just arrived.

"Bring!" commanded the foreman, outraged disbelief in his face.

He latched and locked the windows. His baby! His child! Drunk, fighting, crazy. Savagely adoring, he took her from Haldane.

Helen ran in.

"Look out! Harry's coming."

Haldane went out, and Edwin closed the door and set Hula down. She stormed and tried to open the windows. Edwin followed her, frustrating her efforts, his face looking as though it were hewed from stone. Helen, wet-eyed, watched them.

Her instinct had been right when it had warned her of disaster coming to them all.

Her mind was intent on Edwin; loving, outraged, unyielding.

Suddenly he flung up a window, shouted out of it in Hawaiian and closed it again.

"Go; see they don't fight—that *haole* and Dehan. Tell Jerry to hold them."

Helen slipped out and wondered what plan of his own Edwin cherished that did not permit these two to fight.

Hula, sobbing, beat herself upon the floor, furious, frustrated.

"I will go out! I will! I will!"

The old man looked down at the wreckage accomplished in a few hours. She was "running blind" like a crazy colt. He knew the futility of trying to reason with alcohol. Temporarily she was beyond appeal or control. Outwardly calm, inwardly convulsed with fury against the conditions that had proved stronger than his love and the years he had devoted to strengthening her character, he stood, waiting.

"That's all right, Hula," he said. "I guess he too old for you. Better you marry Harry. He young, he do what you like. He your kind, after all."

The girl looked up at him astounded.

"But—but—you said—"

"I old. I make mistake sometime, Hula. You know which one is best. I see you angry because Haldane no like you get drunk. Harry no mind. He let you. No good to fight with the man you marry."

Pressure of feeling and the blind and instinctive wisdom of love made him choose his words oddly but wisely. The better English he had tried to use for Hula's sake was submerged in the old careless, cowboy jargon of his youth. With lowered lids, he veiled the glitter of his eyes while he listened tensely for sounds from without.

"But, Uncle Edwin, you lied to me! You said he—loved me—and I saw him holding Mrs. Bane!"

Edwin looked at her in feigned astonishment, for Haldane had already explained the happening to him, so he could better cope with Hula when he had to.

"I love him—he's my Anthony—but he doesn't love me." Her voice broke.

"No can be helped then, I guess," Edwin spoke casually. "That Mrs. Bane nice looking woman."

"She isn't! Oh, Uncle Edwin," she scrambled to her feet and clung to him. "I did it—got drunk to make Anthony sorry and because I was so unhappy."

Her head thumped down on his heart.

"Never mind," soothed the foreman. "Uncle Edwin still loves you."

"But tell me he does. I'll die if he marries her!" She drew off and shook him. "Oh, he can't. He's married!"

she cried triumphantly; then her lips drooped. "But then he couldn't marry me, either. Oh, Uncle Edwin, take me away, take me away to somewhere there's *only us!*"

She shook her head like a young animal crazed with too much punishment.

"Wait," commanded the cowboy; "I fix you."

He opened a locker and poured out a drink of whisky and gave it to her.

She drank it unquestioningly but her eyes were amazed. Edwin watched. The effect he desired was accomplished almost instantly. A shudder passed through her. He caught her and placed her compassionately on the hard Hawaiian bed.

For her some hours of oblivion . . . respite . . . before reckoning.

He waited for a moment, holding her hand. He knocked his hat to a more violent tilt as if to express his contempt for the circumstances that had triumphed over him. Limp, flattened out, she lay . . . his baby, his broken baby.

The stark and terrible caliber of his love shone in his face. Ruthless, without law or limit. Then he dropped her hand and, flinging open the door, went out.

Below the steps, his back to the veranda, stood Dehan, facing young Jerry and Haldane. Livid, enraged, brought to bay, waiting for an opportunity to spring.

Haldane looked up. He ached to be in upon him, venting his feeling, but respect for Edwin held him back. His was the greater love—the greater right.

Without a word, but with a look of command for every one to keep out of it, Edwin vaulted over the railing, bringing Dehan to the ground with him.

With the silence of deadly intent, the two men clenched and fought in the dark, rolling over each other, bumping against the steps, crashing into the ginger that grew under the railing. The dull impact of furiously given blows, the gasp of quickly taken breath, the grunt of wind suddenly expelled by sharp concussions came to the ears of the watchers.

Cowboys, roused from their slumbers in adjacent cottages, appeared, disheveled, inquiring of eye, silhouetted against their lighted doorways.

Jerry spoke sharply, commandingly to them, and Helen gestured to them to keep out.

A pot of ferns on the veranda, jarred by the banging of their bodies, fell upon them and broke, scattering them with roots and earth. Moments of tense silence held the dark when the two adversaries were locked in deadly grips which ended as suddenly by the heavy thump of bodies flung back upon the earth. Gingers and ferns bent, flattened, snapped off or recoiled with a backward spring as the two rolled back and forth among them. Stertorous breathing, scufflings, stifled grunts and occasional glimpses of striving forms, eloquent with their deadly intent, were revealed, then engulfed by the dark.

There was something appalling about the struggle. It was a spirit contest, felt, but not clearly seen. Terrible, because of the impossibility of following it. A combat unlike any other Haldane had ever seen in all his wanderings. A young man fighting for possession of a girl's body, an old one for possession of her soul.

Helen gasped and caught her lower lip in her teeth. What if Edwin were killed! She dared not contemplate such a thing, but she dared not attempt to stop them. Fierce, great-hearted, he would brook no interference; but she could not listen to it any more.

She must get Hula.

"Wake up!" she cried, shaking her limp shoulder.

The child sat up dazedly, then dropped back upon the vivid patchwork quilt.

Helen listened; they were still at it.

"Hula! Hula! Harry is killing Edwin. Go out! Stop them!"

The girl roused herself and shivered.

"Helen, you here?"

"Yes." The woman swallowed nervously. "Listen! Oh," she cried, maddened by her contest with alcohol, for Hula began to droop again. "Hula! Hula! Can't you realize that Harry and Edwin are fighting, and Harry's killing him—in the dark!"

The girl drew a deep, shuddering breath. Her face became alive; then it grew incredulous, then terrified. Her love, aroused, lent a moment of illumination; then her mind, stupefied with alcohol, began to drift again.

"Uncle Edwin? What are they doing to him? Who is doing it? And why?"

"Harry, Harry! He and Edwin are fighting by the steps. Can't you hear them!"

Hula sat tense, then scrambled unsteadily to her feet. The room swam. She felt unhappy and ill. Roused unnaturally from prostration, she could not assemble her faculties, yet her love for the old cowboy spurred her to action.

She took some lurching steps across the room, grasped the handle of the door, essayed to turn it, failed and burst into tears.

"I remember—he locked it."

"Turn it," commanded Helen.

The girl wrenched it open and stepped unsteadily on the veranda. Men and women with horror-stricken faces crowded every cottage veranda. Jerry and Haldane, white-lipped, stood on the edge of the dark.

An awe-struck Hawaiian voice said, "Hula!" and the child peered into the dark below the railing. The sounds of deadly, silent fighting penetrated her fogged brain. A fierce white light flashed into her dimmed eyes.

"Hit him, Uncle Edwin! Hit him!" she cried. Loyally and unerringly her heart went to him.

Some one laughed. Her words seemed to bring the struggle to earth. It was no longer the vast and hideous striving of spirit beings but a battle between men.

A moment she wavered above the railing; then she vaulted over it, and the dark swallowed her up.

"Hula, stay out of it!" shouted Haldane, rushing forward, but Jerry halted him.

"Let her stop them; she can."

For a few minutes the inarticulate sounds and poundings continued, broken into by Hula's voice.

"Hit him, beat him, Uncle Edwin. Good for you!"

Dimly outlined by a ray of light from a distant window they could see her sitting in the shambles of what had once been a ginger bed. A few forlorn stalks stood in dejected angles about her. Like a baby, propped up on stiffened arms, leaning slightly forward, she watched with parted lips and with eyes dilated and alarmed. The ferocity of the struggle fitted her mood, appeased her. Then she made a short, inarticulate protest, and her hand went out detainingly.

"Harry! Damn you! Let him go. Don't do that!"

"Hula!" the half-white's voice came, incredulous that she should be there.

"Hula," gaspingly, commandingly Edwin's sounded, "*Hele* (get out)!"

"Stop, Harry!"

"On one condition only." There were sounds of labored breathing.

"What?"

"That you'll have nothing more to do with that God-damned Englishman."

"She going to marry him," Edwin's voice asserted, and the sounds of fighting recommenced, with doubled violence.

"Pau!" Hula's voice, desperate, outraged, tore the air.

"Let him go! Harry!"

With a scramble she was into it, clinging to his pounding arm, hampering him.

"Stop. Uncle Edwin! Stop, Harry!" in a fury of protest. "Do as I tell you. That's not fair, Harry!"

Once more the fighting was arrested.

"Hadn't we better step in?" asked Haldane, in a suppressed voice.

Jerry shook his head.

"It's an old hate."

Haldane's whole body was ringing. Perspiration trickled down the back of his legs and dripped off his wrists. Some day . . . he would have his inning. For Edwin's sake, this time he had kept out of it. He felt as beaten as if he had been engaged in the actual combat, so varied, so intense had been the emotion of that day.

He felt mighty concussions of fury, of love, of desperation breaking through him. What was this excess of emotion leading up to? What appalling culmination was in store?

They were at it again. He stiffened.

His fists clenched; his fingers ate his palms. There was a sudden thud followed by a peculiar tearing sound. What were they doing?

Then Hula's voice, horrified, stifled with terror and fury.

"Damn you! Don't *spur* him, Harry, you beast!"

Haldane could stand it no longer. Dehan had knocked Edwin out and was "rib-roasting" him brutally. That was the explanation of the ripping. He plunged into the dark, clenched with Dehan and threw him backwards.

Stunned, but still fighting, the half-white struggled to

get up. Haldane pinioned him and held him in a sitting position. After a moment Edwin sat up also.

"*Pau,*" cried Hula flinging her arms about him, "don't fight any more. Oh, you're bleeding; your shirt is all torn."

"Ai," assented the *paniola* in a calm voice of great fury.

And Haldane, holding Dehan, knew that no one would ever discover by what foul trick Dehan had obtained his advantage; but he knew also that the old man would never forget. He had the disadvantage of years, but his hearty mode of life balanced that. Odds were even enough as long as the fighting was fair.

"Come," Jerry broke in, "*lawa* (enough) *lawa,* old man. Call it off. *Pau!*" and he shook him and taking his arm assisted him to his feet. Haldane pulled Dehan up violently and stepped back.

"Well, how about it, Edwin?" asked Dehan with studied insolence, his lips drawing back like a cat's. "Are you licked?"

With a curse Edwin lunged at him. Haldane pulled Hula aside.

Blows, curses, grunts, gasps, and they were down and at it again.

"Stop them, Anthony! Stop them!" cried Hula, beating his arm with clenched fists. Her voice mounted in a crescendo of terror.

"Hush, kiddie," said the man, holding her tightly against him. "You don't want the whole house down here. They've got to have it out. We'll see that the fighting is fair. They're in the light now."

"But I don't want to look!"

"Don't, Hula. There," he held her head against him.

"You're shaking—so—Anthony. Do you think that—Uncle Edwin—"

"No, Hula!"

"Then I can stand it."

She bit her lip, tearing at it with her little white teeth. Then she wheeled suddenly and watched with horror-wide eyes, quivering, following each blow. In a very passion of destruction Edwin and Dehan pommeled one another.

The color and roundness left Hula's face; her nostrils paled.

"Oh, Anthony! won't it ever be *pau?*" she cried, turning to grasp him and beating her small, spurred heels up and down.

"Steady, Hula, ride yourself on the curb."

"Is he winning?" came in muffled tones from his shirt-front.

"I think so. They're getting tired."

He listened, lean-cheeked, grim-jawed.

The grunting and pounding began to grow less. There came longer intervals, more breathing spaces, a silence, then Edwin got up. Slowly, unsteadily.

He looked at the various spectators, then back to Dehan, prone at his feet, one arm flung above his head. Motionless. Inert.

"He *pau,*" he observed laconically; then he looked about as if in search of something. His eyes lighted on his hat that had flown off when he leaped the railing. Stooping, he picked it up, dusted it off and replaced it upon his head at the old defiant angle.

His chest still strained and heaved. His blue shirt hung in ribbons. Where it gaped at the sides there showed a succession of blue-edged red weals where Dehan's spurs had torn.

"Come, Hula," he ordered, and, taking her hand, he led her slowly into the house.

CHAPTER VI

"Well, that was a pretty row last night," said Von Erdmann laughing, when he saw Haldane next morning. "Harry, he is a ruin."

Haldane did not smile.

"It may prove serious before it's done."

"Bah! You don't know the Islands or Islanders. I've lived here for years. Nothing lasts—effect of the climate and surroundings, I suppose. Insects lose their venom, plants their poison, after they've been here a while. Harry will rage for a day or so, then he'll get sullen. After a while it will wear off. The two old boys, Tom and Bill, they'll have a drink on it. In six months it will be forgotten. The lava crusts as soon as it hits cold air."

Haldane wondered just how right this cold-eyed German would prove to be. He pulled out his pipe and stuffed tobacco in it viciously.

"You look upset," observed Von Erdmann; "it offends you?"

"Not exactly."

"I know, it is not 'good taste,' as you would say in England. Well, it is a pretty layout, at the best."

Haldane smoked without replying.

"Wishing you were clear of it?"

"Yes."

"Bah! You take these happenings too seriously. You are English. If they are not to your taste why do you not go?"

"I cannot."

"Business?"

"Of a sort."

Von Erdmann glanced at him. Business? He had imagined this man to be a casual guest. Was his presence in any way connected with Howard Hamilton's being there? What were these two up to? Possibly they were after the Calhoun lands. Why? They were mortgaged, of little real value. It must be some deeper thing. He must keep on the alert. If Hamilton was in it, it must be worth while. He tilted at no windmills. When Harry recovered, he must talk to him. If that Hana land was good for something beside sugar growing, they must get onto it.

He turned his pale eyes on Haldane.

"How much longer do you expect to be here?"

"I don't really know."

A little later Haldane encountered Howard. He was strolling on the terrace, his eyes on the distant, shadowed plains. Austere, immaculate, untouched, he had walked through the tempestuous nights and days.

"Seen Dick this morning, Haldane?"

"No."

"He wants to talk to you."

"What about?" . .

"I don't know. He's been up all night talking to Edwin and trying to talk to his father. His hands are rather full there. There'll be nothing doing around here to-day. Every one will be—recovering. Care to take a ride out there?"—he gestured slightly toward the plains,— "it'll give you some idea of the extent of land that will be available for cane growing some day."

"There's nothing I'd like better to do."

"I'll tell Edwin we want horses. Have you seen Hula this morning?"

Hamilton asked it without curiosity but with interest.

"No."

"She showed them a bit last night what she can and will do. A wonderful child, but she possesses rather ghastly possibilities. Edwin will regain his hold over her; she's accustomed to being dominated by him. Several outbreaks like this will occur before she really gets off."

Haldane's chin squared. Howard looked at him. Just how deeply was this man interested and affected by that hurricane-like child? And by the happenings of the last twenty-four hours. It was hard to tell.

All that day, riding the blue and scarlet reaches of the wind-swept plains, Hamilton studied him. His eyes held a deeply thoughtful look. Was he intent on the project ahead or upon other matters?

Haldane's eyes rested on the wet, dark line of the forest to the eastward, and his mind followed the bulge of the mountain back to the country of thundering streams and dripping gulches.

Mounting a slight rise, Hamilton checked his horse.

"Who owns—all this?" Haldane indicated the plains about them.

"I do. It took me years to get it. I bought it in sections . . . carefully, for I did not want any one to suspect why I wanted it. Now I have it all. Some day this isthmus will be one of the great sugar-producing regions of the world. Now I have possession of it, I can set things in motion. Water can be got to it; every drop of it will mean gold. I've married recently; I couldn't before. One day my sons shall be the first men of this Island. I've become a power in Hawaii by a lifetime's effort—I'm nearly fifty, and my real work's just begun."

For the first time something sparked in him, and Haldane realized that there was fire in him, encased in ice.

"When I've brought Dick to terms I'll feel safe. With every day that goes by, I am afraid that some one else will see the possibilities of that ditch."

Thought of Von Erdmann flashed into Haldane's mind,

but he said nothing. He would talk with Dick, first. There was no need to make Hamilton uneasy. A strange man of deep passions. The indelible brand of his lean youth stripped him of all outward semblance of feeling. His passions were cold, but they went deep. Every step of his life had been thought out, and Haldane knew that some day he would be acclaimed the sugar-planter without peer, the man who had anticipated by two decades the development of the sugar industry of the whole Island of Maui.

Some day those red plains would be clothed in a growth of green fields, wound through by brimming aqueducts, threaded by tree-shaded roads, dominated by a giant mill that would stand as a monument to the Island.

"I shall talk to Dick, to-morrow," said Hamilton.

Riding home, Haldane turned once or twice to look behind him, not so much to look at the land as to feel the wind on his face. The hours in the sun and saddle had brought temporary respite from Waikapu, but they served to contrast and emphasize the atmosphere of the place he had left behind.

He was too tired to think. Life had taken the bit in its teeth and bolted with him, shamefully, he felt, when he looked at the self-contained man at his side.

In the late afternoon he sighted Edwin and Hula, riding alone. The foreman nodded to them and drew rein on a red bank of earth to let them pass. Hula looked at Haldane; her whole attitude was eloquent of shame and remorse. Poor punished baby! Haldane longed to take her in his arms, to restore her, but Edwin interposed his spirit between them.

When they had passed, the girl turned to the cowboy.

"I feel sick inside. Oh, Uncle Edwin, take me away!"

"No can."

Sternly he said it. It was part of his punishment to make her face them. Hula drooped. Her eyes went to Edwin's face. It was battered and faintly discolored, but unrelenting.

All day they had been out; galloping and walking their horses. At noon they had halted to rest, and Hula had cast herself on the ground and slept with her head upon Uncle Edwin's knee, holding his hand fast, disregarding the terrible silence of his displeasure. Some one she must have to love, to cling to. She had estranged and disgusted Anthony—forever, Uncle Edwin said.

In an agony of desolation, for she was very young and the world in its beauty seemed to have gone from her, her bruised spirit clung to the *paniola's* strong one.

Hot and cold alternately, seized with violent spells of nausea which she fought down with a wild sort of fear—for she had never been sick a day in her life—her alcohol-shocked system punished her as cruelly as did her mind. With set teeth, she fought the physical and spiritual revolt in her, seeking for healing in a dumb way from the sun and the wind and her horse.

Briefly, when some familiar odor of cattle or grass came to her, life seemed as it had yesterday; but the recaptured bliss would not stay with her. Elusively as it had come it had gone, leaving her stranded.

She longed to abandon herself to the flood of tears that worked in her, but Edwin would not permit it. Self-control must be knocked into her, cost what it might in agony.

When they got back to the house she followed Edwin pathetically about his duties. She filled mangers, got water, anticipated and executed his every order in an avid desire to create an illusion with herself that things were as they always had been.

When they came to Silver Wings' stall she stood gazing at him.

"And he's mine," she breathed. Her eyes passed over him, and she noticed a bandaged hock.

"What's the matter with his leg?" Then with a gasp of terror, "Did I do it?"

Edwin nodded, and his eyes were accusing.

"How!"

"Last night, when you drunk, you took him inside. Coming down stairs he slip. His tendon got cut."

Edwin did not trouble to say how little.

Hula's eyelids quivered downward, and her throat worked convulsively.

"No cry, Hula!" commanded the old man. "Come, we go *kaukau*."

Desolate as a punished puppy, she followed on the old man's heels.

"I'm not hungry," she protested tearfully.

"Eat! Make you feel better."

With long pauses between each mouthful, the girl endeavored to obey. The food, little as she took of it, was fuel to her exhausted system. A little of the nausea passed. He was right; he was always right. Why had she not heeded him the previous night? But she had gone mad. The sight of Mrs. Bane in Anthony's arms had robbed her of her reason. There must be some explanation, but she could never ask it of him now. She had disgusted him. Her hurt little soul crept deeper into its shell.

She had been drunk, a damned fool, like the rest.

Rising from her seat, she went hastily to him. Edwin divined what was coming and rose. Not yet would he allow her the relief of tears. He knew her. Pain and sorrow were strangers to her, they frightened her. She wanted to be rid of them, free, free to be loved and happy again, with everything wiped out, but this lesson must be driven home.

He placed a hand on her shoulder.

"More better go to bed now."

Her face was beseeching, but a reminding look in the man's eyes checked her.

"All right." It was a cry of despair.

When she slept the old man went out to his seat on the steps. He lighted his pipe and regarded the wrecked ginger bed. About ten, Haldane came down.

"Hula? May I see her?"

His face was concerned.

The foreman took the pipe from his tightly shut lips.

"*Aali* (no)," he said. Then in English: "She is sleeping."

"How is she?"

"All right."

He waited and Edwin smoked.

"I'd like to see her to-morrow; I want to talk to her." Haldane jerked it out.

"More better no."

"Why, Edwin?" Haldane challenged. Anxiety ate him. Memory of Hula's face as he had seen it that afternoon haunted him. He wanted to take her in his arms, to comfort her. It was intolerable to be separated from her when every instinct bade him be with her. Limp, beaten by life, temporarily dispossessed of everything—left to the cruel kindness of this old man.

"But, Great God—"

Edwin removed his pipe slowly.

"I think more better she stay only with me."

Haldane wondered if, after all, this man distrusted him.

"But, Edwin—"

"I sorry. But no."

"Very well."

There was respect in Haldane's voice. After all, this man might be hard, but there was no doubting the quality of his love for Hula. It put to shame anything of its kind that Haldane had ever known. He stood, mentally, uncovered before it, said good evening and retraced his steps to the house.

Edwin watched his departing figure until the aisles of the garden closed it out, then he took out his pipe and refilled it.

"Ah, Helen," Haldane said as he mounted the steps.

"I was waiting for you."

"How is Mr. Calhoun?"

"Not so good. I've just come from his room. Dick's there now."

"I'd give a lot to be away from all this!"

Helen smiled. "So would we all, Anthony. The old let-down. I know it so well, only this time it's intensified."

There was a tired wisdom in her voice.

"The party will begin to break up to-morrow."

"You?"

"I shall return to Honolulu."

"I shall miss you, Helen."

"That is sweet of you." The woman looked at him. "Well, what is it, my dear? You look desperate."

"Edwin would not allow me to see Hula. He said she was asleep. I'm inclined not to believe him."

Helen laughed.

"Profound old man," was her thought, but she did not voice it. Instead she said:

"In all likelihood Hula would prefer not to see you—poor baby."

"Why!"

"I don't doubt that Edwin has informed her of her—well, immoderate behavior of last night. She'll be prone to shun everybody, more especially those she loves. This is her first offense. She'll take it desperately to heart."

"But I've got to see her, Helen; I must tell her that nothing she can ever do would make me do anything but adore her. I can't rest for thinking about her."

"She's best with Edwin."

"Perhaps. He loves her, I know, but he's—hard."

Helen drove her white teeth into her lip to still her mirth.

"A little punishment won't hurt her."

"She's been punished enough. Can't you talk to Edwin, explain that I only want to tell her—"

"What?"

"That I love her so damnably much—"

He broke off.

Helen laughed. "Can't finish it, can you? Well, I shan't attempt to interfere with him. He knows better than any of us what's best for her, for he loves her more than any one of us does."

Haldane suppressed the words that leaped to his lips.

"He's given his life to her; he'd give it for her!" Helen's lovely lips ceased moving. She looked away, then spoke in the polite and impersonal tone of drawing-room conversation. "Well, you've seen some heights and depths of living, Anthony. They've left some impression on you for all that—"

With sweet maliciousness, her eyes reminded him.

"Cruel, Helen," said Haldane, but he smiled.

"I was right?" she challenged.

"Yes."

"I prophesied something else. Is it, has it come true?"

"I'm afraid it has, Helen."

The woman's long and lovely hand fell upon his.

"If that's so, you are the luckiest man in the world. To love and to be loved by Hula. Marvelous!"

"Don't I know what it could be!"

Helen looked at his harassed face with a sort of dainty disdain.

"What it can be, if—"

The man caught her thought.

"Perhaps I am not capable of feeling—greatly."

"You are."

They looked at each other deeply, weighingly.

"When you do—"

"I'm listening, Helen."

"Remember, that love overcomes everything."

Haldane stood, deeply moved.

"But it must be great enough, Anthony!"

Helen stood like a torch lighted from within.

"I can see no way out at present, but I suppose it will work out, somehow, eventually."

"Nothing works out," said Helen, "unless it's faced."

"You accuse me of what?"

"Of not wanting to face this situation."

"I don't," said the man honestly.

"But you're going to—have to. And now go to Dick, he wants to talk to you."

"It's about that land business, Tony," said Dick without preliminary when he went to old Calhoun's room.

"Yes?"

Haldane looked at the ghastly sleeper in the four-poster bed. The air rasped out of his lungs and rattled in his windpipe like that of a broken-winded horse. Dick glanced anxiously at his father.

"They gave him a shot a while ago, to put him to sleep."

He stood, frowning distractedly.

"What decision have you come to, Dick?" asked Haldane, putting his hand upon his friend's shoulder.

"I can't think of it."

An extraordinary sensation went through Haldane. If Dick would not sell, if the ditch was not to be constructed there would be nothing to detain him in Hana. He would have to go. Blankness seemed to hedge him around.

"You see, Tony, it's this way: Dad's old, he can't face

the thought of change. Nothing would suit me so well at the present moment as to pull stakes and go."

Dick desisted from speaking and stared anxiously at his father.

"After the—other night, I realized a bit for the first time where all this is leading to." Haldane saw his shrinking from bringing Hula's name into it. "It's best for us all to get away from Hana. God knows I've loved it; if I go, I shall always look back upon it with great affection. . . ." This time he stopped to swear, in a man's endeavor to ease his feelings. His white face was shadowed with blue, and Haldane realized that he was suffering. After a life-time of heavy drinking, to be entirely without it!

"Damn it, Dick, old man—," he said compassionately.

"Hell, it's all right, Tony, you brute! Let me go on. The other day I talked to Dad about what we owe Harry and told him of Howard's offer. Of course he was a sport about it, but I could see it broke him all up. He said, 'Do what you think best, Dick, but don't force the pace. I'm old.' That ended it as far as I'm concerned. Dad comes before everything else. I wonder, Tony, do you appreciate what a wonderful man he is?"

"I think I do."

"Most people don't. He drinks too much, we all know; he's spent a fortune on racing and all that goes with it, but, when it comes to his dealing with his fellows, he's got them all put off the board." Dick looked at the laboring chest of the old man and pulled the sheet over it. His dark blue eyes dimmed, and he said with a sort of furious affection: "This is the sort of chap he is, Tony. Yesterday he was pretty bad, and I was up with him. They had to give him a drink, and he offered it to me. I told him I was through. You might have thought, after the life we've lived and the state he was in at the moment, that he'd have flung it back at me, but he didn't. He just lay on his pillows and said, 'You are a better man than I am, Dicky. Luck to you.'"

Dick clenched his hand.

"So you see it can't be done. I thought for a bit Dad was going to flick out yesterday. . . . I'm going to turn over all we made to Harry but it's nothing to what we owe him. I'm not looking forward to the job, I've a fancy he'll refuse to take it. But while Dad lives things have to go on as they have gone. Damn it, the old boy shall finish royally, as he began."

"Just a moment, Dick; there were two alternatives on that deal: one to lease and one to sell."

"I remember, but any change would bother him. No, it's *pau*." Dick lighted a cigarette and smoked feverishly. "I'd give my soul for a good stiff drink; I can't collect myself; I can't think."

"It won't be so bad after a while."

"After a long while, Tony. I've drunk pretty heavily for thirty-six years."

"Wish there were something that I—"

"There isn't. I didn't realize what I was taking on. I felt so remorseful about everything and didn't know how else to make clear to Di—"

He jumped up from his chair and paced the room.

"Tell you what, Tony! Stave these fellows off a bit. When Dad is ill everything comes to a stop for me until he is well again. Edwin is going back to Hana to-morrow by way of Haleakala. Deanie's decided to go along with them; she's never seen the crater. Think Von Erdmann plans to go as well. Odd beggar. Loves beauty, although you would never suspect it of him. You better make the trip too. Wish I could go with you all, but I guess I'll have to stay with Dad."

"He's better?"

"A bit."

"Pity you can't come then, Dick. It would help you to get out."

"Hell, don't talk about it. I'd give my eye-teeth to be off on horseback up there for a day or two. Inspiring place. I'd like Di to see it. Well, you talk to Howard; I've got to tackle Harry."

"Righto. Dick—"

"Yes?"

"I shall tell Howard that the deal's off temporarily; but will you give him first option on your land when, if, it goes up for sale?"

"Harry!"

"I appreciate that, but, after all, if you can repay him in cash out of what you are paid for it, surely—"

Haldane's face moved Dick to grasp his hand.

"Damn you, Tony; I can't refuse you anything. Yes, here's my hand on it. Howard shall have first say, over every one else."

"Then it's only a question of two or three years," said Hamilton when Haldane told him the result of his interview; but there was disappointment in his voice. "We'll get it in the end. I've waited so long, I can afford to wait a little more."

"The old man may hang on longer than they anticipate," said Haldane, feeling intense compassion for Hamilton.

"Thinking about your own part, Haldane?" asked Hamilton, fixing him with basilisk eyes. "I realize you can't afford to stay here doing nothing."

"You mistake me entirely; I was thinking of you—of your disappointment."

"Good of you, but I am accustomed to waiting. I shall get it eventually. You got Dick's word on that?"

"I did, and whenever you close this deal I'm your man, wherever I may be. You'll have to send me word."

"Thank you," said Howard stiffly. "I shall catch the boat back to Honolulu to-morrow. You?"

"Dick suggested that I make the trip through the crater."

"Quite right. You should see it. The greatest sight in Hawaii. Call me up when you get back to town."

"I will."

"Oh!—and, Haldane."

"Yes?"

"Might remind Dick again about his promise before leaving."

"I will."

CHAPTER VII

"Well, it's 'good-by.' Shall I see you in Honolulu?"

Helen stood at Haldane's stirrup.

"As if I should go through without looking you up!"

She moved impatiently, lifting her chin, regarding him intently with her beautiful eyes.

"Then you are going! When?"

"I don't know. Things are held up temporarily."

"I know. Dick talked to me, so did Howard. He wanted me to try to persuade Dicky to sell."

"Did you tackle Dick?"

"I wouldn't; I respect his affection for his father too much. It took all the powers of persuasion I have to make him go with you. I'm going to stay with Uncle Bill. Dick isn't in any shape to be overtaxed now. I may go back to Hana with him on the boat."

"Then I shall see you again before I leave?"

"Uncle Bill won't be fit for the trip for some time, I'm afraid."

"Then I shall miss you entirely, Helen. There's no reason for me to impose on Dick's hospitality any longer. The deal's fallen through."

"Anthony, may I ask you a question?"

"Assuredly."

"Will you—be alone?"

"Yes. You forget, everything else aside, I'm married."

"I had forgotten." She looked at the man in a deep way.

A sudden breath of air passed through the tops of the Norfolk Island pines, making the day forlorn. Both man and woman felt as if they had been left stranded momentarily on a forsaken shore.

There was a movement among the horses. The cavalcade was starting. Reaching down, Haldane grasped Helen's hand.

"Good-by!"

The girl stepped back, slim, beautiful as a plumaria blossom.

"She'll be on your conscience."

Her red lips framed the words deliberately, accusingly.

The end of the first day's ride took them to the Garrison Ranch, in Makawao, a stately place set among sightly hills. Haldane got no opportunity to speak with Hula; she rode at the head of the cavalcade with Edwin, won back, temporarily at least, to his life.

When they dismounted, Dick went to her.

"Coming in with us, Hula?"

She shook her head. Her cheeks were rather pale, and her short dark hair curled into her neck pathetically.

"I'm going to help Uncle Edwin."

"Righto. Don't forget to come in in time to get cleaned up for dinner."

Deanie giggled. This brotherly solicitude from Dick! Amusing.

Von Erdmann regarded the pale child thoughtfully.

"You look tired," he observed.

Hula looked up. "I'm not, Tancred," but there was infinite weariness in her voice.

Edwin's hand fell upon her shoulder compellingly.

"Ready to unsaddle?" she asked, quickly turning around.

She followed him like a puppy, and the old fellow drew a breath of relief. Her affection, her respect for him and for the soundness of his judgment, had not altered. Even as a colt which has run to the end of a rope and thrown itself will return bewildered and shaken, so had Hula come back to him after her brief and disastrous break for strange pastures.

He looked at her. As long as she remained of his world, he could safeguard her.

The cowboys of the Garrison Ranch crowded forward to help in the unsaddling and watched Hula with admiration and respect. They had heard of her prowess with horse and rope; they had seen her ride Silver Wings to victory. They noticed, in the hustle of unsaddling and feeding, she never made a false move. She knew every detail of their work, from rubbing up the hair on a horse's back, damp from the saddle, to the exact spot in which to insert her thumb between a horse's jaw to make it take the bit.

At first they held off, shyly friendly, fearing she was not as knowable as the Hana cowboys averred she was, later finding her more so. The distant, scarce-known ranch on East Maui became invested with distinction. While the horses fed, Edwin leaned against a post, smoking and conversing with the foreman of the Garrison Ranch, a gigantic, noble-faced Hawaiian called Holomalia. Hula chatted with a group of cowboys.

Edwin knew a moment of respite and deep content. His child, his again. Safe for a while.

When at length she departed for the house, at the summons of a Japanese house boy sent by Dick, he relaxed even more completely. He knew John Garrison and honored him. English, well-born, a lover of fine horses, he had been instrumental in introducing polo and racing to the Islands. He was a sportsman, a lover of his fellow men, high minded, forceful and vigorous. He had been a model father to his motherless sons. No influences emanated from that household that he need fear.

Edwin drew a breath of relief and filled his pipe.

A young fellow detached himself from his comrades and walked forward.

"*Pehea, kela keiki mahini?* (What about that little girl?) What she going to be when she grows up?"

Edwin roused himself to study his questioner. His words proved him to be a thinker.

The boy, for he was not more than twenty, although he was over six feet, watched Hula's vanishing figure intently, a puzzled expression on his face. Edwin noted that his features were too fine to be purely Hawaiian. His personality was arresting, his forehead noble, his lips those of a lover and a fighter.

Edwin prolonged the silence deliberately, a suppression at his heart. That this fellow cherished any untoward thoughts in regard to Hula, Edwin did not believe. The boy was unaware of his own potentialities, but his strength and deliberate, unthinking grace were magnets to draw women. There was a vital, though suppressed, quality about his person. Always on the alert to anticipate danger, Edwin drew back, on guard instantly. Reared as Hula had been, having looked on such men as comrades, it was possible that, in her revulsion of feeling from her brief and painful contact with a new mode of existence, she would fling herself too wholeheartedly back into this one. It would be the way of youth, and might not the youth in her, restless and waking, answer the youth in this man, should she see too much of him or another of his type? He commanded interest; he had the unconscious dignity of youth; and he possessed a vivid sort of masculine beauty found sometimes in men of mixed race.

The rapt, thoughtful expression on his face alarmed the old man.

"Why do you ask?" he demanded in an iron voice.

The young fellow looked at him as if he had only just recollected that some one else was there.

"I saw her, the other day when she rode the gray stallion. I cannot think of her in a house, like other women, having babies. I cannot help but wonder. She is—" But something in the grim eyes holding his warned him the rest of his thought was best unsaid.

A widening silence made the younger man smile, as if a thought dawned slowly in his mind. He looked at the bitter face opposite and, turning, walked slowly away, still smiling as from some source of pure happiness.

Edwin, his arms locked across his chest, felt a terrible and stifling anger, anger that was not directed against Hula, but that included her somehow. Anger not against the outward child, but for the mysterious and potent allure that emanated from within. To look at her, were one a man, was to feel a delicate stinging fire running newly through one's veins. Fool, ass that he had been to fancy that there was any security for her! Depression filled him, followed by savage and unreasoning anger against Haldane. Why did not the fool speak? He must know Hula's heart was his for the asking. Could it be possible that he did not want it? The thought was inconceivable. He had showed—that night—that he cared, and he looked miserable enough now; but he made no move to bring matters to a head. Deliberately he had kept Hula from him to see what it would drive him to do. Could he be indifferent to the look on her face? It tore at the old cowboy's heart. Every natural impulse bade him forgive and comfort her, but too easy forgiveness would not do. And he loved enough to hurt her, if by hurting he could help.

He was no weak and doting parent to mistake indulgence for love. As he would have punished an outlaw colt that periled its own life by bolting, crazed, unseeing, so he must punish this child he loved lest she break herself.

Haldane was necessary to Hula's future. He must be forced to give what remained of his life to her. Somehow pressure must be brought upon him sufficient to force him to act.

So went Edwin's single-track mind. For her . . . anything . . . everything. . .

Next morning they mounted at three. Brightly the stars shone above the dark tops of bending eucalyptus trees. Lanterns flashed athwart men's legs; horses snorted and backed when they were led out to be mounted. Dick ordered Edwin to hold Di's horse while he put her up. Haldane helped Deanie, who laughed excitedly when her horse started to sit upon its haunches, like a dog. He struck it smartly on the quarters, and it jumped up. Von Erdmann mounted warily; then Haldane threw his leg across his horse's back, and his eyes searched for Hula.

A little aside from the rest she sat, laughing down at a young cowboy whose eyes and teeth flashed in the lantern light. His strong brown hand grasped her horse's mane, as if he would lift himself to a level with her by it. His face revealed much more than he was aware of. As Hula gave herself wholly and unashamedly to those she was moved to love or care for, so he bared his heart, unconscious that he did so. The imagination of some white progenitor, who should never have intruded himself into the making of him, tricked him. Lifting his shining face, while his fingers worked deeper into the horse's mane, he spoke, and so pitifully is feeling lessened by words, all he managed was:

"Bime-by come back one more time to Makawao, eh?"

He was uneducated but, despite it, somehow appealing.

"Perhaps," laughed the girl, thinking he had a singularly attractive face.

"Some time I come to Hana, maybe."

It was a tentative promise and an unconscious feeling of his ground. Feelings surged through him that he did not comprehend. They delighted and daunted him. He had never felt interest in girls; they were not worthy of thought, though they had played the same part in his life as they did in that of his fellows. Then, in a moment, he had become aware of a living, breathing being, compounded of star-shine and fire and dew, garbed in woman's flesh, bringing sensations strange and beautiful. His brain worked as in the beginning of intoxication, but beneath the joy was a great despair. He stood, looking up at her, just one of a throng of Hawaiian cowboys, yet, because of a remote and treacherous dash of white blood in his veins, not wholly of them. He possessed, what his mates did not—imagination. He had watched her at the track with the light of glory on her face. He had never expected to know her, to speak to her, but she had possessed his thoughts. Then last night he had looked into her dark eyes, watched words fall, addressed to himself, from lips as crimson as *luau* roses.

"I should like to see you rope a wild bull," he switched into Hawaiian. "I saw you ride at Kahului—" A sudden thought came to him and he took off his hat, removing the crimson carnation *lei* from about its crown.

He lifted it to her.

Hula accepted it as she had accepted a hundred others from men of a like station but different caliber, but instinct made her know that he liked her. And because she had been so bereft of love, of approbation, her grateful and affectionate nature leaped toward him. She smiled divinely, as only Hula could smile, and Haldane was not astonished to see an icy blast of anger sweep Edwin's face. His fury was unmerited, unjust, for the girl was innocent of anything but a passionate gratitude, the gratitude that makes a puppy rush clumsily toward any one it feels might be kind, and the man was innocent of everything but admiration.

"Hula!"

The girl stiffened, her eyes dilated. She was ignorant as to how she had offended, but she knew that voice. For a moment she could not even answer, then said in a dazed way:

"All right, Uncle Edwin. *Aloha.*"

"*Aloha,*" echoed the cowboy, stepping back into the shadows out of which he had come.

Haldane watched Hula's distracted little face unhappily. He spurred forward to ride by her, but she, with ever so pathetic and wondering a glance, fell in beside Edwin.

Turning out of the dark masses of trees planted by Garrison, the night burst upon them, navy blue, boundless.

Glancing backward to assure himself that every one was there, Edwin headed for the mountain. Haldane rode in a depressed silence. Somehow he got from the fabric of the night the depression and desolation that filled Hula as she rode, her eyes fixed upon the dark bulk of Haleakala. Above its rim-line the beautiful stars of morning shone with passionless brilliancy.

The cavalcade rode for the most part in silence, save when some horse blew out its nostrils or a bullock called in the hills. Occasionally Deanie giggled or Dick spoke to his wife. His face looked pale in the starlight and somewhat drawn. Haldane rode, his mind intent on Hula, but she seemed as unaware of him as though he had been an inhabitant of a distant world.

Dawn began to break. Stars enlarged and paled. A clear

yellow light grew in the east. Morning stalked upon the mountain top with cold blue feet. Plover wheeled overhead; cattle called; cock pheasants crowed from the ridges. In stately blue masses, the hundreds of thousands of trees planted by John Garrison to add to the beauty and value of his ranch showed against the green of the rolling hills. Distant islands swam, cloud-like, in the splendor of the sea.

Like a gigantic palette of mingled colors, lay the isthmus and the plains. To the south the barren reaches of Kahoolawe showed like a fiery streak above the dove-gray water. And bounding every view rose the tremendous, untroubled horizons of the Pacific.

One of the cowboys riding ahead broke into a song. Clear, reckless, his voice floated back, swaying to the primitive hula rhythm. It sent a queer sharp pang through Anthony, making him increasingly conscious of the boundless blue realms of sea and sky about him. It drew his eyes to the mountain above. It bore evidences enough of its volcanic origin, but the agony of past ages had burned itself to an impressive and all-encompassing peace.

Rudely uptilted cones showed purple against the blue sky; drifts of ash, rivers of congealed lava were on all sides. Dizzying, boundlessly blue the sea swam up to meet the sky and the sky reached down for the sea. Tremendously the mountain seemed to plunge down toward the plains, but the passing ages had cooled its heat to a vast peace.

A chill struck Haldane. So would life be when he left the Islands. The emotions and sensations of the past two weeks would end. Life would cease to move forward—would become again the dull and deadly thing it had been. Was he capable of anything beyond work and drifting? He loved Hula as he had never loved any one, and yet he could not bring himself to trample down the traditions on which he had been reared; to divorce his wife to marry a child! Rather than have his love mistaken for passion, he would abandon her to her fate.

He looked ahead to where the two rode and realized the exhausted stoop of Hula's small shoulders. She could ride a grueling race like a man, but could not survive the displeasure of one she loved.

Then without preliminary she reined her horse aside from the trail. Edwin looked at her, then rode indifferently on. The girl was given the impression that she was no longer any concern of his.

White-lipped, desolate, she looked after him; then her eyes glazed. Haldane's heart came to a stop. He knew she was waiting for him.

"I want—to—see—it—with you," Hula said, unsteadily nodding toward the crater's rim.

"Why, Hula?" Stupidly he asked it.

"Because it will be much nicer." There was a sort of distracted daintiness about her lips. Her face had a closed look.

A brief, sharp scramble brought them to the edge. They sat on their horses without speech, their hands locked.

Immense, silent, rimmed with cyclopean walls, splashed with barbaric color, harboring strange shadows beneath its cliffs, the vast crater cradled its giant cones. The day was breathless, but sudden winds came up out of the pit in gusty swirls and with peculiar noises, even as gases had come in ages past. Precipitous walls brooded above the distorted landscape, perhaps remembering the time when mad blue flames danced demon dances beneath crimson-dripping crags and rocking lava islands grated against seas of melting rock.

Across the farthest rim, in contrast to the color and the chaos at their feet, the serene mountain-tops of the island of Hawaii showed above packed masses of trade-wind cloud.

They dismounted and walked to the brink of the pit.

Hula's face quivered, broke for an instant, then set again.

"It's beautiful, isn't it, Anthony?"

"Yes, Hula," but it was at her he was looking.

"What's he angry about? Do you know? I can't breathe —when he looks—like that."

Before the force of that mighty pit the man could not lie. He put his arm about her shoulders.

"I'll tell you to-night, Hula."

She looked at him adoringly, and turning her face against his arm, kissed it through the shirt. The man's hold tightened. Side by side, in silence, they stood looking down into the vast and silent crater.

"Couldn't you tell me now? It's agony—waiting."

"Not very well, sweetheart. I need time to talk to you, else you will not be able to understand why he is so upset. Let's go." He turned from the pit. "I can't stand much of this."

Hula looked at him, smiled as if from a great distance, and remounting rode to some stone corrals.

"Here, you loiterers," called Deane, "lunch is almost gone. Or have you looked so long at Haleakala that you've feasted yourselves with beauty?"

She eyed them closely, for she suspected that Anthony, at least, had been looking deeply into other things as well. Her perceptions were keen. She realized that Haldane was in torment. Imps sang and danced in her. How would he meet his problem?

Her lashes flickered, and she laid her hand upon a spread coat beside her.

"Sit here, Hula."

She would keep the drama near her. The child obeyed limply. Until the last few days she had never known fatigue. She picked up a sandwich and tossed it to Anthony. Then her little face resumed its gravity. Languid, possessed by memory, she seemed to look back at something that had gone forever from her.

"Why aren't you riding your great horse?" asked Deane.

Hula looked her disdain.

"And get his legs all knocked to bits on the lava!"

"I'm afraid I'll never have any horse-sense," mourned the little woman; "but that's because I was brought up in a city. Would you like to go away, Hula?"

"No."

"Don't you ever long to see the rest of the world? It's very fascinating; isn't it, Anthony?"

Carefully she maneuvered toward her object.

"Rather," said the man, "and some day you must go and see it, Hula."

Hula did not reply. Diana glanced sharply at her. Her little face was subtly changed. She looked at Haldane. His face was pale under its tan, the jaw rigid. She frowned. Conscious of her intense scrutiny Haldane looked around. He saw the doubt in her eyes and felt curiously outraged. Extraordinary woman! How could she question his acts or intentions toward that beautiful child? And after her brief moment of suspicion, the woman felt abashed. She wished that this man were years younger or Hula years older. He was somehow competent to handle that distracting girl, Hula; he could be pal, lover, friend. He had a great capacity for loving; he had humor, understanding. He would interest himself in the myriad interests of her life and bring learning and appreciation for other things which had not, as yet, touched her.

She rose and walked to the rim of the pit. Thinking of her own unhappy marriage—for despite Dick's generous surrender, the gulf of their great difference persisted between them—she clenched her hands. Dick was sick and exhausted from the battle he was fighting—for her. She knew he could never be truly happy divorced from his old life. She wandered on. Finally finding herself out of sight of the others, she cast herself down upon the scorched earth—grasped the sharp cinders and crushed them in her hands.

Exhausted, she lay against the ashes looking at the marvels of volcanic upheaval about her, frozen now with time into a soul-shaking peace. Would time bring a like boon to her?

She did not hear Dick's searching footsteps. He was shocked when he saw her lying on the cinders, her body vibrating to her grief. He could not realize he had brought any woman to such a pass.

"Di," he said, falling upon his knee beside her, "for God's sake, my dear—"

She sat up, shockingly pale.

"It's nothing; I'm tired."

"You're lying, darling."

"Yes."

"What is it, then?"

"Everything."

"Am I making you unhappy?"

"No—life is."

Dick's face was pinched, showing the effects of his past dissipation intensified by lack of stimulants.

"I've been a brute, Di, a blackguard; but I love you. Can't you forgive me in your heart? I know I don't deserve it. No man deserves forgiveness for some of the things he does to his wife—" He wrung her hand, hanging like a miserable, apologetic boy above her.

She looked away.

"The sacrifice you're making—for me—is too much."

"It isn't, it isn't. It won't be easy; for I've loved it, and I'll want it again."

"It makes me sick to think of having to go back to Hana."

Dick winced. He regarded his home with the passionate attachment characteristic of Islanders.

"Don't say that, Di. I can't leave while Dad lasts. I've got to stay."

"I don't want my child to be born there."

Dick's white face took on a tinge of blue.

"That can be arranged, dear; you can go to Honolulu, anywhere. That matter is entirely up to you."

"You wouldn't mind it very much?" she asked doubtfully.

"I'd mind frightfully, for I love the damned place. But I understand, Di, how you feel."

The woman hesitated before speaking.

"I can't afford to risk my child's knowing that atmosphere. It's too deadly. You know, Dick, the influence of environment!"

"I know," he replied in a dead tone, "but couldn't you chance it—for me?"

He looked at her with dragged eyes.

"I don't know, Dick. It's risking so much."

"Try me out. If I fail you"—it was wrenched from him—"you may go, and I'll never ask you to come back."

Di looked at him, feeling he would ask, many times—as men of his type always do ask—unbelievable sacrifices of the woman he loved.

"And if I do not," he continued, "couldn't you believe that I would bequeath some strength of character to my child? After Dad goes—I'll pull stakes. It won't be more than a couple of years at the most. It's impossible that a child of that age could be affected."

Beseechingly he watched her.

She drew a deep breath.

"Dick—I'll—for love's sake, but not for our love; for

as yet it's not worthy of the name. I'll try, but, God help me, if you fail, I'll go!"

Without waiting for more, Dick took her in his arms.

"I wish . . . please, Dick, don't make it too evident that we have ended our difficulties."

She said it with pain, knowing that he could not understand her desire to keep the intimate side of their life from the world.

He looked bewildered.

"Surely, Di, you can't expect me to keep my distance when I'm so damn happy that you'll risk it for me. I want to be near you!"

"I know it's silly, but I hate outsiders to know everything."

"They don't know—everything," laughed the man gently.

"They might suspect."

"Would it be so awful, Di, if they did?" he teased.

The woman blushed and Dick kissed her, entranced.

When they got back Edwin was ready to start. He was keen to be moving. Anger had devastated him. He had alienated his child. Cruelly, unjustly. After all it was not her fault, rather her misfortune that life had fashioned her in the way it had.

He took a quick look at her from under his angry eyebrows, and their ferocity concealed the adoration of his gaze. Hula's face was pale, wistful. Her eyes rested upon Anthony as though she expected surcease of misery to come from him.

"Are you happy?" she asked disconcertingly, turning upon him.

"No, Hula. I don't think I am. Perhaps it's because I know I'm going away."

She frowned.

"Why do you? Do you have to?"

"Yes," he answered, "I'm afraid I have to."

She sent a long look at him and in her bewildered young face wisdom began to grow, and with it despair.

"He doesn't love me. He wants to get away—to be away from me."

She half shut her eyes and stood as if transfixed by the thought; then she hastily mounted.

The cavalcade started, Edwin in the lead, Mahiai following with Silver Wings, eagerly stepping, his carefully bandaged legs flashing dusty white above the fetlock deep cinders.

A delicious sense of remoteness from the world came to Haldane as the long trail wound down the sliding sands. Great walls towered higher; colors grew more violent, the silence more impressive. Desolation was on every hand. Lakes of congealed lava, masses of smelted rock, sphinx-like cinder-cones lifting their heads hundreds of feet above the cluttered crater floor, while the frosty foliage of Silver-Sword glittered on the long sand slopes and from the blue shadowed cliffs.

Occasionally, as they passed along the floor, strange cries came from the towering cliffs, and, looking up, Haldane saw bands of wild goats swarming, ant-like, on the precipitous cliffs. As the afternoon waned, they began to descend from the *palis* for the richer feed on the alluvial flats, the dust of their going rising like brown steam from volcanic cracks.

Edwin lifted his hand in a signal to halt. Below them the floor was covered with a species of scattered vegetation. Through it bands of the little animals ranged.

"Look," said Hula in an excited whisper.

The busy little feeders were foraging through the *mamani* forest that covered the ancient lava flow. They were almost human in their antics, playing in open glades, feeding on the trees, their forefeet braced against the trunks.

Hula and the cowboys took off their ropes and fastened the led horses to fragments of rock.

Advancing cautiously when they got to the lip of the depression, they drove home their spurs, and the horses raced full speed into the flock. Like a little red devil Hula raced in the lead, old Edwin on her heels.

The band scattered; a fine amber dust rose; little hoofs pattered like rain over the rocks; trees and brush crashed as goats and horses broke through them. Lassos swung and whined. The shouts of the cowboys came back to the watchers. An old billy-goat abandoned his flock, which had headed for the rough safety of newer lava and the greater security of the cliffs. Hula wheeled after him, her rope swinging with beautiful precision. The goat zigzagged in a series of rushes and stops. She threw and jerked him down.

Sliding from her horse, she threw herself upon him. From somewhere behind her a kid bleated, delirious with terror. Its mother halted, realized the futility of attempting to fight these pursuers, and bolted. The kid screamed in despair and Dick, who had roped it, pulled open his noose and let it go, because his own heart was still soft. Like a rabbit it darted after the dust of the vanishing herd.

Hula, her legging knife in her hand, looked at the wild yellow eyes of the goat. He struggled but would not cry out. In the very act of cutting his throat, her hand dropped. For the first time in her life she couldn't do it. She looked at her brother. What had happened to them both?

Anthony galloped up, his brown eyes alight.

"Bully, kid!" he shouted; "I wish I could swing a rope like that."

The child looked at him and pressed her foot harder on the billy's wiry neck.

"He's been caught before and let go," she observed. "See!" She touched one horn with her forefinger . "D.H.B.," she laughed. "Well, I'll put ours on the other. Doesn't he smell!"

The old billy-goat struggled as if in protest, but her horse moved, deftly tightening the rope.

"Your pocket-knife, Anthony; this is too big."

The man handed it to her, and she carefully carved an H and then an A.

"What are you doing to that unfortunate animal?" asked Deane riding up.

"Not hurting it!" cried Hula indignantly as she tried, with a hard-pressed knee upon its neck, to still its writhing and kicking.

Edwin galloped up and grunted to gain her attention.

"What did you get?" she called without looking up.

"Fine fat nanny for your supper. The boys are skinning her."

Suddenly the breach between them had healed.

"Fine," said Hula, rising and brushing the dust off her knees.

"You like I kill for you, kid?" asked Edwin dismounting.

"No, let him go."

The man looked curiously at her but made no comment.

"All right, I let go for you."

Hula smiled; shut up the knife and handed it back to Anthony. Edwin pulled off the noose, and the goat snorted and bolted. Re-coiling the lasso, the foreman handed it to her.

"Now *wikiwiki* (quickly) to Pali Ku. I like make camp before dark."

A half hour's ride brought them to the eastern end of the crater. Diana looked about her in amazement. There was a small green plain at the base of the eighteen-hundred-foot cliffs and a small golden-green forest.

She looked at Dick.

"What a contrast to the aridity of the crater we've come through. How do you account for it?"

"Easily. The trade-wind clouds that blow over the wet woods above Hana hit the cold air and the cliffs; the moisture is precipitated. . . . Shall I lift you off?"

Camp was rapidly made; horses unsaddled and turned out to graze. Di and Deanie lay face downward on the lush grass. There was an elemental peace filling the vast blue bowl of the crater. It brought soothing to body and mind.

Supper was announced.

Deanie was childishly enchanted with everything.

"Well, Hula," she said, looking at the child a-sprawl on the grass, "I know a little why you love going off on these trips, and why you are so nice."

The child disregarded the compliment. She flipped an insect out of her cup.

"I love it," she said in a dreamy fashion, looking about at the towering walls. "I love it up here."

Haldane studied her, wondering how often she had been up in the crater with Edwin. In all likelihood a hundred times since first she had begun to ride with him. What a profound impression such a place must make on the mind of a child!

He looked about him attentively.

The first chill of night had crept into the vast, quiet place.

Sunset is the loneliest hour in the pit. Terrific blue shadows lengthen across the crater-floor, emanating an uncanny chill. The sound of horses grazing, the thin cry of goats high up on the *palis*, the bubbling of sea birds in the crags, cannot dispel the appalling quiet of the place. Swinging walls are silhouetted sharply against the calm evening sky, and the cones rear more and more impressively above the cobalt shadows that steadily engulf the crater floor. Then, indeed, does Haleakala seem kin to the enormous burnt-out craters of the moon that it approximates in size. And it is filled, like them, with the eerie loneliness of a planet without inhabitants and filled with a majestic peace accumulated from the ages.

And always, the cones are what impress one most; each individual in shape and coloring, but alike in that they were all vents to the furnace that built a vast mountain mass up out of the sea. Silent, shapely pyramids of scoria and ash . . . aloof . . . brooding . . . mysterious. . . .

Haldane, stirred by the spell of the hour, rose to his feet. Encircling walls towered remote, with shadows like navy-blue chiffon hanging under the cliffs. About him was sound; over in the crater proper a terrific silence. It filled him with rest and unrest. He wanted to walk for a while, to be alone with himself. But he could not go, else Hula might be hurt. He had no intention of trying to evade the issue ahead, but just to be without her bewildering presence while he attempted to think. But, even as he rose, he was conscious that her eyes sought his.

"Let's take a look at the horses, Hula."

She scrambled up, and they swung off toward the cliffs of Pali Ku that became increasingly green under the gold of the leveling sun.

Edwin looked after them.

"Damn him; he must speak. If he keeps silent, he is no man."

He kicked at the fire; then busied himself coiling a lasso. He knew, even as Diana knew, that those two could give great happiness to each other. Oh, that Hula's life might run securely, decently, as it ought!

Hula and Haldane made their way across the plain to a rise that commanded a view of the entire pit. About them rose the fragrance of ferns and damp grass. Grazing horses never lifted their heads. The towering cliffs grew momentarily brighter, as the sun fell down the last slope of the sky with gathering speed.

They turned to watch it drop.

Of a sudden it met the highest pinnacle of the walls; blazed a moment blindingly, terrifically; then vanished. For a few moments the gold light lingered, then the crater became a strange place of shadows.

The man looked at the thoughtful child beside him and took her hand. Her fingers clung tightly. He looked about for a log on which to sit and drew her down beside him. About them rose the fragrance of ferns. Hula looked at him with a sort of desperate expectancy. Her thought of the afternoon recurred. He doesn't love—he doesn't want me—he wants to get away.

"Hula," he began, looking anywhere but at her.

"Please—don't say it. I know." She spoke with difficulty. "I knew this afternoon, for the first time." Then she was a child again and added with tremulous lips, "It hurts. It's funny, like that puppy running away when I tried to love it. Like when Silver Wings jerks away from my arms. I love too hard. It's funny, but it hurts!"

"What do you mean, Hula? What do you know that hurts?"

The child's face seemed to become tense, as if she were galloping at a high fence.

"I knew, to-day—that you can't love me. That's why you are going away. I knew it when you said, 'I'm going. I have to.'"

"Sweetheart," cried Haldane, shocked at the expression on her face, and, turning, he grasped both her hands.

"It's the truth, isn't it, Anthony?" Her throat worked, but her eyes were despairingly calm. It was over—the worst agony. Now numbness would come as it had after she had seen him holding Mrs. Bane. A chill shook her, then she burned. But this time there wasn't anything—anything—to help to make her forget. She wouldn't go crazy. She'd go to Uncle Edwin, if he didn't get unreasonably angry again. If he did, then to Silver Wings, though he sometimes drew back from her too violent embraces. But he loved her and always put down his head again. Sorry. So the thoughts flitted through her distracted little head.

"No, Hula, it isn't!" cried the man fiercely. "I love you —God knows how much! I've been tormented, but I brought you here this evening to ask if you could ever think of—of—some day marrying me."

The girl made a sudden movement and grew pale.

"Oh, Anthony," she gasped, turning her cheek against his arm.

"Dear, have I upset you?" he asked, bending to look at her.

"No," she said lifting her head. "I was, I was so *afraid* you'd never ask me to, now—"

"Why, *now*, darling."

"Because I got drunk. Because I rampaged around and hurt Silver Wings. I thought—Uncle Edwin said—that you were disgusted."

"Hush, sweet."

Their locked hands burned together.

"Don't you, Anthony?" she asked breathlessly.

"Don't I what, Hula?"

"Don't you hate me?"

"God, no! Not I!"

She drew a rapturous breath. "I can't breathe I'm so happy."

"Hula!"

"Yes?"

"There are many things I must say to you, dear."

"I don't mind, even if they are horrible. You love me."

The man put his arm about her and pressed his lips on hers. She quivered and thrilled as a colt does to a new caress. She felt the man's heart laid upon her mouth with his kiss. Then he lifted his head, and his face bore the same intense look that Hula's had when she had told him she knew that he did not love her. The girl saw it, but did not heed it. Heaven was hers.

"Hula, sweetest," he said in a sort of deadly despair, "I've no right to ask you to marry me, for I'm married, as you know. But I can't leave you—"

"Then you'll stay. How beautiful."

"No, I'll go. I'll have to, more than ever now. I must go to England."

"To be divorced?"

How easily she said it.

"Yes."

"Anthony."

"Yes, Hula?"

"I'm glad you are married, for I'll know how much you love me if you have to get un-married to have me."

"Yes, Hula; even yesterday I thought that I couldn't do it. It's a sad and terrible thing to have to do."

"If she loved you, but she doesn't."

"She'll say she does."

"And you'll believe her, a little?"

"Probably." Savagely he said it.

Hula looked at his grimly set face and touched the rock of his chin with her lips.

"I love sticking-out ones," she observed in her throaty love voice.

"Rascal!" Haldane smiled but shook her. "I've got to talk to you seriously. Don't deprive me utterly of my reason."

"I'd forgotten, but go on. What made you change to-day?"

"I don't know, Hula—to be perfectly honest."

"Maybe it was this place." She looked about with awed eyes. "I'm not afraid of it, Anthony," she explained, "but—you know the feeling it gives you. As if God were here."

Haldane's arm tightened; he could not for the instant command his voice. His eyes followed the ragged rim-line, above which stars were pricking the deep violet sky. A vagrant line he had once read wandered through his mind.

"Only God and I know what is in my heart."

He studied Hula's upturned face, then bent and kissed her, holding her close. It was pure, it was deep, it was compassionate: his feeling for her. It was nothing of which he need ever be ashamed. He loved her intoxicating exterior, but more he loved her desperate little soul. She was life: beautiful, amazing, upsetting.

"When you kiss me like that, Anthony, I feel—oh, I don't know how to say it," she laughed, with a sort of breathless excitement, "but as if Silver Wings were winning millions of races and I were roping wild bulls, and all the wonderful feelings of the world were inside me, all at once. But you were going to talk. Go on."

Haldane smiled.

"Can you listen, attentively, sweetest, for a few minutes?"

"Yes."

"First, remember that I love you, and because I do, I must leave you and go back to England. It may take a couple of years. What I must do takes time. I shall worry about you while I'm gone. You are too beautiful, Hula, though as yet you haven't realized it. But men and time will teach you so. You have a marvelous nature but a dangerous one. It will lay snares for you. I cannot endure the thought that mischance may come to you. I wish to God that I were free and could marry you and take you away from Hana. But even if I were not tied, I couldn't yet. You're just a baby. Can you be faithful to me?"

"If you love me enough!" she cried.

"I love you so much I'm afraid to think about it, or to go away—or stay."

Hula laughed, through rising tears, at the driven expression on his face.

"But I don't want you to go. Stay!"

"Dear heart, I'll have to go if ever we are to be really happy."

"Oh, yes. Your damned wife! I hate her."

Haldane laughed. "So have I hated her. Frequently. But I loved her once."

"As much as me!"

"Hardly. It was a different kind of love, Hula. You couldn't compare the two feelings. The other is dead, killed."

"But if you see her again, you might—"

"No, Hula, not after having loved and been loved by you. It isn't possible."

"Oh," cried the child, "what a darling you are!"

"I hope you will always think so, but what I want most to say is, I shall go, free myself and come back. In the interval you will grow up. If there is any one else when I come back, more suitable, whom you could love more than you do me, I'll give you up, dear. I love you enough to do it."

"No!" she cried, her face red with approaching tears. She slipped from the log to her knees and held him fiercely. "I wouldn't give you away, to any one, ever!"

The man laughed and bent his lean cheek to her hair, soft and fragrant as fern.

"Neither will I 'give you away,' dear, unless you ask it of me. I think I loved you from the minute I saw you. That I'd ever ask you to marry me I didn't believe possible. Now

I know that the only thing that would have been impossible was—not to. I felt that I mustn't tell you."

"But I knew!" cried Hula clenching her fist, "and it hurt because you wouldn't tell me. You've always been my Anthony; that's why she hated me."

"Mrs. Bane?"

"Yes. She wanted to marry you."

The man laughed.

"She had some plan, idea, of a sort. What it was, though, is beyond me. She's an extraordinary woman."

Hula looked at him doubtfully. Did he remember? She must know.

"Do you remember what she said that night after I pulled you out of the creek?"

"I do, but I don't believe it, Hula. Whatever you have brought or may bring to me couldn't be wrong."

It was quite dark. Stars burned above the walls. Haldane caressed the girl's hair, and she leaned confidently against his knee.

"Oh, I'm happy," she breathed from her seat in the sweet ferns.

"Are you, Hula? So am I. For a while," he added to himself. He looked at the peaks silhouetted against the star-strewn sky. Birds made strange sounds in the cliffs; horses tore busily at the grass. The man could sense the imperceptible fall of the dew. Above the trees of the little forest the smoke of campfires uncurled their rosy spirals. Eerie peace brimmed in the vast, shadowy bowl.

After a while he began talking again, looking into Hula's eyes, counseling, advising, explaining. With a quiet desperation he endeavored to make clear to her the things that menaced her.

She listened to the end.

"That's why he was angry: poor Uncle Edwin. But he

mustn't be any more. I'll be good; I'll be good now I am yours! He ought to know that."

"Why?"

"Because, oh, well that day on the hills, he talked to me, said he wanted me to marry you. That I must, for you would be good for me. I hadn't thought of it till then. I only liked you better than any one else I ever met."

"And I you, from the first. You know, that day when I came upon you two sitting in the grass, I felt in a dim way —I know it now—what had been said between you. The old rascal, so he'd made his mind up to it even then!"

Hula studied his grave face and got to her knees. She put her arms about his neck.

"Anthony, the moon will be up in a minute."

"God bless you, I'll kiss you; then we must go back."

"Ever such a long one, Anthony."

When he lifted his head, the crater was flooded with light. There came the thought to the man again, as it had at sunset, that this huge pit was, indeed, kin to those that pocked the moon, and it was filled, like them, to the brim, with the peace of the ages.

His arms tightened about the girl. With passionate intentness he studied her face. Would fate or destiny or whatever governs men's lives, grant that he should see it again? And, seeing it, would he ever find the bewildering, the adorable Hula that he left?

PART III

THE DEVIL'S GARDEN

CHAPTER I

Dick lifted his head. It was done. *Pau.* His father, the old order. For a moment his eyes would not focus; then they righted and he saw Hula sitting on the opposite side of the bed.

Outside, on the gravel driveway under the window, he could hear a man and a horse pacing up and down. It had been his father's wish—that he die with the sound of a horse's hoofs in his ears.

He stood up and went to Hula, unconscious of Dehan and Fitzmaurice, of Deanie weeping in her husband's arms. He smiled, rather terribly.

"Poor old boy!" Dick spoke the words calmly, but he could not look at Calhoun. Very still and enormous he lay in his four-poster bed. Hula got up and took her brother's hand tightly. Dick had loved him best . . . always.

"Come outside for a minute," she said.

They walked into the sunshine. The afternoon was full of peace; a peace that weighted their hearts.

"I'll tell Mahiai that he can go," said the girl. She burst into tears which she angrily quelled. "Wait, Dick."

She ran down the stairs and gave the order. The world seemed to end when the cowboy led the gray stallion away. When the sound of crunching gravel ceased she turned back to Dick. His face was dragged, his lips ashen.

"Don't mind—so much!" she cried, and her arms went about him. He winced at the violence of her hold, but its hurt comforted.

"It's all right, Hula—but I can't realize that the old boy has gone! Let's go for a ride!"

Instinctively they turned to horses. Galloping furiously along the green bluffs, Dick looked with a wild sort of despair at his land. Whatever came, Hana would pass out of his hands. They did not deserve to possess it—they who had squandered it away. In a few days Harry would come—he looked at Hula—then Howard Hamilton, perhaps others.

Rounding a curve, they met Edwin.

"The old man?"

"*Pau*," said Dick with savage grief.

The foreman took off his hat and stared at the rain-squalls that moved ghostlike upon the sea. His jaw squared and his eyes hardened.

His child—what would become of her? His muscles grew rigid, then tipping back his head he replaced his hat.

"More better I go," and he headed his horse toward Hana.

Dick and Hula rode until the evening lights made the sea beautiful; then they turned back to the house.

The next two days were a blank to Dick. He went through them conscious of people coming and going, of events that moved to an inevitable end. A strange delusion persisted with him; that afterwards he must recount all of it to Calhoun. The flowers, the grief of his labor, details that imprinted themselves on his mind . . . nightmarish . . . aching . . . unreal.

He was roused by Dehan.

"Take a drink, Dick, you can't go on like this."

Kindly, concerned, came the voice of the half-white. His black eyes were wet. Dick accepted the glass, took a swallow and set it down.

"I forgot. I can't—Di."

"Hell, if she were here, she'd insist upon it. Don't be an ass!"

Fitzmaurice pressed it upon him and he finished it. He waited until he felt the alcohol strike revivingly through him;

then he looked around, at the room, at the sunny garden. A dazed sort of recognition grew in his eyes.

He was home; his father was buried.

He clenched his fist and got up.

"Thanks, boys, you've been bricks!"

"Dry up, you ass," said Fitzmaurice, his brown eyes full of compassion. "How's to another, then a ride? Harry, find Hula."

Dehan departed and returned presently alone.

"She's with Edwin," he announced.

Fitzmaurice looked thoughtful. "Bet the old chap is talking to her," was his thought; "no grass ever grew under his feet. Wish Haldane were here, I'd feel better somehow. Stable sort of Johnny. Wonder how things stand between him and the kid?" So went his mind while he busied himself with Dick. The next few days would be difficult. Di would come. The affairs of the estate would have to be settled.

Calhoun's seizure had been sudden, brought on by a spell of heavy drinking. In twenty-four hours he had gone. At intervals he had been conscious but unable to speak. His brown eyes had rested with compassion on his son. Greatly had they loved one another; greatly had they lived; and only he and Dick knew how heavy was the penalty they must pay for the joy they had had.

Dick spoke suddenly. "Fitz, here's Dad's will. Will you read it?"

The veterinarian took it; broke the seal; cleared his throat; and put it down. Across it, scrawled in Calhoun's vigorous hand, was, "Sorry, kids—this is all bunk. You know. 'With all my worldly debts I thee endow.' Dad."

"I—can't, Dick. Sorry, old man."

Fitzmaurice walked to the window and blew his nose vigorously and resentfully. It seemed, for the moment, as if Calhoun's breezy and life-loving presence had entered the room.

Jestingly he had written the words, above the ache in his heart. The Irishman thought over the years he had spent in Hana. Careless, happy years that would never come again.

"Here's Hula, Dick," he announced. "Let's go."

And once more they galloped the green headlands and gorges, striving to ease their hearts by riding. It brought temporary relief, even to Dick.

"How's to spending the night at Kipahulu?" suggested Dehan.

Dick had an impulse to go, then resisted it.

"Thanks, old chap, I guess I'll go back."

Fitzmaurice glanced at him. Poor Dick. He could not face the thought of leaving his father, back there, alone, under the brown earth and flowers that covered him. He must be near him while he could.

A few days later Dehan came to him.

"I'd like to talk to you—when you feel like it."

He moved restlessly, like an animal in its cage. Uneasy, seeking escape.

Dick knew what he wanted. Now as well as to-morrow or the next day.

"What is it, Harry? Fire away."

"We're—we're—it's all square between us, Dick. You don't owe me anything."

Dick looked at the half-white.

"Is Hula going to marry you?"

"I haven't asked her yet."

"Then how are we square, Harry? I don't understand."

"I don't know how to explain. It's—my *aloha*—for the old man."

"Harry!"

Dick's head went down on the table. Agony tore him. Harry had loved his father, greatly, but Dick could not accept this impulse of his generosity. Had he known the battle Dehan had had before he won Von Erdmann's consent to it, he would have appreciated it still more. As manager of Dehan's plantation, the German had felt called upon to contest it. But it had been in vain.

"Well, if you want to be three hundred thousand dollars the poorer," he had stormed, "it's your lookout. You're a fool. You have no sense of the value of money!"

"I have!" Harry had retorted in such a manner that Von Erdmann had taken a second look at him. Then the thought flashed through his mind:

"The price of a girl. Of Hula!"

But he did not ask him, as Dick had, if he had spoken to her. He concluded that he had, else he would never have decided to wipe off the debt.

Dick looked at Dehan for a long time.

"Thanks, Harry. It's decent of you, but I cannot accept it, even for Dad. You've been a good friend to us—too good—but there's a limit to everything. This last year—" He choked and could not finish.

Dehan placed a compassionate hand upon his shoulder.

"Better do it, Dick. You're head over heels in debt, to others as well as to myself. You can't sell this place for any decent figure."

"I've an offer for it, here," and Dick handed him a letter.

He watched Dehan's face. Disbelief, incredulity, wonder showed in it. When he finished reading he looked at Dick.

"What's there on it that justifies his offering you such a price?"

Dick hesitated. After all, there was no reason now why Harry or any one else should not know. He lighted a cigarette and told him of Hamilton's project.

Dehan listened, then his eyes narrowed.

"Does that mean that Haldane will come back to be their engineer?"

"I don't know what arrangements were made. I believe he went to England."

"If he does—" Dehan's voice quivered.

"If he does, what possible difference can it make, Harry? He's—married."

"If he does, Hula will never marry me!" cried the half-white passionately.

"You had better talk to her before he comes, if he does come. She knows nothing of this," and Dick gestured toward the letter.

"Wait!" Dehan lifted his hand. "I'll give you what he offers for the place. Von Erdmann and I can put the ditch through ourselves. Howard's schemes are all sound; if he thinks it worth attempting—"

Dick held up his hand. "Sorry, Harry, but I gave him my word that he should have it."

Dehan's face grew rigid.

"Then I'm to understand that you—" he broke off, stifling with the pressure of his feelings.

"What, Harry?"

"I won't have him here!" he said violently. "I'll—I'll kill him if he comes."

Dick looked at him wearily.

"There are—other ways, Harry, that are more intelligent. What makes you think that Hula loves him? To me, it appeared just a childish infatuation."

"She was damn well crazy about him, as I am about her. In the same way!"

"But she mightn't be now. Be sensible. You and I can't settle this. Talk to her. If you can persuade her to marry you, I shall not stand in your way. You've been a wonderful friend to us. I shall not forget it."

Dehan stared at him.

"Edwin will fight. Tell him to stay out of it!"

"Very well. Send him to me."

Dehan departed and Edwin appeared, truculent as always, but his eyes were uneasy.

"Edwin," said Dick without preliminary, "I've sent for you to talk to you about Hula."

"I know."

"You must know," Dick spoke in Hawaiian, "that this place is heavily in debt. I'll have to sell it. I owe Harry more than I can ever repay. He's generous; he offered to wipe off the debt."

He waited to see the eagle face relent.

"Harry loves Hula, he wants to marry her."

A terrible light leaped into Edwin's eyes, but his face did not alter, save that it got very white. Dick looked away, out of the window, at the pale, polished sea. Against it Kauwikī stood grimly, as this old man had stood, always, against Hula's environment, against her family, against herself.

"Well, Edwin, have you nothing to say?"

"*Aali* (no)."

"What do you think?"

"You know."

The two words rang out like iron that is given a terrible blow.

Dick divined the fury that strangled him.

"Harry is talking to her."

"I talked to her the day the old man was buried."

Dick smiled in spite of himself.

"She loves that *haole*, I like her to marry him."

"So would I, Edwin, but he's married."

"He went home to bust up all that."

"How do you know? Did he—did Hula tell you?"

"*Aali*, I only know—inside. Bime-by he come back."

"And in the interval," Dick got up and roved restlessly

about the room, "I owe Harry more than this place is worth. He's been a good friend."

"Not a good one," interrupted Edwin, "he gave because he hoped to get."

"What do you think Hula will do, Edwin?"

"She'll do as I tell her to—wait."

"You cannot run her life, Edwin."

"I must, because she cannot."

"She's like the rest of us, eh?"

Edwin nodded without looking at Dick.

"I know, we're a set of fools, all of us!"

Edwin made no reply.

"You can go."

The man walked out, and Dick listened to the chink of his spurs; then sat down heavily at the table. After a little Hula came. Her face was pale, her eyes dilated. She gave her brother the impression of a scornful, young ghost.

"Dick, give me a cigarette."

The oddness of the request unnerved him. Hula never smoked. She seemed remote, removed from him. He handed her one.

"Dick!"

"Yes?"

"Is it true that if I don't marry Harry we'll have to sell Hana? Go away from it?"

The words seemed torn from her.

"He put it rather crudely, sweetheart."

She stood by the table, a desolate, long-legged child, loving the land greatly, as Dick himself loved it—perhaps more.

"How—how—wasn't there enough money, Dick?"

"There should have been if we'd managed more intelligently."

Miserable, harried, the man sat looking at her. There was a distracted daintiness about her as she stood hesitatingly before him, in the breeches and boots which seemed the essence of her. A thing of the forests and hills, of the green bluffs and blue sea—beautiful, pulsating.

Dick's heart smote him. How pretty she was, how pitifully young. How they had neglected her. She had grown up like a tree, Edwin her only gardener.

He felt run over by life.

"I suppose you couldn't—"

"What, Hula?"

"Oh, Dick, Dick," she burst out, "how can we go away from here! From Uncle Edwin, and the horses, and this place!" Her throat worked; then she finished, "Oh, if only Anthony were here!"

"Hula!"

Dick laid his hand on hers as she sat down in a chair and began crying.

"Do you love him, sweetheart?"

"Ever so much. Always. From the moment I met him! But I love Hana, too," she added.

Dick contemplated her. And between the two loves stood —Harry.

"I'm sorry, frightfully, that Dad and I have muffed things up so for you."

"Don't," interrupted the girl, "but I wish that he were here."

Dick knew she meant Haldane.

"I wish I could talk to him, have him hold me. I wish I could hear—know what is happening. It's been so long since he went!"

"Hula."

"Yes, Dick?"

"Did you—were you and he engaged?"

"Yes. He asked me to marry him—in the crater. Oh, Dick!" She moved from the chair to her brother's knee and clasped him fiercely. "I'd been so sad; then I was so happy! I've tried to do, to be, as he wanted me to, and like Uncle Edwin."

"Ah, Hula, I think a man would love you no matter what—"

"Dicky, you dear!"

Her lips quivered and her arms tightened.

"Isn't there—any other way?"

"For us to keep Hana?"

She nodded.

"I'm afraid not, dear."

Then he told her of Hamilton's offer.

"Anthony talked to me of that, of the ditch, when he was here."

A silence poignant with desolate thoughts hung between them.

"And, then, I promised Di that when Dad died—I'd go."

She sat very still, her arm about her brother's shoulders.

"I'm sorry, sweetheart."

"Don't!" she cried.

"What did you tell Harry?"

"That I couldn't, that I love Anthony."

Dick grew rigid. "And what did he say?"

"He didn't say anything. He was thinking."

"Do you think Tony will come back?"

Hula's eyes opened.

"He said he would."

Dick studied his sister.

"Dick?"

"Yes, sweetheart?"

"Don't you—think he will?"

"Yes, I know he will. Any man would. To you."

Hula hugged him, then went and stood by the window. A breeze, warmed with sunshine came in from the forested hills, rustling the trees and flowers of the garden, bringing their fragrances.

"It's hard to choose. You have to, though."

"Choose how, Hula?"

"Between Hana and a person you love. But you don't love her as I love Anthony, do you, Dick? Do you?"

"I do love Di—in a way," he said, as if to refute something.

"But she can't understand our loving Hana so!" protested Hula. "Why did you marry her, Dick? She doesn't make you happy."

"God knows I'm not happy. We aren't, we never can be, one."

"Anthony and I are."

"I believe, in spite of the differences in your age, that you are—or could be. Oh, what's going to become of us, Hula?"

"Let me talk to Howard when he comes."

"He'll be here in a few days."

Dick dropped his head onto his hand.

"Don't mind so, Dicky. This place can't stop being ours, because we love it so."

Dick stared at her. Did love seal things and persons to each other? Perhaps, in some obscure and profound way, it did. Love had sealed him to his father, Edwin to Hula. He could not conceive how Hana could cease being theirs. Because they loved it, because it could never mean to any one else what it meant to them.

"Well, Hula—"

"Let's go for a ride, Dicky," interposed the girl hastily. Then she smiled wistfully. "It's lucky we have lots of horses to ride or they'd be tired from this week."

CHAPTER II

"You're a fool, Harry!"

Von Erdmann flung away from Dehan in a fury of disgust.

Dehan stared resentfully at his partner. He liked Tancred, respected his ability, but felt worlds removed from him. He was a fish.

"You've got Dick nailed, and Hula, too, if you'd only use your intelligence. Let me handle this!"

"What course would you suggest?"

"I'd put the whole thing up to Dick on the basis of friendship. You've been a good friend to him, and it's his turn to be one to you. That'll get him. Hula's only a kid; she can be talked into anything, so long as there is no one else!"

He made an effective pause.

"Edwin'll fight it."

"Bah! what can he do beyond talk?"

Dehan looked thoughtful.

"Talk to Hula, Tancred. I can't; I love her too much."

"I appreciate that. I think that if you leave things to me, I can accomplish—something."

"You know, Tancred, I will!"

When Dick saw Von Erdmann he knew what was coming. He walked to meet him.

"I've a matter I want to discuss with you, Richard."

"Very well."

"I should also like to talk to Hula later."

Without preliminary Von Erdmann waded into the subject he had come to discuss.

"After all, Dick, your old man accepted Harry's help knowing that he could never repay him. Hula's young; she doesn't know her own mind. If she marries Harry, she'll love him. It's her disposition to love, and you'll have the place. Where else could either you or she be happy?"

"I don't know."

"With the debt wiped off and with reorganization, this plantation can be made to pay."

"I don't think," Dick broke in, "that it could mean the same to me if I felt that I had it at the price of Hula's happiness."

"Sentimental rot! Hula could be happy with any one. This other—is just a fancy. Have you no sense of gratitude? Can you take all and—"

"I'll pay him back everything out of what I get from Hamilton."

"But that is not the point. Harry gave you the money without wanting it back. It was foolish; but like him. He thought, and he'd a right to expect, that you would help him to get it back in another way. Through Hula."

"I appreciated that, for the first time, a year and a half ago, when we were at Waikapu. I never gave the matter a thought until then."

Dick got up. In his eyes there was a faraway look.

"No, Tancred, I guess it's on the books—that I lose this place that I love, and Harry, Hula."

"But she will not be happy away from the Islands, brought up as she has been."

So he harried Dick through the afternoon, and in the end he gained a little ground.

"Talk to her," Dick said, and he descended the steps and paced the terrace, his hands locked behind him, thinking the long, gray thoughts that come at times to every man.

"Well, Tancred, what do you want?" asked the girl resentfully, when he found her. "You've been at Dick for two hours. Now me."

She threw up her chin.

"I've come to talk to you about Harry."

"It's no use. I like Harry, but I love Anthony."

"You believe he'll come back. Credulous youth!"

Von Erdmann laughed and Hula flashed around.

"Why do you say that! Anthony *said* he'd come back. He asked me to wait."

"And it is now nearly two years!"

Amusedly the pale eyes regarded her.

"Well!"

"Surely, had he been so very ardent he could have managed to return by now. What excuses does he offer?"

Hula's face reddened, then paled. A thought flashed to the German.

"He doesn't—he hasn't written?" he asked as if he could not credit it.

"He said—he wouldn't—write—till he was free, able to marry me, that—"

The words seemed wrenched from her lips, one by one.

"He said—what?"

"That it would test my fidelity, build up my character. And Uncle Edwin said so too."

"I'd have given Edwin credit for more sense."

Hula experienced a terrified, inward fluttering. Von Erdmann wasn't trying to coerce her. He seemed almost to be talking to himself, thinking his thoughts aloud.

"Tancred."

Terror sounded in her voice.

"Yes?"

"Tancred!" Her throat moved painfully, and her fingers went to it.

"Ah, Hula"—he put his long, tallow-colored hand upon her—"you are sick?"

"No, but why did you say that—that—you'd have given Uncle Edwin credit for more sense!"

"Because, poor child, he ought to be wise to that old lie."

"Why is it a lie! What is a lie!"

"Men have said that and women have believed it since the world began. It makes a man's going easier. Time does the rest."

A chilly and dreadful sensation permeated Hula's body. Remembrance came of the conviction that had crept to her in the crater that afternoon, before Anthony spoke.

Had he, had her Anthony, told her that he loved her, that he would come back, in order that he might go the more easily? But his kisses had not been lies! But then had he not said, "A man would not be human who did not want you. You are a magnet to draw any one"?

Madness seized her. She looked about wildly.

"I—I—feel like tearing up trees and beating the ground with them! Why did you say that?"

Flaming, she turned on him.

Von Erdmann regarded her compassionately.

"It's a shame, Hula."

"It isn't; it can't be true!"

The German had a moment of compunction. How like Hula to take it so to heart.

"I'm going. I must find Uncle Edwin and ask him if what you say about men is true."

"He'll deny it, for his own ends; but I'm afraid that you'll find it to be true—in time. So long, and not a word! If I were your promised, Hula, I could not keep silence so long. It would not be possible."

"But Anthony's different!"

"All men are alike. Poor child. You are so beautiful. So young!"

"Don't! He said that!"

"When?"

"In the crater, when he told me he loved me. He talked to me afterwards. About me."

She stared back, visioning the encircling blue walls, the rare peace, Anthony. . . . Choking, she ran from Von Erdmann.

He looked after her and went his way, knowing that he had opened the gate of the Devil's Garden—doubt—for both Hula and Dick to walk in.

Edwin was on the steps of his house. The moment he saw Hula, he divined that something was amiss. She blundered up the steps and collapsed beside him.

"Uncle Edwin!"

"Ai," he said. Then warningly, "Steady, Hula."

She struggled passionately for self-control.

"He, Tancred, says, that Anthony told me he loved me, that he'd come back, to make it easier for him to get away. He says that men always do—Uncle Edwin, is it true?"

Like a cry it came from her. Edwin answered sturdily, denying it, and yet his mind halted a moment in doubt, and Hula felt it. Terror possessed her. A world, hers, seemed spinning to pieces.

"If—if— Oh, he has to come back!"

"He will come back."

With glittering eyes Edwin spoke. If Haldane had lied, it would prove the final disaster for Hula. Faith in his love, desire to prove worthy of it, had kept her feet in the narrow path that Edwin desired she should walk in. Devil of a German who had put doubt in her mind—and in his own!

"Everything is wrong!" she cried passionately.

She looked at the stables and the trees, at the road that led down to Kauwiki.

Edwin's hand tightened. Yes, everything was wrong.

"Bime-by," he began, "we see, Hula—" But he could not go on.

Their hands locked.

"In two days Howard will come," it was an inspiration—"and I'll ask him if your *haole* is coming back, for make that ditch."

As always, when inner pressure grew too great, Edwin lapsed in his speech.

Hula shivered violently. Two whole days of waiting, of agony, before her.

"Let's walk around, Uncle Edwin."

So they made the old tour of the stables and corrals, hand in hand, silent, depressed. They ended at the stables, lingering in the quadrangle, going to kennels and stalls.

Silver Wings thrust out an inquiring head, and Hula caressed it, her hands lingering upon the velvety softness of his muzzle and the bony and noble swell of his jaw. Her eyes ran down the long line of thoroughbred heads. Edwin put his arm across the girl's shoulders. Neither could utter the thoughts that strained in them. Then Hula cried as she had cried to Von Erdmann that afternoon:

"I—I feel like tearing up trees and beating the ground with them!"

"*Homanawanui* (Hang on and make the best of it)," he said. "We will go to Kaupo to-morrow and into the crater. When we get back Howard will be here and we shall know."

Before Howard came, Di arrived.

"I landed at Kahului and rode overland," she explained brightly. "I knew you would need me."

"Good of you, Di. That's a long ride. What did you do with the kid?"

Dick kissed her.

She looked sharply at him.

"I left him with friends of mine in Honolulu. You don't look well, Dick. Your poor Father! But it was to be expected. The thing you need now is to get away, to new scenes, to new people."

Her hand pressed his encouragingly.

"Yes," Dick agreed. So Di had not forgotten; she was set upon going. He looked about him at the rooms and the garden.

"Let's go in; you must be tired from your ride."

"Tell me everything, Dick. I wish that I might have been with you."

"I can't very well, Di. You'll have to excuse me. Ah Sam, bring tea."

They sat down in the *lanai*, looking at each other. Then the woman gazed about her, slowly, as if she were weighing something in her mind.

"Have you made any tentative plans yet, Dick, for the future?"

"Howard's offered to buy this place at a very good figure."

Diana looked at him.

"But you don't want to sell it?" There was reminding, there was reproach, in her voice.

"I haven't a choice," Dick said, as if he had fought with the knowledge many times.

"I know it will be hard, Dick, for you and Hula to leave. But in the end it'll be the best thing that could happen for you both—for us all."

The woman could not conceal the gladness in her voice, and Dick knew that his wife felt freed from the life she had hated. She had lived almost entirely in Honolulu since Little Billy came, pleading to Dick and to the world that the climate of Hana did not agree with the child. The lie served as well as any other.

"I can't think, can't realize, yet, but things will get done, in a while. I can't picture going away and not coming back. I wonder sometimes if Hula will go."

"She will have to; she can't stay."

"No one can count on what she, or any of us for that matter, will do."

Diana looked at him sharply, fear clutching her heart. Had he been drinking? His tired face, his dead eyes, reassured her, but she asked:

"You've kept your promise, Dick?"

"With one lapse, the day Dad was buried. I took a drink when I got back."

"That's excused, Dick," but there was an edge to her voice as though she resented and blamed Hana. The man sat, looking about him, sick to his soul, loving the place with a great passion that this woman could not comprehend. A thousand thongs of memory bound it into his being.

"Howard's price will enable you to square your debts?"

Dick nodded. "And it will leave sufficient to invest in bonds to bring us a moderate income."

"Oh, Dick!" Di went to him. "Oh, husband, aren't you happy to be clear of it! I feel as if our life—together—had begun. This," she gestured about her, "has always stood between us, a barrier that no amount of love could surmount or break."

Dick put his arm about her dutifully.

"I'm afraid, my dear, that you'll have to be very patient with me. I love Hana; I shall always remember and regret it. I would give anything to be able to keep it, if just to come back to once in a while. I can't imagine it—without us—"

"It'll be hard," said the woman, endeavoring to encourage and console, and Dick was given the impression that he was a weak, wayward child being petted into compliance with an elder's wiser wishes. He smiled. Diana need not concern herself. He would have to go. Hula would never marry Harry, and, even if she did, Di would never consent to his staying on. He had given her his word; in decency he must stand by it. He felt as if he were a spectator of life, no longer a glad participant. He wished suddenly for Helen. For her arms, for her understanding. She would have appreciated the desolation that filled him; she would have comprehended all Hana meant to him. She had led a life similar to his—and been despoiled of it.

Howard arrived the following day. Dick was glad he had not brought Mitchell. It would have been distasteful to have had that promoter in his home at such a time. Howard was fine. He did not jar. No reference was made to his father, but Dick felt the compassion transmitted to him by Howard's hand-clasp.

"I got your letter," Dick said as they drove to the house. "Did you have a smooth trip?"

"Excellent. I hope you excused and understood my writing so soon."

"I do. I did."

The man looked away, and Dick was conscious of the passionate impulse of his mind toward the green wetness of the hills. From himself a dream was going; for Howard one was being fulfilled—after a lifetime of waiting. He could not hate him, could not even resent him. He understood how one could love and want to possess—that up there. His eyes went to the folded forest ridges, soft in the afternoon light.

"I've cabled for Haldane," said Hamilton, as they drove past the mill.

"Where is he?"

"In England. I've kept in touch with him. He's a brilliant man."

"Hula will be glad!" the thought leaped into Dick's mind.

"He said, when he left," Howard spoke in his level voice,

"that he'd come back to do the work for me. It'll take some time for him to get here."

Dick got the unspoken thought, that Hamilton did not want him to feel that he was being rushed out.

Di greeted him graciously. This man was instrumental in freeing her from Hana. She was overnice, and Dick winced. Howard, even as he sat talking with assurance and ease, was conscious of the awful quietness of the house, although the Lightfoots and Fitzmaurice dropped in. The spirit that animated it had gone. The light had been put out.

After tea Hula came. Some expression in her face gave him a curious inner stab. Lovely changed child! She watched him as if she expected something to come from him. Did she know that he had come to buy Hana?

When the company began to disperse, she lingered, and he, feeling the command of her mind, waited also.

"You're taller, Hula, and thinner than when last I saw you," he said, walking over to where she sat on the railing. "This has been hard on you I'm afraid."

"Is Anthony coming back?" she asked, without answering his question. How the great dark eyes watched his gray lips, waiting for the words to come! The man experienced an odd pang. This beautiful orchid-like creature loved Haldane. Fortunate and unfortunate fellow.

He heard the desperate exhalation of a held breath, as of one in agony.

"Yes, Hula. I've cabled for him."

"Did he answer?" the words came with difficulty.

"Yes. I got word yesterday that he would come as soon as he was able."

The girl stood tense and said, "Thank you, Howard," as if she were thinking of something else. Then she shivered violently and burst into tears.

Hamilton was nonplussed. He put his cold hand on her shoulder and felt the quivering of her whole body.

"Hula, my dear."

"Oh, Howard!" The words burst from her, and she shook her head as if she were trying desperately to free herself from something.

"What is it, Hula; tell me! Are you unhappy? Don't you want to see him again?"

"I'm so happy, so happy!" She seized him fiercely by the arms. "Have you ever been so unhappy that you couldn't breathe, couldn't move without its hurting inside? Howard, have you?"

"I don't think, Hula, that I've ever been very unhappy or very glad."

The girl laughed in a delirium of excitement and shook her head again, and Hamilton realized that it was from sorrow that she was trying to free herself. Sorrow, a thing hideous and foreign to her nature. Pain and punishment bewildered her. He knew, with the keenness of sight when it came to judging his fellow men, that Hula was not as she had been. There was a pathetic attempt toward strength, not because strength was good, but because some one she loved had required it of her. To this passionate child of the blue seas and sun, right and wrong, of themselves, did not exist. To grieve or distress those who loved her was wrong, to please and make them happy was right.

He had an impulse of affection toward her, and his hand, unused to caressing, clasped hers diffidently.

"My dear," he said compassionately, looking at her wet and beautiful eyes, "I don't know what is in your heart or Dick's, but I hope my coming will not add to your difficulties or make either of you unhappier. No doubt you know why I am here, but I don't want you to feel that I'm driving you from Hana."

How easy it was to talk to her. She stood, drinking in every word, absorbing the feelings that emanated from him; compassion, a wish to make things as little difficult as possible.

"As far as I'm concerned, Dick can keep this house and this place. I have no use for it. I want the forest land, but when the ditch is constructed, the work done, Hana itself will be of no use to me. I do want possession of all that," he moved his head toward the mountain, "but if he can arrange to keep this place no one will be happier than I."

"Oh, Howard, Howard, what a darling you are!"

She seemed to overwhelm him with the feelings that charged her. The cold hand of sorrow was taken from her.

Dick came into the *lanai.*

"Well," he smiled from the distance of his grief, "what's the occasion for your great glee, sweetheart? Tony's return —or something too profound for my comprehension?"

"Oh, Dicky, Anthony's coming back and we don't have to go!"

Dick looked inquiringly at Hamilton. He smiled, oddly.

"I've just explained to Hula that, as far as I am con-concerned, you can retain possession of the immediate place. I'll have no use for it, and it can never mean to any one what it means to you both."

"Do you hear, Dicky! I don't have to marry Harry, or anything!"

Hamilton looked away. So that had been pressed on her. Had she been less faithful . . . had she loved Haldane less. . . . He grew cold. How nearly had he lost this wet land of Hana again. To Hula, indirectly, he owed possession of it. He made a mental note of a debt to be paid . . . somehow . . . some day.

Dick's face bore a peculiar expression. Gladness and despair. He spoke, but Howard knew he was keeping his heart to himself.

"Decent of you, Howard, awfully. I can't express what I feel." He choked a little, "I'll talk to you later about it. I can't now."

And he left them with Heaven knows what in his heart. To know that he might keep it, to know that he had given Di his word that he would go! Desperately, resentfully he flung across the lawn in the direction of Kauwiki.

Hula looked after him catching her breath.

"He's going—to Dad."

"Where is he buried, Hula?"

"In the graveyard, at the foot of Kauwiki, by the race-track."

CHAPTER III

"Di—"

"No! You must choose between Hana and me. There can be no compromise. If you keep it, you'll have a thousand excuses why you will have to pass the greater part of your time here. I know."

Dick looked out of the window, at the highly-colored landscape. He loved it better than he loved this woman—better than anything else. Duty bound him to his wife, affection to the soil. His silence was too eloquent of his preference; he must break it.

"But if I just—"

"Dick, you promised me!"

Bitterly she brought it out, knowing that even if he relinquished Hana outwardly, his heart was sealed to it, forever. Di was not great-souled. Vanity demanded that her husband give up this place for her; pride would have made her release him to it. Dick stood looking out of the window. To know that he might keep it, as one keeps a picture for which one has no actual use but a vast sentiment, was physical pain. It was brutal, outrageous, of Di to demand that he part with it, to hold him to his word.

Her eyes were bitter.

"You promised," she said again, accusingly.

Dick made a violent, protesting gesture.

"I know. I'd promise anything under pressure, but I keep—I've kept one promise to you."

"With a lapse."

"Have you no generosity, Di!"

"According to you I have none. Why cannot you accept the fact that this phase of your life is over!"

"Why can't we ever talk without quarreling!"

With vast exasperation Dick brought it out.

"In all likelihood you blame it on me."

"Great God, Di, what a rotten thing to say!"

He grasped the back of a chair and stared at her. After a moment he spoke:

"I don't believe, Di, that we . . . well . . . love each other very much, or we shouldn't be this way."

He looked at her as a child looks at uncomprehending parents. Hopeless. Hoping.

The woman made a sudden resentful movement.

"Does that mean you've decided to—stay?"

"No."

"Then, why such a statement?"

"Because I don't believe we do—"

Burningly his blue eyes regarded her, striving to pierce the armor with which she encased herself. He knew he had never broken through it. Even if he left Hana for her, he would get no closer to her. Her soul was still in a formative process. Must he sacrifice everything to further its development? Would he not, rather, retard it? She was his wife, the mother of his son, but stranger, less known to him than a chance acquaintance.

His marriage had been the supreme blunder of his life. From it he could reap nothing. Their minds and souls were compounded of materials that could never fuse. Must he, because the world expected loyalty from him, sacrifice everything that he held dear? Di would accept the sacrifice without ever appreciating it. Claws seemed to clutch and tear him. The passionate impulse of every human being toward happiness reared within him like a protesting horse. He drove the spurs of his mind into its ribs to bring it down. To earth; to reason, but it balked; it reared; it shied backwards.

Diana waited for his final surrender, hating with a new hatred the place that had forged such fetters about her husband's soul. There was a sort of love between her and this man but not all the love of which either of them was capable. She was happier far, leading her own life away from him, playing to her own chosen circle. She never could be in harmony with him. But she must make him concede an outward victory to save her own vanity, vanity which she mistook for pride. . . .

So they wrestled with each other for days until Dick finally yielded.

"I'll go, Di, I pledge you my word, but don't try to hurry me. I shall stay on until the last possible moment!" And savagely he had gone out to rove among the things of the past, staring at the gardens with desolate eyes, avoiding the stables. And Edwin walked grimly through the days, and Hula rode, dreaming, on the green bluffs that fronted the sea.

One afternoon, as she sat with clasped knees facing the

guava-scented wind, Harry rode up and, dismounting, sat down beside her. Turning, she smiled at him.

"Hula," he said, "isn't there anything I can do to make you marry me? I've been crazy about you ever since you were a kid. I can't sleep, I can't eat for thinking of you."

"Poor Harry!"

"You'd have married me if that—"

"Don't swear at Anthony or I'll go."

"All right."

Burning, his eyes regarded her. His spicy, his crimson carnation. He longed to grasp her, to kiss her. A convulsive shudder passed through him. From being burning hot his skin grew clammy and cold. Hula placed a consoling little hand upon his arm. Bending over he kissed it violently.

"I can't, I won't believe that I won't have you some day. You are mine. You always have been. It's not fair!"

"I wish I were twins, Harry, so you could have one of me," said Hula pityingly. "I hate it that you are unhappy, Harry, because I am so glad."

The lark's note trilled in her throat. Lighted from within she looked at him wishing that she might give him some of her joy, she who had so much. He divined it, and, like a worn-out child, he put his head upon her knee and began to sob, as Hula herself would have sobbed in like circumstances.

"Harry, don't," she cried, her hand falling upon his glossy black head.

"I love you," he gasped, sitting up, his body still convulsed by his grief. His wild black eyes roved over the land, moving from the recklessly flung hills above him to the forests and fesh flowing sea. Then he looked back to Hula.

"I'd do anything; I'd take you anyway!" he cried, pushing his fingers through his hair.

"He doesn't love you as I do," he burst out. "He's cold, he doesn't know how!"

"He loves me—more."

"I wouldn't love you and stay away."

Hula looked at him speculatively.

"But he had to, to get divorced. I wish Dick would."

"Dick's a dog!"

"Why?" she flashed.

"He's double-crossed me twice. I had prior claim to his land; I lent him more than its original value, because of you!"

"But he'll pay you back."

"I didn't want the money, Hula, and he knew it. So did your Dad. And I didn't want Hana. I wanted you!"

He seized her and kissed her, her eyes, her lips, her warm neck. She felt the throbbing of his heart. It frightened her and set her own heart going as furiously.

"Harry, let me go!"

He paid no heed to her.

"Harry—Harry—"

"Hula!"

It was torn from him. He knew he could have had her, had it not been for Haldane. Somehow, still, he would possess her, despite Haldane, despite Edwin. . . .

"Wait, Hula, I want to talk to you."

"Let me go and I'll listen."

"No, I want to talk to you while you're held in my arms."

The girl looked up at him, thrusting him a little from her in order that she might see his face. Compassion made her tender. Harry was feeling as she had felt when she thought Anthony loved Mrs. Bane. As lonely. As forsaken.

"Listen, Hula. If you ever find out that he doesn't love you as much as I do, will you marry me? If he comes back still married or—"

"But he won't! He said he'd come back free, so he could marry me."

Conviction, doubt, mingled in her voice. Dehan continued to hold her. He felt eased, just to have her in his arms, even while her mind clung to this other man, Haldane. . . . He thought quickly and clearly. It was best to remain friends with Hula; then he could be with her, near her. There was no telling what closed door might suddenly open to snap her into his arms. As one cannot relinquish a long-cherished dream, even when it's over, so Dehan could not realize that he would not have Hula still.

Then he released her. She was disturbed and distressed.

"I wish you didn't mind so much, Harry."

"But I do!"

"I'm ever so sorry, Harry. Everything is wrong for you and for Dick. Only I am all right." She said it with exultation and regret.

"I wish we could turn everything back to where it was before—"

"Before Anthony came?"

"No, to when he was here. I'm so afraid that it won't—ever be just as it was."

"It can't be."

"No. Daddy's gone and—" Her voice quivered. "Let's ride, Harry, hard!"

They threw their legs across their saddles and galloped madly. The long lavender road smoked under their horses' hoofs; the wind snatched at their faces. A heady intoxication assailed them, born of speed and the reckless green ridges that rushed toward them and fell behind them, one after the other, unendingly, with a magnificent rhythm.

Dick wondered what had happened when he saw them ride in together. Thoughts were moving in Harry's black eyes. Edwin saw them as well as Dick. What mischief was the dog plotting? He called Hula aside.

"*Pehea?*" he questioned.

Hula started. She had been thinking of Anthony, coming so soon.

"Nothing, Uncle Edwin," she answered.

"Why have you been riding with Harry?"

"He came when I was sitting on the bluffs."

"You must not ride with him, Hula."

"Why?"

The old fellow looked at her. "Because," he said slowly, "because, being the kind of man that he is, some day his love will get too strong and he'll take you."

Edwin did not mince his words, and he looked straight into Hula's eyes. She was curiously affected.

"But he couldn't. I wouldn't let him."

"He is stronger than you are."

Edwin's face was terrible. Anxiety ate him. Haldane was on his way. He had pledged himself to Howard's ditch, but how would he come! He felt as furious, as frustrated, as a mountain bull when the cowboy's ropes hold it helpless. He could do nothing except wait, and waiting was torture to his vigorous soul. If Haldane came back free, all would be well, Hana disposed of, Hula placed in safe hands. His work would be done. He could linger a while until the construction of the ditch ended, releasing Haldane to his own land; then he would return to Waimea to finish out his days, satisfied, and with the memory of the years to solace him and the knowledge that Hula was in the right hands.

"Remember what I tell you, Hula; I know."

"You always know, Uncle Edwin."

"Yes, I know what is good for you."

That night after dinner Hamilton called Dick aside.

"What have you decided about keeping this place? I have to go to Honolulu for a few days, though I'll return when Haldane comes over. I want to settle things, arrange the papers."

"I've decided—that it's best—to let it—go—"

One look at Dick's face sufficed, for Hamilton to know that the choice was not his. Compassion filled him. Dick might be weak, but he was a man of his word.

"I'm sorry. Very. But you know best. Stay as long as you want. You are tired. If there is anything I can do to assist you—in advising—how best to invest—"

So Hamilton fumbled with his words, trying to express the fine sentiments that moved him: compassion, a desire to assist this man whose misfortune had proved his good fortune.

Dick could not speak.

Hamilton took a turn down the room, looking about him. Pictures everywhere; of horses. They hedged him around. Here. There. It would hurt Dick to part with them. In what way would he do it? They were beautiful but useless, unfit for work as were the Calhouns. He looked at Dick worriedly. He might go to pieces, unexpectedly, horribly. He was still stunned, moving like one in a nightmare. It would be a relief to have Haldane come to start work. Perhaps there might be something for Dick to do in connection with the ditch. Hamilton smiled, remembering the sentiments he expressed to Haldane that first day. But he felt in some obscure way responsible for Dick, as Haldane had felt responsible for Hula.

CHAPTER IV

"Oh, 'delirious *Ke Ala Ka*, sweetest to my Heart!'" teased Dick, putting his arm about Hula's neck. "I suppose the ship's sunk a thousand times, in your imagination, between Honolulu and here, since we got word that they're on board."

"No," said Hula, "but I can't breathe. I feel full inside, as I do before a big race."

"I know."

He looked at her and wondered what fate was lurking for her. He felt relieved yet uneasy. Glad that Haldane was at last coming, wondering how he would come. He felt that it was a bit shabby of him never to have written or sent her a word. Faithfulness such as she gave was almost beyond what any man deserved. But her believing youth did not question. Her faith had not, as yet, been shattered by too much contact with life. She was a flower and a flame. It would be ghastly were she ever to be spoiled. But beautiful things usually were. He felt it with a sort of hard bitterness.

When the hour came for the boat to arrive they went down and stood together, with locked hands, on the wharf. Edwin had come with them, then suddenly ridden away. Dick was conscious of the hammering of his heart. He glanced at Hula. A fine moisture showed on her lip and brow. She moved, looking at him with a smile; but the pupils of her eyes were dilated.

The boat came across the gold-sparkled, blue bay, shadowed by Kauwiki.

Haldane stood up in the bows with Hamilton. Two big men coming to do big things! Dick's eyes strained for a closer sight of Haldane's face. Its expression would mean everything.

Hula's fingers tightened.

"Dick!" she said and moistened her dry lips.

"Hold your horses, sweetheart."

What torture waiting was! To know anything, even the worst, was preferable to not knowing. Then he saw a woman, sitting in the bows, near Haldane. Instantly by intuition he knew it was Haldane's wife.

In that moment he could have shot him.

Hula knew too. Her face grew ashen and she shut her eyes.

"I think—I'll go, Dicky."

"Stay, Hula. Be a thoroughbred."

Her throat moved and he feared she might faint, but she rallied herself. He looked at Haldane. His eyes were miserable. Something flashed from him to Dick, and he knew instinctively that his wife's presence was as much of a surprise to Haldane as it was to Hula. He looked dashed, appalled.

"Hula," he said, "keep up the flag. She's with him—against his will. I know it."

"Oh Dick—"

"He loves you still."

"Is she—beautiful?"

"Oh, Hula, not like you. There isn't any one on earth—"

Passionate gratitude flashed into her face.

"Dicky, I love you!"

"Hula, he's in hell!"

Side by side they stood, both bereft; Dick of his land, Hula of the man she loved. Then Dick said:

"Buck up, sweetheart. The worst is yet to come—for us both."

And he laughed as if he defied the fates that had been so deadly unkind.

The boat bumped the wharf; Haldane's eyes leaped to Hula's. Dick pitied him. For any man to know that he might have had Hula, and to be so tied! He looked at the woman. Haldane had displayed as colossal a folly in his selection of a mate when he married, as he himself had when he chose Diana. This one was blonde, carefully preserved, correctly and modishly appareled. Brainless yet calculating. Shallow. Suspecting. Her eyes were fixed on Hula. She glanced at her husband mockingly. So there was more. . . . Dick knew a fierce gladness that his little sister was so beautiful. There was nothing garbed in woman's flesh that could touch her.

The passengers scrambled up the rough wooden steps and Dick greeted them; then Hula, with the aloofness of a child. Brooding, her eyes hung on Haldane's. Their hands locked and burned. His unhappy, harassed eyes met hers. "Make an opportunity. Promise. I can explain. Her coming isn't my doing." There was no time for more but Hula experienced a choking sensation. He loved her more than he had when he went away. He was still, more than ever, her Anthony!

Her pale cheeks became like two crimson roses. She laughed excitedly as she greeted Howard, and the spurs on her little heels sang a song as she moved.

"How do you do—oh, I was going to say, 'Mrs. Anthony,' " and she laughed— "Mrs. Haldane. You look as though you'd been seasick. Did you have a rough trip?"

"I'm afraid Mrs. Haldane did have a rather miserable passage," said Hamilton when the woman did not answer.

"I feel quite well, now, thank you." She seemed to recollect herself and become aware of Hula.

Then her eyes went to the little rough wharf, the dusty road and ranked hills, the frowning bulk of Kauwiki. A shudder passed through her. What an awful, what a God-forsaken spot. It daunted her. Some of her triumph seemed to dissipate. Haldane fell back with Hula. "I didn't know she was on board, Hula," he glanced back at the ship with a sort of horror. "It about bowled me over."

She looked up adoringly.

They made their way to the carriage. The depression that had filled Haldane so long began to dissipate. Exhilaration pricked through his veins. What spell did this place exert upon him? Everything was wrong, impossible, and yet—now he was back—the old feeling returned. Anything, absolutely anything, seemed possible . . . here.

At the house, Di greeted them. A faint shock went through

her at meeting Mrs. Haldane. She glanced apprehensively at Hula. The child seemed curiously excited in a suppressed way. After a few moments, she departed stablewards. Haldane looked after her, not caring if his wife saw. She did see and sat looking at him scoffingly.

So this was the girl. She set her lips. Never! Never! Never!

Edwin was waiting. Laughing, crying, Hula went into his arms.

"His wife is with him, but he loves me!"

"What!" cried the old man, his fierce brows swooping down over his eyes. "What you say?"

"She's with him, but he loves me! I was so afraid that he wouldn't any more—love me! But he does. He's mine. My Anthony!"

She clung to him, inhaling the dust of his *palaka* joyously. Everything was beautiful—even dust!

Edwin removed his hat and rubbed his brow.

"That's bad, Hula. It will mean trouble."

"I don't care. He's back, and he loves me!"

"Could a man help it," was Edwin's thought, but he said only, "I wonder what will come?"

"I don't know. I don't care. Let's go for a ride. I must gallop."

When they returned dark had come, with a great smothering rush as it does in the tropics, blotting out everything: the wild outline of the mountain and the deep-sounding sea. In the house, lamps were lighted. Hula went in. Dinner was long since over.

Haldane heard her spurs. He moved in his chair uneasily, hoping that she would come. He heard her voice in the kitchen at intervals, between the chink of dishes being washed. Oh, Hula! Hula! His heart cried to her. She must come, else he would get up and go to her. He was conscious of his wife watching him.

After a while she came, through the great living room with its souvenirs of the gallant past, bringing with her something of the wind and the hills and clean spaces outside, her face flushed from riding or with love. Haldane's hands grew cold on the arms of his chair; his eyes strove to penetrate what was within. She called to him carelessly and sat down, stretching out her legs before her. How at ease she looked; how collected! And he was choking; in torment. Let Margaret watch them with mocking eyes. She had never meant to him what Hula did; there was not enough to her. Memory came to him of the night in the crater. Beautiful, enchanting, enchanted, asking all, all from him, but giving all in return . . . Hula . . . Hula . . .

"This place will be a veritable hive, humming," he heard Diana's voice, "when things get under way." She looked at Margaret, smiling, brightly gay. "It's been such a Sleepy Hollow."

Haldane had a desire to laugh but restrained it. How that speech revealed her and how like Margaret to sit, staring at Hula. Two of a sort. Hana a Sleepy Hollow! Mirth shook him. How life had rushed forward there, like a great river in flood!

Hula sat talking, in that gently spurning manner she had when with people she disliked or distrusted. She looked at Margaret in the same way that she had looked at Mrs. Bane, only there was something subtly triumphant in her expression.

She knew how he felt. Without telling, she knew, and, feeling his mind upon her, Hula looked at him and smiled, and Haldane was given the impression that she walked toward him with opened arms.

Next morning Haldane rose early.

He saw Hula in the quadrangle and knew she was waiting for him. Edwin, who was with her, turned his back and walked away. Haldane could not blame the old man for hating him. His position was false enough to all appearances. But Hula waited.

He hastened up to her and took her hand.

"Why didn't you let me talk to you last night, Hula?"

She smiled up at him.

"I must explain about Margaret."

"Oh, Anthony, don't look so unhappy!"

Miserably he looked at her, at the stables, the horses. All this would go. Hula clung to his hand, her eyes upon his face, adoringly.

"Come into Silver Wings' box and kiss me!"

He moved as though to rid himself of a thought. Hula made an inarticulate sound and thrust his hand away.

"It hurts—inside," she said unsteadily. "Oh, Anthony."

"Dear, don't think I don't want to!"

"What then?"

"Oh, it isn't possible that you can understand, Hula. Damn—everything!"

He flung himself aside, and Hula laid her hand on his arm.

"I can understand. I know you love me. I can feel it."

"Wonderful. Oh, sweetheart," he grasped her shoulders, "I haven't, I won't give you up. I love you, with all of me. I'm yours and I have been wholly yours, since that night in the crater."

"Oh, Anthony," her voice vibrated. She looked like a creature enchanted.

His face gradually became suffused with blood.

"Come into Silver Wings' stall. I shall choke if I don't kiss you!"

"My Hula!"

They held each other convulsively. Momentarily the

world was shut out. Softly the great horse nosed in his manger, and outside a cricket chirruped in the sun.

"Oh, Hula, Hula, how I've longed for you! For this, to have you in my arms again. Can you believe me if I tell you that I didn't know . . . hadn't anything to do with Margaret's coming?"

"Of course, Anthony."

"Bless you, sweet!" There was no doubt in her face, only expectancy.

"But hurry, Anthony, and tell me, I can't get my breath."

He kissed her.

"When I left you and was back in England I went and saw Margaret. She agreed, finally, to a divorce. I made over practically everything to her. Proceedings were started, but such things take a long time in England, Hula. Three months ago Howard cabled telling me about your father and asking me to come back to undertake the engineering of the ditch—" he broke off. "I hated to come to you, to leave before I had my final decree but he was very insistent that I come immediately."

Hula nodded. "Go on."

"I saw Margaret and told her. You don't know her. She suspects me always . . . everyone . . . but me in particular. But she seemed reasonable for once and I was able to leave after a little delay. Hamilton followed up his cable with a letter, giving a rough estimate of what the ditch would be worth in a few years, millions and millions, and he said in addition to my salary I was to have a block of the shares. I left before it arrived and it was forwarded to Margaret by mistake. She stopped the divorce proceedings and caught the next boat for Honolulu. I arrived there last Monday but I had to wait until Friday to get the *Klaukina* here. Another boat arrived from England on Wednesday. Margaret was on it. She's clever. She did not let me know of her arrival until we were both on the boat coming here. Hula, I wonder if you can imagine what I felt when I saw her—I guessed, easily enough, something of what had happened and when I talked to Howard he confirmed my suspicions and told me the contents of his letter. . . . And now she's seen you . . . ."

He broke off.

"Do you think she will stay?"

"I know she will!" he said savagely. "She's avaricious. If I gave her sufficient, I might buy her off, but her vanity—she has no pride—will never let her, now, lose me to you. She's never loved me. . . ."

"But how can she stay when she knows you don't want her?"

"I don't know, sweetheart."

"I wouldn't."

"I know that—nor would I. Sometime, somehow, it'll come right and I'll marry you, Hula. I shan't hesitate; the world can think what it will of me."

"I'll think you a darling!"

Edwin, passing the stall and hearing, was somewhat mollified; but his eyes were still angry when they came out, their faces lighted by the divine fire that burned in them. They did not even see him, so intent were they upon each other. He stood, with arms locked across his chest, as if to keep the emotions he felt from splitting his ribs. Apprehensions strained in him. Harry! Hula! This man's prideless and damnable wife. How would it end, how could it, save in some tragic or horrible way?

He lingered among the horses, scheming to devise some safe method of procedure. The next months would see some tremendous living and he knew depressingly that he could be only a spectator. In this Englishman's hands lay Hula's heart.

Anthony was trustworthy; before anything he would think of Hula, and therefore, somehow, he must have her. But he was slow to act.

Suddenly the old *paniola* knew that he and this man were one, in that they both felt and knew the same thing.

He jammed his hat over one eye.

Ahead was destiny, which waits for no one, which takes heed of no man. Strange, mystic, often terrible, waiting for Harry and Hula, for Dick and Haldane!

CHAPTER V

Weeks passed. A road was torn through the forest up to the level where the ditch was to be run. A line was surveyed; camps constructed along it. Workmen were brought and installed. Hana, almost overnight, became a small but busy metropolis. Haldane spent days and weeks on the mountain, in the forests and hills, penetrating them, surveying them, probing them. He came in occasionally, caked with mud, lean-flanked and lean-faced. Machinery was imported and taken with great labor up the wide road that straggled through the forests. Edwin and Hula rode from dawn to dusk, collecting cattle from the bluffs and out of the woods.

It was the breaking up, the beginning of the end.

Harry bided his time. Haldane had come back, but with a wife. The thought was mead to him. No matter what the conditions under which she was with him, her presence was a fact. So long as she remained and refused to release Haldane, there was a chance that he might get Hula. Von Erdmann watched enviously the tremendous marshaling of men and the arrangement of work. Why had he never visioned the vast possibility of this thing? Why had he not seen that

Haleakala was a titanic water-shed that could be harnessed to man's use?

Hamilton, Mitchell and others who bulked large in Island affairs came and went constantly from Honolulu to Hana. Haldane came in occasionally for a week-end and departed, after twenty-four hours, more jaded still. Hamilton, up from Honolulu, saw it and was worried.

"Look here," he protested, "you're working too hard. Ease up a little. I can't afford to have you go under."

"I shan't."

"You don't look well. It isn't good business to overdo."

"It isn't my work. I love it."

Hamilton lighted a cigar and changed the subject.

"How's Dick making out?"

"Well. He handles men ably and seems interested in the work."

"I'm glad. I shall go up with you to-morrow."

"May I go, too, Anthony?" asked Hula, joining them where they stood on the *lanai*. "Would you mind, Howard, if I did?"

"Certainly not, Hula. I should like you to see the work."

"I've never been up," said the girl.

"Time you went then, young lady."

"You mightn't like it, Hula," said Haldane.

"Are you thinking of what I said that day on the hill?"

"Yes."

"You remember?"

"I think I remember everything you ever said to me, Hula."

Howard looked at them and moved away. He, like Edwin, felt apprehensive. Things were going too smoothly. From what quarter would trouble pounce upon them?

"Anthony, walk with me a while."

They paced the terrace that Haldane had paced with Helen.

"Your wife can't ride, can she?"

"No, Hula. Why?"

"Then I shall come to see you up there."

Haldane's heart stopped like a rudely checked horse. He glanced involuntarily toward the house.

"Oh, why do your thoughts always go to her!"

"Habit, I suppose."

"You're afraid of her!"

"Not exactly, but you cannot understand, not being married, how she has it in her power to make it utterly hateful—for every one."

"She can't for me. It's only people I love who can hurt me. She knows it, too; for she has never tried to talk to me, though she knows. Don't look so unhappy, Anthony. It's so unflattering to me. Smile! Darling! Darling! Darling! To-morrow I'm going to ride up with you to your ditch." She gave him a curious, long look. "And I'm going from the house so that she'll know I'm with you."

Next day, at dawn, they left; Hula and Hamilton, Haldane and Dick and a small group of men from Honolulu. Up through the torn forest, where uprooted bananas flapped miserably and trees lay prostrate over their fellows. The horses' hoofs sucked the deep mud. Up and up the wet road wound through the so-long-inviolate hills, its sides piled with lumber for camps, with machinery, with supplies of every sort, while the bedraggled forest that edged it looked on in a desolate, uncomprehending way. Up and down it, long trains of men and animals toiled.

About noon they reached the ditch line, and Hula halted her horse and dismounted. Her eyes followed the long red winding of its way. Already miles of it had been accomplished. Cleanly cut, deep, it went determinedly forward. There it bent around a bluff to vanish and reappear, diminished by distance, girdling a green ridge. It plunged into mountain spurs and emerged, its sides slathered with earth and uprooted trees. Ferns and bamboo lay crushed under the dirt thrown upon them; gnome-like workmen swarmed in and out of it with plying shovels. Hideous, mushroom-like camps thrust up out of the chaos of uprooted spots in the forest, the uncouth growth of a day or night of work. And still the ditch nosed forward like a vast red earthworm, uprooting everything that came in its path, burrowing through the portions of the mountain which it could not go around.

Hula sighed a forlorn little sigh, and her eyes went to the gracious ridges and blue distances of Haleakala, then to the fall of the woods, below the ditch line to the sea. Her ears strained for the familiar bird notes of the forest. She knew each cry or whistle, of red *iwiwis* and green *amakihis*, of *apapanas* and parrakeets. Gone, all of them, to their last fastness, the mountain top.

"I suppose it's all very fine, Anthony," she said, stamping her foot into a deep pile of earth, newly turned out of the ditch, still smelling of the ferns and trees that had grown in it. "You are a marvelous engineer and Howard will be a millionaire, but it makes me feel lonely."

She raised her face to his, and he appreciated how this violation of the forests and hills, claimed at last by progress and civilization, must hurt.

"I was afraid, Hula, that you wouldn't like it."

"But Uncle Edwin and I can see it from below, when we collect cattle—the red rents in the green, the broken hills. We see it winding along."

"It doesn't make you hate me, sweetheart, as the destroyer of your lovely green land?"

Sadly he asked it, and Hula knew the depression that filled him—for everything.

She slid a fierce little arm about his lean waist, uncaring who might see.

"I couldn't hate you, Anthony, no matter what you might do. It's your job to build ditches, even if it has to spoil my forests that I've loved, that I've chased wild cattle in, and listened to birds in. . . . What's that great thing, tearing at that ridge?"

"A steam shovel."

"It looks like a hungry biting mouth, with great teeth, eating it. See the earth running out of its jaws." She turned from it. "Where do you stay? Where's your house?"

"Four miles along, at the edge of a gulch where we are tunneling."

"Let's go to it."

She looked back at Hamilton and Dick, conferring on some phase of the work.

"Dick looks funny with dirt on his riding boots. It doesn't look funny on you."

Haldane laughed. "I don't know whether to take that as a compliment or not, kid."

"You haven't called me that for ever so long."

"It seems jolly to have you up here. You may not believe me, but it's hurt me, seeing the peace of these hills brought to an end. I keep thinking of how these changes must affect you. If I only were free, if only I might keep you with me!"

"Sometimes I do feel a bit sad, not hearing the mill, seeing the empty flumes and cane cars, knowing it's *pau*—forever! The race-horses and good times."

"What is Dick going to do with them?"

"I don't know. He doesn't say, but he thinks about them a lot, when he goes down to Hana. They *eat* so much and he can't bear to cut down on them. They've always had all they wanted. You see you must cram feed into a young thoroughbred to develop it, else it grows into a weed, with no stamina."

She looked away, and the man's hand closed over hers. "Oh, Hula!"

"It's *pau,* but we—we can't realize it."

Hula blinked the tears resentfully from her lashes.

"Take me to your house, Anthony, quickly; so I won't think about it."

"All right, sweetheart. Just wait a minute; I must talk to Hamilton's guests."

When he returned they set off, riding along a trail beaten along the edge of the ditch by constantly passing feet. They scrambled over earth piles; slid down cuts; avoided newly felled trees. The horses leaped convulsively through bogs and splashed among the boulders of thundering streams that crossed the line, crystal-clear above the ditch, muddied below. Raging, protesting they hurried from the scene of upheaval, seeking to escape the forces that would one day harness them, and far below Hula could see the stain that the hurrying waters carried down to the sea, spoiling its blue.

"The others are coming to lunch at your house?" she asked as they dismounted in front of a small building roughly put up and roofed with galvanized iron.

"Yes."

"It looks an awfully little house for a big man," and she laughed.

"There isn't any sense in having a larger one, for the men have to keep moving it forward as the work progresses. I have to be at the head of the construction."

"I always forget how smart you are, Anthony, a great engineer; I only remember that I love you."

"That's all I want you to do, sweet. Love me!"

He took her violently, possessively, into his arms. Hula throbbed like a held bird, but her eyes glazed and her strong arms clung. About them the hot forests steamed and the distant, satin-traced sea dreamed under the sun.

"Oh, Hula, I love and I love you!"

"Darling! Darling! Darling!"

"Oh, Hula, I want you!"

"My Anthony! I am yours."

With burning faces close-pressed, and hands tightly holding, they stood, disordered hearts pounding.

"Wait," said Hula, pushing him away.

"Did I hold you too hard?"

"No, but I can't stand it—your wanting me so! I'll—I'll stay up here with you."

"I wish to God that you might, but I love you too much to let you do it. When I have you, it must be forever, not just sometimes or for a little while."

"What if your wife will never give you up or die! Oh, Anthony," it was a cry, "why don't you divorce her!"

"I can't without employing methods—"

"I don't think you love me very much."

"Hula!"

"There isn't anything I wouldn't do to get to a person I loved or away from one that I hated!"

"Dear child, it would be a chaotic world if every one—"

"I wonder if it wouldn't be better."

"In what way, Hula dear?"

"It would be truer. You wouldn't be living with Margaret, not wanting her, or Dick with Di, trying to please her. He used to be merry and gay, not caring about to-morrow, enjoying to-day."

"It wouldn't do, Hula."

"But it doesn't do anyhow, Anthony!"

"True, O Queen!" laughed the man. "Now come inside and see the palace you should be sharing with me."

Hula smiled and entered. She looked at the clean, bare floor, at the shelf of books, at the narrow, blanket-piled army cot drawn up to a long table made of Nor'west planks.

"What do you do in the evenings?"

"Work—and think about you."

"In here?"

"Everywhere. I think of you when I'm directing the work, when I'm surveying—"

"And I of you."

"Oh, Hula, what is to become of us!"

The child gave him a deep look, then said:

"Your cook is coming to make lunch, and I see Howard and the others riding along the ditch. Kiss me, Anthony, before they get here. Ever such a long one."

"Well, sweetheart," said Dick cheerily as he dismounted, "what do you think of it all?"

Hula studied him. He seemed different up here, more like the Dick of old, not as he was with Di or wandering miserably about Hana. And Howard Hamilton, glancing at him, was glad that he had made it possible for Dick to stay a while longer. Glad—for Howard was big—to feel that he had rather misestimated the caliber of the Calhouns. He appreciated in an inarticulate way that Dick loved the ditch. It prolonged his stay at Hana. He laughed at the money he earned; he had gambled and betted away many times its amount in a night of poker or the few moments of a race, but he was pleased with it in a boy's way. Dick, like his father, would always be young hearted. He had a boy's enthusiasms and a boy's despairs. Up here in the golden-green forests on the mountain's high flank, he felt freed, temporarily, of the fetters that bound him.

Dick on the ditch line and Dick down in Hana among the ruins of the past were two different beings.

He had been perilously near collapse; now he seemed to have a hold on himself. He would be responsible, faithful to the belief, the trust placed in him—to his work—so Howard believed.

But there was a side that only Anthony knew.

About nine that evening he heard the trot of Dick's horse. He went out to meet him, his face a trifle concerned.

"Hello! You look as cheerful as a corpse, Tony!" Dick greeted him merrily. "Shut up your books and let's have a drink."

They went in.

"When Di finds this out, it'll be the end," he confided, for the moment remorseful; "but I did the best I could for as long as I could. When she insisted on our going, I knew that she didn't love me; or understand. I'm a Calhoun. If I can't be a little happy, why live? I can't keep Hana; it's gone, but thanks to you and Howard my stay is prolonged. I love this place, and while I'm here I might as well enjoy it. I've a feeling that I shall stay, somehow, although I've given Di my word to go and despite Howard's having fixed the papers."

"Less in mine, Dick, old man."

"Suit yourself, Tony. Think I'm all kinds of a rotter?" asked Dick as he corked the bottle.

"Not I."

"You're an understanding cuss. I've always liked you. I had a fight with myself before I fell off, but I've had too much leisure to think, up here. I don't drink a great deal, just enough to give things a rosy glow. I'm tired of being suppressed. Drinking has always been part of my life as it was of my father's. When I'm sad it makes me jolly; when I'm happy it makes me happier. To me, life seen through the stimulus of alcohol has a different aspect. It's—boundless. It's the best and worst friend a man can have. I wouldn't have missed the impetus drinking has given to my life, though I'd have liked to avoid the great after-depression. Dad never had it. Drinking speeds things up, intensifies them. If I could re-live my life, I think I'd do it in the same way.

Glass in hand. I recall race meets and *luaus;* jolly fellows I've known; big nights, the tension of a race or a card game. Would any of it have seemed—" he paused searching for a word, "so glamorous, if my pulses had not been speeded up and my brain prodded by a drink? I'm not pleading that every one should drink, not by a long shot. Each man for himself, but I'm, on the whole, happier, and I like my fellow men better when I've a shot under my belt. Oh, Tony, I've seen life with its veil off in the last months, and it isn't pretty. I'd rather see it the other way, perhaps not so truthfully but more pleasantly. Alcohol may cheat and delude you, but so long as the delusion is pleasanter than the reality—while it lasts—why not be deluded? Sober, I see the dust on a beautiful vase, 'jingled,' only its exquisite outline."

Dick sat looking at Haldane, waiting for him to make some reply. As he did not, he waved his hand at the open door.

"Look outside, Tony, at the ditch. After a couple of drinks I positively love the damned thing. I'm happy up here following your trail. I seem to have left my troubles behind. They don't seem mine any more. I know I have to go back for the final reckoning but I don't realize it, thanks to this—" He lifted his glass. "It's not with me *all the time;* sorrow, I mean. Well, here's *Aloha ka ko!* Dad's old toast," and he drank it down.

For a while longer they sat talking; then Haldane accompanied Dick to his horse. He stuffed some tobacco into his pipe and stood thoughtfully watching him ride away. Not so good! Poor old Dick. He understood the logic of his reasoning. It was applicable to his life and the way he had lived.

He went in, perturbed and uneasy, conscious of a quickening pace in the river of life. He listened to the million rills that gurgled about him, saw the flash of wet leaves in the moonlight.

A vast peace brooded over the gigantic landscape but it seemed charged with treachery.

He sat down to do some calculating on the earth displacement of a weir that was under construction in the next gulch. Here the gathered waters must be spilled down the original stream-bed for a mile, then taken up at a lower level. A shoulder of Haleakala too big and too solid to be bored through blocked the way. It was easier and less costly to run the water down and siphon it up to where the going was better.

He lifted his head. Along the line of the ditch he heard the rhythmic trotting of a horse. No, it was only water; running, dripping, everywhere. He went on with his work. He heard the sound again more distinctly. His heart stopped. Hula. Coming back! Turning his light lower, he went out and looked along the line of torn trees and earth. Clearly silhouetted in the moonlight, approaching at a rapid trot, were a horse and rider.

He had not been mistaken. It was Hula, mad child, returning to him.

She rode to within fifty feet of the door; dismounted; tied her horse to an *ohia* tree. Hastily she slacked the girth and assured herself that no harm could come to the animal in the precarious space torn in the jungle, faithful to Edwin's teaching even in moments of pressure. Then she hurried toward the house.

"Anthony."

"I'm here, Hula; I heard you coming."

Before he could say more, she had clasped him, and his arms went about her.

"Sweetheart—"

"You are angry!"

"No, Hula, of course I'm not, but you shouldn't have come."

"I came!"

"All those miles from Hana alone, up through the forests," said the man as if he were talking to himself, "past those camps of laborers."

"I'm not afraid of them, and I love the forests at night. They smell wonderful and look so beautiful."

Haldane held her. He shivered as if he heard padding footsteps approaching.

"Come inside, sweetheart."

He closed the door, and somehow the hard, red glare of the kerosene lamp inside restored things to something nearer normal. He looked at Hula. Her eyes were shining; her face, although it was cold from these upland forests, flushed.

"I kept thinking about you, Anthony."

"Sit on my knee, I want to talk to you."

She obeyed with a nestling movement, and her arms went about his neck. It was a moment before he could command his voice. Then he said with a savage sort of desperation:

"I've—I've—got to take you back. You can't stay here."

"Back where?"

"To Hana, or at any rate to Dick's."

"You *are* angry!"

"I'm not, Hula."

She drew away, and the light went out of her.

"If you loved me, you couldn't send me away. I just want to stay with you."

It came like a reproachful cry from her. Haldane felt a terrific fury against life, conventions, conditions. Why did he have to send this warm, glowing child from his arms into the damp chillness of the night and the forests? For what? For whom? She was quite safe with him. She withdrew herself from his hold after a moment; shivered; and said with a gasp:

"I believe Harry's right—he said you didn't know how!"

"How to what, Hula?" he asked, holding her close.

"How to love a lot. He wouldn't—send me away."

"No, he wouldn't."

"But you will." It was an accusation and a question.

"Yes, and you'll misinterpret it probably. Yet it's because I love you better than my life or our own immediate happiness—because your well-being comes before anything else. Oh, Hula, Hula!"

He kissed her with furious despair.

"I can't bear to make you unhappy, and somehow I always seem to." Her great eyes hung on his face, bewildered, despairing. "So—I'll go! You—you make me feel that Mrs. Bane was right. I've lived to do you a great wrong. *I've made you unhappy!*"

She choked.

"Hula, don't!"

"Go?" the light blazed up in her.

"No, dear, don't—cry. You can't remain; it's out of the question, sweetheart."

She gave him a long look, noting the unhappiness of his face and eyes. A drear conviction stole like chilly fingers about her heart.

"He loves me, but he's unhappy. He doesn't want me. I'm too much trouble to get. Oh, I know! I know!"

The man wondered what was passing through her mind. He saw the dilation of her eyes, felt the rigidity of her body.

"Hula, what are you thinking about?"

"It doesn't matter."

"But it does. Everything that concerns you matters to me."

She smiled strangely, as if she knew differently. She did know something: that he did not love his wife; that he did love herself, but for some reason beyond her knowing would not fight to get her. She had a high pride, a pride that would not take a gift that was not freely given. She felt lonely, left, as if a cold wave had washed her up on a forsaken shore.

"I understand, Anthony," she said with difficulty; "I'll go back."

"I'm afraid you don't."

"I do."

"Really?" How glad his face looked, how happy his voice—because she was going!

"I'll get my horse."

"I'll go back alone. I'd rather!"

"But I hate to think of you—"

"Please!" It was a cry and a command.

"I don't believe you do, Hula!"

"Do what?"

"Understand why I cannot let you stay."

She sighed, desperate to rid her heart of its agony.

"Let me go, please. I'm burning." She withdrew herself from his hold. "I'll be all right. I'll not stop. I can get back before light."

"Won't they have missed you?"

"No. I waited until every one was asleep."

"Dear, *believe* that I love you!"

"I do. I know you do." But— "I bother him," was her thought.

"I'll walk out with you."

He held her hot little hand. The wet ground pulled at their feet detainingly, the forest dripped. Ridges swam in the moonlight. Hula shivered as Haldane untied her horse.

"Believe that I love you," he said holding her fast before he permitted her to mount.

"I do."

The quality of her kiss tortured Haldane. What did it

transmit to him—that clinging, desperate caress? What message? What resolve?

"Hula! Hula! tell me what you are thinking. What does your kiss say that your lips won't?"

"Nothing. It's all right. I understand."

"But, understanding, you are unhappy, nevertheless?"

The child nodded and mounted.

"Dear—"

He grasped her hand.

"Remember that I love you, though I have to send you away. Ride up to meet me, the day after to-morrow when I come down. I shall be anxious about you, sweetheart, until I can be with you again."

"I'll come."

He watched her vanish beyond a ragged turn. Tense, he stood trying to interpret the message of her kiss. What was it? What was it? The blue landscape spun. He was mad. It was—but it couldn't be!—a message of farewell.

Unnerved, he hurried to the house and took down his saddle with shaking hands. Midway in the act, he halted. The door was pushed open.

Edwin stood in it. A lean figure, with angry eyes, holding leashed the violence inherent in him.

"Edwin!"

"I followed her. I waited outside while she was in here—with you!"

"You know, then—"

Bitter, accusing came the words:

"That you are a fool!"

He said it without care that Haldane was a white, a superior. And Haldane did not resent it. Man to man they faced each other.

"I couldn't let her remain, Edwin; you know that. It wouldn't have been right!"

"Why?"

"Because—people—"

Contempt blazed into the cowboy's eyes. He drew his belt a notch tighter.

"If you loved her greatly enough you would not care what people thought. You would have kept her with you, as I keep her. Safe," he spoke in Hawaiian forgetting that Haldane could not get all of it. "So long as you were square with her and your own heart, what could it matter? Now there's no telling what she may do."

"I was afraid after I sent her away—knowing her. I was just going to get a horse and follow."

"I'm going. Now."

"I'm in hell, Edwin," said Haldane; "you cannot appreciate how tied I am. I love her."

Edwin snorted his contempt.

Haldane looked at him. Helen had been right, the love of this uneducated brown man put all his white love to shame.

"She'll go to Harry!" Edwin threw it at him.

"I'll go down."

"No use. I know Hula. She won't take your love—now."

His aspect could not have been more condemning if he had accused Haldane of murder. Had he murdered Hula's soul, her love, when he had only tried to protect her?

"What do you want me to do, Edwin? What do you suggest?"

The old man measured him.

"Bust up with your wife anyhow you have to and do it quick! If you do that, maybe Hula will believe. If not, if you won't—" he made a quick contemptuous gesture—"then you are a coward and your love is not worth the name. You shrink from hurting a woman who doesn't care for you and for whom you do not care, because she is your wife! Hula," he flamed, "loves you, and you drive a knife into your heart because you haven't the manhood to fight to possess her. You don't deserve her. No man does! She would do anything for you—and you—hesitate!"

CHAPTER VI

"You're pale, Hula," observed Margaret Haldane at breakfast next morning. "Didn't you sleep?"

She hated the child but always assumed a condescending manner toward her, as if, from her own vantage point as Anthony's wife, she pitied her.

Hula looked at her a long time before replying. There was a lost reverence in her eyes for something. Her face was pallid, her expression distracted. Fixing Margaret with her glance, she said slowly:

"I rode up to see Anthony last night and just got in. I'm tired."

The woman strangled. How dared Hula make such a statement at the breakfast table! Before every one!

There was a terrible silence. Fitzmaurice dug desperately into his grapefruit. Dehan, who had ridden over that morning from Kipahulu, grew deadly white. Diana stared at Hula as though she were a monstrosity.

The silence lengthened agonizingly. Then Margaret Haldane made as though to rise from the table.

"Never mind," said Hula getting up. "I'll go. You needn't."

With a pale hand she pushed back her chair.

"Harry."

He did not answer, and finally Fitzmaurice—for no one else seemed capable of speaking—said:

"What is it you want, Hula? Can I do anything for you?"

He rose in his easy gallant manner and went around to her.

"No, Fitzie, thanks. I want to say something to Harry."

Her eyes commanded him, and he followed her out of the room. In the hall they halted.

"Well?" he managed to force the word out.

Hula looked at him.

"Do you want me, Harry?"

Dehan made an inarticulate sound.

"I said I'd take you under any conditions. I will."

Hula smiled a tragic smile the deadliness of which he entirely missed.

"The conditions aren't what you think them, Harry."

"I don't understand, Hula."

His eyes devoured her pale little face.

"I'm not—'ruined.' Anthony's—" she swallowed, "not that kind of man. He's—he's like Uncle Edwin. Good. But he doesn't," she shivered and turned her eyes to the sea, "he doesn't, he can't, seem to love me enough or he wouldn't just keep on staying married!" She said it with a sort of tragic desperation. "So, if you want me, I'll—I'll marry you."

Dehan's head reeled. With what diffidence she offered herself. The gift of gifts!

"Oh, Hula!"

Vise-like his arms closed about her, but their hurt eased the aching lump which was her heart. Harry loved her as she loved Anthony. In the same violent way. Like a flower whose stem is suddenly broken, her head fell against his shoulder.

"Hold me tight, Harry! but don't kiss me—now. I couldn't. I'm not ready for it."

He had got her! He had got her! He had got her! But he was not a fool and restrained himself.

"I told you that I'd do anything for you. I meant it."

He choked.

"Thanks, Harry." Then she lifted her head, "I think I'll go for a ride. By myself."

He released her and watched her cross the garden. He had got her! He clenched his fists and drew a deep breath.

Edwin was waiting at the stables.

"Well?" he asked.

"I'm going to marry Harry," she announced without looking at him.

"I think, maybe, more good. The *haole* make me sick!"

"Me too. Get my horse, Uncle Edwin."

He saddled it with loving care, while she sat in the sun like a sick puppy, shivering continuously.

"I want to go alone."

"I know, Hula."

She returned at sunset and unsaddled slowly. Edwin appeared just as she turned her tired horse into the corral. His was as jaded.

"Where've you been, Uncle Edwin?"

"Oh, little *holoholo*," he answered carelessly as he slacked his girths.

"You didn't mind?"

"Hell, Hula, I no care. Sometimes a fella has to be alone."

"Oh, Uncle Edwin—dear!"

She kissed him, and he watched her walk house-wards with dragging steps.

"Oh, Hula! Hula!" he muttered, "the rain is falling on my heart."

A false move now and she would be lost. And in his silent fierce way he prayed for enlightenment and wisdom to guide her, to stay her hand, her hand that he loved.

Mounting the stairs, Hula encountered Margaret Haldane.

"Little girl, I want to talk to you."

"About Anthony?"

"About my husband."

"You needn't. He hasn't done anything."

"You need hardly tell me that, Hula; I know him rather well."

Hula looked at her.

"I see you are taking this affair desperately to heart."

"I'm going to marry Harry."

"Isn't this—sudden?"

"I told him I would, to-day."

"After seeing my husband? Little girl, let me tell you this; you'll find it never pays to play with married men. Almost invariably you'll find that in the end they'll desert the girls they fancied for their wives."

"Anthony doesn't 'fancy' me. He loves me with all his heart, and he doesn't love you at all."

"Quite naïve. If he cared so greatly, he'd divorce me to marry you. You can count on that. No, Hula, it's just that, well, women are his weakness."

Hula grew cold. But there had been other women, lots of them, lovelier than she was: Helen and Deane and Mrs. Bane, but he hadn't loved them. Only her. He was and had been her Anthony, but he lacked courage or the will to fight. Looking at Margaret, she experienced a strange mental nausea. The woman was like a doll, nice outside but with nothing inside but sawdust. Yet Anthony chose to hurt herself instead of this woman who couldn't—feel.

Hardness filled her.

"I don't believe what you've said is true, Margaret, and I don't think you are very smart. Helen says—"

"Who is 'Helen?'" Margaret asked coldly. "You'll have

to explain. You forget that I've only been here a few months."

"Helen," Hula's face lighted for an instant, "is the most beautiful woman in the world. Everybody loves her. She said once, that it takes an intelligent woman to keep any man wholly hers. I remember it. I know more about men than you do."

"I don't doubt that you've had a liberal education in regard to many things, despite your youth. I've heard a lot about all of you."

"From Di?"

"From many sources."

Hula laughed.

"I bet you haven't been sitting around all the years that Anthony was gone. I—I hate you!"

"And I'm sorry for you." Loftily she voiced it.

"You aren't. You hate me more than I do you, because in your heart you know that Anthony loves me and is ill because you aren't a good enough sport to let him go. Keep him. He'll always be mine in his heart as I will be his in mine—though I'm going to marry Harry."

Margaret's hands clenched. Wait, wait until Anthony came down for the week-end. He arrived late next day with Dick.

"I'd like to talk to you, Margaret," he said when they rose from afternoon tea.

"On what subject?"

He moved unhappily.

"About getting a divorce."

"I think we've discussed that sufficiently."

"We will have to do it again. I've made up my mind."

He looked at her apprehensively, waiting for the ghastly, inevitable scene.

"On what grounds?"

"On any you'll give me."

"I shall give you none."

"Then I shall get it in spite of you. It's come to a point—"

"What has made you so excited?"

She used the word deliberately, hoping to enrage him. He looked at her. What restrained her? Why did she not employ her usual weapons to vanquish him; tears, screams, hysteria?

"Because—because—"

Margaret laughed a laugh she kept to goad him.

"I've—it's come to a point where I've got to hurt somebody, either you or Hula. Things can't go on like this. She loves me, and it's not right. I'm determined—"

"To make a fool of yourself over a baby?"

"See it as you will. The only thing in the world that really matters—"

"Spare me the heroics, please. I've been your wife too long to have them impress me. Go on, I shall not interrupt you again."

"Well, I'm determined to get a divorce, whatever you may do to combat it."

There was a long silence. The woman was the first to break it.

"You've arrived at this decision a bit late."

"In what way?"

"Hula announced to-day that she is going to marry Mr. Dehan."

Anthony passed a cold hand over his eyes. He had not been mistaken, and Edwin had predicted rightly. . . . That had been a kiss of farewell. Coward that he was and had been!

How could Hula be expected to understand the things that had made him shrink from ruthlessly tearing himself free. How could she help but misinterpret—developed as she had been by a man whose love was a flaming sword to cleave every obstacle in her path—his reluctance to resort to violent methods.

"Nevertheless I shall get it."

The woman stiffened, realizing that this man, for the first time, had taken his spirit to a region where she could not reach it to hurt it.

"What good will it do, may I ask?"

"Prove to her, even if it's too late, that the quality of my love, poor as it is beside Edwin's and hers, is real and sincere."

Margaret gave a shriek of laughter.

It was coming. He waited like an animal that has been punished to the point of stupidity, uncaring of further blows rained on its back. The woman filled her lungs, waiting for his old despairing cry:

"For God's sake, Margaret, I'll do anything if you won't make a scene."

It did not come. He was going to go through with it! Frustrated fury filled her. It was monstrous. She had always defeated him. She marshaled her forces, watching him. The expression of his face did not alter.

She gave a shriek of hysterial laughter. Its sword pierced him; she saw him stiffen—knew his well-bred spirit recoiled from a public display of their private differences. And yet he made no move to check or restrain her. In red waves her rage mounted. She screamed, she beat herself on the floor. The household must hear her!

The man waited for a moment, then left the room with great strides.

Arriving at the stables, he saw Dick.

"What looking for, Tony?"

"Edwin."

"He'll probably shoot you. Hula's announced that she's going to marry Harry. You've been a bit on the slow side, old man. Should have started your divorce before coming back here. I understand, but I can't blame her for doubting you."

Dick laughed in an over-strained manner.

"I know that"—Anthony broke off, "I'm going back to the ditch. Margaret"—he looked apprehensively toward the house.

"Broken it to her?"

Haldane nodded.

"Hate scenes as I do, Tony, eh? Beastly messes. Better clear out. Here, take my mare. I understand."

Dick looked compassionately at his friend. Di and Margaret were alike. Both pretenders, Di without knowing it. Both were vain. Margaret was cheap; Di was not. Di had never found herself; Margaret had no self to find. Therein lay their difference.

"I feel an ass running away from a woman—from my wife, but I can't stand that sort of thing."

"Hell, I've run away, too."

Dick led out the black mare and without a word commenced saddling.

"Let me do that!"

"Dry up. You'll find a drink in my locker. Here. Get aboard. She'll be out in a minute."

Haldane mounted.

"I'll see you Monday, maybe to-morrow. Anything I can do for you down here?"

Haldane's brown eyes darkened.

"No, I guess not Dick. I'll—"

"I'll talk to her, Tony—tell her it's useless to try to see you. The sooner you file your divorce papers the better. I'm a bit anxious about Hula. Can't get her idea."

"It's my fault. I've been—"

Dick slapped the mare on her shining black quarters.

"Hell, we all are sometimes," he said, and with a clatter of hoofs she was gone.

He sat down on an upturned stable bucket and laughed immoderately.

Fitzmaurice appeared and looked around.

"What are you doing, Dick; making an inventory of your assets?"

"Nope. I'm saying good-by to them."

"Decided to sell the lot?"

"I'm going to get rid of them." He looked at the long line of loose-boxes in a peculiar way. "They cost too much to keep. I've got Di and the kid to consider."

"Damned pity you've got to part with them. You've got some wonderful blood in that lot, best in the country."

Dick got up. "Don't I know it! Come from the house?"

Fitzmaurice nodded and they both looked away—two gentlemen desirous of keeping life garbed in a semblance of decency.

"Tony has cleared out. It seemed best, in the circumstances. I'm going to talk to his wife to-morrow and make clear to her the uselessness of trying to see him. Great life if you don't weaken, as my dear old Dad used to say. Come on up to my room and let's toast old Tony."

CHAPTER VII

"You are always a bit drunk now, Harry," observed Hula one sultry afternoon as she sat on the hitching rail. "Why?"

"I'm unhappy. I'll never feel safe until you are married to me."

"I can't do it—yet."

"Has he said anything to you?"

The words came through set teeth.

"No; he hardly talks to me when I go up to see Dick on the ditch. He—just looks at me as if he were dead." She clenched her fingers on the rail.

"He deserves to be. Any man who wouldn't fight to have you!"

"*Pau,* Harry! Nobody knows better than I do how that makes me feel."

She turned unhappy eyes on her companion. Lithe, graceful as a young panther, he lounged against the long rail, watching her avidly. His face was flushed, his skin moist. Hula knew the signs.

"Why do you?" she asked again, frowning.

"Because, as I told you, I'm miserable, and drinking makes me forget."

"Does it, really?"

"Ask Dick."

"Is he drinking again?"

Harry nodded.

Hula pondered. That explained it, then, his being more like his old self. Her little desperate face set, and her outlaw soul snatched at thoughts as they passed. If drinking deadened sorrow, why was Uncle Edwin so against it? Was not anything preferable to feeling dead? The sky was blue; birds sang; the sun shone; and yet joy had gone. When she was unhappy she could not think. The warm stream of her blood would not move forward; it seemed to be at a standstill.

She straightened her body as though to make room for her heart. It seemed too big for her. Her eyes filled and she drove her teeth into her lip.

"I wish I knew of something to help—me. I can't cheat you, Harry. I love Anthony, and I'm dead because he doesn't love me enough to get free. If he only would! But he won't, and you love me, and there's no sense in every one's being unhappy; so I'm going to marry you, but don't hurry me."

"I'm so afraid something may happen!"

"Nothing can, unless, Margaret drops dead."

"If she did, would you, would you—"

"Yes, I'd do anything."

Dehan felt crazed. He knew it. Hula loved Haldane as he himself loved Hula. He stalked away to the house and helped himself to a drink from the sideboard. The alcohol steadied him but set its devils working, in his brain. He must possess her, else he would go mad. Red seas of feeling surged through him like lava.

He thought of the wild hills of Haleakala. Abduct her? Edwin would find them. He knew every foot of the mountain. The Island was not big enough, or the world. Edwin would hunt them down. She still loved the old man even though he appeared to have cast her off. Kill him? The law would take him for his deed, and he could never have her. He must wait, inspiration would come.

He walked back to the stable. Hula was still there, sitting in the sun; but the warmth of the day could not warm her body or soul.

She looked at Dehan.

"Does it really make you feel better, Harry?"

"It makes you forget; nothing seems to matter."

Hula's heart was aching. Her mind reached back for the blue distances of joy which had gone. Her body seemed weighted. She felt as she had felt at Waikapu, as she had felt in the days before Anthony came. Why not anything—anything so long as it helped. So long as it could rout this detestable state of despair. Dick did. Harry did. She could at least try it and see if it worked. If it didn't, she could stop; if it did, if it put a person beyond any one's reach, she could survive Edwin's wrath, for it could not reach her.

Dehan watched her, divining somewhat what was going through her head. His mind leaped ahead.

"Like to try once, Hula? I'll make your drink small. It'll relax, ease you a bit."

"I'm sick of feeling sad," she burst out. "I hate it!"

"So do I, so does every one, Hula."

She slid off the rail.

"Uncle Edwin?" she said dubiously.

"He need never know. He's an old missionary now," Dehan snorted; "but he wasn't before you were born. He's had his time. Every one goes through the mill—"

"Except me. I never have, except once." But she shuddered, remembering, and her resolve weakened.

"That was an accident; you were overtired and took your drinks too fast."

He held the forbidden fruit before her, tempting her. Alcohol weakened the will, destroyed resistance. As Edwin would employ any means to save her, so Dehan was willing to resort to any means to get her.

They went in. Hula's face had an expectant expression when they paused at the sideboard where Dick and her father and uncounted others had gone, many times, seeking, as she was seeking, for the golden fleece of forgetfulness.

"I'll give you some Sherry," said Dehan. "Better begin easy."

"I've drunk that before. Daddy used to give me sips out of his glass. But I've never touched anything since Waikapu. Anthony—"

She broke off and snatching up the glass drank it off.

"It isn't—helping," she said after a moment.

Harry laughed.

"It couldn't so soon. Take another, then let's go for a ride."

The girl watched him pour it.

"I'm so cold!" she said resentfully, and her eyes moved mournfully about the great living-room. "Oh, Harry, I'm tired of feeling shut up inside!"

She burst into tears.

"Here, drink this, Hula," said Dehan, maddened at the sight of her tears, and he pressed a third glass upon her.

With a shaking hand she drank the liquor. After a moment a little reviving warmth ran through her sorrow-chilled body.

"It's beginning," she cried with a breathless sort of anticipation. "It's making me warm! Oh, Harry! Give me some more."

"Not too fast, Hula."

"But I want to forget, to be happy, quickly!"

She drew a deep breath.

"I can get it a little now."

"Get what, Hula?"

"Air, it wouldn't go down before. My lungs wouldn't open. Give me some more; I can't wait for this dead feeling to go."

He poured a scant glass and she tossed it off as deftly as old Calhoun. Her heart beat faster, and scurrying blood warmed her chilled hands and feet.

"Oh, Harry, I'm coming alive again!"

It was a pagan cry of exultation. She flung her arms about him and beat her little spurred heels up and down on the polished floor in a tattoo of joy.

"I'm alive, I'm warm, I'm feeling! Harry! Harry!"

So was it done, and Hula's cheeks were red again and her eyes bright—perhaps too bright—but she rode and laughed excitedly on the cliffs with Edwin and the cowboys. But oftenest she rode with Dehan. He watched her sometimes, wondering how much she took that he did not give her.

Edwin absented himself frequently, camping in the hills,

hunting down the remaining bands of cattle. He grew lean and gaunt and savage from desolation. Anthony seeing him at intervals felt that he had abandoned the battle for Hula's soul. But he had not the wisdom of the old horseman. He did not realize that Edwin was giving his filly rope again to throw herself. But he watched her as carefully as he would have watched a colt he was breaking, lest she fall too hard.

Then one day he rode up to see Haldane. He recognized him from far away as he rode the torn line of the ditch, his silhouette oddly at variance with the work in progress, reminiscent of horses and cattle and Calhoun.

Reining up, the foreman accosted him.

"I like talk."

"Very well, Edwin; ride on to my house. I have to talk to Dick about this work. I'll be along."

Edwin glanced over. Drinking again and heavily. That was why he did not come down to Hana. He did not blame him overmuch. With that cold wife and with Hana gone, things were practically at an end for him. He must pay the price of his folly as must every man who will not learn. He rode on to the house and dismounted. Securing his horse to a tree, he watched the work.

Shovels moving up and down, red earth flying through the air and falling with hollow thuds. Mechanical contrivances tearing at the hills. Dull detonations of dynamite. On it went, Hamilton's great ditch, relentlessly as life. Ending beauty but bringing worth. Destroying to build. His grim soul walked beside it approvingly.

He saw Haldane approaching. Locking his thumb into his belt, he waited. He liked Haldene and despised him, but have him he must.

"What is it, Edwin?"

"Have you filed the papers for your divorce?"

He put the question to him in Hawaiian.

"Yes."

"Have you told Hula?"

"No. I shall not say anything until I am free. I cannot, Edwin; you must appreciate that."

The old man debated.

"You cannot, but I shall. Something is wrong."

"I haven't seen her for weeks. Is she ill? I can't go down to Hana any more because of my wife and my work."

"She is a rotten woman," observed Edwin.

Haldane flushed. He had an impulse to hit the cowboy, but resisted it.

"Careful, Edwin," he warned.

"I no care—" he broke off, then added, "You must come down."

Haldane looked into the gulch.

"Couldn't you send Hula up to me? I can't leave; it's out of the question. That dam in the gulch must be finished. It's taken months to build. The work's at a critical stage. If a freshet should come, it might all go out, and it's cost a lot. If it had to be rebuilt, it would delay completion of the ditch. It's damnable, Edwin, but I'm tied here until it's done. A week or ten days, then I can go down."

Edwin looked at him with savage disgust. Everything before Hula. He knew it was not so; he knew this man to be loyal to the interest of the company for which he worked, responsible as no Calhoun could ever be. But he wanted to be angry with him, to hate him, to force him. The very qualities he most admired in him, he most hated, too; for they hampered the fulfillment of his schemes.

"Dick," he suggested.

Haldane shook his head and his eyes looked concerned.

"He'd do his best, Edwin, but it wouldn't be fair to him or the company. Send Hula up to me."

"She would not come."

"I wonder?"

Haldane tore a page out of his note-book and wrote on it. Folding it, he handed it to Edwin.

"Take that to her."

"What did you write?"

"I asked her to come to see me—said I wanted to talk to her."

"Did you tell her?"

"No."

"I shall."

"Use your own judgment, Edwin."

"When will you be free?"

"Not for a year."

Edwin swore furiously at the law, at Haldane, at the universe. Then he put on his hat.

"I go back," he announced. "I tell her. Maybe it help, maybe not."

Dick sauntered over.

"Well, Edwin, what brings you here? Something gone wrong with the works?"

Edwin eyed him. Pretty damn drunk, but the foreman did not blame him overmuch. He had been a doomed horse from the start. He wondered how much longer it would be before he foundered.

"Nothing *pilikea* (wrong)," he answered resentfully.

"Just rode up to kiss Tony and take a look at the view? Well, it's not a bad one."

He stared at the folded forests and distant sea.

"How are the ladies? Do they miss us, Tony and me?"

Edwin grunted, and Dick laughed.

"Take them my compliments and tell them the atmosphere is cooler up here."

Edwin looked at him.

"Oh, I'm a bit drunk, I'll admit, old '*mikineli*' (missionary) but not too drunk to attend to my work. When will Hamilton be up again?"

"Sunday."

"Have the stock ready for him to look over. How many head have you collected?"

"Near twelve hundred."

"That's about right. Where are you holding them?"

"Above Kipahulu, below the forest. Some more yet to get."

"Well, you might stage a hunt for the old duffer. Like to go down, Tony? Ever chased wild cattle?"

"No."

"It almost beats horse-racing. Better go down Saturday and meet Hamilton and stay over for the week-end. I'll keep an eye on the work; I don't want to see Di."

He laughed in a high, unsteady way.

"I'll pass it up this time, Dick. I want to push that dam through."

"Afraid that I might muff the job?"

Dick taunted and challenged, egged on by the devils of alcohol.

"No, Dick, I know that if I were forced to leave you'd be on the job."

"With both hands and feet."

Edwin looked at the two men, lifted his hat and said: "Well, I go."

"Give every one my love and tell Hula she might ride up to see me. How is she? Still going to marry Harry?"

"She says so."

"Tell her I wish her luck."

"I think more better Helen come."

Dick darted a look at him.

"Helen? Why?"

"Something going to happen."

Dick laughed, and Haldane moved unhappily.

"You write, old Siwash, it'll have more weight with her."

"All right."

Edwin flung a contemptuous glance at him and began to cinch up his horse.

"Wait," said Haldane, "give me that note."

He scribbled an additional line on it and handed it back.

Edwin pocketed it, lifted his hat, and rode away.

"Profound old duffer. Wonder what's eating him? What did he want to see you about?"

"He wanted me to go down."

"Hadn't you better?"

"I sent a note."

When Edwin got in he found Hula, but he did not give her the letter. He glanced at her; he had not been mistaken. Her eyes were glassy, her gait a trifle unsteady.

"Hula!" his voice sent a chill through her, then she breathed freely, remembering. Nobody could reach her. Another drink, and she could put herself beyond even his wrath. He divined her thought.

"I take letters up to-day," he announced in a changed voice, "and tell Dick about cattle. He say that the *haole* is sick."

"What's the matter? Oh, Uncle Edwin!"

"I guess he working too hard and he have trouble about his divorce."

Hula dropped her bridle and ran to him.

"Uncle Edwin, is he, is Anthony getting it?"

"He no tell you?"

"No—oh!" She burst into tears. "Oh, Uncle Edwin, dear!"

"But you going to marry Harry."

The girl laughed her scorn and shook him. He scented the

alcohol on her breath and had an impulse to beat her. But he dared not lose his head or his hold of her.

"When—when—will he be free?"

"I don't know; law stuff take a long time."

"Did you see him?"

"Yes."

"Is he fearfully sick."

"Pretty bad. He give me this for you."

Hula devoured the note and paled.

"I'm going up. Saddle Silver Wings for me. Don't let Harry know." She calculated. "It's one o'clock; he'll be back about six, I can make it. Meet me at the road about sunset with a fresh horse, so he won't see where I've been, and wash the mud off Silver Wings before you bring him in."

"But, Hula, sure trouble if Harry find out. He kill the *pelikani* or you."

"I don't care. My Anthony! He's sick. Quick, saddle up; I can't."

"Drunk?"

"A little. Don't get angry. I'm so unhappy and it's the only way I can forget for a little while."

"Hell, I know."

"Oh, dear Uncle Edwin, and I've been so afraid to go near you for a long time."

He put his arm about her.

"I know, Hula, for a long time."

"And you weren't angry?"

"Yes, I angry, but I understand and I sorry for you."

Her arms went about him, and she pressed her red lips to the grim crack which was his mouth.

"I love you—more than any one. You are my Uncle Edwin."

The old man's eyes dimmed. He disengaged himself.

"I saddle up."

He put her aboard the gray stallion and watched them go. Strange journey for an undefeated race-horse; the quaggy woods, the uptorn line of a ditch! Shining flanks would be encrusted with mud, great muscles strained by untoward efforts. Hula would not spare him. Anxiety and her semi-intoxicated state would unite to drive her on, regardless of consequences. Well, if anything worth while resulted from the trip, Silver Wings' life or ruin would be worth it.

He thrust cold hands into his pockets and then walked into his house and wrote to Helen. When the letter was done he took it to Fitzmaurice.

"Please send to Helen. You know her address."

The Irishman took it, "All right."

"Mahalu (thanks)."

Edwin strode back to the stables, uneasy with presentiment. He felt its long shadow in his heart, chilling him, in spite of the sunshine that inundated the land and sea.

CHAPTER VIII

From where he worked Haldane saw Hula coming. He recognized Silver Wings, although he was blue with sweat and caked with mire. Like the proverbial Indian, Hula rode recklessly, lying on the horse's neck. She was up to Haldane before he had taken ten strides to meet her.

Sobbing with exhaustion she slid off, and, fighting for breath, the great horse eased himself from leg to leg.

"Oh, Anthony—"

"What is it, dear?"

He took her into his long arms.

"I came—Uncle Edwin said that you were sick."

"I am, Hula, in truth, though he lied to get you here. Come inside."

"Have a man lead Silver Wings up and down, or he'll founder."

He gave the order to one of the ditchmen.

"Now, Hula—"

"Give me a drink."

He obeyed, and she sat on the cot and held out her arms.

"Hold me—my Anthony."

He sat down beside her and locked her in his arms.

"Why didn't you tell me?"

"I couldn't, Hula."

"But I might have married Harry. Would you have let me?"

"I don't know. My love seemed so poor, measured beside yours and Edwin's. I was ashamed of it."

Hula laughed hysterically.

"What's wrong, kid, besides everything?"

"Oh, I'm a little drunk."

"Hula!"

"I have been for ever so long. Don't get angry. He didn't."

"Edwin?"

Hula nodded, and again Haldane's spirit went down, honoring the old man.

"It was the only way I could forget. Haven't you, ever?"

"No, Hula."

"You and Uncle Edwin," she proudly linked the two.

"He's a man in a million. I'm not."

"You're my Anthony."

"That's enough, though I don't deserve to be."

He kissed her close and long.

"I shall hate—having to tell Harry. He'll go wild. I'm scared."

"Leave that to me."

"No, I'll have to tell him."

Anthony held her, thinking. A queer coldness enveloped him as though the mountain sent down its chilly breath.

"There's going to be a horrible mess. With Margaret and Harry. They'll—they'll—"

Hula shivered with exhaustion and repugnance.

"Sweetheart, lie down, you're played out."

"I couldn't. Just stay close to me. Like this."

She closed her eyes and listened to her horse being led up and down.

"I'm happy, just to feel you," she said dreamily. "I wish I never had to go out of your arms." She relaxed to the fulness of the moment. Her features blurred in the man's sight.

"I don't know what to do, Hula, I'm afraid to let you go back lest something terrible may happen. I can't leave here; it's out of the question. So you'll have to stay with me here."

"I can't; I must go back."

"I can't allow you to."

The girl looked at him.

"Once you wouldn't let me stay."

"I've learned a lot since then, Hula."

He sat holding her, looking at her.

"Hula?"

"Yes?"

"Promise me that you won't drink any more. It isn't safe for you, dear."

"I won't need to now. I have you."

"Oh, Hula . . . Hula. . . ."

"Are you sad again!" she clasped him fiercely.

"No! glad, thankful that I had the courage to bolt my

fences. It's against my nature and upbringing, but I am, or shall be, free to protect you, to have you."

Footsteps aroused them. Dick pushed open the door. Seeing them, he laughed.

"Well, what's the dope?"

"Anthony's divorcing Margaret!"

"A great idea, sweetheart," said Dick as though he did not know. "Have you broken it to Harry?"

"No, but I will to-morrow."

Haldane looked at Dick.

"Hadn't she better wait until I can go down? He might—"

"What? Kill somebody? Yes, he might, at that. Better not say anything, Hula, until Tony or I can go down."

Hula sat, watching her brother.

"When can you come? I hate waiting."

"True disciple of Edwin!" he observed; "but I think it'll be decidedly wiser to hold back that card for a little."

"I hate to let her go down, Dick."

"It's best. Howard'll be here Sunday. You better meet him, and I'll hold the fort."

Anthony sat silent, thinking.

"All right, I think I will."

"What time is it?" asked Hula.

"Nearly four."

"I must go. Uncle Edwin is waiting for me with a fresh horse, so Harry won't know I've been up here."

"Quite an old boy, that *paniola* of ours. All right. Rattle your hocks, Hula."

"Look away, Dicky. I want to kiss Anthony."

Dick laughed, the easy laugh of intoxication, but he felt apprehensive and was glad when Hula had gone.

"Look here, Tony," he said, "I feel there's going to be a hell of a showdown in Hana, when Harry finds out. He's a volcanic sort of beggar. He'll go off. Explode. Wish to God you and Hula could clear out. I'll help you, back you both up; think none the less of you for it. I'll help you to get clear, and Edwin can settle Harry."

"It won't do, Dick. I can't go. I gave Howard my word that I'd see this ditch through."

He spoke harshly, and a muscle in his lean cheek fluttered.

"You're a better man than I am, Gunga Din," said Dick. "I'd do it."

"I don't think you would. It's all my fault, you know—this mix up. If I hadn't been such a—"

"Dry up, you ass! We all are fools and cowards sometimes. It's not your prerogative. I feel a bit uneasy, though. There's no telling what Harry may be moved to do—or Edwin. But we have no choice; we'll have to wait."

He clapped his hand encouragingly on Haldane's bent back.

"Buck up, Tony, the worst is yet to come. Let's take a squint at the dam."

Side by side, they strolled out and watched the work. Haldane stood, remembering the tempestuous two weeks of his first visit to Hana. Even then he had felt fate's soft, persistent knocking at his heart. He was conscious in an awed way of the immense forces—terrible and fine—at work in the world. The lawless wild land waked desires of a like nature in him. To be able to go down and kill Harry and carry off Hula, to be rid of the world, to be free to love and be happy! But honor bound him to the work at his feet. What was honor? What would it matter a hundred years from now whether or not, he, Anthony Haldane, English and thirty-seven, kept his word? How could it affect the destiny of mankind? Why not live as Dick's father had lived, doing the things he wanted to do, sweeping aside the rest? He recalled the night he had spent at Kaenae, and again Calhoun's spirit seemed to come and mock him. . . .

"Live as you want to. I did! I am dust, and you will be. Dust blown on the wind. Take your joy and pay for it. It's sporting; it's all a man can ask!"

Recalling his mottled, purple face, his wide, hospitable arms, his love for his fellow men, his passion for horses, his enjoyment of all the good things of life, Haldane realized why—in spite of his flagrant disregard of the principles of right living—every one liked Calhoun. He had lived true to himself always!

Haldane straightened his shoulders. He must be true to himself. He was no magnificent outlaw of life as the old man had been, as Dick had been and still was, and as Hula was. They reminded him, in their blind fury when life went against them, of elephants running amuck in African jungles. Blindly they charged, tearing up, destroying, without care or count of the cost. Banging themselves, hurting themselves, as Dick hurt himself by consuming quantities of alcohol, knowing it was killing him; as Hula had hurt herself when she had become engaged to Harry. . . .

And what awful price must she or some one else pay for the profitless folly of that act?

CHAPTER IX

"What brings you here, Miss McKaine?"

Diana asked it, her face distorted with surprise and fury. Helen paused on the steps and looked up at her.

"Edwin wrote, asking me to come."

The red spots on Diana's cheeks blazed.

"I don't believe you. You cannot stay here in this house!"

Helen's fine eyes flashed. She had anticipated this. Opening her purse, she handed the woman Edwin's note.

"I came as soon as I got it. Where is Hula?"

"I don't know."

"And care less," thought Helen. "I'm afraid that I can not leave until I've seen her or Edwin. He would not have sent for me unless he felt it was necessary, Di."

"Mrs. Calhoun!"

Helen laughed.

"As you will."

She spied another woman and divined who she was. These two, leagued against all the others! Little souls, caring only for themselves and their own immediate destinies.

"Howard—Mr. Hamilton—came with me. He'll be up presently; he remained behind to superintend the landing of some machinery."

In reality she had advised him to delay his arrival, suggesting that it might be pleasanter. The man had complied with her wish, wondering where events were trending. He felt apprehensive, glad Helen had come. She was daring, fearless and sane. No false motives moved her. Her arrival might be a bomb in the women's camp, Hana, but it would be a godsend to the two men on the ditch—Dick and Haldane. It would relieve the latter's mind for his work to know she was with Hula.

"I cannot permit you to stay here, under this roof. While Mr. Calhoun lived I could not protest. Now—"

"Now, Howard has been kind enough to extend the hospitality of this house to me."

Diana's face whitened, and her lips went into a straight line.

"I will not demean myself by staying in the same house with a—"

Helen mockingly substituted the word, and the woman recoiled.

"I shall go!"

"And I!" said Margaret Haldane, coming forward.

Helen's eyes swept her. Shoddy and trivial. Sufficiently brainless to be dangerous. Anthony was well rid of her.

"Dick—" began Di.

"Dick will never ask me to go," Helen said quietly, and, knowing the truth of her words, Diana stifled.

This was the end. She would not go on. As Hula had once in a moment of rage longed to tear up trees that she might beat the earth with them, so Diana longed to have it in her power to take Hana and all it held in her hands, to destroy them. Outlaw place and people, stronger in their unleashed disregard of convention than she was when allied with the world's majority. But that Howard, Mr. Hamilton—she corrected her thought of him to more proper formalities—that he should condone, champion such as Helen! That he should permit her the shelter of his roof! It was unthinkable.

So Diana flamed and hated, and then went within the hour to Deane Lightfoot's "more respectable roof."

"I shall send for my things and have them shipped to Honolulu," she informed Helen, who sat upon the *lanai*. "The boys will see to their packing."

Helen nodded.

"I've left a note for Dick."

"Shall I give it to him?" asked Helen with delicious maliciousness, looking at her.

"I could kill you!"

"Do so; I shouldn't mind in the least."

Helen looked around serenely, but her foot moved up and down. She disliked scenes; human nature stripped bare. Her eyes went back to the placid and immaculate sea. Di betaking herself to Deane's "more respectable roof!" Delicious! Quite in keeping with the comedy of life. She smiled, knowing some of the hidden pages of the clever little woman's life.

Sitting quietly, she watched the two depart, but her foot kept moving up and down, restlessly. What a more than welcome relief this double going would be to Dick and to Anthony!

When they had gone, she got up and walked thoughtfully about the house. In every room lingered some atmosphere of old Calhoun. She could see him spread back in his wicker chair, a "schooner" of Scotch in his lavender hand. "Old man Calhoun," with his wide indulgence of his fellow men, his deliberate sagacity. His merry and twinkling eyes which had never looked condemningly on any one. A great choking loneliness and longing for him rushed over her—for him and for the days that had gone. She remembered his love for her, a love greater than he had had for his own daughter, Hula. She remembered the first time her lavish nature tripped her up . . . how she had rushed to him, the terrible tears she had wept on his knee! She remembered the understanding in his brown eyes, the words that had come from beneath the "walrus" mustache.

"Don't break your heart over it, my dear. All mankind has gone that way—it's neither here nor there. Some are made that way. Some aren't."

She heard approaching wheels and went out.

"They—Di and Mrs. Haldane—have gone to Deane's."

"Because of you?"

Helen nodded.

Howard looked at her thoughtfully.

"It will simplify the situation—make it pleasanter. Tell the boy which room you want. I think I shall start for the ditch this afternoon. I'm anxious to see what progress they are making. You will not be nervous alone? Surely Hula will be coming."

"I shall not mind even if she does not. I love this place; it's home to me. Have you seen Edwin?"

"No. I believe he's up on the mountain, but I shall send a boy to tell him you are here."

"Thank you, Howard. I wonder why he sent for me? I feel uneasy."

"I am sure, whatever his reason was, it was sound. Edwin is not a fool."

"I lovė him," said Helen.

Howard smiled, thinking of the fierce-souled old man.

"Will you take up a note to Dick?"

"I will." Howard inclined his head with grave courtesy.

Dick arrived from the ditch line that night about eleven. He was noticeably intoxicated. Helen met him.

"Oh, Dicky," she said, going into his arms, "you got my note? You know?"

"Yes," he replied, "it's all right. Don't feel bad. She'd have gone anyway when she found out that I'm drinking—" he broke off. "God, it makes me sick to think about it, but I've got to go and see her—talk to her. It's best to get it over. We have a genius for stirring each other up and making each other unhappy." Then he looked at the woman he held in his arms. "Helen," he said, and they both looked deep—remembering.

"You were my first love and my first and greatest sin." He kissed her. "You know me better—"

"And love you better than any one else. Dick . . . Dick. . . ."

"I know it."

His arms tightened, and he gazed about him.

"Where's Hula?"

"I don't know. I wish she'd come."

"Guess every one's with Edwin, rounding up the last of the stock. Order me some dinner, Helen, and come and talk to me while I get cleaned up."

They sat down at the great expanse of polished table, and

the candles flickered upon a silver racing-cup, flower filled, that formed its centerpiece. Their eyes met, and they raised their long-stemmed glasses in a toast.

"To Dad."

"To Uncle Bill."

The words came simultaneously.

The lips of their glasses touched.

"To Hana and the horses and the old days!"

Helen spoke the words without a tremor in her voice and Dick leaned over and kissed her, his blue eyes wet and adoring.

The meal over, he rose and placed his hand on her shoulder. A moment he stood, looking down at her.

"I'm going. In all likelihood I shan't get back until tomorrow. Pour me another, Helen. Thanks. If Hula and Edwin come in before then, tell them I want to see them before I go back to the ditch. If you want a horse to ride in the morning, until I return—"

"Don't worry, Dicky. I shall make myself at home. Luck to you!"

"To us! Some day! My God, how Dad wanted it!"

"I know."

He looked at her, like a tired, unhappy boy.

"Well, I must be going. You will help me out of the woods, Helen, by and by?"

"That is in the lap of the gods, my dear."

They kissed and he went.

Edwin and Hula did not come in that night nor the next morning. Helen felt increasingly uneasy and driven. She was terribly concerned about Dick. There was something about his face, a deadness, that no face on a living body should have. It haunted her. It had never been there before; it should not be there now, no matter what. A great coldness took possession of her warm body, the coldness that comes to one sitting at the bedside of the dead. Something was dying in Dick, though he still lived and moved about. It was not a spiritual dissolution; some living, vital part of him, of his body, was breaking up, going to pieces. . . .

About ten she ordered a horse and rode up toward the ditch. She saw its winding, mighty tear along the dark side of Haleakala. She lifted the wreath of crimson roses off her breast as though to give herself more air. Then, spurring, she galloped back to Hana. It was nearly noon. Dick should be coming.

She rode into the garden, and a cowboy took her horse away. There was a curious, shocked expression on his face.

A few minutes later she heard Dick's step on the *lanai* and hurried out.

"I've—I've—shot them all!" he announced, coming toward her with a peculiar gait. His face looked boiled, and he lurched sideways into a chair. Then his features changed to wood, as if all the blood in his veins had ceased to circulate.

Helen went to him.

"Dick! You've what?"

"I've shot them all—the thoroughbreds!"

"Oh, Dick! Oh, God!" cried the woman, trembling. "Oh, Dick!"

But she did not ask why. After a moment he spoke, and her eyes riveted themselves on his face. Continuous ripples seemed to be passing over it, like squalls across the sea. Its expression did not alter; it was stony, dead; but the flesh was in quivering, constant motion, as though each minute cell and atom of it was vibrating against the other. She drew a deep breath and closed her eyes. They were the vibrations from a brain in decay from alcohol, dissolving rapidly.

Her arms tightened about him.

"You see—give me a drink—indirectly the horses were behind it all. Di hated them. She—I— Oh, hell, seeing her was dreadful! Had it not been for them, had we stuck to sugar-cane," and he laughed immoderately, remembering the sumptuous, purple years, "things would never had ended as they have."

"Yes?"

"I think I'm crazy, or going crazy, Helen, for doing it—for talking all this rot. I don't mean a word of it."

"You're sick, Dick."

"I think I am; I seem to be—jarring to pieces, if you can imagine such a thing. Could you help me upstairs? I'd like to lie down a bit before I start back. Oh, Helen! Helen!" His arms nearly broke her with their despairing hold. "I shot them all! All! O, God—my horses. Something snapped inside my head, and I went and did it. I shot all of them, Awapuhi, and Crusader, old Champagne, Silver Wings, and—"

He wrenched himself to his feet and stood, swaying unsteadily, the wreckage of the years in his unhappy eyes and on his breaking face.

"O, God!" he cried, as if the soul had been torn out of him. "Get me a drink, Helen, for God's sake! I must—I must—forget!"

He swayed, and she caught him strongly in her arms.

"Here, Dick," she said, valiantly reaching for the half-filled glass and putting it against his lips. He drank and stiffened for an instant in her hold.

"Helen!"

"Yes?"

"Have you ever heard that there comes a time when alcohol ceases to have any effect, when drinking won't help?" The words were wrenched from him.

The woman thought quickly.

"I've heard it said, but I've never known of an instance."

"Nor I—yet. I'm afraid, Helen, I'm reaching that point. If I should—"

He looked at her.

"I'll give you a hand—out. I promise it!"

"What a woman you are!"

He looked unseeingly about.

"It's getting dark, Helen. What time is it? Late?"

"About five—six," lied the woman. "Here, let me put you to bed on the *puune*.

He staggered toward it with her assisting arms.

"Don't leave me; I've a funny feeling in my head. It's getting numb."

"You've reached your limit, Dicky. You've got to the breaking point. It was bound to come."

She eased him down. He lay, breathing terribly. Convulsively she held his hand, looking about her. Then her eyes went back to his devastated face.

"Helen."

"Yes?"

"You'll remember."

"My promise? Yes, Dick."

But she knew there would be no need for that final and greatest test of love. In a few minutes . . . a few hours. . . .

"Ah Sam," she called, and Dick opened his eyes at the familiar name.

"Tell the old duffer to rustle us a drink. Your arm, Helen, under my head. That's it. It feels—infernally—numb, but I'll be right as a bank presently. It about knocked me out—seeing Di. But that's done. Thank God! I feel free, like a horse with its bridle taken off."

Helen grew tense, lest he recall what he had done, but he only said thickly:

"Tell Sam—to hurry with those drinks!"

HULA

CHAPTER X

When Edwin came in, Helen met him and told him about Dick. He evinced no surprise, and she knew from his face that he had been to the stables.

"I think that this would come, for a long time," he said. "You tell—Hula. She coming behind with Harry and the boys."

"Send one of them up to tell Howard and Haldane."

He nodded, then added, for he was still thinking of Hula: "All right, they be here in a little while."

He looked at the tall, pale woman and said: "I glad you here."

"You had better have Silver Wings buried before she gets here."

"Yes. Good for Dick that it is *pau*." Helen nodded, and her eyes filled with tears. Her hands were as cold as those of the dead man inside.

"Where are the *wahines*?"

"At Deane's."

"Now they be coming back, I think."

"Probably—of course."

"I no like Hula stop. Better she go somewhere till it's all *pau*."

"Where can she go, Edwin?"

He thought.

Helen studied his face. It was worn, concerned, the eyes angry and troubled. How he resented everything that menaced Hula. The unending marvel of being loved! Why? Why should any one be loved, greatly, or at all?

"I'll go out and meet her."

Edwin nodded his approval and walked away toward the red-roofed stables. Helen stood listening to a louder sounding note in the sea. . . .

Edwin had a horse saddled when she got out. He helped her to mount and watched her ride away. One good woman, one he could absolutely depend upon for anything. No one had ever called on her in vain. Like the thoroughbreds when race-day came, she gave valiantly of her best, of her all. He turned back to his task. No tears could come although this wholesale destruction affected him profoundly—they were burnt up as they rose by the intensity of his feelings. He had loved the Calhoun thoroughbreds, and he was terrified by the thought of what their killing might do to Hula. Anthony must be fetched immediately. He called one of the men from his work, Mahiai was the most reliable, but this once he would not do. He was prostrate, stubborn with grief. He could not be torn away from Silver Wings; he would not forego the last services he could render him. . . . Faithful retainer of an equine king.

Edwin despatched another boy and moved about his duties, but his mind rode out with Helen to meet Hula and the cowboys coming in. How would she tell her, how break the news? His deadly premonition of disaster had been correct.

He waited, braced for the sound of hoofs on the road. When he heard them, he notched his belt until it almost cut him in two and walked out. One look he threw at Hula's face, and his heart turned over sickeningly. Tear-dabbled, distracted, she rode beside Helen. At sight of him she slid off. He met her and held her tightly.

"No, Hula," he commanded, "no can go inside, no can see—"

She struggled with him a moment, then collapsed against his breast.

"No, more better no," he repeated, "Uncle Edwin no like you to. He know best. . . . Hula. . . . Hula. . . ."

She seemed stupefied and looked about her as if she did not recognize the place.

"Dicky—" she said.

"He all right, Hula, better for him. No be sorry. Be glad."

"Silver Wings!" it came out like a cry.

"Oh, Hula, already I bury, Hula."

Her head hit his breast, and he held her with iron arms.

Helen looked away, and Dehan dismounted. His face was white. He walked over and took Hula's arm.

"I'll ride with her, Edwin."

The foreman looked at him weighingly.

"All right," he said.

In his own way Harry loved her; this once he could be trusted, be used until Anthony came.

"Uncle Edwin."

"Yes?"

"Couldn't I kiss—Dicky?"

The old man stiffened and spoke hastily. Helen realized that he was frantically alarmed.

"No, more better no. Make you feel bad, Hula, and Edwin no like you to feel bad."

She turned sickly toward her horse, and the old man swallowed his heart.

"Wait!" he commanded, and, taking her arm, he spoke to her in a low voice. Some of the misery left her eyes. Harry stood by, a distracted expression on his handsome face. His whole body was rigid, but he did not speak. He watched Hula as Edwin did, fearful as to how this might be affecting her.

"Edwin," said Helen, "give Hula a drink. It'll steady her. Then send them off."

"I'll get it," said Fitzmaurice and Harry followed him into the house. Edwin stood with his hand on Hula's shoulder. When Fitzmaurice returned he took the glass from him and gave it to her himself. Hula drank with a shaking hand. In her eyes was an expression of desperate expectancy, which changed to thankfulness as her system yielded to the alcohol. Edwin raged. Her action was eloquent of too close an acquaintanceship, but to-day he had no choice. He must give Hula into the guardianship of his ancient enemy. He could not risk her realization of all that had occurred. Better to haze her mind, deaden it. To-day alcohol must be his friend, his assistant. . . . To-day. . . . To-day. . . . He ground his heel into the ground and put Hula upon her horse.

"Go—ride!" he said, for a moment losing hold of himself. His eyes were red with angry tears. He struck the horse savagely on its quarters with his hat. It leaped away, throwing up its head, and Harry, vaulting onto his saddle, clattered after Hula.

Edwin stood, looking at them go; then, with a gesture of fierce resentment, he turned back to the work that must be done before they returned. Helen dismounted and laid her hand on his arm. Her spirit bowed to his love.

She signaled to Fitzmaurice.

"Would you go to Deane's?"

"Of course, Helen."

"Thanks, Fitzie."

Evening came down from the hills, stilling the sea, bringing peace to the trodden garden grass. When the last spear of light went out above the brooding mountain mass, Edwin came to the house.

"Helen," he said curtly from the steps, and she came out.

"Yes?"

"*Pau?*"

"Yes, everything's done, Edwin. Have they come yet—Howard and Haldane?"

"Not yet."

"They ought to be here soon. Hula?"

"I hear her horse coming, now."

From afar came the sound of galloping hoofs.

"Meet her, keep her away from the house until Haldane is here."

"The *wahine-haoles?*"

"They came a while ago. They are inside."

"With Dick?"

"No, I'm with him and Ah Sam."

"Good. I go meet Hula."

Helen went indoors and sat down silently in the living-room where she had dined the evening before with Dick. She felt no sorrow, only an aching void. Looking at his face, so deathly white and drawn, she shivered suddenly, and then something scorched her heart. She had seen it like that once before, as if the soul had died in his living body. Once, long ago. He had grasped her by the shoulders and looked at her, and his face had been like that. As if he were dead. His words of the previous night came back to her.

On her lovely lips grew a stony little smile. She got to her feet and stood by him; then, bending, she kissed him, the candle-light flickering on her slender, supple form. The Chinaman who sat across the room from her moved in his seat. He had loved his master, too. Helen stood looking down at Dick. She had held him through the years. The love he had had for her since that first, unhappy, passionate boy and girl episode, he had never given to another. No other woman could wake that feeling in him. Taking, giving, standing aside. . . . Then she sat down, her hand over his where it lay over his heart, memories thronging about her. Once Diana came and went away, seeing her there—her face like a white gardenia in the golden candle-light.

Steps—Edwin's—roused her. They came across the lawn and she recognized something terrible in their sound.

She got up hastily and went out.

His face appalled her. Gray, ravaged, cast in stone above the raging fires of his heart.

"What is it, Edwin?"

"Come."

She followed him across the trodden grass, hastily, but without a word. Entering his house, she saw Hula sitting on his bed, and in her eyes and upon her face was a look she recognized—remembering!

"Hula!" she said, and, falling on her knees, she took the girl in her arms.

Hula shuddered, and her lips, under Helen's, were cold.

"He says—Uncle Edwin—that I mustn't tell."

Her eyes wandered about the room.

The woman was sickened by her own heart-beats. One after the other the mighty concussions shook her. She drew a deep breath, angrily, to still them.

"Hula—how did it happen?"

Edwin moved, and the sound of his feet on the floor chilled the blood in Helen's veins.

"I—I—told him"—she swallowed and her hand went vaguely to her throat— "told him Anthony was getting his divorce." She swallowed again. "And I wasn't going to marry him. I had to think about something nice—and—and—"

"And, Hula?"

"And something happened to him as it did to Dick when he shot the horses, and he—pulled me—pulled me off—"

Edwin moved ragingly and, looking up, Helen was sickened at the expression in his eyes. So one, bound, looks on at the torturing of a beloved. Hula's shuddering recommenced, and her little boots chattered on the floor. The sound distracted Helen and maddened Edwin; and, looking around a second time, the woman realized that he could not speak, so great and terrible was the fury of his intemperate soul. Brain and limbs were paralyzed, but his soul looked out of his eyes, tortured, crazed.

"Edwin!" she said sharply.

His response to the necessity of the moment was instant. He threw up his chin like a jerked horse.

"Ai?"

"Get hold of yourself."

Then she turned to Hula. She looked vague, as if her mind was not in her body.

"Hula, listen."

"Yes?"

Her body quaked in Helen's arms.

"I feel—sick," her voice broke, "and there are noises in my head."

"Listen! Anthony will be here at any moment. He will come right to you. He loves you, and he'll stay with you until everything is over. You love him, don't you?"

"Oh, Helen!"

"Then get hold of yourself, sweetheart. Edwin is right; he always is. Anthony must never know, must never be told, that this has happened."

Hula listened with distant eyes.

"Under no conditions, feel as you may about it. He'd kill Harry, and then he would be hung."

Hula moved as though a knife had been thrust through her body. Her eyes were as tortured as Edwin's, and hopeless; but in his there burned a great, increasing light.

Hula stamped her heel on the floor in a fury of exasperation, and the old resentment against trouble flamed in her. Helen's arms relaxed.

"Listen, sweetheart!"

The child winced, remembering that Dick had always called her that.

"You must be a thoroughbred. Set your teeth; remember

that whatever happened it was not your doing. Your slate is as clean as if it never had happened. You are shocked—upset. I know."

"You, Helen! How can you know? It's never happened to you."

With a sob, the woman kissed the despairing lips.

"I know, Hula—just the same—and I know more—that you must promise me, on your honor as a Calhoun and on your love for Anthony, that you will never tell him. If you do, you'll make him a murderer. Some day, in your happiness with him, you'll forget it entirely and forever."

"Ai," agreed Edwin.

Hula sat, her arms braced upon the bed. Her eyes went from Helen to the old cowboy.

Above her silky black head, their eyes met. She, being Hula, would tell him undoubtedly; but if the telling could be delayed until they were gone from Hana, until she was in his arms, completely his, it would make him only love her the more fiercely and compassionately.

Then the girl spoke.

"But Harry! He might—tell!"

"I shut him up."

Edwin's voice, wrenched up from the depths of his despair, stopped both their hearts. Hula gasped:

"Don't kill him, Uncle Edwin, or you'll go to jail!"

"Hell. I no damn fool. I no kill, but I fix so you no need scare that he tell anything when I *pau* with him."

"Uncle Edwin, dear!"

"Listen. Horses coming. It's Howard and Anthony."

Hula began to palpitate like a caught bird in Helen's arms, and her eyes dilated. Helen moved her head commandingly.

"Get him here," she signaled.

Edwin went out, and almost at once Haldane came with

long-legged strides out of the dark. Without a word he took Hula from Helen, kissing her, holding her against him.

"Hula!" he said chokingly.

"Oh, Anthony," and her arms went up about his neck, and the red blood flowed back into her face again.

Helen walked onto the porch. Edwin stood staring at the dark like an old and angry bull. His ragged brows were drawn down until they almost concealed his eyes. The skin of his face was gray, his mouth a bitter and calculating crack.

Her hand fell on his arm.

"Edwin," she said, "use your head. Don't be a fool."

"I no fool," he retorted, "I no do anything *pupule* (crazy)!"

But the woman saw murder looking out of the red-rimmed, angry eyes.

CHAPTER XI

Morning came vividly with white clouds and a brilliant sun. Pacing the *lanai*, Helen saw Hula and Haldane sitting on the terrace, with clasped hands. Hula's face, in spite of its whiteness and the bigness of her eyes, had an expression of dreamy happiness. Anthony had remained with her throughout the night, walking with her through the silenced rooms, remaining beside her when she slept on the couch in the wide *lanai*. Despite the fact that his wife was there, despite her bitter, scoffing face! The woman realized that this man over whom she had had such complete dominion had deliberately, with a courage born from his love, put himself beyond her reach.

Helen contemplated them. Still in her riding clothes of the previous day, with faint stains of forest earth on her boots, the child sat, holding Haldane's brown hand clasped between both of hers. Something plucked at Helen's heart. Hula—despite everything—was happy as few persons ever are. She had him, her Anthony, his love and his truth. She was at peace with the world, as one can only be with the human being that one loves.

She had been quite calm when Haldane brought her in from Edwin. She had gone with him to see Dick and walked through every room of the quiet house, a being apart, beyond the world's power to harass or distress. She would face the greatest ordeal of the day with courage, because she had this man she loved and in his deep, still way he looked up to her for it. It was the miracle of love which put even this passionate creature beyond pain of outer things. Haldane, looking for a moment into Hula's eyes, realized it too. How nearly he had missed it, the glory and the revelation!

Hamilton came out and went to Helen.

"Di wanted a reading of Dick's will. I sent a boy up last night for his effects, and I found one, made out quite recently. I'm afraid he was rather expecting—this."

"I think he was."

"She wants it read—publicly, as it were. I think it's best, Helen, for us all to be present. Don't you?"

She nodded.

"Then I'll speak to Haldane."

When they assembled to read the will, Helen looked about her.

"I'd like Edwin to be here, Howard," she said, "I think he ought to be, for he has been more faithful to—to—their interests than any one else."

The man detected anxiety in her voice and a wish to have Edwin within her sight.

"Certainly," he agreed, and dispatched a man to find him.

Diana looked at Helen in a peculiar way, but she appeared unaware of her. She stood with clasped hands looking at the sunshine on the lawn. Edwin arrived, and Helen had a moment of agony in looking at his face. How life had trampled on his heart. He came into the room and stood holding his hat against his breast.

Howard read the will in a voice as cold and steady as the waters of his ditch. Helen's eyes never left Edwin's face. At the words, "and I give the guardianship of my sister Hula to Anthony Haldane," the old man's eyes, which had been fixed on the array of flower-filled racing-cups, went to where Hula and Haldane sat. Satisfaction and ferocious anxiety mingled in Edwin's face. He saw the girl's eyes go to the man at her side, and his fingers tightened about hers in a silent promise that he would never betray her love and trust or Dick's faith that Hula's happiness would be a sacred trust in his hands. Edwin saw some of it and divined the rest. A look of resolution grew in his face that filled Helen with anxiety and alarm. In Edwin's eyes was a look that asked whether he should chance the ultimate working out of his great scheme or should take his sword to it.

The reading over, Edwin's eyes lingered thoughtfully on Hula. He still held his felt hat pressed to his breast. Hamilton halted Helen as she made her way toward him.

"I had thought surely, Helen, that Dick would—"

"He left me nothing, Howard, because he gave me all. I prefer it this way, and Dick knew it."

In her face was the glory of fire, and Howard bent his head slightly. With a great man's greatness he appreciated the quality of that love. Without ever having experienced a great human passion himself, he recognized and honored it. He stood, his eyes upon her lighted face.

"Later I want to talk to you. There is something I want to say."

"After—" she could not say the word, then added, "I think I know what you want to do and I thank you, Howard."

Haldane, standing at the doorway, heard. He knew what Howard wanted, for he had talked to him, fearing that Helen might misinterpret and refuse, but he knew she was great enough to accept a gift in the spirit in which it was bestowed.

"I want," Howard had said, "to deed this place to her, with sufficient to keep it as it should be kept. Diana is amply provided for, and I had wanted, eventually, to give Dick a small interest in the future profits of the ditch."

Haldane had not smiled, remembering an afternoon when Howard had asserted something quite different. Aloof, descendant of missionaries, regarded by the world as frozen and cold, something apart from his fellow men, a being not quite human, yet he was the most human and understanding of them all! From the vantage point of his security he got a vast perspective on life and men. He saw without condemning, appreciated without having known, gave with the giving of two-handed generosity.

Edwin glanced sharply at Haldane, as if he were aware of his thoughts. He had not been mistaken in his man. Gently, but with wisdom, he was seeing to it that Hula was not spared a phase of the day. With him she must go through all of it. There was to be no running away from life for either of them any more. Together they could and would face it gallantly.

There was no longer any need for him. Hula was no longer his responsibility. In this man's keeping her soul and body were safe. He took a long look at them, and Hula's voice penetrated his consciousness.

"Say that again, Anthony, so I can understand."

There was something feverish in her manner. Edwin grew tense. So deep had he been in his own thoughts that he had not realized that they were speaking.

"Say what again, Hula?"

"What you were saying."

"Nothing beautiful in the world can ever be really spoiled!"

Hula clasped him and began to shudder violently. "Then—then—no matter what—I couldn't be spoiled for you—because—because—I love you beautifully, Anthony?"

"Oh, Hula, don't I know it."

His arms closed about her in a dumb, fierce way, and he looked again at Helen, whose life had given him the thought.

"Look at me, Anthony. I love you."

He looked down at her upturned face.

"Oh, Hula, Hula, what have I ever been or done that I should deserve to be given you!"

The girl's face grew pale with bliss. Watching, Edwin made his resolution. He looked across at Helen. Howard was talking to her—would keep her occupied until he could get safely off. He put on his hat and went down the steps.

Saddling his best horse, he rode toward Kipahulu along the vivid bluffs, wind-swept and fresh from the splashing showers of the Trade. To the south Hawaii showed indigo-hued, piled with cumulus cloud. He jogged along steadily, saving his horse. His deep set, red-rimmed eyes regarded the familiar landscape resentfully, as if he were angry with the world.

The fresh wind snatched at the *halas* that clung to the brows of the bluffs, shaking them fiercely. Against the bold headlands the great seas smashed and smoked and recoiled to assault them afresh.

Edwin unloosed his rope and let it trail behind him, glancing back every so often to assure himself that there were no kinks in it that might mar a good throw. It slipped and glistened in the long Hilo grass. His eyes followed the rising and falling ridges, from the wet edge of the woods down to where tropic birds wheeled and flashed in the sun and the mighty seas thundered their wrath.

After a mile he took the lasso up, coil by coil, laying it

across his palm while his eyes scanned the lawless land. Something there was in it that always suggested horses stampeding, ears laid back, hoofs flashing, eyes gleaming white. The sensation always was his that this land of East Maui was an outlaw land, running away . . . and nothing could halt the speed of its great going. He whipped out a few coils of his rope and threw at a guava bush as he passed. Sighting some cattle, he put them to flight and caught one of them. He loosed it. His eye and hand were working in perfect accord, in spite of the fact that sleep and he had been strangers for many nights.

His glance swept and reswept the land as he steadily neared Kipahulu. Then he sighted some running objects on a ridge ahead. Cattle running, being pursued by a rider on a black horse! Here and there, catching them and letting them go. Edwin drew into some guava bushes and watched.

It was Dehan, assuaging his hate and assuring himself that the fury of his soul had not upset the machinery of his body!

Out roping—for him!

All right, man to man, horse to horse, and rope to rope they would finish it forever. Edwin got off and carefully adjusted his blanket; shook his saddle into place and cinched tightly. As he worked, his brain cleared, and he was able to think for the first time since Hula had come in with her tale. Mind and body had been paralyzed. He had been quite unable to plan ahead; he had done and said things, one by one, as they had come to him. To save her, to safeguard her, to give her to Haldane. This was his last work. Edwin realized the consequences but did not consider them. What came afterwards did not count. But he must put Dehan into the black silence from which there is no coming back to tell any tale. . . . That the price of that silence must cost two lives, Dehan's and his own, did not deter him. It must be done so no specter could haunt Hula's happiness.

Feeling his spurs and gathering up his reins, he mounted and rode up the gully bottom in order to get above where Dehan roped the running cattle. He noted trivial things as he went along: odd shaped rocks and a weed that threatened to overrun the land. But his mind—his whole being—was intent upon the thing he went to do. Reaching the head of the gully, he rode his horse up a steep and sticky trail. Emerging cautiously and keeping in the guavas, he halted to watch.

Dehan was riding like a madman, this way and that, roping and throwing the bewildered stock brutally and violently in a passion of destruction. Dismounting, he would tear the noose from about a throat, only to put it on another one, and Edwin knew that in Dehan's raging brain each neck was his.

He watched from under his tilted hat with a face of iron. Let the idiot wear out his horse. So much the better! Its sides were bloody from the spurs, its flanks heaving.

Edwin edged down toward him, and a great bull that had been hiding in the bushes leaped up with a snort and went charging down the ridge. With lowered horns and knotted tail, it raced. Brindled, heavy, graying about the horns, Dehan saw it coming and with a face of exultation went for it. It passed him like a hurricane, and he threw, without swinging, high over his head and to the left. The rope jerked taut, and with great plunges the horse followed. Something in its gait and something in the man's movements made Edwin drive home the spurs and ride in pursuit. On and on down the steeply sloping ridge, the wind muttering in his ears, he galloped; but faster went the two ahead. He saw the horse's plunges, the rider's efforts to extricate himself from the coils in which they had somehow become entangled.

Down the vivid green bluffs the trio sped, Dehan trying to get his horse close enough to make some slack; but there is no horse that can outrun a bull downhill. Like a taut wire, the rope glistened in the sun. The wind snatched at the bushes and rattled the long sword-like leaves of the *hala* trees exultantly. Straight toward the bluffs the bull raced, and horse and rider perforce followed it.

Edwin drew a little closer, but not close enough to see what had occurred. Dehan made one effort to check his horse and throw the bull, but the agony of the cutting rope could not be endured. There was a deadly wrench. Edwin, winking the wind-tears from his eyes, saw the horse's plunge and the man's writhing. Then on they went for the brink of the cliff.

Edwin knew what must come. Blinded with rage, the bull did not look ahead. With lowered head it ran, jerking Dehan and his tired horse after it. Guava bushes fringed the edge. The bull broke through them as a lava flow breaks through the forests of Mauna Loa when it rushes for the sea.

It pitched over, tried in mid air to right and check itself, and vanished. There was a forward rush. The horse drove in its hoofs and braced gallantly against the wrench when the twelve hundred pounds of bull reached the end of the rope. There was a jerk, a bound, another brace, another jerk as the horse endeavored to hold its beast. Inch by inch, foot by foot, it gave up the narrow strip of vivid green grass that ended in nothingness.

Edwin halted his horse and watched.

His fierce heart knew a grim compassion for the horse that must go to destruction because of the man upon its back. It braced, it strained until the muscles cramped and the veins stood out like worms beneath its soaking skin. Its eyes bulged, its flanks heaved. How the rope that bound Dehan was cutting him! There was no possibility of its coming loose, for it was tied solidly to the pommel. Dehan rode, as do all the real riders of Hawaii, "tied to death," to translate an old Spanish term, and death was coming to him on the windswept bluffs.

Seconds lengthened into minutes. The rope did not break, and the tired horse yielded its ground. Edwin's iron heart went out to it, but he made no move. To rush forward, to extract a promise from Dehan to save him did not enter into his head, or, if the thought came, he disregarded it. Compassion fought with love; for, though Edwin was adamant, he had a great heart for the fine things of life. His body was as taut as that of the straining horse; his breathing as labored. He heard the hollow boom of the assaulting seas, and he saw the smoke of the great swells rising and drifting back against the serried headlands. . . .

Then, suddenly, it was done. There was a violent scramble, a rush, a wild last plunge, and they flashed out of sight. Edwin's muscles relaxed painfully. He took off his hat and wiped his face. His white hair bristled fiercely in the wind, and his eyes rested grimly on the great, shifting dunes of the sea. He rode forward to inspect the tale that the torn grass told. A story tragic and gallant. A saga of the bluffs . . . the saga of a brown man's adoration and fight for a white child's soul. . . .

There could be no telling now. Hula's future was secure beyond any undoing. He looked back across the vivid miles to Hana. He saw Kauwiki standing against the driving seas. So had he stood against life for Hula, and its crashing waves had been unable to best his love or beat it down. Stronger than life and undaunted it remained, a beacon-light for other great loves to be guided by.

Riding back he saw Haldane galloping furiously. The road smoked under his horse's hoof. His face was drawn and alarmed. Seeing Edwin, he checked his horse violently. Something, satisfaction or peace, showed through the rock-like strength of his face and figure.

"Edwin! For God's sake, what have you done! Helen sent me—she told me—"

"What!" cried Edwin in a dreadful voice.

"That—that she was afraid you had gone out to kill Dehan."

Edwin smiled:

"No, I not have to kill him—God did it for me!"

THE END